New York Times Bestselling Author

ALLISON WIN

in
twenty
years

a novel

PRAISE FOR THE AUTHOR

NO LONGER PROPERTY OF ANYTHINK LIBRARIES / RANGEVIEW LIBRARY DISTRICT

THE THEORY OF OPPOSITES

"Willa's brave trek to find her true self is charming, with some laugh-out-loud moments. Sure to appeal to fans of smart women's fiction."

—*Library Journal*

"Readers who enjoyed Scotch's *The Song Remains the Same* will find much to like in this satisfying tale of a woman changing her fate."

—*Booklist*

"We're loving it . . . [and] can't get enough."

—*Glamour* magazine

"You can't help but be sucked right in. Before you know it, you are pausing in the subway station to keep reading before you go into work. Let yourself sink into this one come holiday time."

—*OK!* magazine

"Rife with lighthearted humor and memorable characters."

—*Publishers Weekly*

THE SONG REMAINS THE SAME

"Bestseller Winn Scotch sparkles in her captivating fourth novel. Readers will love Nell and won't be able to put the book down."

—*Publishers Weekly*

"A dry-eyed modern take on healing and forgiveness."

—*Kirkus Reviews*

"Readers who appreciate women's fiction that investigates serious themes will enjoy Scotch's fine novel."

—*Library Journal*

The One That I Want

"With a thriller of a conclusion . . . keeps readers in suspense until the final electrifying pages."

—*American Way*

"The real magic is Scotch's ability to create authentic moments between her characters that push this fast-paced story to the edge and joyfully brings us along with it."

—*The LA Books Examiner*

"Well-told . . . a good choice for fans of women's fiction and book clubs. It's fast-paced and feels light yet still packs a satisfying emotional punch."

—*Library Journal*

"Scotch creates eminently relatable characters, with a particularly excellent understanding of the way sisters interact, and has the ability to craft scenes of real emotional weight."

—*Booklist*

"An aching, honest look into the death and rebirth of relationships . . . a wise, absorbing narrative."

—*Publishers Weekly*

"You'll like this book because it's not all about a guy. It's layered with friendships, family ties, heartbreak, and the excitement of a new crush."

—Glamour.com

in
twenty
years

ALSO BY
ALLISON WINN SCOTCH

Time of My Life

The Department of Lost & Found

The One That I Want

The Song Remains the Same

The Theory of Opposites

in twenty years

a novel

ALLISON WINN SCOTCH

LAKE UNION
PUBLISHING

This is a work of fiction. Names, characters, organizations, places, events, and incidents are either products of the author's imagination or are used fictitiously.

Text copyright © 2016 Allison Winn Scotch
All rights reserved.

No part of this book may be reproduced, or stored in a retrieval system, or transmitted in any form or by any means, electronic, mechanical, photocopying, recording, or otherwise, without express written permission of the publisher.

Published by Lake Union Publishing, Seattle
www.apub.com

Amazon, the Amazon logo, and Lake Union Publishing are trademarks of Amazon.com, Inc., or its affiliates.

ISBN-13: 9781503935242
ISBN-10: 1503935248

Cover design by Ginger Design

Printed in the United States of America

For the women of 3930 and for everyone I met at Penn.
How lucky I was, how grateful I am, how fondly
I remember.

Dearly beloved,
We are gathered here today,
To get through this thing called life.

—*Prince, "Let's Go Crazy"*

1998-LATE MAY

PROLOGUE

BEA

Admittedly, it was an overly nostalgic idea. But, so what? If there were ever a time for nostalgia, it was tonight, our last night together at Penn, our last night under the same roof, our last night as a six-point star. Besides, if I didn't insist on it, none of them would have been willing. Frankly, and this is the part that somersaulted my stomach, none of them would have even considered it, thought of it in the first place. Well, maybe Annie. Annie would have considered it, but she'd never have spoken up because she'd worry that we'd all call her cornball or cheesy or judge her in some way for loving us more than we loved her.

We didn't. We all loved one another equally.

Or maybe not. I like to think we did. But love is never quite egalitarian.

"Get down here!" I shouted up the two flights from the living room. "Colin! Come up!" I yelled toward the basement.

The throb of the bass from the speakers in Lindy's room thundered overhead, rattling the old wood banister. I marched upstairs and knocked. She didn't open the door, but sweet Annie did across the hall.

"I'm getting ready," she said, though she was already more done-up than I ever was. The scent of her burning vanilla candle wafted toward me. "I need ten more minutes."

"You look perfect."

Annie scrunched her nose, then wiped her lipstick off with a balled-up tissue.

"I hate this lipstick."

"It's nice," I say, though the crimson hue was indeed a bit too murder-red.

"You think?" She winces. "I don't know. It's new."

Annie always went heavy on the beauty products—though Catherine had bought a makeup book at the university bookstore and, after practicing on herself, had given Annie lessons. She'd toned it down since freshman year, but the eyeliner was still too thick, the blush still a little too unnaturally vivid. She was pretty enough without it, but telling her as much only embarrassed her, made her lips turn down at the corners, made her hands bat in front of her face as if she were literally shooing the notion away.

Tonight she was wearing a maroon baby-doll dress that she'd splurged on at Urban Outfitters last month. I tried to buy it for her as a half-birthday present, but she shook her head and pulled wrinkly bills from her backpack. Frankly, she seemed a little confused, like she'd never celebrated a half birthday as a kid, like her mom had never surprised her with a cupcake just because she was halfway to a new start. After the cashier rang her up, I realized that, in fact, her mom probably never had.

I stopped celebrating half birthdays when I was eight, so I got it.

That's one thing that Annie and I had in common, one secret we understood about the other: being orphans. Me, literally, her compared to the other four, with their (mostly) happy homes. She and I were on our own.

Lindy popped her head out of her door, the music blaring. Dave Matthews.

Where you are is where I want to be.

"What?" Then, across the hall to Annie: "You look nice."

Annie flapped her hands like I knew she would.

"Not really," she said.

"Come downstairs," I bellowed over Dave Matthews. "Before we go out. I have something."

"Ugh."

"Not ugh!"

"Is it something nuts? Like, are you about to make me jump out of an airplane?"

"I am not about to make you jump out of an airplane. But you should. You know. One day. You'll never forget it."

"Ugh." Lindy rolled her eyes.

"I'm just saying." I wiggled a finger toward her like a schoolmarm who knew more than she did.

"Fine. One second." Lindy shut her door, and the music dampened.

"Catherine!" I called to the third story. She, Owen, and I lived on the top floor; they were across the hall, had been for two years now. They were the only ones who shared a room, but they were also the only ones who were solidly coupled—or coupled at all. When we rented this place the fall of junior year, it was understood that they came as a unit.

"I'm coming!" she called back, her voice muffled through the walls. Then she scurried out and down the flight of steps to meet me, her chambray tank top billowing above her belted jeans, her Steve Madden sandals flopping down the steps. She looked like an Abercrombie & Fitch model, her hair bouncing in a high ponytail, her cheeks golden in a way that she encouraged Annie's to be. She'd made the tank top herself, or at least fashioned it out of an old, baggier button-down from freshman year. She'd found a pattern at the crafts store she haunted on the weekends, sliced off the arms, and sewed up the back seams.

"Owen and Colin are out. But should be back any minute," she said, tucking in the hem of the shirt, disguising the slightly awry stitching. She was still navigating her seamstress skills.

As if on cue—because Owen rarely, if ever, let her down—Colin and Owen, like Batman and Robin, unlocked the front door and strode inside.

"Who's ready?" Owen shouted. "Because *we're* ready!"

"You're also drunk!" Catherine laughed and scampered past me to the living room. She kissed him for a beat too long (they always kissed for a beat too long), and said: "Hmm, yes, definitely drunk."

"Lindy! Annie! Come on!" I said, and Lindy's music finally quieted.

"We did the bar crawl downtown," Colin said to me. "You should have come."

"I can cream you in any sort of bar crawl, and you know it."

Colin purred and curled a palm like a cat.

"Besides," I said, "it's our last night. I wanted to spend it all together."

"Well, now we are!" Colin was as tipsy as Owen. He pulled me closer, braiding his arms around my neck. He always got touchy-feely whenever he drank too much, which wasn't as often as Owen, but wasn't so unusual that I couldn't read the signs. It had been this way since freshman year, after that bottle of Absolut in the student lounge, when I declined his proffered adoration, and we mostly got over it in the years since.

I savored the weight of his body pressed against mine for a moment, and then untangled myself when I heard Lindy's and Annie's footsteps clomping down the steps. Annie's lips were reslathered in murder-red.

Annie gazed at Colin quickly before averting her eyes to the floor. I wished she would tell him. Late one night sophomore year when she and I were lying in the grass on the Quad, staring up at the satellites because you couldn't see the stars against the Philadelphia lights, I told her she should tell him. *Jesus, Annie, life is short! You're only young once. Live like it! Tell him.* Or maybe let me tell him for you? But she stuttered and said, "Oh no! *Never.* Please don't. I'd rather die." So I didn't. And she didn't. And now she just averted her eyes to the floor.

"OK, now that we're all here, I have something," I said.

"I'm not getting a tattoo," Catherine said. Owen rubbed her bare shoulder as if he couldn't imagine marring her milky skin.

"It is *not* a tattoo." I groaned, even as mine peeked out from the waistband of my jeans. Wings. It felt a little clichéd four years later, but what was I going to do? I'd turned eighteen and had been emancipated from my grandparents and celebrated accordingly.

Tonight I was being a bit of a cliché too, but it was now or never. So I'd planned it all out: gone to the campus bookstore yesterday for supplies (they were running a 50 percent off sale on Penn 1998 hats, and I thus stood weeping in the hat section until a salesperson asked me if I needed to call someone) and rehearsed my pitch to the five of them. I grabbed the bag off the flaking pea-green dining table that Catherine had found at a garage sale and attempted to repaint to a shabby-chic white, but had managed only to dull the once-bright lime color. Sometimes, when you were eating your macaroni and cheese, you found a tiny shard of crusty white paint on the tine of your fork.

"Here," I said, offering them each a new notepad and shiny gold-inked pen. "Write down your hopes for the next twenty years. Where you think you'll be in 2018. Where you want to be."

Lindy rolled her eyes. "Bea, come on."

"I'm serious! I'm making a time capsule."

"A time capsule?" Colin pulled out a dining chair and seemed ready to mock me, but I glared at him, and he shut up.

"Yes, a time capsule. You'll be glad we did it. We'll open it at, like, our twentieth reunion. Write it down! Or . . . of course, we can just go get tattoos. Your call."

"We'll be, like, *forty* in twenty years," Owen said. "Jeez."

"Forty-two, Owen," Lindy said. "In other words, fucking ancient."

"Whatever," I said. "The future. The path that lies ahead." I flourished my hands like a circus magician.

"I love it!" Catherine grabbed a pad and pen, and Owen followed. They smushed together on the couch by the back window, even though there was room enough for four. (Five if we all piled on, like we did when we watched *Friends*. Six if Lindy lay across the top of the couch's back, which she was usually happy to do, flicking us each on the ear whenever the impulse seized her.)

"Fine," Lindy mumbled, then offered Annie a pad of her own.

"Oh," Annie said, "I don't know. I don't have much to say."

"Just think of the first thing that comes to mind! Your wildest dreams." I smiled at her, but I could see the blush rising up her neck. Annie furrowed her brow like she couldn't imagine her wildest dreams. She chewed on her lip and reluctantly accepted the pad from Lindy.

"Come on, I'll help," Lindy said, and she opened the front door, plopping down onto the stoop outside, Annie plopping down one step above her.

The heat from the abnormally hot May air blew in, and I closed my eyes and savored it, welcomed it. The rest of them never considered time, how it moves both so quickly and so slowly that it's always just beyond your grasp. But I did. I considered it always. I knew. I knew because time had robbed me of the years I deserved with my parents when I was eight, and the ocean off Australia turned black and swallowed them. I knew because time had also granted me life, literal life: if the doctors had caught my leukemia a few months later—at twelve, not eleven and a half—remission would have been just a word they used for someone else, or if my ski had caught an edge just a second later on that chute in the Alps, I'd have been paralyzed from the waist down forever, not just left with two nasty surgeries and a dull ache whenever the skies turn gray.

I also knew because these four years with them, my friends here, had cocooned me from everything else: the grief, the isolation, my cancer. I knew because nothing had gone wrong while I was here, while I was with them, even if I insisted on tempting fate a little too often.

I understood time. I knew its value. That's what I hoped for myself for the next twenty years: that I had time. Just . . . time. But I was wiser in this way than they were: I lived cavalierly, recklessly even. I swam with sharks, bungee-jumped off too-high cliffs, skydived a chance too many. But I knew that none of us are made any promises, none of us are ordained to be here forever, or even for as long as we want to believe. This is what nearly being robbed of time does to you: it leaves you glancing over both shoulders, wondering when it will catch up to you, wondering when its pace will quicken so you can no longer outrun it.

So, for now, for tonight, I wanted to preserve it. Forever. Or at least for twenty years. Besides, twenty years from now felt like forever.

It was the last night of college before graduation, and if we'd felt anything other than sky-high, we would have been doing it wrong. Tomorrow Annie and Lindy were off to New York: Annie had lined up a job in PR; Lindy was intent on being a superstar; Owen and Catherine were set to domesticate outside of Chicago. Colin was driving west to Palo Alto for medical school. A neurosurgeon. Colin was always a fixer, so I had no doubt he'd be the guy I'd want to work on my brain if it ever came to that.

He'd asked me to join him for the road trip, and I was considering it. I had vague plans to head to Central America to volunteer at an orphanage, but like so many other things in my life, nothing was cast in stone, nothing was definitive. The only definitive things were these five, the roots we'd planted, the way our lives had flourished and intertwined with one another.

"Listen," I said, and they all peered up from their pads and gold pens, Lindy and Annie craning their necks from the front stoop. "Promise me that after tomorrow, nothing will change. That no matter where we all end up, we'll stay family." The air got caught in my throat, and Annie rose to grab my hand, ripping her paper, tossing her draft into the trash, as if she thought I wouldn't notice. "You guys are my family. So please. Promise."

"Bea," Annie said, "don't say it like something bad's gonna happen. Don't say it so ominously."

I wanted to say: *You don't know. You don't know how time works. How it can sneak up so quickly you don't even realize what it's stolen from you.* But Annie was so sincere, and besides, this was my burden, not theirs.

"Just promise." My voice still shook.

They did. We all did.

We said it aloud. We said it to each other.

We promised.

"We're streaking the campus police later," Owen said, handing me his folded letter. I tucked it into an envelope. "Wanna come?"

"Streaking!" Colin thumped his fists against the table. "It's going to be legendary!" He set his pen down. "Come on, Bea, you in?"

"Maybe." I smiled.

"I'll take that as a yes." He grinned back, because he knew me well.

"I've seen your naked ass before, you know; it's no great shakes." I leaned in and kissed his cheek.

"Says just about no other girl on campus." Owen laughed. "Bea's in!" He raised his fists in triumph.

"Like I could say no," I said. "I practically live for streaking."

"Please don't get arrested," Catherine fretted. "Our parents are all in town! And we're graduating tomorrow!"

Not everyone's parents were in town, but we were past offending one another by parsing words. Only Annie's mother was here. And my parents not at all.

But it didn't matter. What mattered was the six of us. What mattered was our star. What mattered is that in this moment in time, we were unbreakable. We were light and destiny and a meteor shower of invincibility.

We were twenty-one. We were allowed to believe impossible things.

2016-JUNE

1

ANNIE

Annie is not at all happy with the way Gus is smiling in the photo.

Why does he look like he needs to take a poop? she thinks. *Why can't he smile like a normal ten-year-old?*

She immediately regrets the thought, because what sort of mother thinks her son isn't the epitome of handsomeness and looks like he's constipated in a picture? She narrows her eyes and stares at the image on her phone. *No. He is handsome. The cutest ever.* He looks more like Baxter than her, which is OK, because theoretically—though she fights the good fight (the best fight)—Baxter is better-looking than she is, even now that he's forty.

Forty. Jesus.

Her fortieth is right around the bend in October. Annie tries not to think about it too much because she finds the concept of middle age to be depressing, and no one likes her when she's depressed. Maybe her mother does. She sets her phone on her marble kitchen counter and remembers how, after Gus was born ten years back, just nine months after she and Baxter married, she found herself sinking deeper and deeper, mired in darkness, pedaling through the quicksand, with no idea how to pull herself free. She called her mom more often then; in fact, she was the only one Annie called. Every night when the hours grew too long, and sometimes in the mornings too. Annie's mom always answered, and Annie could hear her sucking on a cigarette in her La-Z-Boy—her breath a long gasp, then an exhale—while Annie curled up on her white-tiled bathroom floor and confessed her guilt, her shame at her bleakness.

Annie nods to herself now: yes, her mother probably liked her, but no one else likes a stick-in-the-mud.

She shakes it off and refocuses on the task at hand: a suitable filter on Instagram to perhaps whitewash the pinched look on Gus's face and thus capture their euphoria (and her very lean biceps and really cute bikini) from their weekend spent in the Hamptons. She settles on one that makes the ocean much bluer than it actually was that day, but the bluer the ocean, the better the picture! And the better the picture, the happier they seem.

So she uploads it and then almost immediately regrets her choice—maybe she should have included a shot with Baxter to show off his handsomeness, his wavy chestnut hair, his eyes that match the sea, their triangular, perfect threesome—but it's too late now; she already posted it, and besides, he hates her obsession with social media, hates it when she uploads photos of him without his permission.

It's not professional! he says. *My clients can see them!*

Annie attempted to sway him a few months back while she was pressing Hershey Kisses into the center of heart-shaped cookie cutouts for one of Gus's school bake sales, but Baxter had already dismissed the notion, returning his attention to his own phone, his oxfords clicking on the marble floor as he headed back toward his home office.

It was hardly the worst of his dismissals; hardly, also, the worst of hers.

She'd started up with the pills after Gus was born, gulping them like they were jelly beans, the better to ease her postpartum depression, and then simply to ease, well, everything. So when she discovered that Baxter was seeking refuge, seeking *affection* elsewhere, she couldn't blame him. Or at least, she didn't blame him. She'd only discovered his indiscretions in a fit of paranoia, scrolling through his texts while he showered, and since she shouldn't have been spying on him in the first place, she never quite worked out how to point fingers. She didn't have the spine to dig too deeply into his old texts, more-than-likely-guilty e-mails; she wasn't the type of wife who chased bad news with more bad news. So it was what it was. She was who she was. He was who he was. That was that.

He still took care of her, after all; he still offered her more than she'd have without him: the Upper East Side apartment, the tuition for Gus's tony private school, the occasional dinner companion, and access to charity galas and theater and all sorts of interesting people who would never deem her worthy without him.

Sometimes it was simply better not to know, not to investigate too deeply into betrayal.

She'd mostly forgotten about the affair. Made her peace with it. Her pills helped, had a way of blunting the pain, distorting the truth of it. Then, on Valentine's Day four years back, something shifted. Baxter clutched her wrist over dinner at Gramercy Tavern, then nudged a Cartier box around the candles and wineglasses. A diamond necklace. Her eyes welled, and his did too. Annie had read enough posts on CitiMama to know that unexpected generosity from a spouse often correlated with an affair (or the end of one), so she scrolled through his texts again that night while he slept, and indeed, he'd ended it on New Year's Eve, while they vacationed in Aspen.

And thus, right there and then on Valentine's night, Annie rose in the darkness of their bedroom, stumbled to the white-tiled master bath, and flushed the Klonopin, the Xanax, and the remaining Percocet she hoarded, for good. Once and for all. Really, this time.

Baxter never knew about the pills. Or at least she didn't think he did.

Instead, in the years ensuing, Annie found other ways to quell her anxiety, her dissatisfaction, her guilt. Like Instagram. Or volunteering for the PTA once Gus hit kindergarten. (The all-boys private school Baxter had attended: they wore jackets and ties, which were just adorable. Annie incessantly captured shots of Gus on the way to school. It was too cute not to.) Or developing her long, lean biceps, which she liked to display on Facebook.

Slowly they found their way back to each other. Or at least as close to that as they ever had. Two years ago, Baxter's father keeled over on the ninth hole at Shinnecock, and as they were driving home from the funeral, Baxter announced that he was making changes. That *his life was passing him by!* and that *he wasn't getting any younger, for God's sake! It is all about family, and you are my family, and by God, I am going to be HERE now.*

Annie exhaled, the wind from her open window whipping against her blush-covered cheeks, and reached her left hand over to the nape of his neck, letting it rest there until she felt self-conscious. And knew it had been worth it: her silence, her nonconfrontational manner, how she buried his secrets until they became her own secrets too.

Baxter cut down on his office hours at Morgan Stanley, pawning off work to his underlings, then took up yoga, bought himself a Porsche, and for a very brief period, went on an ill-fated raw-food diet, which seemed to wreak more havoc on his digestive system than it was worth. He went from a passing ship in their household to an anchored liner in their port, and though they aren't perfect, now, together, Annie believes they are happy. They started having sex again—usually twice a week after a few years of every now and again. (Annie refuses to even imagine him having sex with the other woman, whoever she was.) They go out to dinner, and he holds her chair, then scoots it in. He asks her if she likes the Porsche, and she doesn't even tut, even though she's terrified to ask how much it must have cost. She knows she should be used to niceties like a new Porsche by now, but every time she sinks into the supple leather seats and inhales the musky scent that just screams "filthy rich," she feels a little sick, like the gods might smite them for their ostentatious display of new money.

She would never breathe a word of any of this to Baxter, though.

Today she picks up a dead sunflower leaf that's fallen on the counter next to the crystal vase. She bought the flowers at the farmer's market just yesterday, and here they are, already dying on her.

Annie's phone buzzes. She swipes her screen, hoping for at least five or six "likes" to her Instagram shot in the past minute. But there is only a solitary text. She squints at it because she doesn't recognize the number. It's a Los Angeles area code, and she can't recall anyone she knows who lives in LA. Well, there was that family from preschool who moved because the dad was a bigwig at Sony, but surely that mom, whose name she can't recall—maybe Cynthia?—but whose child once bit Gus on the arm (and was a bit of a sociopath, Annie thought), wasn't texting her now.

Did you get this shit in the mail today?

Annie rereads the message three times. She never checks the mail—her housekeeper usually does it for her—but even if she had, what sort of *shit* is to be expected? She fishes around in her kitchen drawer—the messy one where she allows Gus and Baxter to throw all their crap—for the spare mailbox key. But she can't find it, and then her phone buzzes again.

Seriously, this is fucking weird. I mean, WTF?

Well, she can't not reply to that.

Annie doesn't get many WTF-type texts. She gets texts about sales at Bed Bath & Beyond and reminders for Gus's dental appointments. Very rarely, nay, never, is there a WTF-type text.

She thinks of a million things to say, like:

If this is Cynthia Burton, then I hope you can apologize for when Henry bit Gus. He required three stitches! And I considered a rabies shot!

Or:

Perhaps you have the wrong number?

She taps her fingers along the perfect white Carrera counters. She wishes those sunflowers weren't already dying. She really thinks they're a pick-me-up for the kitchen.

Finally, she types:

Oh, I didn't think it was weird at all!

She opens her Sub-Zero to pour the lemonade she made last night, satisfied that she's covered her cluelessness well.

Before she can add ice to her highball, there's a reply.

Annie, cut the shit. Check your mail. Text me back when you do. It's Lindy.

⌖

Annie's fingers are shaking by the time she has the wherewithal to slide on her Manolo sandals, jab the elevator buttons to the lobby, and retrieve the FedEx from her doorman, Frank. She clutches the envelope to her chest on the ride back up, her heart coursing blood so quickly through her brain that she loses her train of thought entirely.

She finds herself back inside her kitchen with no memory of the prior few minutes—if she properly thanked Frank, if she said hello to her neighbor in the elevator, if, in fact, her neighbor was in the elevator at all.

She hasn't seen Lindy, hasn't seen any of them, in thirteen years.

She thinks her heart might stop at the notion.

Thirteen years. Has it really been that long?

Of course it was for the best; it was the only way Annie knew how to move on: to simply *move on*. After the disaster of Catherine and Owen's wedding that June, after Lindy ran off to Nashville a few days later, and then, well, after Bea so soon after. It was like a ball of yarn that came unspooled too quickly: there wasn't any way to roll it back up. She's friends with Owen and Colin on Facebook, but Colin never posts, and Owen's posts are usually just stupid sports stuff. She Googles him—Colin, of course—all the time, too often, then quickly deletes her history, her cheeks cherry-red, like she knows it's silly, knows it's almost shameful that she's still out there wondering. He's probably not Googling her back.

That was the last time she saw them all: thirteen years ago on that horrible, overcast day in October. The funeral. Annie tries not to think about that day too often—ever, really, if she can help it. She still thinks of Bea fondly every once in a while: when she hears the Macarena at a kid's birthday party (nobody did a Macarena with more zeal than Bea) or spots a woman in a sunny yellow dress in Saks, in nearly the identical, impossible-not-to-stare-at hue that Bea wore to Catherine and Owen's wedding. (The rest of the bridesmaids wore plum—it wasn't the most flattering—but Bea read a special poem, and because of her special role, she wore a special dress. It was all so natural, so Bea, that none of the other bridesmaids thought twice about it.)

But the funeral? That day? No, Annie can't bear to think of that. She's found, after all, that if you force yourself not to think of things, they lose their power; they shift from reality to mirage, from true to almost imaginary. And Annie would so much rather pretend that this was nothing but make-believe.

Colin had been the one to call them all with the news. He'd heard it from Bea's grandmother. It had been a car accident, though the specifics were hazy—just that Bea was the only one hurt, a solitary fatality. Annie remembers all this now, more than a decade later. How she rushed from the pews at the funeral to escape her fraying nerves and tumbling stomach, as well as the tension with Lindy; how Lindy trailed after her, hissing under her breath, perhaps trying to forge peace, to apologize, but unrepentant in doing so and thus failing entirely; how they stumbled into the bathroom and nearly collided with Bea's grandmother, who was waxy and wan and resembled a ghoul. Annie remembers this even now. How she looked like something out of a horror movie, out of some zombie film she'd be too squeamish to sit through. Annie offered quiet condolences, spun around and strode back to the pews, never once acknowledging Lindy, never once relinquishing her anger.

At the funeral, they sat in the pew on opposite ends, like bookends, buffered by the three in between. Annie. Catherine. Owen. Colin. Lindy.

Afterward, in a catatonic state, they wandered to a Greek place on Third, not because any of them particularly wanted to, but because it felt wrong to just scatter. Bea wouldn't have stood for it.

"I just don't understand," Catherine repeated again and again. "I just don't understand."

Annie forked at her rice pilaf and wished this could all be over: Lindy here, Bea dead, the humiliation of facing Colin after how she'd behaved.

"You know Bea," Lindy said.

But Catherine was still pissed at her from the wedding, so she rolled her eyes and said, "Explain it to me, Lindy. Explain Bea's psychology to me, because I'm pretty sure she shouldn't be dead."

"What? Who said she should be dead?"

"You did."

"I didn't say that. I said, *You know Bea.* Like, she wasn't exactly a Girl Scout."

"She wasn't exactly a Girl Scout?" Catherine was clutching the tablecloth, and all their plates slid a tad askew. "What does *that* mean?"

"Cathy." Owen touched her arm.

"She did things on her terms," Colin interjected. "I'd like to think that whatever happened, it was on her terms too."

"Right," Lindy said. "Jesus! That's all I was saying."

"No," Annie finally said. "That's not what you were saying at all. You were *blaming* her, making it sound like she *did* something."

"You don't have any idea what she did," Lindy said, too loudly. "None of us do. Isn't that why Catherine asked?"

"She's dead, Lindy! Shut up!" Catherine blurted out Annie's thoughts exactly.

Annie remembers that Lindy stood abruptly and threw down some cash. She had a plane to catch, a gig to play on the road, though it was a convenient excuse. Who was she opening for? Annie squints toward her kitchen window, trying to recall.

The Goo Goo Dolls.

Catherine said, "*Sit down*, Lindy, you can't just run away. Not tonight."

And Lindy said, "I'm not sitting down; I'm not taking this shit. I don't want to deal with this; I don't *need* to deal with this."

Catherine snorted. "Well, everything is always about what you want. You're all take, take, take. So you did, and it ruined everything."

Even Annie was shocked, but she couldn't blame Catherine because she didn't disagree. Also, they were so strung out, so wrung dry from the news of Bea's death that no one was thinking straight. Like they were wearing their hearts outside their bodies, and every little pulse felt like a detonation.

So Lindy sneered. "Oh God, Catherine, you and your perfect self-righteousness. Perfect, perfect, perfect. I don't need this anymore! I don't need *you guys* anymore. I've moved on. Too bad you can't do the same."

Then she spun around and tromped away, leaving to go open for the Goo Goo Dolls, and when she left, so too did any chance for them to stitch up their wounds collectively, as a six-point star. A five-point star now. That made it all the worse. Lindy left, and whatever remained among them shattered.

Annie rests the FedEx envelope on her immaculate marble counter and flattens her palms against it, inhaling and exhaling, trying to slow her breathing. The midtown law office on the return address is unfamiliar. Annie can't think of anything that she and Lindy would share these days—no friends, no interests. There's no reason why they'd each receive matching envelopes. Annie refuses to "like" Lindy's fan page on Facebook or download even one of her songs. (She did buy one for Gus a few weeks ago because he was begging. But that was the exception. She makes all sorts of exceptions for the men in her life.)

And yet, here Lindy is, polluting her tranquil kitchen, muddying her quiet afternoon while Gus is at day camp. All Annie wanted to do today was read a few cooking blogs, squeeze in a Pilates class, maybe do some online shopping. And now there's this! Of course there's this!

Because Lindy never had any boundaries in the first place! Annie's flattened palms curl into fists. Of course she would weasel her way into her serene afternoon. This is just *so like Lindy!*

Before she can give it a second thought, Annie rides her crest of anger, shredding open the top of the FedEx envelope as if it's actually the offending party.

She regrets it immediately and wishes she hadn't been so impulsive. Because now she has to look to see what's inside. Something's been opened, and it's not like she can just pretend to seal it back up like it was never opened in the first place.

If she could, she'd check Pinterest to see how to DIY this: *how to seal something back up like it was never opened in the first place!* Of course, if Annie could do that, then she'd bottle up those days of October 2003, stuff them right into a mason jar, tie a gingham ribbon around the lid, and throw it off a cliff. What she'd really do is bottle up Bea's accident and breathe her dear back friend to life.

Annie eyes the FedEx.

No.

Bea is dead. There will never be a Pinterest board for such things.

From the desk of: David Monroe, Esq.

To: Former Residents of 4120 Walnut Street

Dear Ms. Armstrong, Mrs. Cunningham, Mr. and Mrs. Grant, and Mr. Radcliffe,

I am writing at the request of one Ms. Beatrice "Bea" Shoemaker. She designated me as the executor of her will on September 15, 2003, and asked that this notice be sent to you in June of 2016.

Ms. Shoemaker approached me at the behest of her grandmother, whose estate I have managed for forty years. I tell you this so you understand that this letter is not a joke, nor a prank, and our firm's relationship with the Shoemaker family is easily verifiable. If you have doubts, please, by all means, feel free to ask questions.

Shortly after your graduation, Ms. Shoemaker purchased your former residence, 4120 Walnut Street, on the campus of the University of Pennsylvania. At the time, and henceforth, it has been used as an investment opportunity. Since her death I have managed the row house, and per her will I have vacated the premises for the summer of 2016 and am officially extending an invitation (at Bea's request) for the weekend of July 3–6, on the eve of Bea's July 4th birthday—her fortieth. Bea has set aside something important for you all, and at her request you cannot receive said item until the five of you are together on her birthday.

Your travel expenses will be covered via Bea's trust. Please call my office to make travel arrangements.

It was her deepest wish, expressed in her will, that all of you are able to return to campus and to the house on Walnut Street. If you are unable to do so, please let me know at your earliest convenience, and I will attempt to rectify any roadblocks. Though again, she reiterated that she hoped for and expected attendance. She expressed that she thought you would understand.

At Ms. Shoemaker's request, I am at your service to assist in any way.

Yours,
David Monroe, Esq.
Webster, Monroe, and Proctor
Attorneys-at-Law
New York, New York

2

LINDY

Lindy's trying to find her groove but failing. It's been this way for a couple of weeks, and though she's suffered through occasional bouts of writer's block before, she's usually able to shake it off through her tried-and-true methods: tequila, casual sex, sometimes a decent three-mile jog (if she isn't half-dead from the tequila).

This time, though, she's off tequila, and for all intents and purposes, she's now committed to Tatiana, though there was that hiccup (hiccups, plural, if you want to be technical about it) with Napoleon a few months ago (and then again a couple of weeks ago) after the recording session in New York for her new album. So booze and casual sex are out, and she's too exhausted to drag herself over to the treadmill, which stands dormant in her guesthouse/office/writing studio.

She knows she has something here in the chorus. She rattles the pencil against her desk like a drumstick—trying to stir up the magic—but she can't draw out the verses, can't pin down the melody or the lyric that will elevate this song above the rest of her catalog. Not that it matters, really. The label sends over manufactured pop songs these days. No one is interested in a Lindy Armstrong original—not because she's not up on her game, not because her compositions aren't the best they've ever been, but simply because to stay relevant, they need her to be *younger*. Sales on her fifth album dwindled, and that was all the label needed to intervene: first they insisted on a cowriter; now she's been erased from the process entirely.

"Hipper, you know, hotter, sexier. Like everyone still wants to fuck you even though you're forty," one of the assholes on a conference call said when they were discussing her new record.

But she's writing her own stuff anyway. Gonna lay down these tracks anyway. They'll never make it on the album, and she won't argue with that: Lindy knows that what sells, what gets radio play, is what matters, and at her age she's lucky not to have been pushed into adult contemporary or the alt-lite station that semicool moms listen to in their carpool. She still gets Top 40 play, but mostly because she's singing songs intended for twenty-three-year-olds.

She flips her pencil across her desk and checks her phone. Of course Annie hasn't texted her back. No wonder she can't write a fucking word! No wonder she can't conjure up a decent chord arrangement. All she's thinking of is goddamn Annie Eisley, and also occasionally about Tatiana, and then sometimes about Napoleon ("Leon" for short, thank God), and how maybe she should tell Tatiana about Leon, but maybe Leon wasn't worth mentioning, but that things are a little more complicated right now, and why the fuck hasn't Annie replied?

Napoleon! Who names their goddamn kid after a tyrant with size issues?

Lindy slides open her desk drawer and retrieves another pencil, pressing the graphite to her sheet music. Everyone writes electronically these days, but not her. Shit, she really is a dinosaur; she'd almost laugh if it weren't so goddamn depressing. All those fucking twenty-three-year-olds. Hell, the eighteen-year-olds too. With their taut bellies and baby-voiced singing. None of them have as much talent in their entire lithe bodies as Lindy does in her left pinky, but so what? Talent doesn't rule; talent doesn't even necessarily sell. This is what middle age looks like in the world of rock: assimilation or extinction.

Lindy's gonna be around long after the cockroaches. She laughs to herself at this. Her four framed platinum albums on the wall behind her seem to laugh too. She'll do what she has to do, even if it means selling herself down the river while still writing the best goddamn music of her life.

Welcome to forty.

This new pencil offers no help. She throws it across the room, where it skitters next to the previous one. She reaches for her phone again.

Nothing.

How hard is it for Annie to check her mail and text back?

Lindy had impulsively texted her when maybe she should have chosen one of the others. But it's been, what? Thirteen years since the funeral? She can't possibly still be mad.

Of course she could still be mad. Which is probably why Lindy impulsively texted her in the first place. To test the waters. Lindy was always testing something.

Lindy rises, cracks her neck, and debates the treadmill. Then she catches a glimpse of her reflection in the window. She didn't sleep well last night, not after the FedEx, and she doesn't bounce back like she used to. Also, she looks bloated, puffy from her eyes to her hips, and she's expected to pour herself into a low-cut catsuit for the show tonight.

A leather catsuit! Megan, her costumer, had picked it out, and the producers had approved it, and it was hung in her dressing room, all without as much as a consult with Lindy. Sure, they'd asked casually, but it was already understood: this is why they paid for her trainer; this is what keeps her relevant. Of course she was going to wear the catsuit. Even if she *was* forty, which she'd just turned last month. People. com had devoted their top story to it—*Lindy Armstrong Through the Years!*—a portfolio of pictures from every year she'd been famous. It wrapped with a recent photo of her leaving a London nightclub with her fingers linked with Tatiana's. Lindy didn't linger on the spread, but she glanced quickly enough to recognize the very first shot—the one from when she'd just started out. When she was twenty-four and landed a one-off gig as the opening act for the opening act of a Tim McGraw charity concert in Nashville. Everyone—all five of them—had flown down to cheer her on.

Forty.

Her sister tells her that it's time for her to figure out what she wants out of life. Lindy tells her sister that she's a goddamn superstar—what else could she possibly want? Her sister sighs heavily and tells her to take care of herself. But her sister has two dirty-fisted toddlers and a minivan, so it's not like she has any idea, not like she can relate one iota to Lindy's life. And yet when Lindy hangs up the phone, she's also semi-aware that her sister isn't entirely wrong: that Lindy often has no clue what she wants—or wanted or should have wanted—and spends a lot of time regretting things she was sure she coveted (but didn't) and things she was certain she should have left behind (and later wished she hadn't).

That's what rock 'n' roll is! Not having any fucking idea about anything other than the music! She's long since forgotten that her first love was country music. And not that *her* music matters that much now anyway.

She stares at her bloated, exhausted reflection and hesitates.

This fuck-all sentiment used to be true for her, but now, just for this passing second, she wonders how honest it really is. If you were to make a graph on where Lindy's truths lined up these days, you wouldn't exactly get a straight arrow.

She turns from the window and checks her phone.

Annie still hasn't texted her back, which, Lindy thinks, is so goddamn typical.

Her text beeps just then, and she swipes immediately.

It's from Napoleon.

Blow off the walls tonight at the show.

She checks the time: two hours until the car picks her up.

"Christ." She exhales. "Like I need this right now."

Lindy has no idea what she actually needs right now, though a text from Annie would help, and the premiere taping of *Rock N Roll Dreammakers* surely seems like it won't.

When they'd approached her to be a judge, Lindy immediately said no.

God, she'd said to Tatiana, *a reality show? Have they ever found anyone remotely decent on a reality show? What happened to busking? What happened to earning your goddamn stripes? Everyone just shows up with an acoustic guitar and says, "I can sing 'Hallelujah!' so make me famous!"*

Tatiana, a seasoned publicist (though not Lindy's—don't shit where you eat, and all that), pointed out that plenty of remotely decent people had been discovered on reality shows and that Lindy herself had been helped by exploding on MySpace back when not everyone exploded on MySpace. Lindy saw her point but was only swayed when her manager informed her that they were offering her $4 million for the season. Also, it would really bolster the fall tour (thirty-two cities in six weeks—Lindy has no idea how she'll have the stamina to endure it).

Lindy ignores Leon's text and instead Googles "Catherine Grant." Maybe Catherine's checked her mail, gotten the FedEx too. But if everyone's checked their mail, she wonders, why hasn't anyone called *her*?

She taps her phone into her palm and debates whether she should be offended. She *is* offended, come to think of it. Catherine had been such a bitch at her wedding, after Lindy had endured mind-numbing phone calls and e-mails about calla lilies versus tiger lilies, about those hideous plum (*"eggplant,"* she remembers Catherine insisting) bridesmaid dresses, about first-dance ideas, about party favors. Sure, maybe Lindy's attitude wasn't exactly *sparkling*, but Jesus, could you blame her? Who *wouldn't* want to jump off a bridge at the notion of another discussion about seating charts?

Not to mention, Lindy wasn't exactly in favor of marriage in general.

But the way Catherine derided her at brunch the next morning?

Lindy splays back into her Eames chair behind her desk and bounces eight times—like a beat, like a rhythm—to calm herself.

She figured maybe they'd all just move the fuck on after the funeral. Jesus, Bea was dead; she figured they could at least forget the wedding. But no, she saw it immediately in Catherine's stupid stoic jaw, in Annie's weak eyes that refused to meet her own. So Lindy decided right then and there, even at Bea's funeral, to *screw that.* It's not her fault that their dinner that night went south, that what should have been an evening where they reminisced about their old friend, when they should have found their way back to one another, was instead the night things detonated for good.

What had Catherine said to her? Lindy squints, focusing on one of the framed platinum albums on the wall.

That Lindy "ruined everything." Ah yes, that was it. That she'd wrecked their friendships, the bonds among the six of them. That everything was always about what Lindy wanted, that she was "take, take, take." And she took, and then it ruined everything.

What bullshit, Lindy thinks now, just as she did back then. A lot of things ruined them, like Bea dying.

She bounces again in her chair.

Bounce. Bounce. Bounce. Bounce.

Bea is dead.

Why did she send us a letter?

Bounce. Bounce. Bounce. Bounce.

When did she have time to buy our old house?

In quarter time.

Bouncebouncebouncebounce.

Bea is really dead. Jesus, Bea is still dead.

For the first year or so after the funeral, it plagued Lindy, it probably plagued all of them, but she was done with them all, didn't stay in touch, so she couldn't be sure. Still, though, she'd find herself awake at 3:00 a.m., staring into the darkness of a hotel-room ceiling or listening to the clattering of the tour bus's wheels and wondering: *Why is Bea dead?* And not just in a metaphorical sense, like: "Why her?" but also: Really, how did it happen? Peeling around a curve too quickly? Asleep at the wheel? Drunk driving? That last one made sense: the just-so combination of reckless and animalistic that embodied Bea when she dialed things up. Over time, Lindy came to take this explanation as fact: when she thinks of Bea now (which she rarely does, if she's being honest), her next thought is something akin to: *Oh, my friend who died in a drunk-driving accident.*

This rationality provided solace. And solace meant that she could forget.

So now, why all of this?

A knock on her office door, then the hinges opening before Lindy can reply.

"Hey, babe."

Tatiana.

Instinctively, Lindy reaches for her phone and drops it in her lap, concealed. Like Leon's text is a land mine that Tatiana might happen upon. No need to blow anything up.

Lindy feels Tatiana's arms wind themselves around her torso as she folds over her from behind. She kisses her neck, and Lindy detects a hint of mandarin orange, some new body lotion, a gift from one of her clients.

"Hey," Lindy says, dropping her head back against T's shoulder, then righting herself as Tatiana does the same. "Just give me a second. Just . . . checking something."

Because she can't help herself (she is very bad at helping herself, actually), Lindy clicks onto Catherine's home page, The Crafty Lady. She's built herself an empire, but Lindy's not particularly surprised. Catherine was always more ambitious than any of the others gave her credit for: she was intent on selling the most baked goods for their sorority spring charity event; she was constantly toiling in their shitty little kitchen, testing and tossing recipes, trying to best the one before.

French toast. That's what Lindy remembers about Catherine. She'd make it for them every Sunday, tweaking the ingredients until finally, in April of their senior year, she declared it perfect. The rest of them thought it was close to heaven already: gooey and crunchy and honey and cinnamon tangled together. The house smelled like love the rest of the day.

"Crafting? Please tell me you're not interested in crafting." Tatiana laughs like this is a foregone conclusion.

Lindy laughs too, but skims through the how-to tips on Catherine's site: *How to Make Lip Balm from Scratch! How to Build a Country-Chic Birdhouse! How to Host Thanksgiving in July!*

"What do you think of Thanksgiving in July?"

"Sounds like a lot of carbs." Tatiana, a pin-thin publicist whose clients view carbs with as much disdain as Lindy does twentysomething songwriters, shrugs. "Also, who needs extra time with our extended families?"

Lindy nods like T has a good point. "My sister *is* driving me crazy."

"And your parents?" Tatiana semi-snorts.

"I'm not sure my mom believes in Thanksgiving anymore. Taking up the injustice of the Native American. Or the sacrificial turkey. Maybe both." Lindy rolls her eyes. But still, she wonders if anyone would ever cook her Thanksgiving in July, which actually sounds kind of sweet. "Yeah," she says. "What a stupid fucking idea. Thanksgiving in July. Why not Christmas in April? Halloween in March?"

Tatiana leans in and kisses her perfunctorily once more.

"I just popped in to say good luck tonight. I gotta run: crisis on a CW set. I'll see you at the after-party."

Lindy waits until the door latches shut to reread the Thanksgiving menu. She wavers, then prints it out to suggest to her chef.

Then she clicks on The Crafty Lady's contacts page, her finger twitchy, and pulls up Catherine's e-mail address. (Like this is actually Catherine's e-mail. Catherine's company is about to go public: Lindy had seen a tweet about it a few weeks ago while she scrolled through Twitter late one night, plagued by a bought of insomnia—the insomnia brought on by Tatiana and Leon and all the possible ensuing complications. The CEO's e-mail address would hardly be announced right there, on the contacts page. Lindy knows this. Her own assistant usually tweets or Facebooks or Tumbles or whatever for her. Lindy doesn't really have time for all that, and she's guessing Catherine doesn't either.)

And this leads Lindy to an epiphany.

I don't need this shit, she thinks. Why go poking a bear when it's better left alone?

Instead, she yanks open her desk drawer, full of sharpened but unused pencils, and drops the FedEx in, slamming it shut with such force her entire desk trembles. She'll figure out what the fuck this is all about after the show. More important things are waiting, like earning her $4 million. More important things like finishing up the best song of her life, which might finally make her label say: *You still got it.*

She stands abruptly and ignores her puffy, sad reflection as she strides out the office door toward the waiting catsuit. No one ever said Lindy wasn't capable of proving everyone else wrong.

3

CATHERINE

Catherine is in the test kitchen, her staff of eleven swirling around, and nothing is going as planned for the HGTV taping exactly thirty-nine hours from now. This was supposed to be their trial run for the pilot she's filming, and the pilot she's filming could very well save her company, or at least buffer it until the deal with Target comes through. But the flesh of the apples is already browning! And they're Granny Smiths, for God's sake! Is no one on her team aware of the fact that Granny Smiths are *green*, not *red*, as she specified? Why would she want *green* apples on a Fourth of July shoot? And the plates—*the plates!*—are showing water marks! Oh, and she requested royal-blue napkins, and these are unequivocally a deep shade of navy.

"Stop!" she says to the photographer, whose name she can't remember but who is snapping, snapping, snapping away to capture stills for The Crafty Lady website. *"STOP!"* she barks louder, and he peers an eye above the lens, as if just hearing her for the first time, and lowers the camera.

"Sasha! Please call Owen and tell him I'm taking a later car home." Catherine snatches the napkins off the table. "Ask if the kids want to FaceTime after their showers."

Sasha, her twenty-five-year-old assistant, with blotchy cheeks and terrified eyes, scurries around a lighting tent, her phone already to her ear.

"And please be sure that Mason has studied for his spelling test!" Catherine calls after her. "Tell Owen that I don't want to get another e-mail about him not living up to his potential."

Is it spelling? Catherine isn't sure. It could be a math test, actually. She can't remember the specifics. Something. It's something about Mason not living up to his potential, like third graders need to worry about potential. But these days, Catherine guesses, maybe they do.

Sasha rushes back in, the phone against her shoulder, and drops a pile of printed e-mails on the disastrous Fourth of July table.

"Forgot to give you these," she mouths, pale and skittish, and then is off. She reminds Catherine of an overcaffeinated fox.

Somehow, out of the 543 e-mails in Catherine's inbox, Annie Eisley Cunningham made the list of print-worthy must-reads. Catherine rubs her forehead, regretful at her piercing tone, regretful that her assistant (and the rest of her staff) scurry around her, regretful that she'll be missing another dinner at home. That's six in a row, something Owen will surely remind her about.

Owen also tells her that it's *just amazing* how she can run a nearly-billion-dollar company but can't figure out how to schedule sex with him. She tells him (she doesn't really, she just says this in her head because all she actually does is apologize and feel guilty), that it's *just amazing* how fortunate he is to be a stay-at-home dad when he decided that he loathed being a lawyer and his wife happened to blow up in the blogosphere and then, in the span of a decade, sits on the precipice of taking her company public.

Yeah, she thinks now, swapping out navy napkins for a more patriotic royal tone, even though Owen isn't here and has nothing to do with this particular problem. *It's goddamn amazing, Owen, it really is.* What she also doesn't say to Owen is that The Crafty Lady has seen a treacherous slide over the past year; copycat bloggers have produced content faster and fresher, with younger demographics and hipper ideas. So if she *doesn't* work these late nights, doesn't slave over the right color of napkins, then the treacherous slide will evolve into a full-blown avalanche. And then what? They've built their whole lives around her success. Owen included.

But Annie's name makes Catherine smile. She runs her fingers over the paper, like this brings them closer, and she wishes they'd stayed tighter, been in better touch. But life got busy: children were born and work took up so much time, and there were dinner parties with preschool parents, and there was that catastrophe from their wedding, and of course, once Bea died . . . If she hadn't, Catherine knows they'd never have splintered, the six of them. But she did, and they did, and as Owen likes to say so often now, "You've made your bed, so lie in it."

Actually, what he says is: "You've made the bed, Catherine! And the sheets, and the pillows, and the bedside candles, so just go lie in it, and I'll be right here managing the kids' homework and sports schedules!"

Usually, she's so tired that she pretends he's not being sarcastic and, in fact, goes to their bedroom and passes out.

"Catherine." Sasha has returned and hands her a green-tea energy drink. Catherine drops the e-mail stack on the table. "I hate to tell you this." Sasha's voice drops to a whisper. "But I was just scrolling through some images from last year to compare . . . and . . . well . . . we used these same napkins last year. And that cookie design too. I mean, I know this is for the pilot, but since they're going live on our site too . . ."

Catherine can barely hear her now.

"What?"

Sasha clears her throat. The air vacuums from the room.

"The firecracker cookies. We did those last year. And . . . the mason jar centerpiece." She's whispering again. "Very similar." A pause. "That's why I was checking."

Catherine leans forward to hear her. "What?"

Fred, her lead designer, appears beside her.

"They're not the same."

Sasha stares at her feet. Catherine stares at Fred. Fred finally withers and says: "They're similar, but not the same."

Catherine knew it! She beats a fist against her thigh. Catherine knew she shouldn't have put anyone else in charge.

"Goddamn it, Fred."

Fred tucks a flop of blond hair behind his pink ears and looks like he might cry.

"There are no tears in craft design," Catherine says, incredulous, and Fred swallows too much air and hiccups.

"I'm exhausted," he says, as tears do begin to seep out. "Tapped dry. We turn these around every other week, Catherine! I can't . . . I can't keep up."

"So you thought stealing from last year was the best way to go? That no one would notice? Stealing is *never* the solution! It's the worst form of crafting, Fred! The lowest of the low."

Catherine starts to say more, but suddenly clamps down, her mouth pressing into a thin line, her lips then morphing into an angry comma. She worries that she's said too much, that her overzealous rebuke might actually betray her own guilt, her own notebook full of others' ideas that she pulls up, prints out furtively late at night, and tucks away for inspiration. Never, she tells herself, for plagiarizing.

Catherine sighs loudly and grabs the stack of e-mails, marching off the set, her staffers parting ways, like the Red Sea for Moses, to give her space. She slams the test-kitchen door and exhales, savoring the silence, the solitary moments when no one is asking her for anything, no one figuratively tugging on each arm, needing something more. She starts down the hallway, rounds one corner, then rounds another. Over and again. The walking clears her head, lets her *think*, refuels her neurons. She tosses her shoes by the elevator and takes another lap, then remembers the e-mails, the papers in her hand.

Annie Cunningham.

Why on earth is she e-mailing?

She stops abruptly by the women's restroom. Her shirt feels sticky now, the silk clinging to her lower back, the sky-blue fabric turning a deeper shade where sweat has seeped in. She tugs at her waist, then at her neckline. The air smells like vanilla honeysuckle because they were testing scent sticks as part of a new product line to lure Target into partnership—a partnership that would infuse the company with much-needed cash—especially if the pilot doesn't go. A partnership that Catherine needs more than Target needs her.

She leans against the door of the bathroom.

> Dear Catherine:
> Wow. It's been years! I love watching your
> segments on Good Morning America! And
> The Crafty Lady . . . I check it every day!
> Also, I really loved your Halloween decorat-
> ing ideas from last year: I am on our build-
> ing's co-op board, and I followed them to a T
> for our lobby!! They were such a hit that I've
> been asked to head up the decorating com-
> mittee again this year!
> Anyway. Gosh, now I feel silly. Maybe this
> won't even get to you. But . . . did you get a
> FedEx today? From . . . Bea? Or Bea's lawyer?
> Well, I did. And Lindy did because she texted
> me out of the blue.
> It is all very weird, and I'm not sure what
> to make of it. It seems that she owns our
> house. Our old house on Walnut Street. I
> know. It doesn't make sense to me either.

When would she have done this? Why would
she have done this?
Anyway, let me know.
xoxo,
Annie

Catherine's brow creases (she doesn't do Botox because it does not play well with her middle-America demographic) as she tries to connect the dots.

Catherine hasn't thought much about their old house on Walnut Street over the last two decades. She doesn't have a clue what Annie is talking about or why on earth Bea would have bought it, or what a FedEx bearing this news would mean. But when she does think about that old house on Walnut Street, just for a beat of a moment there against the door to the ladies' room with vanilla honeysuckle in the air, she senses a tiny flourish of nostalgia, a pulse of a memory when life was simpler and she—they all—were so happy. It was almost twenty years ago—*eighteen years!*—but the feelings come easily, quickly, catching Catherine off guard, flooding her lower lids with tears.

She bats her pink-polished fingers to dry the dampness and glances around to ensure that no one bears witness to her weakness. There are no tears in craft design.

Then she tilts her head against the wall, her body sinking against it, its weight the only thing propping her up, keeping her from sliding like jelly onto the ground.

It couldn't have been so long ago, she thinks.

It stings like it was just yesterday.

4

OWEN

Owen looks like a startled deer when Catherine unexpectedly drops her tote in the mudroom and skulks into the kitchen. He literally jumps a few inches from his perch on the stool by the granite kitchen island and yells, "Holy shit." His Heineken bottle spins to the floor and shatters.

"I'll get that," Catherine says, already heading to the pantry to retrieve the broom.

"I can do it," he offers, though he doesn't move, doesn't feel like moving. "What are you doing home? I thought . . . Sasha called me and said . . ." He trails off, not wanting to sound displeased that she's home. Because he's not. Though her arrival changes the tone of the evening, a colder wind blowing through what he thought would be a warm, breezy night.

Catherine reappears from behind the pantry door and starts sweeping, her temples pinching. Owen takes a little pity and grabs the paper towels to wipe off the counter, still slightly dismayed by her arrival, now that he's tasked with conversation rather than relaxing on the couch with his phone.

"Have you eaten?" he asks, balling up the paper towel and aiming it at the sink. "The kids are showering. I was going to order a pizza." He hesitates. "But . . . I guess I can cook now?"

It's a question hoping for only one answer.

Oh no, a pizza is fine.

Even though when they agreed five years ago that he would stay home with the kids, he cited his passion for home cooking (and gardening!) as one of the reasons why. "I want to be the dad who makes lasagna from scratch for them!" he'd said. "You go do the heavy lifting outside of the house; let me do the heavy lifting here."

The paper towel bounces off the porcelain farmer's sink and onto the floor. He sighs. It's just as well. He'd have to put it in the garbage either way.

Catherine squats and ushers the glass shards into the dustpan, a few stubborn splinters refusing to eke their way onto it.

"I'm not hungry," she says, sweeping harder.

"I'll get you something just in case," he offers. "A Greek salad? Garlic knots? Or we can order something else. What would you want? Or . . . I mean . . . I can cook. I think there are chicken breasts in the freezer." He makes a show of opening the giant freezer drawer and fishing around, even though he knows that she sees through his act.

"It's fine. I have to work anyway," Catherine says, scanning their gray wood-planked floor, searching for any shiny remnants that sparkle under the glare of the kitchen light, but apparently seeing none, she is satisfied.

No easy feat these days, Owen thinks. *Satisfying her.*

"You really have to work tonight? You're finally home."

He regrets this as soon as he says it because that's not what he means. Not that she's *finally* home. Well, that *is* what he means. But that's not how he wanted it to come out. This is how their fights always start these days—someone misinterpreting something, some tone too harsh, another tone too passive-aggressive.

He watches her set the broom back exactly just so, as she found it, and disappear around the corner to dump the glass scraps into the trash. He runs through all the scenarios, bracing himself for all the ways this is about to turn south. *Shit.* It would have been so much easier if she'd worked late, which he hates thinking, because all he wants is for her to be here, more present, with them.

She emerges from the mudroom with a FedEx envelope in her hand. *Work. It's always work. Maybe it's just easier this way,* he considers. *She'll close the door to her office, and then we won't have anything to argue about.*

But she surprises him, sliding the envelope across the counter toward him, resting it a foot from where the Heineken spun to its peril.

"What's this?"

"It's for both of us."

Owen pulls the document from inside, cocking his head, his face a puzzle. He can feel Catherine watching him, like she used to when he'd bring home his own work from the firm, and he'd spend hours sifting through depositions, through fine print, trying to find logic in all the rhetoric. He raises his eyes to meet hers, wondering if she remembers that time too: how she'd lean against the door frame and smile, telling him he was the smartest man in the world, and that there wasn't any stupid deposition he couldn't make sense of. He wills her to move to him, to pull him tight enough so he can smell the lingering aroma of whatever she hatched up in her test kitchen, so she can smell the half-drunk beer on his breath.

She meets his eyes and offers a limp shrug. "What do you think?"

It takes him a beat to realize she's referring to the FedEx.

He refocuses, trying not to think that he hadn't moved to kiss her hello when she got home. And that she hadn't moved toward him either.

"I don't understand," he says. "A reunion? At Bea's behest? A delivery we have to be together for?"

"I don't understand either."

He likes that: that they're a team again, on the same page, even if it's about something as off-kilter as a letter from their dead friend's lawyer.

He opens the stainless Sub-Zero and grabs another beer, holding up one for her, but she shakes her head no, which she always does. He knew she'd say no even before he offered. She doesn't do beer these days. Instead, she grabs the bottle of Grey Goose from the liquor cabinet and twists off the top, pouring a splash into a Tiffany crystal tumbler (a wedding gift), then pouring a little more.

"We should go," Owen says, the crest of certainty rising suddenly. Wouldn't it be great to be back there, on their old stomping grounds, where they were happy and life was easy, and maybe he could actually reach over and kiss his wife again?

"We should go," she agrees, her index finger tracing the rim of her glass.

"But?"

"But." She laughs hollowly. "Well, there are a hell of a lot of 'buts.'"

"There aren't any 'buts'!" he says, aware that his voice is rising but unable to quiet it. "Why are there always 'buts' with you now?"

She stares at the ceiling, sips her Grey Goose, then sips it again.

"We haven't seen them in *years*, Owen. After our wedding—"

He cuts her off. "You took sides after the wedding, not me."

"I might have to work."

"It's a holiday weekend, Catherine. For Christ's sake." Owen interrupts her and sets his bottle down a little too hard, its echo clanging in the space between them.

"There are . . ." Her voice quavers. "There are fires at the office to put out now."

"When aren't there?" There are always fires to put out at her office. He doesn't ask for details because it's not like she's sought his advice in years. He doesn't need to feel irrelevant for one more second.

Catherine turns to him, pale.

"Oh my God," she whispers. "I just realized. The Fourth of July. It would have been her birthday. She would have been forty."

Owen swallows his beer. Three long sips. The taste of the hops in the back of his throat.

"I want to go," he says finally. It's not a question; it's not a request. It could be considered a plea, but he says it firmly, and he hopes she'll respect it.

She chews the side of her lip, then nods.

"OK," she says, so softly he almost misses it.

Owen takes a long swig, polishing off the bottle, and listens to the clatter above them, the stampede of their freshly showered children reverberating above—Penelope, already eleven, and Mason, a gangly nine. The stampede of their lives plowing forward without her, without Bea.

"Jesus. Forty. How could we have forgotten?"

Catherine doesn't answer. She pours herself another vodka. So Owen reaches for the phone to call for the pizza.

5

COLIN

Colin is flying down Pacific Coast Highway, the sun on his back, the centrifugal forces of the wind turning his hair wild, the radio on loud—too loud—for him to even hear his own singing. He shifts into fifth gear as Eddie Vedder wails, his gravelly voice screeching out of Colin's Maserati convertible into the ocean air and then into nothingness. Colin's hands play drums against the steering wheel; his head bobs along with Vedder.

"She lies and says she's in love with him, can't find a better man."

Colin sings along—yells, really—the tune irrelevant.

He has a surgery to get to and needs to be at his office in an hour, which he'll never make with afternoon traffic, but so what. He's never late, and just this once he's going to enjoy himself, fly through Malibu, pretend that the FedEx envelope on his backseat never arrived, that it isn't a ticking time bomb.

He hadn't known she'd do this, of course. Maybe he should have, but he didn't.

He'd just been a stupid resident. What did he know? Why did she decide to confide in him? Part of him felt special: that he was the only one she confided in. The other part of him didn't even think about what came next, what came after, what came via FedEx today, a ghost delivered right to his doorstep.

Bea had called him in August, two months after Catherine and Owen's wedding. They'd fallen out of regular touch, as old friends sometimes do—mostly a quickie e-mail here and there, and she was in Honduras doing her charity work, with spotty phone service and unreliable Internet. They'd promised to be better about it at the wedding. But they hadn't been, of course. In fact, they hadn't spoken since, and so he didn't even recognize her voice at first when she said, "Hey, it's me," then "Bea, you idiot."

He figured she'd called to chew him out about Lindy, about the stupidity of the situation. It *was* stupid, but Jesus, people, can't we all be grown-ups about this? We're twenty-seven. This sort of shit happens. (In fact, it happened fairly often with Colin: with his fellow residents, with pretty—if boozy—LA girls he met at West Hollywood bars, with friends of friends of friends whom he promised to call, but never did.)

Catherine had been furious, and Owen looked a little peaked (mostly because Catherine was so furious), and then Annie split early, and Lindy stomped around, fiery like a volcano about to blow, and Bea had stood there with her hands on her hips in that magnificent canary-yellow dress without saying a word. So now, he figured, she was calling to say all of her words, even though chastising wasn't Bea's speed. But maybe now it was. Because he'd done something that had splintered them. And to Bea, that was the worst possible sin. In fact, there weren't any other sins, really. Not to her. Just loyalty. Just preservation of their six-point star.

He remembers starkly, even now, that he'd just ordered a double espresso from the hospital lobby's coffee cart because he was about to start rounds and he'd been out too late the night before on a fix-up that wasn't going anywhere, but his date hadn't gotten the hint.

He braced himself for her lecture, but was relieved, all the same, to hear from her. *Bea.* God, he always loved her just a little bit too much. Whatever she was calling to say, he would graciously accept it and then apologize. She was right, he thought as he waited for the barista and the double espresso. He was stupid, and he'd say so and repent, and figure out how to fix it. Because he would fix anything to make Bea happy.

He started in. "Bea, look, I know why you're calling—"

But she interrupted. "Shush. I have to say this before I can't. I don't want to lose my nerve. You're the only one I can call. The only one I'm telling."

He remembers that he stopped then, so abruptly that a nurse ran into him, and the espresso bubbled out of the lid and onto his thumb. He knew something was wrong by her tone, immediately, certainly, without question. And it had nothing to do with him and his impulses at the wedding.

"The cancer's back," she said.

"What?" He squeezed his eyes shut, then opened them again, then shut. Like he was waking from a dream.

"My cancer. It's back. From when I was eleven."

"It can't be," he said, though he'd gone to medical school, and knew of course that it could be. "That's impossible."

"Anything can be. Nothing is impossible."

"I just saw you. We just saw each other!" He jammed his eyes closed again, shaking his head furiously. *Wake up! Wake up!*

"Well, I'm sick. I *am. I just am.*"

"But you weren't sick! You were perfect. You were wearing that yellow dress, and you danced until the lights came on, and—"

"Colin." She cut him off. He pictured her snapping her fingers, bringing him to, centering him because that's what Bea did. Centered him.

"Bea," he whispered. He knew how stupid he sounded, like one of those naïve patients who asked philosophical, senseless questions when the science had proved otherwise. *You were perfect!* Like anything on the outside determines what's happening on the inside. He'd gone to Stanford Medical School, for God's sake.

He puffed up his chest, though she couldn't see this, of course. Regrouped, came out swinging. "You'll fight it. Who are your doctors? Who are you seeing?"

She didn't say anything for a long while then, long enough that Colin overheard the hospital intercom page an on-call resident twice.

"There's nothing to be done," she said finally. "I've been back in New York for a few weeks now."

"There's always something to be done!" he said too loudly, and a nurse turned and scowled at him.

"Colin," Bea said, and he saw her curled up in an armchair in her apartment that came as part of her trust fund, feet tucked beneath her, eyes tired, probably closed, accepting the truth about things because Bea had never had a choice. Her parents, her accidents, her leukemia.

He reached for a wall to hold himself up.

"I need your help," she said.

"Anything," he replied immediately. "But I thought you said there was nothing to be done."

"That's not what I mean. That's not the type of help I need."

He didn't understand.

"Bea, let me ask around, get you a referral, get you into Sloan Kettering. A guy I went to med school with is a resident. Let me make a call."

"Colin!" she snapped. It was as close to exasperated as he'd ever heard her. He knew she was sitting up straighter now, agitated. "It's done."

"It's not done, Bea!"

She quieted. "It's terminal. I've been to Sloan. There's nothing else they can do. And now I need your help."

"Please don't give up." His voice broke.

"Don't say that. Don't say that to me. It's an insult, and you know it. Like I'd ever give up on anything if I had a choice."

He thought he was going to be sick, felt that espresso rising back up and swirling on the back of his tongue. He swallowed it down. Bea calmed down on the other end of the line. And then he listened. He already knew that he would say yes. He was never able to say no to Bea.

He shifts the Maserati into fifth gear, squinting behind his Ray-Bans in the California sun. Now there are going to be questions from the rest of them: the will, why she planned so far in advance, what she knew, what everyone else knew. He guns the engine fiercely around one of those treacherous curves around the rocky side of the mountain, and his back wheels spin too quickly. She did this that time they'd driven across the country: flown around curves too fast, recklessly. His heart would leap into his throat, and she'd cackle and call him a baby. Today, he overcorrects in time, but just barely.

He turns the music up.

Goddamn it, Bea!

Of course she couldn't leave the past alone. Bea was obsessed with the past, with time, with all of that shit. He remembers how he had to deliver the news to them all: he called Annie first, Annie called Catherine, and so on. How Bea begged him to just say it had happened quickly, "a car accident," and her grandmother pursed her dry lips and nodded her head and concluded that was for the best. He didn't understand it, truly—there was no shame in cancer, he told her over and over again—but Bea didn't want them to remember her as having suffered, didn't want them to remember her as anything less than the vibrant, radiant firework she was. Born on the Fourth of July. Indeed.

"Goddamn it, Bea!" He shouts to the open sky. Vedder finishes his lament of a song, and Colin jabs the replay button on his Bose sound system. He paid an extra six grand for the upgrade when he traded up to his latest car.

Colin cares only about the future. Jesus, isn't that why he got into plastics? Shifted off the neurosurgery track pretty soon after the funeral. Yeah, yeah, it doesn't take a shrink to see why. Plastics aren't about preserving time, molding better versions for the years ahead. You want new boobs, a firmer ass, a neck that doesn't sag like unleavened dough? You got it—it's not about who we used to be; it's about where we're going.

He eases the engine to a stop at a red light not far from the turnoff down Sunset back to Beverly Hills, back to real life. He quiets Vedder and his angst, and gazes up at the same cloudless, crystal sea-glass-blue sky he shouted into just a moment earlier.

"Shit, Bea." He sighs. "Really?"

He wonders if the others have moved past the wedding, wonders if they've forgotten how it undid them. He'd rather do just about anything than reopen those old wounds, the sticky history between them.

But he has never said no to her, ever. He knows as well as anyone that he isn't about to start now.

JULY

6

ANNIE

Annie nearly vomits twice on the Acela, and not from motion sickness. She swallows down another round of nerves in the cab from 30th Street Station to their old house on Walnut Street. She hasn't slept much since receiving the letter from one David Monroe, Esq., and her exhaustion isn't helping anything.

"You look . . . different," Baxter said two nights ago when he caught her staring at herself in the mirror. "What's with this?" His hands waved in front of him as he tried to pinpoint exactly what was different about her.

"I highlighted my hair," Annie said. "And got a little new makeup."

Baxter squinted like there was more, but maybe he hadn't been paying close enough attention to say exactly what. There was, of course. There was plenty more. She had spent a full day at the Mandarin Spa last week, detoxifying and exfoliating until her skin was practically stripped down to cellular level, and yes, she'd stopped at Bergdorf's to redo her wardrobe. Which may explain Baxter's batting hands: five-inch platform stilettos and suctioned-on leather pants (the sales girl assured her stilettos and leather was very "summer 2016") were not her usual PTA look.

"You really want to go?"

"I can't *not* go, Baxter! They're counting on me!" She'd eased down from one of the stilettos and felt off-kilter enough that she might topple over, like a wobbly cake ornament. "And this will be fun for you and Gussy! A boys' weekend!"

"You're . . . just . . . well . . . you're a little hopped up."

"I'm *excited*," she said, hunching over, sliding off her other shoe, hoping Baxter didn't notice her fingers shaking as she did so. "Don't misinterpret." And then, to ensure that she could in no way be misinterpreted, she logged on to Facebook and typed:

Can't wait to catch up with old friends at Penn this weekend! Wow!! I don't feel a day over twenty-five! #timeflies #lovinglife #oldfriendsarethebestfriends

Not that Baxter ever uses Facebook or even has a profile page, but if he did and if he saw that, he'd know there was no backing out now.

He wasn't wrong, though: she did feel frantic, jittery, felt herself slipping into that uncertain fog from those years back when jitters like those were squelched with benzos; like this fog was ebbing in from the coast over the sunrise, creeping up slowly but creeping up all the same. So perhaps she should have been less surprised when she innocently eased out of bed last night to check on Gus, who was snoring underneath his Yankees sheets (Pottery Barn Kids had an entire MLB collection), and she discovered that patterns repeat themselves, after all. Always.

Baxter had drifted off to sleep on the couch in the den, some movie from the '80s on HBO still bouncing shadows around the room, and his phone having dropped onto the Flokati rug. She wasn't snooping. Really. She was innocently retrieving it from the rug. Being a dutiful wife! She was just going to flip off the TV, pull a chenille blanket over his feet and up to his shoulders, and pad her way back to her own duvet.

Still, though, the staccato pulse of her anxiety certainly felt familiar, and perhaps she sensed a familiarity about something else too: the way that dogs feel earthquakes before they happen. Perhaps she unconsciously knew something was brewing in the crevasses of her marriage simply because she'd felt the tremors before. Perhaps that's why she *really* went to the den to check on Baxter. To check *up* on Baxter. She was a German shepherd who knew the earth was about to break.

She didn't even have to try to snoop. The text was there, right on the locked screen.

Yes, around all weekend. xo Cici

Annie hovered over her husband, whose palms were folded across his chest, whose lips were imperceptibly parted, relaxed, content, at peace. She felt her nostrils flare, her eyelashes fluttering wildly, her mouth pursed to suppress a heart-piercing scream.

No. *No.*

Maybe she was being crazy, delusional, even. Maybe she was reading all sorts of things into a harmless four words (and salutation) because they were skeletons from the past, echoes of the shreds of those years and their marriage and Annie's bleakness. Maybe it was just a work associate, who happened to be a woman, who happened to be named Cici. That was plausible.

She pressed her eyes closed and curled her fists and told herself that it was perfectly plausible: Cici, a work associate, here all weekend in case Baxter needed her. She told herself this over and over until she was calm enough to slip out of the den, the television still on, and back to her own room, dragging the sheets up so high that she was buried beneath.

Today, she rubs her exhausted eyes—her left eyelid keeps spasming—and gazes out the dirty window of the taxi, which smells like a fake evergreen tree and turns Annie's stomach just a bit faster, the roil of nausea cresting upward. The Philadelphia skyline and the Schuylkill River are fading behind her, the campus drawing nearer. A red, white, and blue sign hangs from the gritty overpass, rust stained and mildewed, welcoming guests to campus:

JULY 4TH WEEKEND: COME WALK THE ROAD TO FREEDOM!

Freedom. Annie hasn't had a weekend to herself—really, an afternoon to herself—since Gus was born. She's not complaining. She made those choices. To fire the full-time nanny so she didn't miss a moment; to rise through the ranks of the PTA so she had a way to fill the endless hours while Baxter worked. She whipped up cakes for bake sales, volunteered for book drives, jumped in to help at science projects and art fairs, and put together an absolutely knock-your-socks-off teacher appreciation breakfast last May. She hoped all this would magically unlock the gates to those alfresco mommy lunches, the wine-pairing dinner parties she heard about at drop-off. Not yet, though. Maybe this year when she's PTA vice president. She'll work twice as hard. Maybe then.

xo

The pesky, too-cordial sign-off on Baxter's text needles her brain.

No. Annie shakes her head as if shaking off the notion. She refuses to consider it. They were so good now, so much better now. The way concern washed over his face two nights ago, his posture upright and tense, his words tender and paternal. No. She must be misinterpreting.

"You going to the festival?" The taxi driver shouts over his shoulder, meeting her eyes in the rearview mirror.

"I'm sorry?" His accent is thick, and Annie hopes he's not offended she can't understand him. "I'm sorry," she says again.

"Colonial festival. All weekend! Lots of fun."

"Oh no, no festival for me."

"Too bad, very fun. Good hot dogs. I'm from Pakistan. We do not have good hot dogs."

Annie mindlessly fiddles with her phone and thinks about how much Gus loves hot dogs, how maybe she should have brought him along for these few days, shown him off. She bets the four of them would be enamored with him. How could you not be? She scrolls through some unbearably adorable photos of Gus to pass the last few blocks.

xo

No. No, no, no, no, no.

The cab deposits Annie on the corner of Forty-First Street and Walnut, and she stands there for a minute too long, frozen, lost in the drift of the eighteen years that have passed since she was a senior at Penn and this was her home and everything was different.

In those years, forty wasn't even on her radar. *Forty is ancient! Forty is one foot in the grave!* Forty was a blip, like a myth, like a UFO sighting or the Loch Ness monster, like the story of the rabid wolves her mom used to tell her when she was just yay high, and they were uprooted from yet another dilapidated house, or she'd lost another waitress job, or been dumped by another lousy boyfriend.

"There are wolves here, dear," she said. "We have to get going. We'll be better off with a fresh start. It's my job to keep you safe, and I can't protect you from rabies!"

Every time her bedroom window would rattle in the wind, Annie worried it was the wolves, no matter how many times she rose to peek out into the dark, empty landscape, no matter if, rationally, she knew that rabid wolves didn't eat people in southern Texas. But what if they did?

Wolves, it turns out, look nothing like you expect them to.

Her throat tightens, her stomach clenches. She is frozen on their old sidewalk in front of their old house, chased by their old memories.

"Lady, you OK?" the taxi driver finally yells out his window. "Wrong address?"

She worries that she hasn't tipped him enough—she's always worried she hasn't tipped people enough—so she reaches into her purse to give him five more, but he waves her off, and then he guns his engine and he's gone, and she's still there, staring at the row house, trying to remember the girl who once lived here.

She adjusts her new haircut and wipes her palms on the leather pants she already regrets. The July heat is damp, unavoidable, sweltering, and the leather appears to have rubberized around her thighs. The stilettos are digging into her pinky toe, blisters ripe and pink on both feet and also developing on her heels.

Breathe. This is what that therapist used to tell her, the one her OB-GYN insisted she see when she broke down on the exam table at her six-month postnatal appointment, her legs still aloft in the stirrups, the rest of her quaking so much the thin paper sheet beneath her shredded in two. *Breathe. In. Out. In. Out.*

She collects herself and, though her hands are shaking, she holds her phone up to capture the moment. The sun is just starting to fade behind the front façade, which, she thinks to herself, makes the image all the more precious. Maybe she won't have to toy with the pigmentation too much to shift it from a photo of a sort-of pretty, but nothing special, house with navy bricks and white shutters (they used to be teal bricks with purple shutters—no one was ever sure why, but they affectionately nicknamed it "Bruiser," and the moniker stuck) to something magical. Something emotive. Something that the women from school or Pilates or spin class (none of whom Annie really thinks of as friends because, well, she doesn't have a lot of real friends) will see and think, *OMG! Annie, I wish I was there with you, wherever you are! Xoxoxoxoxoxo!!!!!*

She takes the photo four different times, satisfied with the last version, aware that the distraction has calmed her nerves, blocked out the dizzying noise clattering inside her mind. She posts it to Facebook. Filter: vintage.

～ා

The letter from David Monroe, Esq., implored them to convene for the full weekend. Annie would not like to convene at all, despite her protests to Baxter. She felt foolish about the way things had ended at the wedding, the way she'd fled like a spurned teenager. But also about the way that it still stung, like a slap that was still fresh, even though she was a full-fledged adult who was on her way to PTA vice president! It's not like she didn't recognize how childish her grudges were, not like she didn't wish she wasn't the type of person who let those grudges slip away like grains of sand in her palm.

She forgave Baxter for his indiscretions years back because he was her lifeline. But Lindy wasn't. Lindy isn't. Even if Bea implored them, all six of them, to be just that. Annie figured if Lindy were her lifeline, she'd never have betrayed her in the first place. So the grudge occupies a small but present place in her heart, dormant but ticking all the same. (She long since forgave Colin because, well, he was Colin. Easy to forgive, easier to hang the moon on. Also, she understood that he was too good for her in the first place.)

So, yes, Annie would have been perfectly A-OK skipping out on the weekend, dipping her toes in the Atlantic with her chiseled husband and doe-eyed son, boiling lobsters and melting butter on grilled corn, and admiring the fireworks from Georgica Beach.

But Catherine had e-mailed that she and Owen were flying in from Chicago, and of course, there was Lindy, who texted from Los Angeles (Annie never replied), but who later texted Catherine to say that she was in, even though the last Annie had heard, they weren't much on speaking terms either. And rumor had it that the elusive Colin, plastic surgeon to the stars, was jetting in too. Annie fretted over what they'd think of her if she couldn't even muster up the temerity to hop the train down from New York.

She told Baxter she had to come this weekend because she'd encouraged everyone else to—she was the cheerleader, Baxter! She couldn't very well not show! She really came because she worried what they would say if she didn't.

David Monroe, Esq., had e-mailed that the keys would be left under the front mat. Annie peers around. The street is dormant, sleepy, her taxi long gone, the remaining row houses silent. Twenty years ago, leaving the keys under the front mat would have been an open invitation to armed robbery—literal armed robbery—but now the neighborhood has shifted. Annie stares left, then right, then left again, dubious, as if there can't be anything safe about returning, about these square blocks. She wills her legs to get going, and then, before she can think otherwise, she's on her old front stoop, and then she's crouching down and the keys are there. She wants to be the first one here—she *prays* she's the first one here—but she raps her knuckles against the door to be sure.

Nothing.

So she clicks the latch, and then she's inside.

It still smells the same. That's what hits her first. An unmistakable blend of old wood, pine air freshener, and spilled beer. Annie gags—not because the scent is rancid, rather because it's a time capsule. If she closes her eyes and slows her pulse, she could be twenty and on the brink of everything, the scholarship kid who found her way out of her Podunk Texas town: the girl who managed to shed her accent because it was the shadow that betrayed where she came from. Where she came from was a footnote to where she was going.

David Monroe, Esq., hasn't changed the house all that much. Fresher paint, yes, but the walls are still a shade that skews closer to dull yellow than white, the banister still wobbly and faded pine. There's a corkboard by the wall off the kitchen, blank and full of tiny holes, where they used to post fraternity-party invitations, flyers for charity drives, notes to one another on corners torn off notebook paper, saying things like "Studying in Van Pelt until forever." Or "If you order froyo, get me a swirl."

A couch still abuts the back bay window; a flea market dining table still resides just off the kitchen, where the six of them would gather on Sunday for Catherine's French toast. Or where Annie and Bea would nurse cups of tea while the rest of them had gone out drinking (Bea often went out drinking too, to be fair), and Bea prodded her about what she was going to do with her life. Every once in a while, she'd pull out a self-help book she'd bought at the bookstore and ease it toward Annie—not because she was being didactic, but because that's the sort of thing Bea did, and that's the sort of kindness you accepted from her.

Annie brushes her hands across the dining table. It's the first time in years, maybe since the funeral, that Bea's death has felt so visceral. The first time that the five of them will be here. Without Bea. Her nose pinches, and she flutters back tears. This seems like an impossible thing. She wallows in this until she worries the others will be here any second, and she can't be a mess, can't be anything like who she used to be. She wearily climbs the creaky steps toward her past.

She's upstairs staring at the ceiling in her old bedroom, lying on its Ikea bed, her mind spinning, calculating, racing with just how much longer she can bear to be here, when she hears the door unlatch.

Shoot. She thinks. *Please don't let it be Lindy. Please be Catherine. Neutral ground.* She sits up too quickly.

"Hello?" The voice echoes up the creaky steps and scratched bannister.

Colin . . . damn it! She hasn't even changed these ridiculous pants. She unbuttons them quickly, then realizes she'll never make it in time—they may have to be suctioned off her—and flops down again, flummoxed by her idiocy. Her nerves rise up from her stomach to her throat, but she swallows them down and blows out her breath.

Then she shouts, "Colin! I'm here!" She stills herself and hopes that he comes to her so her anxiety-plagued, leather-clad legs won't be forced to make the trip down the steps. She hears him clopping up the stairs—taking them two by two—and then the door swings open and he's there, standing in front of her, smiling and wide-open, and oh my God, as handsome as he always was.

"Annie!" He jumps on the bed beside her, and she falls back, and he pulls her into a tight hug before they both sit upright and assess.

"You look like you're twenty still," he says.

She feels the heat rise up to her cheeks and lets her hair tumble over them to conceal the glow. Yes, this is why she didn't nurse a grudge, this is why he was impossibly easy to forgive.

"No. I'm old." She hopes he can tell that maybe she doesn't mean it.

"We all fucking are." He laughs, and his deep hazel eyes linger, and her face burns hotter. He could do that: make you feel like he was lingering on you for a reason, like you were a prize he coveted, even if it was only in your imagination.

His smile grows a little fuller, and he squeezes her hand.

Annie is a little nauseated, clammy at his grasp.

He takes a beat and glances around.

"Did Bea . . . or whatever, her lawyer . . . make this look like your old room, or am I just imagining it?"

She unbraids her fingers from his and runs hers over the floral duvet that resembles the Ralph Lauren one she'd saved up for from her waitressing job back home and then bought on sale at the outlet in Houston, and nods, partially delighted that Colin remembers her old room. *Why didn't you spend more time in my room? Why didn't you wake up in the predawn hours tangled in my Ralph Lauren sheets, brushing your fingers down my spine, along my cheeks, down my fluttering eyelids?*

"It's weird, right?" Colin says.

"I think it's great, superfun, actually!" Annie chirps in a pitch that she loathes, a tone that sometimes emerges at dinner parties with Baxter's blue-blood associates, and Annie tries hard—too hard—to blend in. "I mean, we haven't seen each other in years! I'm so excited!"

He shrugs, then catches her eye in the mirror on the wall where it always was, where she'd paint on her eyeliner and flatten her bangs and think that maybe that would be enough to sway him her way. "You do look great, Annie. You really do!"

Annie has never been good at taking compliments, so she says, "I don't know." Then adds, "You too," and looks away before she can betray the true honesty of her words.

And Colin does look great. Too great. Annie doesn't know why she's surprised; he lives in Los Angeles and probably dates, like, *Sports Illustrated* models and plays, she doesn't know, beach volleyball for exercise. She wants to peel those leather pants off and chuck them out the window. Who does she think she is? Not a *Sports Illustrated* model. Not someone Colin would even consider.

"What do you think the surprise is? That we all have to be here for?" Annie asks.

It takes her a beat to realize that Colin looks worried. He never looks worried. "I dunno." He peers out the window. "Have you kept up with any of them?"

"A little. Owen and I are friends on Facebook, so there's that. I guess . . . well, Catherine and Lindy are so important, so not as much."

She doesn't add, *Lindy and I stopped talking years ago.* He must know this anyway. It wasn't a secret, the way she stormed off, the way Lindy flew home and moved out, then went down to Nashville. She hopes she hasn't offended Colin; he seems pretty important too. She's well aware that he is the Boob King of Los Angeles, but she doesn't dare make mention of that because that would imply she Googled him. Which she still does at least once a month when the apartment falls too quiet.

"Yeah," Colin says. "Owen and I text every now and then. He seems pretty happy. I guess with those two, you always knew they would be."

"Yeah."

Colin laughs. "They suck!"

Annie says, based on nothing, "No, I think we all seem pretty happy. I mean, I am!"

Colin is silent. Then, "I dunno. It was hard, I guess, after Bea."

"Being happy?"

"Staying in touch." He looks out the window for a moment too long. "Maybe the other thing too."

She doesn't answer, so he says, "I guess it's not like we didn't try."

"Being happy?"

Colin laughs, though there's not much joy behind it. Annie doesn't remember him sounding hollow when they were twenty. Annie remembers him full of life, vibrant, the magnet she couldn't break an attraction from. He turns from the window, his beautiful, sculpted face with its just-so cheekbones, with its firm jaw covered in stubble and its strong chin with just a kiss of a tiny cleft, fragmented almost undetectably, but detectable to Annie, who studied that face for what felt like forever.

Annie wants to take his hand and clutch it to her racing heart, but she fiddles with a clasp on her bracelet and instead thinks, *We didn't try, though. We didn't try at all.*

"Anyway."

"Anyway."

Then the front door unlatches, and there are "Hellos!" that echo upstairs, and Colin's face morphs into something more buoyant as he shouts, "Lindy!" and Annie has no choice but to take his lead and barrel down toward her.

7

LINDY

Lindy could really use a drink, but since she's attempting sobriety, she squelches the urge. Actually, what she could really use is something stronger—some sort of benzo—but that seems out too. She debates the harm of one drink. Just one. What sort of damage could that do? Not a lot, she tells herself. Anyway, she only has two more weeks to endure, until she knows what she's doing, makes a plan for what's coming next, and she thinks she can stay sober for that. Fourteen days. Then she'll drink herself blind.

They're all here now and gathered around the kitchen table, dodging eye contact and feigning friendliness as if bonds hadn't soured like skunked beer. Owen is opening up Amstels that they've found in the fridge.

"I'm on antibiotics." She waves her hand from her perch on the steps leading to the second floor. "Also, super beat with jet lag."

None of them even bothers taking notice.

"I had the worst bronchitis," she adds. "Off and on for two months. Killer to sing live."

"That sucks," Owen says.

"Thought they were going to have to perform surgery."

"For bronchitis?" Owen asks.

"Yeah, I mean, for a node. It's complicated. The doctors weren't sure. Trying meds again. We'll see. If we can't lick it now, it could ruin my voice forever." Lindy's not sure why she's elaborating, she could have stopped with "antibiotics."

"Colin, I cannot believe you're still single," Catherine interrupts, passing out napkins.

"I was engaged for three months," he says, and Annie, who has been incessantly uploading photos to Facebook, glances up, her face slackening.

"What happened?" she asks.

"Didn't stick," he replies, and her jaw eases, her eyes soften, and she returns to her screen.

My God, Lindy thinks. *She's still mooning over him.*

Then, to Colin, "I can't believe you're in LA. I'll have you over sometime. I have a sick view from the Hills."

She watches Annie to see if this needles her, prods her in the ways that Lindy has grown used to prodding everyone. She thinks she notices Annie freeze for a split second, but she's not certain. It irks her that she's not certain, that Annie has learned to hide from her.

"Dude, I can't believe you're famous," Owen says. "Remember how we took that songwriting class senior year?"

"Yeah."

"Shit, *I* got the A. You practically tanked it." Owen laughs. "Maybe I should have given a music career a go."

Lindy does remember the class, how peeved she was that their professor didn't find her special, didn't think she was any more worthy than the other sad sacks in the seminar. Owen, for Christ's sake! She basically kamikazed her grade just to be a dick.

"Fame isn't everything." She shrugs. She's used to feeding this line to journalists, particularly lately, when she's on a junket for *Rock N Roll Dreammakers. It's about passing on your knowledge, breaking open doors*

68

for others! She'll sometimes say, *Fame is just a label other people put on you.*

Lindy doesn't believe a word of her own drivel. Because fame? Yeah, she does fucking love it.

Owen drills her with questions, apparently the only one who has really kept up with her career ("I have a lot of time on my hands," he shrugs apologetically, as if there's something wrong with being well versed in the life of Lindy Armstrong), and Lindy's irritated that Annie hasn't shown more of an interest, even though Annie has made it clear her interest level is hovering right around rage-hate. After graduation, when they lived in that hovel in the West Village that was, like, four hundred square feet between them, and Lindy would play some shitty show for drunk NYU students who would catcall about her boobs, Annie always showed an interest. It was Annie's interest that gave Lindy hope. She would sell approximately four CDs, and drag herself home after, and Annie would wake up, even though she had to work the next morning, just to ask her if she got discovered that night.

It's been thirteen years, Lindy thinks. *When is she going to grow the fuck up?*

"I don't know how you almost failed that class," Owen is saying. "The stuff you write now is amazing."

"Thanks!" Lindy says too cheerfully, failing to mention that virtually none of her radio-worthy songs have been her own. "And now I have this TV show," she adds. *TV!* She'd rather be playing gigs in dive bars across the Southeast, but gigs in dive bars don't pay $4 million. And Lindy isn't dumb enough to pretend that she doesn't love all the stuff accompanying that cash. Still, Annie sits stone-faced. Lindy narrows her eyes. "Seriously, Col, I know lots of hot girls. You'll see."

Annie jabs something on her phone, then crosses her legs in those stupid leather pants, which Lindy actually adores and would probably wear, but which do not suit Annie at all.

"Nice pants," Lindy says. "I think I own the same pair."

"Mason and I are watching!" Owen interrupts. "I love that girl you chose for your team from, where was it, like, some small town in Wisconsin?"

"Kansas." She doesn't ask who Mason is, because she has a vague sense that she should know that he's Catherine and Owen's son, but she can't for the life of her remember how old he is or if their other child is a boy or a girl.

"I'm never home," Catherine says. Then, as if she realizes it's time to bury the hatchet for causing a scene at the wedding, adds, "Or I'm sure I would."

Lindy raises her eyebrows. Catherine didn't give her much of a chance to explain after Annie fled the brunch, and then Bea chased after her, and Colin nursed three Bloody Marys. She marched over to the buffet line, where Lindy was eyeing the scrambled eggs and debating the bacon, and seethed, "How could you?"

"How could I what?"

"You know what you did, Lindy. Stop being so goddamn unaccountable. You knew how she felt. You knew what she wanted."

"It didn't mean anything." Lindy tried to feign innocence, but Catherine was never anyone's fool.

"Which makes it all the worse. And at our wedding. You did this at our wedding. You were my bridesmaids!"

"She's a big girl," Lindy said. "Everyone should grow up."

Catherine scoffed, her bright eyes turning gray. "You should grow up, Lindy." Then, "She's your friend! *I'm* your friend. And you just made this weekend about *you*. Which, if I'm being honest, isn't particularly surprising."

Lindy thought she was being a little overdramatic, and Catherine *had* been a bit of a bridezilla, what with her insistence on those ridiculous plum-colored bridesmaid's dresses that reminded Lindy of curdled pudding, and all of the peach-scented, hand-crafted candle favors they'd had to tie in twine on Friday, and home-pressed invitations Catherine had e-mailed them about, oh, a hundred times.

"Give me a break, Catherine."

"Give you a break? I'm sorry that we can't all be as important as your new cool friends, that you could barely bring yourself to wear the dress I picked out, that you being here feels like an inconvenience to your super-awesome life that is way cooler than mine! But this is the last straw, Lindy. I wanted you here, standing with me, because we were old friends. But you haven't been acting that way at all." She paused to take a breath, then kept on like a dam unplugged. "So I should give *you* a break? And then . . . and then this! With Colin! When we all knew how she felt! Jesus, he wanted Bea for years, and she would *never*, ever resort to this. There was an unspoken code."

"There was no code! What code?" Lindy stared across the buffet to see if Bea could come defend her, put a rest to all this code business, save her from the spiral this was quickly taking, but Bea was still chasing Annie, trying to abort her own emotional hemorrhage. *"What sort of bullshit is this code?"*

Bea was nowhere in sight.

"Oh, you know what code. Don't pretend for one second that you don't know the code. You just didn't care."

"Fine." Lindy flung her plate onto the buffet table, where it clanged against a carafe of orange juice, which promptly toppled to the carpeted floor. Catherine immediately dropped to her knees, grabbing wads of cloth napkins from the buffet, mopping up the orange stain like it was pooling blood. *"Fine! You're right! I'm a shitty person, I'm a selfish asshole. But I gave up a gig at The Bitter End to be here, when, I'll be honest, I couldn't give less than one shit if you have calla lilies or tiger lilies, when I don't give a rat's ass about your stupid peach-scented candles. I don't need this shit, you're right, Catherine, and for that, I'm the worst friend in the world. Happy wedding! Congratulations!"* And then, because Lindy never felt safer than when she was running *away* from whatever obstacle lay in front of her, she fled out the same doors Annie had, though far enough behind not to catch up, not to feel the tremors from her wake.

Now, Lindy wonders if Catherine is sorry for the way she so easily blamed her, accused her, cast her out. Or maybe Catherine is waiting for Lindy's own apology. Lindy almost snorts aloud. Like she should be sorry. It was sex. It was stupid sex, but Jesus! *Been there, done that.* She holds her chin high and waits for someone else to offer an olive branch, to grab hold and say, *"Let's just all move on."*

"Listen," Catherine says now. "Let's just get this out of the way. What's going on here?"

"You first," Lindy tuts. "I'm waiting."

Catherine cocks her head, like she has absolutely no idea what Lindy is talking about, which, Lindy quickly realizes, she doesn't.

"What I mean is, why on earth did Bea own this house? Why would she have made a will with this directive in it?"

Colin clears his throat, and they all swivel their gazes toward him. He presses back against the sand-colored couch, the late-day light from the bay window shadowing his face.

"No . . . nothing," he says. "I don't know."

"Who has a will at twenty-seven?" Catherine asks.

"Bea," Annie suggests earnestly.

Lindy rolls her eyes.

"Was . . . something going on with her? Did anyone talk to her after the wedding?" Catherine says, "It's strange. Like she was almost preparing for it."

"The wedding?" Annie says.

"Dying." Catherine shakes her head.

None of them says anything then.

"I spoke with her a little bit," Annie offers softly. "Just . . . well, when *she* left. Moved out." She raises her head toward Lindy. "But then she was back in Honduras. I tried to e-mail her, but she never got back to me." She shrugs, a sad gesture.

Lindy debates whether she should be flattered that Annie finally acknowledged her or pissed that she can't bring herself to say her name.

"She called me a few times," Catherine says, like she's just remembering. "Left me a few messages, but we were on our honeymoon . . ." She looks to Owen like maybe he can fill in the blanks. "And when we got back, I can't . . . I can't remember if we ever got around to talking. No. No, actually, we didn't. That was it, the last time I spoke with her was at our wedding." She sighs. "I mean, if something was wrong, like, if she had a will for a reason, I didn't know."

"She didn't have a will for a reason!" Colin snaps. "God. You're acting like, she was, like suicidal! She had a huge trust, and I'm sure she was told to be responsible about it. It's not like she was a stranger to people unexpectedly dying."

The other four consider Bea's parents and nod.

"Well, anyway. Is there something here for all of us?" Catherine looks around. They all look around. The living room is empty, other than the odd furnishings and well, them. "Why else did we come back?"

"We came back because we got the letter," Annie says.

"Please." Lindy doesn't mean to sneer like she does when she says this. "Please, what?"

"*Obviously* we are here because of the letter . . . Hello!"

"Lindy!" Catherine says. "Please don't start already, please. Let's put our best faces forward."

"This *is* my best face."

Catherine sighs, too dramatically.

"You're not happy with my face?"

Catherine pinches the bridge of her nose, like Lindy is a monster headache, a giant literal pain in her brain.

"OK, why don't we start over?" Colin says. "Everyone is happy with everyone's face."

"No, please explain what exactly you don't like about my face," Lindy bleats. She knows she should drop it. God, why can't she just let it go? Stop picking this fucking scab until it's ripe and pink and bloody?

"Oh God," Catherine groans.

"Catherine." Owen steps closer. "Not now."

"I'm fine," she says, though spit flies a little from her mouth.

"Really?" he asks.

"Owen, please don't start." He sits down abruptly, dismissed, his chair squeaking, his skin flushed, his lips curled, as if he wasn't trying to start anything before, but now very much may be considering starting something. Then, to Lindy, "Look. We're all trying to get off on the right foot here. So let's try that, OK?"

"Fine."

"Great."

"Fine," Lindy says again, not sounding fine, not feeling fine. She thrusts her hands onto her hips, calculating how quickly she can get to the airport. The first flight probably isn't until the morning. *Shit.* She juts her chin. "Fine, let's talk about it then. Why the hell *are* we back here?"

"Bea asked us to," Colin says, like this is the explanation that clarifies everything.

"And you did always do whatever Bea wanted," Lindy replies.

"Lindy . . ." A long sigh from Colin.

"We all did," Annie interrupts. "We all tried to do what she wanted. Not just Colin."

"Well, she made us promise to be family, remember that?" Colin fiddles with his watch, his gaze fixed on the weathered wood floor. "So I guess we didn't always do everything she wanted, after all."

౿ు

The strangest thing about returning to an enclave that encapsulated your youth is that you feel like nothing should have changed. Like you still have the right to be twenty and carefree and irresponsible. Like you still are twenty and carefree and irresponsible. Lindy has ditched the suffocation of their old house, of the rest of them, sitting around saying things like "Fine," and "Great," when nothing is fine or great at all, and now she's racing down the sidewalk toward Smokey Joe's, the old dive bar where they used to queue up the jukebox to Prince and grind on whomever they were hooking up with for the month (or the night), when she considers that this is the closest to freedom she's been in ages. That she is irritated and pissed off and claustrophobic, but still, she's irritated on her own terms.

She waits for the **DON'T WALK** sign to change, dipping her toe off the sidewalk, then stepping back quickly as a green Jeep flies by, too close, her thin white T-shirt clinging to her from the draft.

Colin chases her down the sidewalk.

"Come on, Linds. Wait up." He jogs to a halt. "Don't run off without trying. We're not so bad." He grins.

"I'm not running off. I'm going out for a drink."

One drink, she's decided, won't matter. She's played with fate in much more dangerous ways than this before.

Owen rushes through the shadows, out of breath.

"Wait, wait, I'm here too!"

Lindy groans. "So much for enjoying some solitude."

"Sorry!" Owen says. "Jesus."

"Forget it." Lindy sighs. "Personal space has never been our forte."

"Since when have you ever wanted solitude," Colin says, more of a statement than a question, so she lets it go.

The light flips, traffic halting in front of them, and they fall in line with each other like they used to, silent for a bit, Owen's flip-flops keeping beat against the pavement.

Owen shoves his hands into the cargo pockets of his shorts. "I think I've forgotten how it feels to be twenty. Like, no responsibilities, no worries. Shit, man."

"What *did* we worry about at twenty?" Colin looks befuddled.

Lindy shrugs. "I didn't worry about much, don't worry about much now. What's the point? Life happens."

"Hey." Owen perks up. "Don't you have a song called that?"

A police car flies down the block before she can reply, its siren reverberating around them, its lights bouncing off the neighboring stores. Twenty years ago, police sirens were like background noise, ever present, a part of the fabric of the campus: so too was the nervous apprehension if you walked home solo too late at night or found yourself locked out after dark. It was ironic: the rich kids thrust into the inner city. Of all of them, Annie was the only one who had even come close to understanding the perils that lay in wait behind the shadows.

Lindy risked it once—she'd broken up with her boyfriend the hour before and then couldn't convince him to escort her home because, well, she'd been a real bitch when she dumped him, callously, unceremoniously, just after he asked her to a fraternity formal—and she was mugged outside the McDonald's two blocks from their house, just kitty-corner from where they stood now, though a Jamba Juice had long ago replaced the McDonald's.

Lindy tries to remember that guy's name, the one who stood his ground and refused to accompany her home, but she can't recall. Greg? Craig? She remembers him being cute but maybe annoying. She isn't sure. Bea and Annie told her she was a moron to dump him—he was hot and kind and smart and already had a job lined up at Goldman—but Lindy felt suffocated, like maybe he was too into her, more into her than she was comfortable with.

"I think that sounds pretty wonderful," Annie had said. They'd been pouring cereal into plastic cups, dinner for the night. "Who wouldn't want to be loved in that way?"

"There does need to be a balance," Bea remarked. She mixed some Cocoa Puffs in with Honeycomb. "But I did once read that it's better to be the one less in love than the one more so."

"So that's your plan? To always be the one a little less in love?"

"I have you guys. I don't need to be in love." Bea shrugged. "I need an occasional warm body and tequila."

"Not the worst plan," Lindy concurred. Though she watched Annie spoon her own Cocoa Puffs and wondered what it would take to convince her that she was worthy of being loved too.

Anyway, regardless of Greg/Craig's positive attributes and/or Annie's urging to keep him around, Lindy dumped him. And then she got mugged. And now she's here, in that same spot, twenty years later, staring at the neon glow of the Jamba Juice sign, and the sidewalks aren't littered with empty cigarette packs and used napkins and sometimes much more disgusting things like old condoms or the occasional syringe. Greg or Craig is long gone, and she can stand up for herself against any sort of threat, and she is famous and a millionaire and invincible.

"Let's do this!" she says, once the whirling sirens have faded southward. "Let's party like it's 1999!"

Owen slaps her five, and Colin shakes his head but grins.

"Lindy Armstrong," he says, "you never change."

"Fuck you, Colin." She smiles as she says it, but she's really thinking, *No, fuck you, all I've done is change.* After all, she's a worldwide brand now, a meteoric star, a VIP with an entourage and celebrities on speed dial, and certainly not the girl who cared about making these fools happy. They didn't get that: that she *did* actually care.

At Smoke's, all three of them are carded, not because they resemble actual teenagers, but because this is an old Smoke's tradition. State your name into the microphone and video camera. Lindy had forgotten about it until the microphone is thrust in front of her. But then it's all so natural to her—the mic out front, the (imaginary) spotlight. So she howls and says, "Lindy Armstrong, bitch!" and the bouncer, who's dressed as George Washington, does a double take, and then howls back, "Holy shit!" and insists they snap a selfie, which Lindy happily does because finally, *finally*, someone recognizes that she matters.

The upstairs of the bar is dark—dimmed sconces punctuate the walls, muted halogen bulbs hang over the booths, shadowy enough to conceal the enormity of Lindy's fame for now. Her eyes take a moment to adjust.

Though it's summer session and most of the undergrads have retreated to their jobs as camp counselors, or vacations with their parents (or if they're really lucky—the Wharton students, most likely—internships with self-important companies like McKinsey or Goldman), it's still crowded for a Thursday night in July. The air conditioner is feebly cooling the humid air that's seeped in from outside, and all the girls have tossed their hair into messy buns, exposing their long, nubile necks, highlighting their subtle collarbones, their youthful cleavage. Lindy used to be young and wily too.

She trails Owen and Colin to a booth in the back, near the jukebox.

She watches a particularly lithe undergrad, in a tiny tank top and vacuumed-on jeans, thrusting her hips to the beat of the music. The girl knows everyone is staring, and she lures them in with her long legs, her perfect rhythm. Lindy loves this glorious undergrad for a flicker of a moment until she hates her too. Hates her for her beautiful legs, her lush skin, her gust of immorality.

Everyone always says that youth is wasted on the young, but that's horseshit, she thinks. *Nothing is wasted on them. Look at them. Look at how happy they are, how invincible they feel.*

She slides into the booth next to Colin and feels the solidness of his legs as she presses next to him. He doesn't seem particularly put off by this, so she leaves her leg where it is. She tugs her V-neck a little lower—her boobs were always her calling card—and then she bounces around until her crimson hair cascades down her shoulders.

Owen catches her preening. "Aren't you a lesbian now?"

Colin cackles. "There is no way you're a lesbian now! Come on."

"Well, I'm *sort of* a lesbian now," she says, fidgeting with a used coaster left over from the person who sat there before. The table hasn't been wiped down properly. She flicks off some crumbs left behind from old chicken fingers. "I don't like hard definitions." In fact, she was always a bit of a lesbian, she just never told them. Tatiana is the first woman she's been public with, but not the first one she's loved.

She wonders if they'll call her on her bullshit answer, but neither seems to care too much about her bullshit in general, which is both a relief and an insult. Colin busies himself flagging over the waitress, and Owen orders two pitchers of beer, which used to be five bucks but are now twelve.

"So. Are we done with the Lindy Armstrong attitude, and can the evening now commence smoothly?" Colin asks.

"Screw you."

"Seriously, Linds. Why come back if you didn't want to? It wasn't like this was mandatory."

"No, seriously, Colin, fuck off."

Colin seems to find this endearing, so he wraps an arm around her and pulls her into his shoulder, which is just as well, because Lindy doesn't have an answer for him. What is she supposed to say? That she wanted to keep tabs on Annie? That she wanted Catherine to apologize? That she wanted them all to understand how she'd triumphed without them? That she couldn't think of anywhere else she'd rather be, not because she wants to be *here*, but because she didn't want to be in those other places either. Not playing the Fourth of July show tomorrow night, not really even making out with Tatiana. Is she supposed to explain, here, over stale beer and a grimy table, that she might need a break, just for a day, twenty-four hours, from her bright-lights, big-city life while she contemplates what comes next?

"What about you?" Lindy asks. "Why'd you come?"

"For Bea, of course. You weren't wrong before. I never said no."

Before she can reply, a riff rings out of the jukebox, and it takes Lindy a moment to grasp it, maybe because it's too familiar, something she's slipped into so many times she can't even recognize it's home. But then the waitresses (in too-small, too-tight colonial corsets) squeal, the other patrons' applause builds to a low thunder, and she realizes it's *her song* (last year's hit single "Don't Apologize—You Already Lost Me"). She uproots herself, standing on the bench of the booth, and bows rather dramatically, and they cheer louder, and then everyone descends around her, snapping selfies, requesting autographs, generally remind-ing her why she's royalty and the rest of them are not.

✑

Lindy's mouth cramps by the time they're done. She's used to photo shoots and faking it for the cameras, but she's weary in a way that drains her mus-cles from the inside out, like someone took her body and wrung it dry. She tells herself it's from all this reminiscing, all this overdone sentimentality. She doesn't do public sentimentality anymore; she saves it for her writing, and since no one sees that much these days either, it's mostly boxed away, keyed off and private, invulnerable and unavailable for public consump-tion. Still, though, nearly dizzy with fatigue, she finds herself wishing for solitude again, wishing that maybe she could just have some peace.

Lindy finds a free stool at the bar and leans over, her boobs doing the work to grab the handsome bartender's attention. He smiles from the opposite counter and makes his way toward her. "We have a Fourth of July special. Blue beer with red limes. You look like a girl who might like blue beer and red limes. Can I interest you?"

"If that's the type of girl I look like, then I think your radar is broken."

He laughs easily—great teeth, rich, dancing eyes—and Lindy mulls the option of a one-night stand. How complicated could that be? Not too complicated not to make it worth it.

The bartender pours her a club soda at her request and tells her he's at grad school here studying Chinese art, which Lindy pretends to be interested in. She fiddles coyly with the swizzle stick and nods her head often while her phone vibrates in her pocket. She ignores it the first time, but by the fourth buzz, she reluctantly gives in.

Well, shit.

She'd forgotten about the lies she'd told her team (including but not limited to: publicist, manager, *Rock N Roll Dreammakers* producer, trainer, nutritionist, stylist, assistant, and, well, Tatiana) to make her escape back east. That she had a wretched stomach flu. That a house-call doctor had been summoned. That he'd insisted on bed rest for at least three days. That she couldn't perform at tomorrow night's show because of her tenuous frailty. That she was so exhausted he suggested they release a statement saying, "She was exhausted." (He was a house-call doctor to the stars, after all.)

Evidently, at least half of Smoke's has posted to Twitter, with a few especially adept patrons blasting out photos to Twitter, Facebook, and Instagram simultaneously. Under other circumstances—frankly, right up until this particular circumstance—nothing would delight Lindy more. However, given the breadth (and depth) of her untruths, said circumstances prove different.

The texts from her publicist are not happy.

The texts from her manager come with expected fatigue at her irresponsibility.

The texts from the producer, particularly since he'd scrambled to find a replacement for tomorrow night's show and was now paying Christina Aguilera double the usual rate, are really pretty fucking pissed.

The texts from Tatiana are confused:

I don't understand . . . are you in Philadelphia? Why would you be in Philadelphia? I thought you were sick? I was worried. I AM worried!

The text from Leon is elated:

Philly! You're there solo, right? I'm revving up the Jag!

He's already on his way.

8

OWEN

Owen has had one beer too many. No, actually, he's probably had about five too many. He stands for the first time in hours, when the lights glare on at 2:00 a.m. after last call, and now it's time for all of the drunks to go home. (For the record, Owen finds this 2:00 a.m. closing time entirely too early—outrageously early! Who the hell needs to go home *now*? If you've made it to 2:00 a.m., you should be entitled to keep going, for Christ's sake! Also, he hasn't been out past 11:00 since he doesn't even know when.) He clutches the wood framing on the back of the booth for balance and tries to shimmy out.

OK, maybe six beers too many.

Shit, he thinks. *Catherine's gonna go apeshit.*

Then he thinks, *Oh well.*

"We shut this place down, dude!" He smacks Colin's back and then burps loudly enough that Lindy is distracted from her incessant texting, which she's been absorbed with for the better part of the hour.

"Finish off the pitcher." Owen thrusts the remains of the warmish, deflated beer toward her, but she flicks her hand, disinterested, so he raises it to his own mouth and chugs. His aim is mostly dead-on, but some of it dribbles down his chin to his salmon-colored polo, and now it kind of looks like he's been neck-sweating.

He squeezes Colin's shoulder.

"We're staying out, man! We can't go home yet!"

Colin has been cheek-to-cheek, deep in conversation with a woman who claims she's in grad school for social work, but Owen suspects is a junior . . . or senior, if he's being generous.

But he'd never say a word, never do anything but gaze on with, well, yes, a little touch of jealousy. She might be twenty, and that might be a little gross (is it gross—maybe it's actually impressive!), but *damn . . . hit it, Colin!* Who is he to cock-block Colin? Every once in a while Colin is tagged in a shot on Facebook, and he's always got a smokin' blonde or a lanky brunette by his side. *Good for him, man!*

I'm not a cock-blocker, man, he thinks. *He should get his.*

Not that Owen's been in a position to really cock-block for the past decade. Sometimes, yeah, back when he was still working at the firm, and they'd all go out for closing dinners or deal drinks, and a few of his buddies (both married and single) might try to score for the night because they were celebrating. But those days are far behind him—five years behind him—and now, as far as Owen is concerned, at this exact moment no one should ever not tap what he wants, who he wants, when he wants. *Goddamn it! Why shouldn't we always get exactly what we want?*

When was the last time Owen got exactly what he wanted? Five years ago, maybe, when he quit. Five years is a long time to wait to feel gratified. Not that he doesn't love the time with the kids. Piano lessons and tennis matches and science projects and all that. Still, it turns out that five years of science projects does not exactly lead to personal fulfillment.

But Catherine pays the bills, and he'd known this was the deal. He'd *wanted* this to be the deal. He just didn't realize how much he'd dislike it. But what's to be done now? He's not a hot property in the legal field, and even if he were, he can't ask Catherine to stay home! It's not like she can just up and quit the way he did. This notion makes him even less happy: that he was utterly disposable in his own little world, whereas she sits atop hers. No one noticed when he gave his walking papers—well, his assistant brought him a pumpkin muffin on his last day, and a few of his "work friends" pitched in for a decent bottle of wine.

Owen miscalculates the depth of the bottom two steps leading out of Smoke's and stumbles out the front door onto the still busy sidewalk, the thick air assaulting his already clammy face. Lindy grasps his elbow, steadying him, as a summer student strolls past and yells, "Bitches, I need a cheesesteak!"

"Shit, man," he says, mostly to himself, since Colin is plugging the possible sophomore's number into his phone, and Lindy is ducking her head so no one else recognizes her. "I really want a cheesesteak. Do you know when the last time I had a cheesesteak was?"

Lindy doesn't answer, so he says, "Senior year, man! Senior fucking year!"

"How important can a cheesesteak be to you?" Lindy asks.

"Goddamn important!" he yells. "Also, what is with your attitude? I love you, Lindy, I love you!"

"I don't have an attitude."

"You *do*," he slurs. "You *do*."

She stares at her phone rather than dignify him, as they hover under a street lamp waiting for Colin to close the deal.

"She's, like, *twelve*," Lindy says finally.

"Don't cock-block," Owen answers. "Don't be a bitch and cock-block." Then, "I didn't just skip out on my job, FYI. In case you think I'm, like, some pathetic, emasculated househusband." He stumbles over "emasculated," and Lindy leans in a little closer, as if proximity will help his enunciation.

"I didn't think—"

"Catherine *wanted* this," he interrupts. "Jesus Christ, Colin, can you hurry the fuck up? I've never needed a cheesesteak more in my life!"

Then back to Lindy. "We agreed on it! That it would make everything easier. That *someone* needed to be home with the kids, and it sure as hell wasn't going to be her." He rubs his collarbone, which surely smells like old beer. "I mean, she's not a bad mom. I didn't mean that. Shit. I'm drunk. I really need a cheesesteak."

"It's hard, I'm sure." Lindy tries to fake sympathy.

"Don't have kids," Owen says. "It complicates everything." Then he slumps against the lamppost. "No, that's awful. I love my kids. Oh my God, I love them so much."

"Mason?" Lindy's face is hopeful, like maybe she's gotten the name right, but Owen doesn't notice.

"He's the best, man. And Penelope. She's gonna be twelve. Oh my God, my baby is almost a teenager." He drops his chin to his chest. "Being a dad is the best thing I've ever done. I *like* being home with them. Since when has the world decided that's a terrible thing? Shit. Maybe we could get a babysitter, but it's not like I'm that employable. I mean, I kind of sucked as a lawyer . . . well, I didn't suck but . . . I brought it up to Cathy a few weeks ago . . ." He shakes his head. "*That* went well."

Lindy's brow creases into tiny chopsticks, like she's worried that Owen is about to start crying.

"Oh God, please don't start crying!"

Owen lifts his head and rolls his eyes up at the night sky. He can't recollect the last time he was this drunk. Or drunk at all. Catherine isn't home often enough for them to build a proper social life in Highland Park, and Owen's not the type to go to dinner parties alone. Sure, he has a few guy friends—husbands of the women he knows from around school (his "work friends" fell by the wayside after a few texts about plans that never materialized)—but these aren't toss-five-back-and-pour-your-heart-out friendships. They talk about the Cubs and the

White Sox and the Bears, and sometimes, when conversation is really waning, the Blackhawks. If the Bulls are on a streak, them too. You don't have to have three pitchers of Budweiser (and that's just your own portion) to talk about the Bulls. Also, they all have careers, work talk, client horror stories. Owen just sits there and nods, his shame quietly boiling in his gut, rising up, rearing its head until recently. Now he can no longer ignore it.

"My wife hates me." He sighs.

"No," Lindy says.

"She's such a fucking genius. I mean, the choice was obvious: her or me. Of course it was her. Have you seen her company? She, like, rules the world."

"I don't know. You're smart." It comes out like a question.

"No," he slurs. "She's perfect. Always was. Remember?"

Owen loses himself for a sliver of a minute to that time: how they shared a full-size bed with no complaints of toes poking the other; how they would sneak away during finals week in the library stacks and make out where no one could see them; how, while everyone was planning boozy spring breaks to Mexico or Florida, they went home to her parents' house, where they did things like look through her elementary-school photo albums and help her dad move his tools around his garage. They were perfect.

He wishes he knew when they took such a strident detour from their happiness. It's impossible, though, and not just because he's wasted right now. Rather, because it's not like there's one event that imploded them—no infidelity, no betrayal, no awful abuse that he could point to and say, "That's when we began to sour." No, their contentment just trickled away, bit by bit, as each of them drifted out on their own separate waves, the water lapping beneath their feet, and they each, separately, pretended not to notice the current pulling them apart.

Lindy takes pity on him.

"Remember how Bea used to say that if you were miserable, you were the only who could change it?"

Owen is surprised to remember this, and from Lindy's wide-eyed expression, she's surprised that it came to her too.

"That's weird," he says.

"What?"

"You being insightful."

"I can be insightful!"

"In your music," he says. "Not in your life."

"Shut up."

"Well, anyway, I'm not miserable."

"And I'm not always a bitch."

"I'm just drunk," he rambles over her words. "Really. Catherine basically rules the world. We're happy. We're perfect. I couldn't ask for anything more."

9

ANNIE

Annie lies in bed, her hair fanning across the pillow like a crown, and keeps checking the time on her phone, wondering when Colin is going to get home. Wondering too why he had to chase Lindy down the street rather than stay and reminisce with *her*. Someone was always chasing Lindy down one street or another, but not Annie. She'd rather lie here like a bug in a rug than dash after Lindy, thank you very much.

Annie wonders what it would take to make Colin chase her down the street. Probably nothing; there's nothing Annie could do to make herself worthy enough for Colin to pursue her. She opens the front-facing camera on her phone and studies herself through the dim, muddied light on her screen. Even with some fine lines here and there, she's prettier than she used to be: The freckles across her nose no longer embarrass her, the glow of her skin has gone from youthful indifference to downright illuminating. Her lashes are lush, her brows are thick and arched like all the current runway models. Her highlights blend so seamlessly into her base color that you'd never know they weren't natural.

She drops her phone to the duvet.

Even with all this . . . no, he still wouldn't chase her down the street. That's just how it is, that's just how it will always be. She's not the type of woman who gets chased down the street. Well, Baxter had chased her in their early days, but that was years ago.

xo

The sign-off worms its way into her mental space—disruptive, unwanted, but there all the same. She cracks her thumb knuckle, then the other one. *He couldn't be.* It couldn't be. She must be reading more into it than it really is. It's two stupid letters, just a casual way of saying good-bye. She pops her index fingers, then her pinkies. Her pulse accelerates with each delicious pop. She couldn't have missed it again, the signs, his distance, not now that she was sober, coherent! She cradles her head in her hands and twists, squeezing out something unfamiliar, something unsettling: rage.

POP.

She rolls her neck back and forth across the pillow, breathing deep yoga breaths.

She thinks of her favorite website, CitiMama, where loads of anonymous women post questions like this: *My husband got a text that was signed with "Xo." What would you do?*

She already knows what they'd say. She spends enough anonymous hours of her own on there to know they'd pile on Baxter like a pack of rabid wolves: shredding him until there was nothing left that Annie recognized.

She pinches her thigh, then pinches harder. She doesn't like being angry, she doesn't like these strange roots of fury blossoming into something bigger, something real. She digs into her flesh until she snaps out of it.

At 2:15 a.m., she turns off her light and tries to settle into her old bed. Or whoever's bed this is now. She waits three beats, three breaths, then decides it's no use. She's not going to be able to sleep at all, and then she worries what she'll look like in the morning: ghastly! Gruesome. With ogre-size bags under her eyes. With blotchy skin that even the best foundation might not be able to conceal. What will Colin think?

She clicks the light back on and checks her e-mail on her phone. No one is e-mailing Annie at 2:20 a.m., but she holds out hope. Maybe someone on the West Coast is awake, even though she really doesn't have friends out there.

Annie rereads her text to Baxter from earlier in the night—right after Colin bolted down the block after Lindy, and after she and Catherine had shared all the pictures of their kids from their phones, and after Annie had peppered Catherine endlessly with questions on how she conceives all of her magnificent (truly magnificent!) ideas for The Crafty Lady. Eventually, she could tell that Catherine was growing weary of the subject, so they retreated to bed.

She reads the text once more.

I love you! I miss you! Give Gussy ten big kisses for me!

Baxter hadn't written back until nearly midnight. He must have fallen asleep on the couch again, waking to pee, checking his phone. He'd replied with a solitary emoji thumbs-up.

She rolls onto her side and stares at their text exchange, with the pseudo–Ralph Lauren sheets around her shins, and the pine-beer scent wafting all around her and the familiar creaking of the stairs as Catherine paces around her bedroom down the hall and her own history here, and she thinks, *xo*.

Why couldn't he at least say that?

She props up on an elbow, considering. *Who showed Baxter how to use emojis?* Baxter's a dinosaur about these things. No social media. No clever smiley faces or winks or frowns fashioned out of punctuation marks. She hadn't shown him emojis. Maybe Gus. Gus knew how to do all sorts of things that his old-fart parents didn't understand. Annie always tried to keep up, but it was like quicksand. *Gus must have shown Baxter.*

Or maybe, a surprising voice clatters deep in her cerebral space, *it was Cici.* Annie swallows hard, like she can literally swallow the thought, but *Cici* lingers, like a rotten aftertaste, like regret over a bite you thought would go down easy but in fact, might turn your insides green.

Catherine knocks on the door, and Annie starts, dropping her phone like it's evidence of a murder.

"You still up? I saw the light on." Catherine pokes her head in. "I can't sleep. It's too weird to be here again." She musses her hair. "God, I haven't thought about this place in forever."

Annie thinks about this place more often than she wants to admit, even to herself. She still Googles all of them (well, except Lindy). She still sometimes flips through her photo albums stacked in their den-library, the ones chock-full of collages and cut-out sentimental quotes like, *"A Friend Is Someone Who Knows All About You and Loves You Anyway!"*

"I know what you mean. Why look back when you can look forward?"

Catherine chews on her fingernail. "I don't know. Maybe I should be more sentimental about college."

"Well, it *is* where you met Owen!"

"It is," Catherine says. "But that was forever ago." Then she asks, "So things never got better with you and Lindy? That was never resolved?"

Annie instinctively sits up straighter, her shoulders arching back, her chin pushing forward. "Oh God. Oh, that was ages ago. I mean, we never actually *resolved* it, I guess. But . . . you know." She shrugs, then fiddles with a loose thread on the duvet.

Catherine purses her lips, puzzled. "I guess . . . well, I feel bad about it. How I acted at the wedding. That we managed to turn . . ." She pauses. "Well, that we managed to turn Bea's funeral into a fight." She sighs. "Not that I'm being good about it now. I should. I need to be nicer to her."

"You're so nice!" Annie says.

"Not to everyone. Not anymore."

"I think you're too hard on yourself," Annie offers.

"Hmm." Catherine considers this. "So you and Lindy never—"

"Oh." Annie jitters her hands. "Well, I have Baxter now, and life is so busy and great that I don't dwell on all that stupid stuff from before. Like, I truly just feel fulfilled now, so . . . why dredge up all of *that* stuff?" She retrieves her phone. "I was just texting him, actually. Saying good night. He texted me back an emoji." Annie smiles and hopes that it's convincing. "I mean, how cute is that?"

Catherine laughs.

"Cute, I guess! The only thing Owen texts me about is why I'm not coming home for dinner."

"Oh, stop. That can't be. You guys were always the epitome of happiness."

Catherine shrugs. "Maybe. I don't know. I work a lot."

"Well, I quit as soon as I got married. Working was never for me, not once Gus came along anyway." Annie instantly regrets her honesty, worried she's offended Catherine. *Idiot! What a stupid thing to say to Catherine Grant of all people!* "I didn't mean . . . I think moms who work outside the home are great! I think what you do . . . it's amazing! I've already told you that a million times!" She overcompensates: "I'm very active, though. All sorts of jobs at Gus's school! And I'd like to volunteer more. And of course, until recently, Baxter was almost never home. I was practically a single mom! No, no, I don't mean that how it sounds. He's a wonderful father." She catches her breath. "Anyway, now I'm vice president of the PTA!" She claps her hands together, like a cymbal, like this is the apex of her aspirations.

"Well, that sounds pretty wonderful. As long as we're happy."

"It does seem like we're all really happy," Annie says, regretting blathering on like the chatterbox her mom always told her not to be. "Like, flash-forward from graduation, and we're living the lives we should be!"

"Not Bea," Catherine offers quietly. "Shit. Sorry. That was terrible. God, do I ever know how to kill the mood. I should go back to sleep. I never have enough sleep. Never."

Annie smacks her palms against the duvet.

"Let's go out," she practically sings. "Why are those guys out while we're staring at our belly buttons?"

What she really means is, *Let's go find Colin.* Then what she asks herself is, *Why are you thinking about Colin?* Then, she reminds herself: *xo.*

"I guess we could go out . . . ?" Catherine sounds unconvinced. "Owen left me a fairly incomprehensible voice mail a while ago . . . I think they're getting cheesesteaks." She checks her Cartier watch. Baxter gave Annie something similar for her thirty-fifth birthday when she noticed that all the moms at school had one. She stopped wearing it within a year when the moms had moved on to something else, an Hermès bracelet. She didn't ask Baxter for that too because she was doing her delicate dance of trying to remain utterly unassuming to her husband, as if her undemanding nature would get him to notice her, get him to come back to her. In some ways, it worked. In some ways, he did.

"We should definitely go out!" Annie is already on her feet. Why did she practically have to make herself invisible for her husband to fall back in love with her? Colin would never ask this of a woman! Annie shimmies into her shoes, clopping down the hallway and then the steps.

It's only as she's reapplying her matte peach lipstick over and over again, ironing out the wrinkles in her linen capris with her sweaty palms, that she realizes that maybe she's already invisible to Colin. At least Baxter noticed her in the first place. At least that's something. Maybe she should be grateful for that.

⁂

Annie lasers in on Colin in one of the back booths as soon as they step inside Pat's. He's got an arm slung around Owen with an effortlessness that reminds her of how easy he was to love: his casualness, his lack of pretense. Of course, Annie was never anything close to casual, which is why she knew he'd never love her in return.

Colin leans a little closer to Owen, saying something with intensity. Owen shakes his head and shoves the remains of a hoagie, with meat and peppers and some sort of processed filler they claim is cheddar cheese (but Annie never believed it) into his mouth. Cheesesteaks, the infamous after-hours ritual of Philadelphia college students (particularly inebriated college students), were never really Annie's thing. As a kid, she'd survived on enough crap—hot wings left over from her mom's waitressing shift, Pop Tarts and Hi-C for breakfast, state-supplemented school lunches—to appreciate the benefits of not inhaling various artery-blocking, chemically preserved, shriveled-up meats as dawn rounded the bend.

Colin raises his eyes and spies Catherine and Annie in the doorway and waves them over. Catherine sighs loudly when she catches a glimpse of Owen's state of drunkenness, and then kisses him perfunctorily and recoils. Annie can only imagine his breath.

"Cathy!" he shouts. "Oh my God, Cathy! I'm sooooooo happy you're here. Come have a cheesesteak, you have to have a cheesesteak." He tries to pull her onto his lap, but she swivels her hips just so, and his arm flails and thuds on the table limply.

"Well, this is lovely." Then to Annie, "I can't imagine your husband would stuff himself with cheesesteaks and an entire keg at two in the morning."

"It was *not* an entire keg," Owen says, while Annie stutters.

"Oh . . . well." She doesn't want to insult Catherine, make her feel bad, because Owen is indeed a bit of slob right now. Fairly disgusting, actually. And no, Baxter would certainly not stuff himself with cheesesteaks at two in the morning. "He's sort of vegan, so that's all."

Annie contorts her mouth into a sympathetic smile, all the while lodged in the memory of that stupid raw-food diet Baxter had insisted on. She had willingly obliged, recreating uncooked carrots in as many ways as she could find on The Crafty Lady. She'd taught herself how to cook after they got married, thinking it was the sort of thing a good wife did. Her own mom had never cooked, never done much more than bring home drive-through fast food or heat up a can of beans and hot dogs. In the sixth grade, for a school fundraiser, other moms had baked lemon tarts and peanut-butter blondies and coffee cakes with mouthwatering brown-sugar crumbles on top. Her own mom sent her in with two boxes of Twinkies and a bag of doilies. *Twinkies.* Annie walked into the gym where the other parents had laid their lovely handcrafted treats full of love on silver platters, and quickly spun around, shame rising up her neck like a heat rash, and dumped the Twinkies and the cheap drugstore doilies into the trash. When her mom asked later that night if they sold quickly, Annie pressed back tears and simply said, "Yes."

No, she was not the woman her mom was. She'd vowed not to be since the sixth grade. Even if it meant recreating carrots. She'd recreated herself, after all. Carrots weren't the most challenging things in the world.

At the booth just behind them, three kids with backward baseball hats and skin that still shone with the glory of youth start pounding on their table.

In metered time, they shout, "Stuff it, stuff it, stuff it!"

Lindy, who's been distracted with her phone, swivels her gaze upward, delight spreading across her face in the form of a lopsided grin. She cackles and joins in with the three of them. "Stuff it, stuff it, stuff it!" Her fists shake their own table. Owen mistakes them as chants for him, as if they're a cheerleading squad there to buoy his bingeing. He swallows the remaining half of his second cheesesteak without so much as taking a breath.

"Stuffed it!" he shouts, like he just scored a touchdown.

Lindy breaks out in furious applause and gives him a standing ovation. Owen tries to bow but just sort of tilts over, his reflection shining in the metal table, until his forehead falls all the way down in near slow motion, thumping down on its surface.

Colin pats him on the back. "It might be time to get you home, man."

"I think it *is* time to get him home," Catherine says, not particularly warmly. To Annie she says, "He's on Lipitor. So this is really wonderful. Really smart. Gorging on cheesesteaks."

"It's just one night. He'll be OK! I mean, there are worse things."

Like ridiculous raw-food diets. Like texts that end in *xo*.

Catherine shakes her head like she's not an idiot, that it's not like he's going to have a heart attack *right then*, *right there* on the linoleum floor that's pocked with melted cheese and meat residue.

"It's the principle."

"You only live once," Lindy says, overhearing. "So screw principles!"

"You would know," Annie snaps, before she can censor herself. Her forehead furrows as if chasing the surprising sentiment. What compelled her to say that? (Other than the obvious fact that Lindy does often screw principles, not to mention the love of Annie's life.)

Owen finds this to be the most hilarious thing he's ever heard and flattens himself against Colin, who nearly has him upright now and is attempting to ease him out of the booth and safely out into the night, away from these murderous cheesesteaks, out of the immediate withering gaze of his wife.

"So we're still being pissy from before?" Lindy says to Annie.

Annie has no idea if she means from a decade ago or from their earlier dustup in the living room of Bruiser, so she simply says, "I didn't mean it!"

"Oh, you *did* mean it!"

"I think *you* were the one who was pissy before," Colin says, over his shoulder to Lindy, and Annie relaxes just a bit because they're not all referencing that disastrous night of Catherine and Owen's wedding when Lindy and Colin screwed each other (and subsequently, Annie).

"Fine," Lindy concedes. "I'm *sorry*. To everyone. OK?" She doesn't sound particularly sorry, but Annie is too caught up stumbling around her own thoughts to push it. Not that she'd push it anyway. She can't believe she pushed it just a second ago by firing back at her.

"Hey, Catherine, I'm sorry! OK?"

Annie sees Catherine debate it, wrestle with her grudge and the complications of the past. Then, because she *is* kind, and Annie knew it, Catherine nods. "OK."

"But you." Lindy pokes Annie's arm. "Don't take that back, don't say you didn't mean it. *Screw principles.* Fair enough. You got your jab in. We're even. Can we move on now?"

Her eyes meet Annie's, and this time it's clear she does mean from a decade ago.

Can we move on now?

Lindy glides past her like that's that, they're square, even-Steven, as Annie would say to Gus.

Annie loses her breath for a moment and sinks back into the booth.

Can we move on now?

That's it? Is she just supposed to *let go* because Lindy has?

Is forgiveness that easy? Is it easier with old friends because you've known them forever? Or is it harder for those same reasons? What about yourself? What about the fucking world? What about Bea? Would she forgive them for not keeping their promises to her—that they'd always be family, always be a six-point star?

Annie inhales and exhales in the revolting, filthy booth at Pat's, watching her old friends shuffle out the door single file. She wants to get a grip, she needs to get a grip, and let the bruises of the past fade into nothingness like everyone else seems to. She breathes deeply once again, then pulls her phone from her purse and angles her arm and then her cheek just so, and captures the moment with a quick snap of a button.

It's not the best selfie she's ever pulled off, but she looks pretty decent for 2:45 in the morning, and with the Amaro filter, she can pass for thirty. Twenty-eight, maybe.

2:45 a.m. and back in the old haunt! Can't remember the last time we had this much fun. #penn #lovinglife #oldfriends #thebest

She debates adding an emoji of a wineglass or maybe a martini, but she doesn't want to overdo it. She's not an undergrad, after all.

It does the trick. Annie gets a grip. And yet, by the time she posts the picture and scampers toward the street, the four others are halfway down the empty, litter-clogged block, darkened shadows underneath the streetlights heading toward home. She has to squint to eke them out.

Finally, she sees them, and rushes to catch up, cursing herself for always being one step behind.

10

CATHERINE

Owen is pawing at Catherine, his kisses sloppy, his breath pungent with beer and mustard. She wants to be enthusiastic, she tells herself to be enthusiastic, but he feels like a tranquilized bear on top of her, and she was never good at faking it. She turns her head to the side, and he moves to her neck. The bed groans unhappily beneath them, and Catherine thinks, *That makes two of us.*

"You're not into this," Owen mumbles.

Catherine's surprised he notices.

"You're just too drunk."

"Jesus!" He barks and rolls off her. "Is it too much to just want to have sex with my wife without her criticizing me?"

"Shhhhhhh! Be quiet!" Catherine sits up quickly. Owen has flung both arms over his face, and she's unclear whether or not he's lapsed into an immediate inebriated sleep. "I'm not criticizing you! You're just really drunk," she whispers.

"Ugh," he says. "Nothing I do is good enough for you."

"I don't know *what* you're talking about," she says, but actually thinks, *Well, half the stuff you do* isn't *good enough!*

"We agreed that I could quit, and now you resent me."

"I don't want to talk about this right now. It's three in the morning."

"You resent me," he whines.

"I don't resent you. And can we talk about this when you're sober? At home?" She sighs like a parent does during an epic toddler temper tantrum.

He's right, she *does* resent him—even if they did agree on it. It's thornier than that now. It's not just that she's the sole breadwinner; it's how he stopped asking about her day, about the complications of running her empire; it's how his own complaints seem trivial—*Ugh, I had to drive two different carpools today!*—compared to hers. *Try managing an inept designer who steals ideas from last year's ideas! Try competing with a twenty-six-year-old decoupaging protégé who was just offered a book deal—on decoupaging!*

"When we were here, we were so happy," Owen mumbles. "Then it went to hell. Why did it go to hell, Cathy? Why did it go to hell?" He flops an arm out toward her.

"Stop it. It didn't go to hell! Please, Owen, just go to sleep."

"I shouldn't have quit," he says. "I should never have quit. That's where we started to go wrong."

"Oh, please, come on. Just . . . sleep."

His chest rises and falls, and then, as if because Catherine is the boss, he heeds her plea and within seconds, tumbles toward dreamland.

❧

Now Catherine can't sleep because Owen is snoring so loudly. *Honestly, he needs to see someone about this,* she thinks. *Like, a surgeon, because it's fucking ridiculous. How can he possibly sleep through this?* It's like a goddamn volcano erupting next to her.

She shifts and pulls the duvet up to her neck.

How did they ever share this tiny bed? When they first met, before they moved into this house with the others junior year, they squeezed into a twin bed in her sorority room. Catherine doesn't remember complaining, doesn't remember being so uncomfortable she felt like she was breathing the same air as a stranger. Why does his leg keep twitching? How can he sleep so solidly, without worry, while her brain runs haywire, armed like a fuse to a grenade fueled with anxiety? She answers her own question: *he sleeps without worry because he has none.* Nothing to *worry* about, no shoulders on which a company rests, no creative well from which he must squeeze drops from arid ground.

Owen emits a particularly annoying crescendo that culminates with the bed literally quivering, akin to the earthquake Catherine had the misfortune of experiencing when she was in Los Angeles two years ago shooting some spots for *E!* She pushes herself up on her elbows, and then onto her feet, grabbing a blanket and pillow off the bed. She finds the light in the closet, its glow casting shadows, half illuminating the room, and for a moment she worries this will rouse Owen. Until she realizes that nothing could rouse Owen. Then she steps inside and nudges the door a little bit closed.

She stares at the ceiling in the closet, leaning back, buttressing the wall, then resting her head against it. Maybe it's for the best that he's snoring; at least it's something to fill the quiet space. The house was never quiet back then: someone was always tromping down the steps, late for a lecture; or sneaking up the steps, with someone drunk in tow; or blasting Pearl Jam (Bea) out her third-story window, loud enough that it reverberated all the way down to the alley.

But Bea was dead now, something that all these years later Catherine still doesn't quite comprehend. Like, she'd remember the way Bea shimmied to "Let's Go Crazy" at Smoke's, or the way that she—with her slightly too-wide eyes and off-skew crooked smile that hung lower on the left side, and her billowy mahogany hair that mesmerized those

Wharton boys—would disappear for a day unannounced, returning when the rest of them were winding their way home from the library (or Annie from her work-study job at the bookstore), with shopping bags sagging her arms, presents from Manhattan for all of them. She couldn't have been shopping for the entirety of those trips, but they didn't always ask where and how she'd whiled away the rest of those hours—inevitably, Bea was off restoring her adrenaline high. Or she'd remember the way she always devoured Catherine's improvised recipes even when they were wretched—the types of recipes that The Crafty Lady's readers would rate with one star and complain gave them diarrhea. (Users on The Crafty Lady message boards could be particularly eviscerating. Catherine chalked this up to the fact that many domestic goddesses were actually closet bitches. She'd met Martha Stewart, you know. Not an easy nut to crack.)

Catherine would remember all these tiny moments with Bea—the moments of humanity, the slivers that made her *her*, indelible, unforgettable, invincible—and it was as if, for that brief bubble within the memory, Bea wasn't dead, because dying at twenty-seven felt impossible, too strange to consider. Stranger still that it has been thirteen years now.

Catherine stands suddenly and peers upward. She wonders if it's still possibly there. She'd forgotten about it until a second ago. Their junior year, on the very last day, just before the airport shuttle pulled up to their front door to whisk Catherine home to Wisconsin and usher Owen off to an internship in Boston, they'd carved their names in the back corner. It had been Catherine's idea. When you're twenty and in love and about to be pulled apart for three months, this is the sort of thing you do. They'd already had sex twice that morning, and she'd double-checked that she had the right phone number for his apartment up there, and they'd both cried and wondered how they could accelerate time. How they could leap over the divide of those ninety days and reunite so their hearts (and loins) could be full again.

Now, at nearly forty, Catherine wouldn't mind three months apart—she'd sleep better for one, and for two, well, three months isn't that long in the span of a lifetime, now is it? She almost laughs at their juvenile angst, almost laughs at the memory of the ache in the pit of her stomach when they parted like a wishbone at the airport.

She cocks her head and cranes her neck and squints to make it out among the shadows.

Owen had put a Toad the Wet Sprocket disk into his portable CD player, and they woefully listened to "I Will Not Take These Things For Granted," and Catherine pulled out an X-ACTO knife she'd used to create rubber stamps. (She also used to write Owen love letters on homemade stationery. She'd slip them into his backpack on his way to a poli-sci class or leave one under his pillow if she couldn't stay the night.) Catherine had etched her name, then Owen his, and then together, they each carved a half of a heart until the halves became whole.

Oh my God. That was another life. Different people. A different sort of love.

She rises on her tiptoes, checking the other corner of the closet. Maybe it was the right side, not the left. She hates that she's so irritable these days, hates that she misses out on Mason's hockey practices and Penelope's gymnastics. Sure, she wishes something could give, but what?

Owen told her last weekend that she should cut herself "a little slack," which was so typical Owen. She still hasn't told him about the downward projections, the faltering blog traffic, the speculation that advertising rates will have to be lowered, that once the board catches wind of this next week, the IPO might be delayed. Or that now she's desperate for the HGTV pilot and to lock in the Target deal and rein-fuse the nearly red bottom line with cash.

And then there's the fact that part of Catherine always wonders if this all wasn't a spectacular mistake. She's good at crafting, sure. She's decent enough at it, but is she really something special? In college, she needed recipes to master her French toast. In her early years starting out, she had to rely on patterns to shape her clothing designs, craft magazines to inspire her holiday décor, online tips for all of those endless candles and potpourri jars and homemade scented soap. Bea used to tell her that no one made a better brunch than she did— that so what if she glanced at a recipe; that didn't take anything away from the love she put in—but Catherine never quite believed that. A true creative revolutionary would spin something from nothing, and Catherine suspected, deep down, in a place she was too ashamed to share with Owen, that maybe she wasn't the crafting visionary her fans hailed her to be, or worse, that she's passed herself off to be for all these years.

What would Owen say about that?

She presses up a tiny bit higher on her toes, hoping something will make its way out to her in the dimness of the solitary bulb in the closet. She cranes her neck again and again and again. Then Owen's snoring rattles the closet door, and Catherine's toes give way, and just like that, she's back on sturdy ground, back on her solid two feet.

It was a stupid idea, she thinks. *To try to find it. I'm sure it's long gone by now. Sanded down by a carpenter. Painted over one summer when they spruced the place up.* She shouldn't pretend that old notions can be so easily resurrected.

11

LINDY

The doorbell echoes in the living room. Catherine—wide awake—peers over the stair railing from the second-floor hall where she's been pacing, but Lindy is already barreling past her, thundering down the steps, a wake of nervous energy quaking behind her.

"Go back to sleep! It's for me!"

"I wasn't sleeping. Who on earth is at the door at this hour?"

"Owen's snoring is outrageous." Lindy races toward the entry, ignoring her inquiry. "I have a white-noise machine that I travel with—go use my bed."

Catherine doesn't need a second offer and slinks into Lindy's old room, locking the door behind her.

Lindy flings the door open and for a split second prays that it's her publicist, who's pretty goddamn pissed at her for pulling "this disappearing stunt," because her publicist is part of her staff, and her staff she can manage. But, as she already knows, it's not her publicist.

It's Leon.

She impulsively texted him her address when he first wrote—she was so delighted that he'd make the trip from New York in the middle of the night that she hadn't even hesitated. Not many people who weren't on her payroll or who weren't looking for a favor would make their way all the way here just for the pleasure of her company. (In fact, not that many people these days—or in a long while—would even describe her company as particularly pleasurable. If Bea were here, then probably she would, because she was always up for an adventure, but Bea's dead, so she doesn't count. Probably Tatiana too, but Lindy's been picking fights recently, ever since she started unintentionally sleeping with Leon, so perhaps not even Tatiana.)

As soon as she realized what she'd done (fallen prey to a very un-Lindy-like notion of romanticism—*a prince in a sports car on his way to rescue her!*), which was almost immediately, she retracted her enthusiasm, texting him at least twenty times, imploring him not to come.

"I texted you, like twenty times, telling you not to come," she says, staring down the stoop, his tanned skin and shaggy goatee taking shape through the night shadows. A fire-engine-red Jaguar is parked crookedly in the street, a tire rubbing against the disgusting Philadelphia curb.

Leon steps closer, his tattooed arm pushing him up along the railing, then leans in to kiss her, but Lindy doesn't meet him halfway.

"Well, hey to you too, babe." He reaches for his phone from the back pocket of his dark denim jeans. He waves it in front of her. "No texts."

"What the hell? Well, I did." Lindy peers down the block. "Whose is that?" She aims her chin at the Jag.

"Mine." A sheepish grin rolls across his face. "A present from Jay."

"Jay?"

"Z."

"A present from Jay-Z." Lindy makes sure she appears indifferent. He shrugs. "What? Am I not supposed to enjoy it?"

"It's a little on-the-nose."

"Like I give a shit? It's a new Jag!"

"Well, it's basically a walking cliché."

Leon shoves his hands into his pockets and drops his head toward the top of his shoulders. "Are you playing hard to get?"

"I'm just saying." Lindy plops her hands on her hips.

"OK, I get it. You're completely unimpressed."

"Not completely. I guess."

"Noted. Semi-unimpressed."

"Are there any paparazzi around?"

"Jesus. I don't know!" He glances to his left and right down the alleyway. "It's the middle of the night. I drove here from New York to see you. And you tell me that you texted me twenty times not to come, and you think the Jag sucks, and now you're concerned that I call the paparazzi?" Leon is often stoned, so this is the closest Lindy has come to hearing him sound annoyed. He rubs his goatee and kicks his biker boots against the step. A truck's axles grind somewhere a few blocks away. Horns follow, echoing down the deserted street to their front stoop. "Linds, you either trust me or you don't."

"I'm still with my girlfriend." Lindy needs to be sure she goes on record. As if going on the record excuses her.

Leon shrugs. "And you're still with your girlfriend. Adding that to the mental checklist."

Lindy glances around one last time, then grabs his belt buckle and ushers him inside.

"So catch me up. You're in Philly, why?" he asks, after she finally acquiesces to a kiss, which goes on longer than Lindy intends it to.

He settles himself onto the couch by the back bay window just a few feet from the base of the steps. The old Philadelphia row houses are narrow and tall, a cascade of stairs leading up, with two bedrooms on each landing. One shorter stairwell heads down below the sidewalk level. Colin took the basement back then and did tonight again too; they'd all scampered to their old spaces like it was second nature, like steps so well worn, they already knew how to retrace them. The space feels compressed now to Lindy, claustrophobic, like she could stretch her arms wide, her fingers wiggling to extend her wingspan, and touch both walls. She tugs the neck of her T-shirt, trying to catch her breath, get some air.

Leon sinks into the pillows as if he belongs there.

"It's too strange to explain," Lindy says. She folds her arms awkwardly, then refolds them, then finally sits cross-legged on the floor a few feet away from him, which cajoles Leon into a howl.

"I don't bite, girl!"

"I know you don't bite!"

"You look like you think I might. I only bite if you want me to!"

"I don't want you to."

Or maybe she does want him to. She doesn't know. She stretches her shirt again, this time at the waistline, fully aware that her pulse is clanging loud enough to echo outside her body, that her usually steely nerve is cratering with each passing second. *Shit.*

She hasn't seen him since she realized her period was two weeks late, and then it took her another ten days to take the test. She took four tests, peed on four sticks, actually, because it seemed so ridiculous, impossible even. Though it wasn't impossible: she'd been reckless, spur-of-the-moment impulsive, and they'd skipped the condom. She was almost forty, and it was just this once, so what harm could come of it?

She hadn't expected to see him again so soon, before she'd decided what to do, before she knew which lie she wanted to chase, which truth she wanted to follow. A baby. *A baby!* Lindy knows what a baby does to a forty-year-old woman who's tenuously gripping a top spot in the music industry. It means she'll shift from man-eater to mommy; it means she'll kiss the low-cut catsuit good-bye; it means she'll devote her days to diapers, not demos. Lindy's never considered the former, not when her life has been so stuffed, so singularly focused on the latter.

She needs to decide, she knows. She's running out of time.

Lindy cracks her knuckles one by one, buying some time, attempting to wrestle herself together. She hates feeling so out of sorts. She's never out of sorts. At least half of her persona is that she never lets them see her sweat. She didn't sweat when her mic dropped out on *SNL*; she didn't sweat when Rihanna picked a Twitter fight with her, accusing her of sleeping with *"my big-dicked man, bitch!"* (Lindy hadn't, but it was great publicity all the same.) If Lindy really considered it (which she doesn't), the last time she truly sweated (figuratively, because she does sweat a fuckload at her concerts) was when Bea died. Maybe she sweated it all out of her that day at the funeral. She could take only so much: first she lost Annie at Catherine's wedding, and then Bea. After that, maybe she sealed herself up, impenetrably, so no one could get close enough to nick her, draw blood again.

She cracks both of her thumbs, feels the relief of the bubble of tension in the joint, and thinks of that little pea in her uterus and wonders how much it would change her. *Should* it change her? Does she need to be changed?

Lindy isn't sure she wants to know. Isn't sure she *needs* to know.

Leon nudges his chin upward, inviting her again to the couch.

Lindy wishes he'd gotten her texts and hadn't come. Lindy wishes she hadn't slept with him in the first place. Or the second place. Or . . . she actually lost count of how many times it had been. She glances at him quickly, too quickly to linger, and tells herself that if she weren't knocked up, she would never have invited him tonight, maybe after the record was done, never have seen him again. That maybe her transgression was a one-off and she'd forget about it (she is very good at forgetting about things) and remain true, or at least true-ish, to Tatiana. But even Lindy isn't sure she believes this lie she tells herself. She's pregnant, and she's avoiding her team and avoiding her girlfriend, and she's at her old house now owned by her dead friend, with a gaggle of people she used to call friends but are now mostly strangers. She has to acknowledge that she's at least a little bit screwed.

Leon pats the cushion.

"Come on, babe. Don't pretend you're not happy to see me."

"I'm semihappy to see you."

"I know. It's complicated."

"Don't speak for me."

He nods.

I'm pregnant!

No, now's not the time. It will never be the time. It's her body and it's her choice, and shit, what he never knows won't hurt him.

She rises to the couch. A compromise. Enough to let him think he's won.

~❦~

Leon has fallen dead to the world asleep on the sofa while Lindy rests in the crook of his arm, her brain in hyperdrive, the rumble emanating from Catherine and Owen's old room upstairs pounding its way into the roots of a headache.

"Jesus Christ, Owen! Shut the fuck up!"

She adjusts Leon's arm, which is wrapped around her waist. He's gotten uncomfortably close to spooning. She doesn't want him noticing the roundness of her belly, the way her shape is slowly shifting. When they hooked up in New York, she was in, well, rock-star shape: lean abs, sinewy shoulders, legs that her mommy-fans would kill for. Now, with the convex swell of her stomach and the softness easing into her hips, who knows if he'd want her, still covet her, still find her desirable in the way that validates her.

Leon sighs in his sleep, and Lindy is surprised to feel the sting of tears behind her eyes.

She doesn't coo at babies in strollers or make silly faces at the kid who's wailing for the duration of a plane ride, doesn't find Gap onesies with cutesy catchphrases like "Got Milk" impossibly adorable.

Motherhood wasn't something she craved, the way that Annie always did. The European tour was what she craved, what she needed. The entourage who come running when she calls; the deference of the hotel concierge at The Savoy in London, The Bristol in Paris, the Four Seasons in Milan; the explosion of applause—like a volcanic eruption— all the way up to the third tier of the arena in whichever city she was headlining that night.

The basement door creaks open, and the thump of Colin's footsteps up the stairs announce his arrival.

His eyes are puffy, his hair a tousled bird's nest, and he's only wearing boxers, through which she can see his boner. He shields his eyes from the halogen light in the kitchen that was left on when they all scattered and passed out, and asks, "What the hell time is it?" Then he realizes his indecent exposure, drops a hand in front of his fly, and says, "Sorry." He spies Leon and shoots Lindy a questioning glance.

"He's an old friend, and it's five-thirty." Lindy grouses. Leon snorts and swaddles her belly once more. "Owen needs an intervention."

"He didn't drink that much. Give the guy a break. He never gets a night out."

"For his snoring, you moron."

Colin falls silent, and then they hear it—the reverberating in and out of air from Owen's nasal passages. Colin, who seems entirely unperturbed by it, shuffles to the kitchen for some water.

More footsteps, this time from the second floor. Annie appears on the landing in her cotton floral pajamas, her hair pulled back in a low ponytail.

"This is awful," she stage whispers. "I can't survive on three hours of sleep! He's right above me, and it's shaking the walls." She pauses, assessing the stranger on the couch. "Who's that?"

Lindy ignores the question. "Go into Bea's room. Try there."

No one had yet gone into Bea's room. Not when they arrived and explored their old spaces, not when they returned home from Pat's, when the alcohol could have been their armor (at least for most of them). The door remains closed for now, securing the ghosts that no one was prepared to face.

"I'm not going to sleep in Bea's room!" Annie barks. "God!"

Colin emerges from the kitchen—Annie hadn't seen him there. His boner has died down for the moment, but if he feels exposed, in his preppy J. Crew boxers with little Scotties wearing bow ties, he doesn't seem to care.

"Hey, Ann." He nods his head up at her. Colin is the only one of them who calls her Ann.

He also doesn't seem to notice Annie's quick hiccup of a breath, the way her eyes grow wider, her cheeks illuminate, but Lindy does. For all of her bravado, for her open, flourishing nakedness, Lindy is an observer. A sponge. She had to be back when she crafted the sort of music that penetrated across all demographics: moms who amped up a song in their Honda Odysseys and blazed down their suburban streets with memories of an old boyfriend; their daughters who belted it out with no inhibitions, daydreaming about their future loves; husbands or boyfriends or pubescent teenage boys who cranked up the melody and considered how much they'd like to screw her. Just because her label isn't using her own music these days doesn't mean that she isn't always subconsciously weaving a lyric, isn't always reflecting on the finer details of life, of humanity, of the beautiful and horrible madness that comprises day-to-day life. She's lost track of the way this used to soften her, humble her, ground her. But she hasn't lost her skills in the art of observation.

So it is Lindy who once again detects Annie's horrified delight or delighted horror that Colin is lingering, half-nude, in the living room, much as he used to when they were in college. Lindy never really liked Colin, meaning she never really had the hots for him like Annie did. She recognized, of course, that he was attractive in a way that was universal— a Malibu surf bum, a Ken doll—but generic was never her thing. She hadn't even really considered sleeping with him until Catherine and Owen's wedding, when Annie was still pie-eyed over him, and Lindy couldn't take it for one more second.

Colin rose to make a toast at the reception, holding his champagne glass aloft, rambling on about some bullshit about first love, lasting love, forever love . . . *and let's raise a glass to Catherine and Owen,* and Lindy glanced to Annie across the table, wondering if she could catch her gaze, wondering if finally Annie would see what she saw, feel what she felt, but all Annie saw was Colin. Her chin tilted upward, her eyes lit by stars, her skin flushed like he'd been speaking of her in his toast, not their old friends.

And that was that. Lindy knew. Lindy got it.

It would never be her.

Why wouldn't Annie notice her the way she noticed Colin?

After so many years of friendship, shared spaces, shared secrets, why wasn't Annie a little bit in love with her too?

They'd lived together for four years in Manhattan. How hadn't Annie known? Why hadn't she reciprocated her feelings? Wasn't Lindy good enough, wasn't she sexy enough, wasn't she kind enough, talented enough?

So, fuck Annie. Fuck her stupid crush and her stupid view of love and her stupid inability to see Lindy in the ways she needed Annie to see her. And so, when Colin left to hail a cab back to the W, Lindy left to hail a cab back to the W too. And thus it only made sense that they share a ride, and since they were both alone and intoxicated, and Lindy couldn't find her key card to the room she was sharing with Annie, they wobbled back to Colin's and ended up fucking.

Bea was in the elevator the next morning when they stepped in as a pair, as a couple, all of them late to the postwedding brunch. Bea assessed Lindy's stubble-chapped cheeks and the shadows under Colin's eyes and said nothing, but Lindy knew she was judging her, knew she'd crossed a line that she would judge herself for, if she judged herself for anything, which, perhaps from that moment forward, she no longer did. They stared up at the elevator lights in silence, ticking down floor by floor, and Lindy thought of a million excuses to absolve her role, to explain it to Bea, but mostly it was that this was Annie's fault, and maybe she should have woken up and realized what was coming to her. Lindy was just giving as good as she got, giving Annie what she deserved. Reciprocating the hurt.

Annie figured it out piece by piece, or perhaps she knew faster than she let on. Maybe she caught a glimpse of them as the doors dinged open and the air still brimmed with intimacy; maybe she saw it in the way Lindy leaned in and stabbed Colin's omelet for a bite after they surfed the buffet; maybe they still smelled of pheromones. Or maybe, actually, Annie was smarter than they all gave her credit for. Or, just as likely, it was that Lindy hadn't returned to their room the night before. Probably a little bit of each.

Lindy wanted her to know. To show her what she could have had, what she was missing. She hadn't showered that morning on purpose, hoping the scent of Colin's sweat still lingered, that her bed-head hair betrayed her in exactly the way she wanted.

Lindy's plan went as flawlessly as she could have hoped. Annie dabbed her lips with her napkin and pushed her chair back so abruptly that it toppled over, and then simply left. Bea called after her, even chased her down to the concierge desk. Lindy dropped her fork with a bit of uneaten omelet still stuck in its tines and refused to watch, wouldn't even grant Annie that attention. She didn't rise to say good-bye, didn't wave; she didn't do much of anything other than wonder why her immense sense of self-satisfaction was already ebbing from her veins, like someone had pricked a finger just microscopically enough to know there'd been a puncture, but not big enough to see the cut on the surface of the skin.

Catherine exploded on her just a few minutes later, and then Bea, who returned eventually and whom Lindy always thought of as an ally, said, *"I can't . . . I don't . . . I need a minute with this, Linds."* She shook her head, like Lindy sometimes sensed her little sister did while on the phone with her.

And Lindy said, "Great, so let's all just take Annie's side!"

"This is pretty hard to defend," Bea said, like she was reading a police report. "You knew there was a line there, Lindy. We all knew there was a line there."

"So because poor little Annie wanted Colin, I wasn't allowed to have some fun too?"

"Just . . . stop." Bea held up her hands. *"Stop talking. Stop making this worse."* She chewed on the corner of her mouth and said, *"You have to make this right. If you don't . . ."* She dropped her shoulders and looked Lindy square in the eye. It wasn't a threat; it was a revelation of disappointment, and Lindy felt her face flush. Bea was their collective conscience, their Northern Star, and in Lindy's quest to hurt Annie, she hadn't considered (of course she hadn't) how much she'd bruise the others too, and how much it would hurt to bruise them.

So Lindy flew back to New York the next morning, springing into their apartment, poised to apologize, poised to repent, and maybe even offer an honest explanation for her betrayal. *I wanted you.* But Annie never showed up that night, and by the next morning Lindy's regret was replaced with indignation. She'd had nibbles down in Nashville: some good gigs, an offer to work on a demo with a hot producer, so she stuffed a hodgepodge of ripped jeans and Doc Martens and flowy dresses and lacy bras into three suitcases, frantic to get out as quickly as she could. Then she hailed a cab to LaGuardia and charged a one-way ticket to Tennessee. She tilted her head against the window as the plane lifted higher, the sprawling concrete of New York getting smaller and smaller, farther and farther behind, and Lindy decided that she was done trying to charm Annie Eisley, done trying to love her. That she didn't owe Annie Eisley one fucking thing.

This morning, at 5:30 a.m., Lindy detects the hint of the twenty-year-old Annie in the blush of her cheeks, as she sits atop the steps and folds herself over her knees. She sees her old friend, and for the first time since those weeks after Catherine and Owen's wedding, wonders what might have happened if she'd made different choices. If she hadn't screwed Colin. If she'd admitted aloud that she knew Annie was in love with him. If she'd also admitted that she was in love with Annie.

If she'd been honest, would that have changed anything? Everything?

"Colin can't hear the snoring in the basement," Lindy says to Annie. "Go sleep down there."

She means it kindly—a peace offering almost, a gesture to say, *"He's not mine,"* though she knows, of course, that Annie is married, and knows, as well, that Colin is complicated for her old friend. So maybe Lindy means it only a little kindly. Maybe it's actually a taunt, really. Which isn't a kindness at all.

Annie's face goes slack, though she tries to quickly recover.

"Oh no. Oh no. I couldn't."

Colin shrugs. "We're old friends now, Ann. It's all good."

Lindy narrows her eyes and wonders if this is Colin's way of apologizing for his own behavior at the wedding. It does take two to tango, after all. That morning at brunch when Bea was done admonishing Lindy, she dragged Colin into a corner by his elbow, and Lindy watched his face morph from neutral to confusion to gloom. He hadn't realized he'd devastated Annie the way Lindy had, but he'd done it all the same. Consequences. Colin was perhaps more adept at accepting them than Lindy.

"I just . . . that's OK."

"I won't peek if you don't." Colin laughs.

"I *wouldn't* peek!"

"*I* would peek," Lindy says. "But I wouldn't need to, thanks to your fly."

Colin's right hand covers his boxers again; his uses his left hand to flip Lindy off.

"I'm going back to sleep. Ann, come on if you want."

Annie sits horrified, her face a frozen statue that reminds Lindy of some medieval gargoyle. Maybe Annie really can't survive on three hours of sleep: it turns her into a gnome.

"It was a bad idea," Lindy says. "Forget it."

But then Annie does something that surprises Lindy completely (who frankly thought she was unable to be surprised).

Annie straightens out the wrinkles in her floral cotton pajamas and says, "Well, all right, then. We're grown-ups. I can behave like a grown-up. Besides, I have Baxter. I don't need to peek." And she marches all the way down to the basement, shutting the door loudly behind her. An exclamation mark, a victory crow, her own middle finger.

Lindy frowns, then smiles, then frowns again.

If Annie Eisley, now Cunningham, can surprise her, then anything is possible.

12

ANNIE

Annie can't believe she's down here, in Colin's basement, sleeping beside him. Well, sleeping is a figurative term, because she isn't. Instead, she's lying rigidly next to him, her body like a wood plank, listening to the steady sound of his breathing, thinking, *I cannot believe that I'm down here, in Colin's basement. OMG! Nothing good comes from being down in Colin's basement!*

Owen and Lindy used to joke about the parade of girls who would tiptoe up the steps, slink out the door—the tank tops and miniskirts and baby-doll dresses and high-waisted Levi's disheveled from the hours spent in a ball at the foot of the bed.

"We should keep a Polaroid camera by the door," Lindy once suggested. "Create a mural in the hallway with every last one of them. So avant-garde."

"We should quiz him on how many names he remembers." Owen laughed.

"We should hold a lineup, police-style, and see who he can identify," Lindy howled.

And now Annie is down here—next to him! Not that she'll be a Polaroid on the wall, another name he can't remember.

She can't believe she agreed to Lindy's suggestion about the sleeping arrangement. She hadn't thought about it clearly, really. What she actually thought of were those two stupid letters: *xo*, and in a brief fit of lucid rage, realized how idiotic she was being, enveloping herself in her naïveté, like she could discount Baxter's indiscretions *again* when this time around she wasn't at fault! No, those letters *weren't* harmless, *weren't* something silly and easily explainable, and *weren't* something she could ignore. Well, maybe she could have ignored it if Lindy weren't sitting on their old couch, eyes like lasers upon her, challenging Annie to a bit of a grudge match. None of this occurred to Annie consciously, but on some level it must have passed through her cerebral space, because before she had time to think about it, she was tromping down the steps, then down another flight, and opening and closing the door behind her. The Annie from before—wife to Baxter, mother to Gus, PTA ladder-climber—would never have done this. But then the Annie from before would have quietly disregarded that pesky *xo* too.

She pulls the navy duvet up to her neck and lets her head ease back on a pillow, and there's no turning back from there. She isn't about to give Lindy the satisfaction of retreating, and frankly, she's a little bit electrified by this. A lot electrified. Maybe this is why Baxter is so casual with his fidelity! There's something wholly titillating about the possibility of the unknown here, in this old room, and for an instant Annie forgives him, her husband, for being duped by this immediate, pulse-pounding gratification. That forgiveness evaporates quickly, but leaves enough space for Annie to forgive herself for lying here, to excuse herself from considering the notion of what could come next.

Why should Baxter be the one who has all the fun?

Annie stares into the blackness of the room, her eyes darting back and forth, her mind racing even faster. Not that infidelity has ever sounded fun to Annie before this, but with Colin, well, yes, it sounds a little exciting—a little bit like driving a race car in the goddamn Grand Prix (or even just in Baxter's Porsche), like flying to the moon and back. *Maybe I deserve to fly to the moon and back every once in a while too.*

Colin sighs in his sleep, not kept awake by his own moral debate of making moves on Annie, not lost in his fantasy of flying to the moon and back with her. No, he sleeps soundly, which punctures Annie just enough that she can almost feel the piercing in her heart.

Her crush planted its roots so long ago, Annie is almost embarrassed that she's still hung up on it. It's childish, really. And it's gross now, she thinks. He's been with Lindy, and it was no secret that he would have hung the moon for Bea way back when.

She met Colin the very first day of school. She was assigned to the freshman dorm, the Quad, a rambling three-story spread of crimson bricks that spanned two blocks of campus. Annie and Colin (and the rest of them too) had the misfortune of getting rooms in the unrenovated section: the overhead lighting flickered; the door hinges creaked; the dodgy linoleum floor chilled your feet, so all the girls shuffled around in these shearling slippers that Annie had never seen in Texas and couldn't afford even if she had. After move-in day, Annie couldn't wait to rinse the sweat residue off every inch of her body (a heat wave was passing through Philadelphia, and their wing of the dorm lacked air-conditioning), so she snapped off the tags to her new, never-been-washed towels and cranked on the shower. But the hot water took forever, and while the pipes whined and moaned and she stood there waiting, sweating, waiting, sweating, Colin popped through the door in a towel of his own.

Annie hadn't realized the bathrooms were unisex.

Her jaw slackened, her sweat glands sped up though they were already in overdrive, and her cheeks flared emergency red. Annie had never had a high school boyfriend, had never let a man see her breasts, had never seen a naked man up close either. (She once inadvertently opened the bathroom door when one of her mother's boyfriends was using the toilet and recoiled in mortification, but that wasn't the same thing. Her mom's parade of men and their flimsy commitments, their disappearing acts, steered Annie off boys through puberty—not that boys were flocking to her or she had to beat them off with a stick or anything.)

"Hey," Colin said, not particularly put out by his near-nakedness and her proximity.

"Hey," Annie warbled, *very* put out.

"I'm Colin." He extended a hand, and Annie worried for a brief moment that his towel would drop, like it sometimes did in the movies. But it didn't, and eventually the steam rose from the shower, and Annie indelicately weaseled her way in, removing her towel and blindly thrusting out an arm to find the hanging hook, only after she'd sealed the curtain as close to shut as she could. And it turned out that Colin must not have found her too horrifying, stranded there like a mute mouse in an off-brand towel from Marshall's, because the next night, after everyone in their dorm shuttled to a mandatory group-bonding Phillies game and back again, he invited her into his neighboring room (his roommate was out, and Lindy, Annie's roommate—still a stranger then—wasn't about to be a third wheel). She tried to make herself as inconspicuous as possible while seated cross-legged on his bed, but he kissed her anyway.

She was still a virgin then (obviously), and she never let him go all the way. It wasn't like she didn't *want* him. She did. But she worried she'd do it wrong; she worried he'd laugh at her; she worried that she'd sleep with him and he'd discover that she was just like her mom: white trash, cheap, flimsy, not the type of girl to take home to his own mother. So for two months she stopped him. And he was kind and respectful, of course. Although his breathing was hard when she pushed him off her, his hand would always flop atop his forehead like he was flushed with fever. Eventually, he just stopped being in his room at night when she would swing by unannounced, and he wasn't waiting for her in the cafeteria when she would stand with her tray in hand, casting about for a place to sit beside him.

The whole thing had lasted only two months; it shouldn't have mattered the way it mattered to Annie for so long—too long, decades. But still, even now, as she lies beside him, the heat from his skin close enough to warm hers, she wonders whether that was why he ended it: if she'd given herself up to him, slept with him, let her become his completely, would she have had more of a chance? Would *they* have had more of a chance? Or was it that he knew deep down she *wasn't* the type of girl he considered worthy, the type of girl whom his mother would approve of? That she was the type of girl whose mom bought Twinkies for the homemade bake sale?

The night Colin officially ended it ("It's not you, it's me"), the fire alarms blared on at three in the morning. Lindy, with whom Annie had forged an unexpected friendship, had convinced Annie that alcohol was the only way she'd sleep after heartbreak. They were dead asleep, practically catatonic, when Bea, their next-door neighbor, banged on their door until Lindy stumbled forward, opened it, and said, "What?"

Lindy winced against the piercing alarm and squinted toward the whirling red lights that bounced off the box on the ceiling. "Oh, shit."

Then their RA ran by, noticeably unpoised, and shouted, "This isn't a drill! Fire on the second floor! Get out!"

Lindy and Bea roused Annie, pulled sweatpants over her legs, stuffed her feet into sneakers, and scampered with her down the steps, out the first-floor exit. Colin was already outside, standing with Owen (who also lived on their hall and had quickly become Colin's sidekick/wingman/bosom buddy), and Bea waved, unaware of the chasm Colin had axed into Annie's heart just hours earlier.

The fire trucks pulled up, so loud that none of them could even hear themselves think, and soon word spread: a Goth girl who was always cloaked in an air of mystery (and black eyeliner) had inadvertently fallen asleep with a cigarette. Rumors spread that she'd been wheeled out on a gurney. Catherine slid up to Owen, folded her hand into his, and whispered that she heard the girl was actually dead.

"Dead!" She whispered again, her blue eyes as shocked as they were wide. This turned out not to be true, but in the moment they didn't know, and the horror was exactly what six not-yet-indoctrinated freshmen needed to find their people. They were one another's people now. They'd retell that story—*remember how there was that fire, and we all stood outside the dorm and watched as they brought down the dead girl?*—forever. And that would be how they came to be, the initial structure of their six-point star. Bea had rescued Lindy and Annie, united them with Colin, and thus Owen, and thus Catherine. What didn't they owe to Bea?

Eventually, nearly at dawn, the fire trucks cleared, and they were allowed back into their nook of the dorm, which reeked like a fireplace had exploded. Parts of the second floor had to be evacuated for the week. They stumbled back to their hall—stunned, baffled, exhausted—and piled into Bea's room, falling on her bed, her floor, her overstuffed armchair.

Annie murmured, "I don't know anyone who's died."

And Bea said, "I almost died. Twice." And told them her story.

They gaped at her, and every one of them silently determined her to be a hero—to be braver than they were, and stronger and more admirable too.

Eventually, restless, unwelcome sleep cloaked them all.

And they woke up changed. They woke up a unit.

Not that this mended Annie's heart. For the next week she curled herself into a tight ball on her bed, underneath those Ralph Lauren sheets, and cried. Lindy blared girl-power music like "I Will Survive" and "It's Raining Men," and told Annie she was better than some dumb asshole. And Bea started coming by regularly, rubbing her back and telling her that he was just an eighteen-year-old guy, and this is the sort of silly shit they do. Bea had been dating since she was fourteen—high school guys for a while and then a guy from NYU last year—so Annie tried to zip up her pathetic sputtering and believe her. Bea seemed wiser than Annie—not just about men, but about everything. She read the *New York Times*; she'd been to almost all the countries in Europe (including Russia, which Annie hadn't even realized you were allowed to visit); she dressed like she had somewhere to be, even if she didn't. *Colin deserves someone like Bea, someone special,* Annie thought when Bea left her to go retrieve a cup of tea. Lindy offered her Jack Daniel's while they waited. It's no wonder she couldn't hang on to him, she told herself, when there were girls like Bea out there.

It would have been healthier to exorcise herself from him, from them, to start fresh and make other friends, find a different crowd, a newer crew to run with. But now they shared late-night snacks (Corn Nuts and yogurt pretzels) and occasional late-night cigarettes (Parliament Lights), studied together, ate their meals together, and survived a girl *almost dying* together. Annie was never good at fighting inertia. Leaving Texas for Philadelphia was enough of a leap to exhaust her. So what was she going to do? She was grateful for their friendship, for their acceptance of her less-than-regal Texas self, and even though she still held out the hope that Colin might turn her doorknob one night and sneak into bed with her, she wasn't about to ruin everything because he didn't. Annie understood that everyone else could be casual, nonchalant, so she pretended that she could be too. Still, today, at nearly forty, she worked on perfecting her act.

Annie turns her head and tries to make out Colin's profile in the blackness of his old room.

No, she isn't going to ruin everything. Not then. Not now.

Footsteps from the living room echo across the ceiling: Lindy or that guy who showed up tromping into the kitchen. Annie allows herself to shift just an inch nearer to Colin, as if his proximity can stave off what she remembers next.

One particularly bleak night, just after she and Lindy landed in New York and it was gusting sheets of rain and their apartment windows rattled and the air inside was thick with curry from the downstairs take-out place and damp from the tears of their early twentysomething angst, Lindy threw back three tequila shots and beckoned Annie close, closer, no, closer still. They were sitting cross-legged across from each other on their apartment's knotty wood floor, and Annie remembers— still, now—her heart beating, her thoughts unsure, as Lindy said, *"No, closer, come here scooch forward, closer."* Annie smiled awkwardly and did as she was told until she was so close she could smell the tequila on Lindy's breath, see the freckle that lay flat just above her top lip.

"What?" She laughed nervously, so Lindy passed her a shot, sliding it a few inches across the floor, and Annie gulped it quickly, unsure why, but she gulped all the same. While the tequila burned its way down, before she even had time to process what was happening, Lindy leaned forward, breaking the divide between them, and kissed her. Annie was so startled, she froze, and Lindy pulled back. She must have seen the shock in Annie's slackened cheeks, her wide eyes, so she cackled loudly and reached for another shot.

"Oh, come on, Annie. I was just playing around," she said. "We can't land a guy worth shit, so I was just teasing."

Annie scooted back a few inches and tried to laugh, but it came out like an uncomfortable, awkward belch. Later, she would replay the kiss in her mind over and again, wondering if it really happened. It was all so fast, and they were both a little drunk.

"No, no, I know!" she said, waving a hand, unable to meet Lindy's eyes.

"We have each other," Lindy said, raising yet another shot. A toast. "To us! That won't change. I promise."

Annie raised up a shot of her own, though her fingers were shaking, and they clinked their tiny little glasses and drank, avowing themselves to each other . . . because that's what best friends do.

∽

After Catherine and Owen's wedding, Annie stayed in Bea's spare apartment in New York until she was brave enough to return to her own, sure that Lindy wasn't there, sure that even if she were, she'd have the strength to face her. Actually, she was never sure of that, and was relieved that she didn't have to be, because Bea, back in Honduras, but who always knew everything, e-mailed that Lindy had made her way to Nashville.

Annie unlatched the door, the lock clicking, her breath caught in her throat, and didn't know why she was surprised to find it empty. A hush settled over the apartment, a barrenness without Lindy there. She stood in the doorway for who knew how long, letting this marinate—that Lindy was gone, and if she didn't want to think about her again, she didn't have to. She stood on the precipice long enough to convince herself of this. Then she strode to Lindy's empty bed, flattened herself on her old mattress, and swore that she was going to change. She'd tried this already, of course, at Penn. With the faded accent and the too-orangey highlights and the knockoff clothing that maybe no one could tell wasn't the real thing. Maybe she needed to try harder to make someone love her, to believe in her the way Owen believed in Catherine—the way that, well, she'd believed in Lindy. Best friends forever?

Fuck that, she thought, staring up at the cracks in the plaster left behind from a faded water stain. Why was Lindy so hell-bent on pushing people outside of their comfort zones? Well! Consider Annie pushed!

She maxed out her credit card the next day at Bloomingdale's, and cut off her shoulder-length hair to a modern bob. She tossed her shoulders back when she walked, and tipped her chin high. She got promoted at the PR firm, though when they called her in for the meeting, she was certain she was going to be fired. She got invited to happy hours, though she fretted she was terrible at small talk and occasionally overcompensated with an extra martini (or cosmo or whatever it was that everyone else was drinking that particular month). Sometimes she even went on dates, and was surprised each time a man found her attractive enough to ask. She nabbed a cheap apartment just south of Harlem and ventured out on her own, eating cold soup from a can for dinner in front of the glow of the TV, but she'd done it all the same—done it without Lindy, done it without Colin, without anyone. It should have made her happy, all of this. It didn't, though. It felt like work; it *was* work. But it was life, and she supposed it was more than she'd thought she'd get back in Texas.

And then Bea died just a few months after that. So suddenly and without warning. The funeral had been their last chance, probably, to make things right, to make a U-turn back to being one another's people. But they'd squandered that too. Still hopped up on their sensitivities from the wedding debacle, and without Bea there left to mend things, well, it was easy to let things unravel.

Annie mourned her for a good year, sometimes a memory sneaking in on the subway or at the deli or late at night in the stillness of her new apartment, making her catch her breath. Memories of how Bea had insisted on bringing Annie home for Thanksgiving because she knew Annie didn't have much to celebrate back in Texas; of how Bea made them all choose a costume theme for Halloween (the cast from *Scream*, the characters from *Clueless*) and go as a unit, an ensemble. Sometimes she still picked up her phone to call her, simply out of habit. Sometimes she checked her e-mail, thinking she'd get a whirlwind update from some glamorous, exotic locale that Annie could only read about in thick magazines at her dentist's office.

But Bea never e-mailed, of course. Annie could never call.

And then Annie met Baxter. And for once, Annie made her peace with Bea's passing. Not because she wouldn't have done anything in the world to bring her back, but because now Annie was unburdened, no immediate history to detach herself from. Only her ancient history, and she'd long since figured out how to outrun that. The accent, the frosted hair, the knock-off clothes, the Twinkies, the wolves—there was simply no one left in her circle who knew her from before.

Baxter was a notorious New York bachelor, a trader at Morgan Stanley, a staple on the late-night scene. They met at a post-5K Goldman-sponsored Fun Run, and Annie was two martinis in. Baxter was three deep. He plugged her info into his phone by his fourth, and then e-mailed her, with her standing beside him, asking if she'd like to come home with him.

Annie knew better, so she declined.

She'd read *The Rules*, after all.

Instead, the next night he took her to a tiny hole-in-the-wall in Little Italy, with homemade gnocchi and to-die-for tiramisu, and they talked about all sorts of things that were out of Annie's league: the opera and weekends in Europe and yachting and childhood country houses. But they weren't out of Annie's league anymore, because now she was whoever she wanted to be. Two bottles of pinot and twelve hours later, she woke in his apartment, under six-hundred-thread-count sheets, a note next to the bed saying he'd gone for a run and to stay for the morning. She pulled the sheets high up to her neck and vowed to be the person he thought she was, be the person she really had become now. He didn't need to know her secrets; she hadn't asked him about his own.

He proposed quickly, after only four months. They'd flown to Antigua, Annie's first time out of the country (she never told Baxter), and he knelt on one knee at sunset on the beach. He cried, and then she cried too, and they both vowed to remember that moment forever. They really did love each other once. Even years later, Annie would remember that gasp of a moment and wish she'd photographed it, wish she'd captured it to share with all her friends.

Baxter had been married once before—a quickie at age twenty-three that lasted nine months—so he didn't want a big to-do. Though Annie secretly dreamed of a write-up in the *New York Times*, she also couldn't bear the notion of her mother, in an electric-blue taffeta gown from TJ Maxx, mixing with his blue-blood family, and quickly conceded to something smaller, something quieter. Something that didn't betray her. Annie flew her mom in for a weekend of pleasantries (at Baxter's insistence), and Annie held her breath for two days straight, so terrified that her mom would embarrass her, give her away, make him stop loving her. But she didn't. Baxter was nothing but gracious—Annie had to give that to him even now. If he thought any less of her, saw through the veneer she'd constructed, he said not a word.

They married a month later at city hall.

Afterward, she thought about e-mailing Bea to tell her the news. Her old friend would be so thrilled for her. Until she remembered that she couldn't e-mail her at all.

They took a real honeymoon to Bora Bora—Annie's second stamp on her passport, and one of the women who was servicing their hut confided to Annie that this was the fertility season, that you couldn't leave Bora Bora without a baby. Baxter overheard from the patio, emerged from behind the sliding glass door, and said: "Ooh, well, let's not leave Bora Bora without a baby."

Annie giggled and agreed, even though Bea, whom she thought of during her lingering walks on the endless beach while gazing up at the impossibly vast, starry sky from the porch of their thatched-roof bungalow, might have told her to *slow down*, that there wasn't any rush, that a lot had already shifted for Annie (and Baxter) in just a few short months. What was the hurry? (Not that Bea ever slowed down on her own: Annie remembered this as well. But she was wiser about others than about herself, kinder to others than to herself too.)

Three weeks after they jetted back to reality, Baxter was already logging dawn-until-midnight hours at the office, chasing a partnership—having long forgotten about Bora Bora's fertility season.

And then Annie started puking. She figured it was from the stress of redoing Baxter's apartment, making it her own; of leaving her job and filling the endless hours with homemade (but disastrous) dinners; of occasionally hearing her former best friend, Lindy Armstrong, on the radio when she flipped the dial.

A week later, she realized it wasn't stress. She sat with her underwear around her ankles and stared at the test for a good half hour. *How could it be?* she thought. *Only five months ago I was a party of one.*

Five months changed everything, though. Annie again thought about Bea—the tops of her legs damp from her fallen tears, and she thought about all the ways her life, and Bea's life, and all of their lives, could have taken different turns. If she'd slept with Colin freshman year; if Colin hadn't slept with Lindy at the wedding; if they hadn't gone to Bora Bora during fertility season; if, in whatever manner she'd died, Bea simply hadn't.

Then she blew her nose, pulled up her panties, and reapplied her eyeliner and mascara. She was going to be someone's mother. And she was going to be the best mother this child could ever dream of. There wasn't any space left for lingering what-ifs. It was time to seal those scars up entirely.

 ⌒๑

Tonight, in Colin's old bed, Annie feels her eyelids dropping lower, heavier, willing themselves shut. She wants one more moment like this, though, in case it never happens again, just so she can be sure she didn't dream it.

Annie rolls to her side and ever-so-softly, as if she almost isn't there, runs her hand over the span of Colin's back, winding down the butterfly of his shoulder blades, onto his waist, which cuts like a V into his Scottie boxers.

She tilts herself away because that's enough, that's all it can be. Baxter got more than this with his affairs, but she isn't Baxter.

Then she shuts her eyes for real this time and tries to not consider the what-ifs that she thought she'd buried ten years ago when Gus was born. It's harder now, though, and frankly, she's relieved when sleep finally comes.

13

COLIN

Colin sleeps soundly and wakes almost refreshed, relieved not to have dreamed of Bea. He used to all the time after she died. He dreamed of her falling off mountains in Maui, of her melting from acid rain in Bangkok, of plane crashes into the Atlantic, and car wrecks on the streets of London . . . and grim reapers from the world over that he never seemed to shake. They became less frequent after a year or so, but never quite disappeared entirely. They'd find him when he was least prepared, when his conscious mind was certain he was over it, but his subconscious mind wasn't ready to forget.

Annie is breathing deeply beside him, a spare pillow flung over her head. He smiles because Annie makes him laugh, even all these years later, even though she doesn't mean to, never meant to. He's surprised to find himself comforted with her here next to him, like a puzzle piece that fits in unexpectedly.

She was always sweet, Annie. He remembers she was a virgin back then, and how he thought that was sweet too. Not weird like he thought she might think it was. Innocent. Colin hadn't known that many girls from his high school who were still innocent in college, not that he was complaining. (He had "de-innocented" several of them.) But even at eighteen, he wasn't such a throbbing hormone that he couldn't recognize he didn't want to be the one to screw Annie up. Not that sex would have screwed her up. He didn't mean it like that. But he wanted to do right by her, treat her differently than maybe he would have someone else: he didn't want a lifetime with someone—he was *a freshman in college, jeez!*—and he didn't think sex was anything other than really pretty fucking fun. But he thought she might. She was wide-eyed enough to think it might mean *everything*, and Colin didn't have everything to give.

So rather than do the thing that a million of his buddies would do—sleep with her anyway—he broke up with her. It wasn't that hard. He shouldn't get too much credit. He wasn't trying to earn accolades for not being the dick who took her virginity and dumped her. Besides, even if he had his doubts and changed his mind, the fire broke out that same night, and that's when he realized it was *Bea*. Bea. She shared her story—orphan, cancer, broken back, for God's sake—and it was love. Like the kind that strikes the hapless high school virgin in the movies. A lightning bolt.

He told her a few weeks later: they split a bottle of Absolut in the student lounge, and he got handsy and tried to kiss her, but she pushed him off efficiently, somehow managing not to humiliate him.

"I don't want a fixer," she said.

"Who said I'm a fixer?"

"Me. I'm saying it. You're premed. You want to be a neurosurgeon! I told you my story, and you want to be my prince." She smiled that crooked smile. "Who said I'm interested in a prince?"

"I would be *such* a good prince, though," he said. It was the type of line that usually worked.

But she bit back a grin and shook her head, and they settled in as friends, then best friends. That didn't stop him from loving her, though. Never stopped him. Later, in those last few days they spent together in her apartment, she told him it was also because of Annie: that she simply couldn't, would never betray Annie. And he started crying then, and she did too, not because of missed opportunities, that they were destined to be soul mates, blah, blah, blah, but because that's who Bea was: loyal to the end, but correct in her allegiances too. She *should* have chosen Annie back then. He loved her all the more, in that moment, for doing so.

No woman had even come close to Bea since. He didn't tell the others tonight, didn't feel like getting into it, but there had been the failed engagement, at least two pregnancy scares, and some less-than-pleasant interactions with an on-call nurse from time to time.

He really thought that Vivian, the last one, would stick. Fucking A, *he proposed*, which is what she said she wanted! But then she was going on and on about how he wasn't "fully there," which he didn't understand because, goddamn it, all he did was be there. *"I'm here! What else do you want from me?"* But Vivian didn't think he was "there, like, enough."

"I can just see it in your eyes," she said before she grabbed her clothes from the top two drawers in his dresser. "You're not there."

"I am," he said, but maybe not forcefully enough. *"I'm fucking there!"*

"Here," she said, and she pointed to her heart, and frankly, Colin almost laughed. But she was a yoga instructor, and a revered one, and took that sort of shit seriously. "You're *not* here."

Maybe he wasn't. Hell, he didn't know. He let her slip out of the bedroom and out the door, so he couldn't have been as *there, here, whatever,* as he thought.

He just didn't really think he'd be forty and still sleeping around. Didn't think he wouldn't have found someone he'd love more than Bea by now.

The actresses he dates bore him. They don't eat. They don't read the news.

He's not so sure he finds being the Boob King of Los Angeles particularly satisfying.

Maybe he'd like a kid someday.

Yes, Colin thinks. *Maybe I would.*

Annie snores softly, muffled underneath the pillow. He rolls onto his back and worries about the lies he told the four of them just yesterday. Thirteen years ago and then again yesterday. He'd like to come clean, relieve his guilt, let them judge him—or ease his burden, if they're feeling generous. But it's been so long now, Bea has been dead for so long now, he doesn't even know where to begin, how to tell them the truth about how she died. Also, he already bears plenty of responsibility for the wedding fiasco; he'd rather not double-down on the blame, the pointed fingers, the culpability. Of course, if he could, he would rewind and retract the stupidity of the wedding, but he can't. Bea forgave him, and that's what mattered most.

He groans and pushes himself up on his elbows. He doesn't want to contemplate any of this: the past and all the ways it still haunts him, or the future and all the ways it hasn't gone as expected. He really just wants a superstrong cup of coffee and maybe some breakfast to settle his stomach. Something smells good in the kitchen, smells like it used to two decades ago. And like an easily distracted dog, he chases the scent that pleases his immediate senses. So he eases out of bed, then folds the comforter back over Annie, and rises to greet the day.

14

CATHERINE

Catherine woke this morning with Lindy's white-noise machine cooing, and she suddenly couldn't remember when she'd last made French toast. When they lived here, it was something of a ritual, at least on the Sundays when they all found themselves in their own beds, which was less frequently than you'd think (mostly on account of Lindy and Colin skewing the odds). Back then, Catherine thought of it like a family sitting down together over Sunday dinner, the irony being that now, her family rarely sat down for Sunday dinner, and certainly she's not mastering French toast in the mornings. The closest she's come is whipping up brunch food on *Good Morning America*, but she really just whisked some ingredients together on-screen before magically presenting the finished plate. But honest-to-God homemade French toast, made with care and thought and love . . .

When was the last time she made that?

Not for Mason or Penelope in ages. Not for Owen either.

So she resolved to make perfect French toast. She stared at the ceiling from Lindy's bed and thought, *Today, I'm going to be who I was when I was twenty, twenty-one. And made all sorts of things for my friends here—in this house, under this roof—that were filled with care and thought and love.*

She ran to Wawa for ingredients while the others slept, and then she cracked the eggs and melted the butter and added in a splash of vanilla extract that she found in the spice drawer and poured in just the right amount of milk. The slices sizzled on the pan. *Yes, today's the day that I remember why I started doing this in the first place.*

Also, she knew that the scent of French toast would wake them all—it used to back then too, when they'd emerge from closed doors one by one, bed-headed and sleepy, but hungry and thankful for her efforts. She'd drifted in and out of sleep in those few precious hours since she'd been granted a reprieve from Owen's snoring, thinking of Bea, thinking of her wedding, of how poorly she behaved, then even more poorly at the funeral. She inhaled the aroma wafting from the pan and imagined that Bea was somehow looking down on her approvingly, like this particular French toast was absolution for the things set in motion that day at the brunch. As if this particular French toast would unite the five of them again.

Twenty years ago, Catherine never believed she quite got the French toast right. She tore recipe after recipe out of magazines, xeroxed them from cookbooks borrowed from the library. There were a surprising number of tweaks to French toast that elevated it from decent to delectable—orange rind, lemon zest, jumbo eggs, nutmeg—and Catherine never trusted her own instincts enough not to heed someone else's formula. Bea would sit with her sometimes while she cooked, dragging a chair over from the dining table whose paint job Catherine was equally dissatisfied with, and ooh and aah about the mouthwatering scent, about Catherine's natural ability in the kitchen ("at everything!" Bea would marvel—"I'm just so terrible with my hands!"). But Catherine would shake her head and reread whatever egg- or milk-spattered recipe lay on the counter, and keep tweaking. She was never as good as she hoped. Never good enough, certainly. Not good enough to gamble and attempt a go from scratch.

On this morning, Colin pops his head up the stairs first, pulling a Stanford T-shirt over his chest. He hasn't changed much, Catherine assesses. Some finer lines around his eyes, but other than that, it's as if time froze for him. He is simple. He is happy. He is unburdened.

It must be nice to be unburdened. To not have readers to satisfy, board members to please, Target to placate.

She slides him a plate, and he growls, pleased. His fork scrapes against the plate before she can even set it down.

"You'd better have saved some for me!" Lindy barrels down the steps, coming from who knows whose room. *Had she slept in Bea's bed?*

"French toast! I'd know that smell anywhere."

A smoldering hipster-looking guy bounds down the steps behind her, and Catherine narrows her eyes, contemplating how on earth Lindy has managed to land a one-night stand, and just how typical that was. And then immediately regrets her judgment—*What if Bea is watching us? What if I could have done things differently?*—because she had earlier resolved to truly make amends. She drops two slices on another plate and offers it to Lindy. *See, Bea? I'm trying!*

Smoldering hipster-looking guy tears off a corner of the top piece and chews slowly, thoughtfully. "Not so bad," he says, his head cocked, his brow wrinkled. "But French toast *is* my specialty." He winks at her, and Catherine sags.

"Leon." He extends his hand. "I'm just playing."

Catherine frowns. "Catherine. This is five-star French toast. It's reader approved."

"Hey, man." Colin bobs his head. "Colin. We didn't officially meet last night." He offers him another slice with his fingers, like this five-star French toast is disposable, like it's not a goddamn work of art.

Lindy grabs it and swallows it in three bites. Not how French toast is meant to be savored.

"Do I smell French toast?" Annie sings from the basement. God bless her, Annie is going to make this right, appreciate it for all it's worth. She bounces up the steps, her ponytail swinging behind her. "Oooh, Catherine! My favorite, you shouldn't have!"

Catherine waves her hand, like, *no biggie*. She hands a plate to Annie, who sits beside Colin but avoids his eyes and instead focuses—intently—on cutting her toast into perfect symmetrical squares before spearing them with a fork and relishing each bite.

"Oooh, this is heaven," she says. "Is this your old recipe? Is it on your site?" She turns to the others. "I check her site every day. She has *the best* holiday suggestions. I use them all the time for the PTA."

Her site! In the early-morning haze of revisiting her grief over Bea and outrunning Owen's snoring, she'd forgotten. She never forgets about her site! And today, of all days, with the critical Fourth of July spread, the one Target would be eyeballing, the one with the stills from the HGTV pilot that surely their executives will be mulling over too. After the disaster of the test run, she'd insisted on a full redo with her own ideas (well, not her own ideas *exactly*: she hadn't *quite* copied anything expressly, just took inspiration, maybe, and some tiny creative liberties from a few unknown mom-and-pop blogs that no one would have heard of, no one would have ever seen!). She tried to manage the shoot from soup to nuts, 100 percent, but what with the board prep and the increasingly frantic e-mails from her CFO, she inevitably had to leave some of the details to Fred.

"Oh!" She claps her hands and pulls out her phone. "I was having so much fun with the French toast that I completely forgot! We have a new photo spread up today." She wipes her hands on a dish towel and hopes the others don't detect the worry that surely spreads like a shadow across her face.

Annie has her mouth full, so she gestures to the chair beside her, and Catherine sits with her phone aloft in her palm, while Leon inexplicably hovers over her shoulder too.

"Leon," he says to Annie.

"That's Annie," Lindy says before Annie has a chance to swallow her bite and reply.

Catherine is immediately sure she'll be caught this time; that this will be it: her cover will be flambéed. Her eyes dart back and forth over the glossy shots, her thumb and pointer finger enlarging the screen for a better view. She'd been at the shoot, of course, the bulk of it anyway—present and accounted for (physically at least)—but now she can see that some small details slipped, even under her own watch. A few of the elements knock it out of the park: the towering centerpieces crafted out of cupcakes, mimicking an exploding firework; handwoven tablecloths braided like the American flag (found on a teeny-tiny homemade site that hadn't appeared to be updated in seven months!); a giant Liberty Bell piñata (which Catherine personally papier-mâchéd after stumbling upon an image from a homeschooling blog out of Iowa), and a Statue of Liberty replica carved out of watermelon (discovered deep in the bowels of Pinterest).

But the flower arrangements are off. *Who approved Gerbera daisies? Do Gerbera daisies scream patriotic to you?* And someone forgot the little American flags in the lemonades, which round off the entire look and were, as Catherine told her staff, just as she ran out the door to try to make one of Penelope's gymnastic meets, "the final flourish, the salute to America, the salute to our readers." She didn't tell them that the flags were fresh off the shelves at Target, a tip of the hat to her potential partners/life raft. Should she have? Was that the only way to get her staff to actually dedicate themselves to the fine print, to the nitty-gritty details?

Those goddamn flags could cost us a partnership, could cost you your jobs, you nitwits! Now, are you listening? Now, are you paying attention?

It's no goddamn wonder that their hits are faltering, that ad sales are sinking. How does someone on her payroll forget a goddamn salute to America?

"It's beautiful!" Annie whispers. She smacks her hand across her chest, like she was pledging allegiance to Catherine. "Wow, Cathy, just . . . wow."

Catherine freezes her face into something like what she hopes is a smile as she runs down the checklist of all the screwups. Her eyes feel wild, her irritation unhinging her. Maybe she should have ignored her irate CFO, maybe she shouldn't have overcommitted to a TV pilot *and* a Target partnership (though she surely needs both), maybe she shouldn't have gotten distracted with all this personal stuff from her past—coming here, dredging up old wounds, losing focus. Or maybe this is her penance for poaching from someone else, for never quite being good enough to play in the big leagues, even though she's firmly *in* the big leagues. Who ever said she was good enough to deserve it?

Leon slaps the table, clattering the plates.

"That's it! That's how I know you. You're The Crafty Lady. Oh, man! I used to watch you on Food Network, like, all the frickin' time."

Lindy side-eyes Leon at the revelation. Catherine spreads her smile wide and hopes he doesn't ask why she no longer guests on the Food Network. (They replaced her with Suzy Carpenter of that stupid Suzy's Secrets blog who was twenty-nine and a mom of four, not to mention a size zero with flawless blonde highlights and a cheeriness that could make birds sing.)

Colin rises and helps himself to seconds.

"Well, hey," Leon says, pulling her into a hug, like they're old mates, like Catherine is at all comfortable with this. "Man, I didn't mean anything with my comment . . . I was just playing . . . if I'd known the French toast was coming from you, well, man . . ."

Catherine doesn't think she can smile any wider than she already is, so she gently pushes her hands against his chest and untangles herself from his lanky limbs, and thanks him demurely. He offers a reverent bow. Though she's not sure that this was much of a compliment: delicious only in name, not in execution.

Leon, evidently a domestic god in skinny jeans and a neck scarf (and whose presence she still doesn't quite understand—*Who are you? What are you doing here?*), takes her phone, peering intently at the photo spread. Catherine worries that he'll recognize something, call her on the plagiarizing farce that she (kind of, at times) is.

Instead, he says, "That looks awesome." He exclaims, "You're killing it! I'd like to go to a goddamn barbecue that looks that fly." He moves to hug her again, but Catherine delicately steps backward ever so slightly, and they both pretend that he's not attempting to invade her personal space with his fawning.

"You're into crafting?" Lindy asks.

"It relaxes me. Also, you should try my coffee cake. Next time you're in the city, I'll make it for you."

Footsteps reverberate overhead, and they all gaze upward, and then Owen plods his way down the steps.

"Good morning!" he says, as if he hadn't ingested approximately seven times the legal alcohol limit twelve hours ago and then kept the rest of them awake since. His baseball cap is slung too low, but otherwise he's in pretty good shape for a guy who arguably could be hospitalized right now. He glances at Leon, utterly unperturbed by a stranger standing in their old living room. "Hey, dude."

"It's practically noon!" Catherine says. It's not like Owen has slept so much later than the rest of them (well, other than Catherine, who rose at 8:30 a.m.). But she can't help herself. *Who does he think he is to saunter down here and act like he hadn't been a ridiculous fool last night?* When she woke, she resolved not to hold it against him all day, but now he's so buoyant and unapologetic that she resolves to nearly hold it against him forever. "And you missed French toast."

French toast is Owen's favorite. She knows this will sting.

"It's also July 4th," Annie says, like this is just occurring to all of them for the first time.

No one says anything for a moment. They all stare at their bare feet (Owen stares at his socks because he fell asleep in them), contemplating the enormity of something so simple as a new date on the calendar. Yesterday was just any old day. Today was Bea's birthday. Twenty-four hours can flip your perspective on end.

Leon just glances at the rest of them because he has no clue what this all means.

"Jesus. It's Fourth of July," Colin says, mostly to himself. "We need to go out and do something. Something like we used to," he says to the others, gazing at each of them. "For Bea."

"For Bea." The rest of them (well, not Leon because he still doesn't know who Bea is) murmur.

For a second, they mean it, they really do.

∽

Colin proposes revisiting Bea's favorite places on campus, each of them sharing a memory at each one, something they loved best about her. They set aside their differences, the vast divide between them, the urge to simply leave and return to their safer havens at home, because each of the five of them is too embarrassed to admit they can't do this for Bea. What sort of friend would they be if they couldn't do this for her?

They walk to Wawa for coffee and convenience-store doughnuts because that's what they ate back then, when no one had heard of organic food, and their bodies could handle a diet of minimal-to-zero nutrients. (Not Annie, though—she usually took a bite to be polite, then stuffed the rest in a wadded-up napkin.)

Owen orders a breakfast burrito at Taco Bell Express, just like he used to, and Catherine sighs because his digestive system at forty is not what it was at twenty. At twenty, it wasn't even all that good.

"Hey." He shrugs. "A college morning isn't complete without a breakfast burrito."

"This *isn't* a college morning," Catherine reminds him.

"You're being technical."

She *was* being technical, but Catherine is always technical. Her irritation runs through her, tangible, an electric shock. She massages the back of her neck.

"Just a decaf," Lindy says, eyes down, though the manager recognizes her, and she agrees to a photo.

"OK, I'll start," Colin says. "What I remember about being at Wawa with Bea is how she was on a first-name basis with the cashier . . . what was it?" He squints, casting for the memory. "Hector? Maybe Hector. Anyway, she'd sweet-talked him one night when we came in drunk without our wallets, and Bea just *had* to have those yogurt pretzels. Remember those things? They had them in bulk?"

"Ew, those bins. Yes. You just reached your hands in and took them." Catherine shudders. "If I knew then what I know now . . ."

"Well, anyway . . . Bea somehow convinced Hector that if she didn't get those yogurt pretzels *right then*, she was gonna, like, die." He stops himself.

"It's OK," Annie says. "You don't mean it literally."

"She asked him about his family and his kids and where he came from, and all of this mumbo-jumbo that who would have thought to ask? And then she promised if he gave her free reign over the yogurt-pretzel bin, she'd never forget any of his kids' birthdays." Colin shakes his head and laughs. "You know Bea. How could he say no?"

"So *that's* why we always got free yogurt pretzels whenever we came in," Catherine says. She resists the urge to check her phone. She's e-mailed her whole team to find out just how the details slipped through on the shoot, and even though there's nothing to be done now, and even though it's a national holiday, she'd like some answers. She expects some answers. But she tells herself it can wait, at least until they've exited Wawa, finished honoring their memories of Bea.

"That is why." Colin smiles. "And honestly, I don't think she ever did forget a birthday. She brought back a Jets jersey from New York once for his son. And a snow globe another time."

The clerk from Taco Bell calls out Owen's order. Catherine sighs again as Owen licks grease off his fingers and exhales contentedly. They all shove their hands into their pockets and stare at the floor.

"Well, anyway," Colin says, "that's what I remember about her here, and I bet Hector remembers her too."

"Bea was good about keeping her promises," Annie says.

And no one has much else to say to that, because they're all keenly aware of the promises of their own they failed to live up to, the promises to Bea they failed to keep.

~⑨~

They opt for their old dorm next; Annie's the one who suggests it. They amble down crimson brick-paved Locust Walk, which cuts like a connective artery through the hub of the campus, on their way to the Quad, where fate and the fire threw them together and made them family. Catherine reaches for a memory of when she lived there with her roommate . . . Susan Ling, that was her name. *What ever happened to her?* They were never close, and besides, Catherine spent all her time with Owen, and then Owen introduced her to the others, and since Owen's roommate had transferred to Villanova the second week, she practically moved in. She remembers that Owen never complained that he needed space, that he wanted to have some breathing room to go out with the guys, or didn't want a girlfriend to drag him down when he pledged Sigma Chi because Sigma Chis were notorious for getting all the hot girls. He let her redecorate with tapestries from Urban Outfitters and a flimsy rug that smelled like hemp she found down on South Street. They were a team, a unit, and neither was ever particularly far from the other. They studied together in the library stacks, they ate breakfast and dinner together, and they fell asleep watching *90210* reruns together.

But that was all so long ago, Catherine reminds herself. Before real responsibilities. Before real problems.

Catherine swipes her phone. Nothing yet from her team. She sets her jaw and grimaces. *Where is everyone when I need them?*

She tries to remember the last time she told Owen she needed him; the last time, really, she needed him period. Surely, if she told him about the trouble the company was in, of the dwindling revenue stream, he'd want to help. Actually, just a few months ago, he *did* want to help. But that was about *him* wanting to work—any sort of work, Catherine gathered, which is not exactly the kind of help she needed.

Anyway, it's her, really. She lost track of relying on him—like she'd lost track of Susan Ling, she supposes—and she's not so sure she wants to retrace those steps. She's not even sure she *needs* to rely on him anymore, even though she recognizes the dangerous slippery slope this recognition can initiate in a marriage.

The Fourth of July Road to Freedom festival is in full swing on Locust Walk. Two men decked out in colonial garb march a few feet behind them, rattling off "Yankee Doodle Dandy" on a fiddle and a flute. Colin does a slightly off-rhythm jig with his feet, then links elbows with Annie and spins her around until she shrieks about dizziness. Lindy sings "Yankee Doodle Dandy" opera-style, and Leon and Colin give her a standing ovation (though they're already standing). Catherine empties the clutter from her mind (though she checks her phone once more) and feels it too, the infectiousness of their old selves—free from the weights of adulthood—nipping at their heels. All of them laugh, a fleeting but perhaps sticky moment of joy, to be back *here*, their mirth traveling up through the towering oak trees that arch and crest above them, insulating them from the reality of the outside world. Or at least that's what the oaks did back then; now they're memories of a memory.

Annie pulls out her phone and snaps a photo for Instagram.

"When was the last time you guys were back here?" Leon asks. "All together?"

Catherine taps her phone against her hip, waiting for Lindy to answer. He's here on her account, after all; she should be the one to explain their history. The rest of them have plenty of other baggage to handle; they shouldn't have to babysit this interloper. But no one else seems particularly put out by his presence.

Instead, Annie looks up from her screen, from her hashtag frenzy, and responds to Leon. "Oh, gosh. All together? Not in a long time."

"Not since the funeral," Colin says.

"No," Lindy snaps. "Not since the *wedding. All* of us. Together."

Catherine steels her eyes at her phone, ignoring her, though she internally blanches at the mention of her wedding, of how she behaved.

Still nothing.

Where is her team? Why does no one care that the photo spread is a mess? She clenches and unclenches her fists, and wishes she could stride on ahead without them, loop around campus or maybe the track down at the stadium, like she does at the office to clear her mind, regroup, realign her axis. Instead, she's walking around as if there's a pebble wedged in her sole, like something is bothering her that she just can't pinpoint.

A row of tents, which teem with summer students, a few professorial types, and local families with cherubic but sweaty children, block their streamlined path to the Quad.

A sign hangs from each tent pole.

LIVE LIKE THE COLONIALS DID!

"Come, come," a revolutionary soldier beckons. "Come join us in the festivities celebrating our great liberation from our oppressor, her Royal Majesty!"

Oh, please, God, no, Catherine thinks, and checks her phone again. *I do not have time for this.* What she really means is she does not have the patience for this.

"Madam, what is that thing you hold in your hand? Is it some sort of enchanting device?"

"What?" Catherine asks, just as Annie says, "Ooh, what are the festivities?"

Another soldier steps out and barks: "Butter-churning contest in two minutes! Who will step up and lead the nation?"

"The nation needs to be led in a butter-churning contest?" Catherine says to no one in particular.

"She'll do it!" Annie claps and points her finger squarely at Catherine.

"I will not do it!"

"You'll be perfect!"

"There are prizes," chimes soldier #2.

"I don't want prizes!"

"I'll do it." Owen steps forward.

You'll do it? Catherine thinks. *Is this your way of proving that you can out-domesticate your domestic-diva wife?*

"Owen's doing it!" Annie claps again, then steadies her phone for a video.

"Oh, fine, I'll do it." Catherine flanks her hands on her hips.

"COME ONE, COME ALL! WHO DARES TO TEST THEIR HANDS AND CHURN A BARREL OF BUTTER FOR THE VILLAGE?"

"I volunteer!" Leon places his hand over his heart, like churning butter is some sort of patriotic duty.

"You don't volunteer!" Lindy replies, but he's already stepped forward, already been anointed with a sash that both Owen and Catherine now tuck over their right shoulder as well, which reminds

Catherine of that scene in *Star Wars* when Han Solo and Chewy get anointed for their bravery at saving the universe. She's surprised at the memory: she hasn't seen *Star Wars* since she was a kid, when her dad sneaked her into the theater even though she was too young and her mother forbade it.

Catherine peers at Owen, then Leon, then two kids who are about eleven who've also joined in, their parents hooting and hollering, like this is actually a *real thing*. But then she thinks of Penelope and Mason and that maybe they'd find this a little bit hilarious, and also that they'd have a chance to see what their mom is good at, why she misses their games and their recitals and isn't home for bedtime nearly enough. So as each of the contestants stands behind an old wooden barrel, Catherine thinks, *I will win this for my children. I will win this because I can. I will win this because I sit atop the domestic-goddess world, and Target and HGTV and stupid Suzy Carpenter can bite me.*

"It's on." She nudges her chin upward, like Rocky Balboa.

"Bring it." Leon smiles but doesn't look nearly as intimidated as she'd like him to.

Owen tries to reply, but he's burping up what Catherine imagines is old beer from last night. Finally he whispers (mostly to Leon), "You have never met a more competitive woman than my wife in your life. Godspeed."

Catherine scowls at him, even if it's true. It *is* true. She won't apologize for that! She *shouldn't* have to apologize for that. Her competitive drive is what pays their mortgage. What sends their kids to private school. What allowed Owen to quit that job that made him so miserable. Catherine hates that she feels like she should apologize for wanting to be at the top of everything, the best at everything. Way back when, when she first rose through the ranks of other crafty bloggers, her newly hired publicist insisted she get media training. Her trainer always said, "Act like the CEO of your household, not an actual CEO. No one wants to be best friends with a CEO. No one wants to make pumpkin coffee cake with a CEO."

Soldier #1 hands her a wooden plunger, and Catherine realizes, *No one does want to be friends with a CEO.* It's not like she's gallivanting out for girls' nights—it's not like she's even invited out for girls' nights. She doesn't get e-mails from moms at school; she doesn't make chitchat in the office kitchen about last night's *Rock N Roll Dreammakers.*

The last time she had honest-to-God girlfriends was, well, here. Back then.

Catherine wipes the sweat off her forehead with the back of her hand and glances at her competition. She makes a slit-your-throat/die gesture toward Owen, which she knows he'll take lightly (he does the same to her over tennis, which they never play anymore, but he used to do it all the time). He smiles. She narrows her eyes. And then Soldier #1 is explaining how exactly to churn butter ("Plunge up and down and up and down"), and then Soldier #2 fires his rifle, and Annie jumps and screams when he does, mistaking it for an actual rifle, and leans on Colin, who rubs her shoulders until she's steady.

"You can do it!" Annie cheers, not to any of them in particular, because she could never take sides.

Catherine hasn't churned butter since . . . well . . . she did it once in the early days of the blog, when she was testing out a branding idea of "Homemade with Heart," and literally all her ingredients had to be homemade. Butter was tough, but she threw in the towel when she tried to tackle olive oil (and one particularly horrible stab at almond milk), and when she realized that very few potential readers had as much time on their hands as she did. Thus, fresh butter is not Catherine's forte.

She doesn't remember it being this exhausting, though. Up and down and up and down and up and down. She's frantically pulsing her plunger, the wooden barrel rattling around, the four other barrels rattling around her. After five minutes, her biceps start to flame out. After ten, her triceps are shaking.

She inhales, trying to catch her breath, the plunger slowing to a pathetically unthreatening pace. Beside her, Owen is looking slightly gray, like a dead fish, with alarming streaks of sweat cascading down his cheeks and neck. But he's still keeping a somewhat steady pace, those spinning classes paying off. Beside him, Leon is looking like he could do this all day. He senses Catherine's gaze, so glances over and winks. Again.

He actually winks at her again!

Well, this is all Catherine needs. She forgets her flimsy biceps and her wimpy triceps and plunges, plunges, plunges—all the while resolving to make more time for the gym—but when is she supposed to find time for the gym? She sometimes locks her office door and does those twenty-minute videos that come with stretchy bands, but always figures that twenty minutes really doesn't do anything, so why bother in the first place? *She should have bothered in the first place!*

Her arms are numb but still moving when the cramp kicks in on her right side. She is wincing, half-doubled over, her once immaculately crisp button-down now drenched in perspiration, when Leon raises his arms above his head, triumphantly announcing, "I have butter! I HAVE BUTTER!"

The crowd that has gathered in a horseshoe around them starts hooting and hollering, like this is actually exciting. Like they literally didn't just stand here for half an hour watching them *churn butter.*

Soldier #1 marches over to confirm that Leon does, in fact, "have butter," and when he does, he bows in front of him (more *Star Wars*) and bestows Leon with fifty tickets to the prize booth, which he notes is five tents down.

"Goddamn it," Catherine mutters, tossing her plunger to the bricks, then massaging her abs like she used to in high school PE after being forced to run a mile.

"That was a bad call," Owen says, looking more gray than ever. "Definitely should *not* have done that."

"Maybe *I* should get invited to *Good Morning America*!" Leon crows, winking again at Catherine.

"Just because you can make butter does *not* mean you're capable of much else!" Catherine says.

"Uh, who wants to hit the prize booth?" Leon turns toward Lindy, who claps her hands together in mock euphoria and mouths, "Yippee!" but trails him down the walk anyway.

"Who *is* that guy?" Catherine says to no one in particular.

"Well, that was exciting!" Annie exclaims. "I posted it to Facebook. I'll tag you."

"I wouldn't call it exciting," Catherine says.

"Oh, it was, though! It was."

Catherine sighs. It was just some dumb contest, and it's not like she's some dog who needs to piss on her figurative territory. *Maybe just a little piss.* A little pee would have been nice. Why did it matter if Leon bested her? It's not like some butter-churning event at her old stomping grounds defined who she'd become or somehow invalidated her.

Annie hands her the Wawa coffee she's been holding. Catherine sips it, but it's gone cold. She spits it back out, then tosses it a little too brusquely into the trash. Just a split second before she notices the recycling bin sitting beside it.

HELP PENN GO GREEN!

She once built an entire house made of biodegradable elements for *InStyle*. She also shot a PSA on how to make coffee without paper filters, and another on how to create a home composting bin on your windowsill for city dwellers. It's not like she doesn't know about environmentally friendly causes.

And yet she pretends she didn't notice the sign and strides onward.

"Cathy!" Owen's pallor has returned, and his shirt clings to him now, the armpits damp, two concentric circles sagging beneath them. He scrambles to catch up to her. "Recycling!"

"It's not the end of the world." She turns around to see him fishing her cup from the garbage.

What is he trying to prove?

He holds it aloft, triumphant.

"That wasn't so hard," he says, dropping it into the proper bin.

Catherine thinks of a lot of ways to respond: *Should I give you a medal? What are you, my errand boy?*

Or, the most honest: *I'm still really pissed off at you from last night!*

She puts on that fake smile that he hates and says, "Thanks. It's not often you clean up my mess."

She doesn't mean it the way it comes out—meanly, cruelly—like a wife who finds her husband subservient. She regrets it immediately—how brittle she sounds, how unkindly she's behaving. But she's angry and tired and completely off-kilter here, with visions of her old dependent, sweeter self colliding with her new autonomous but not particularly gracious self, and no idea what to do with either of them. Besides, once it's been said, she can't unsay it. And the subtext is there anyway, all circling back to his assurances of stepped-up domesticity, of their agreement when he left his job, and all the ways he's let her down since. It's the same fight they always have now, just with different words and out in public rather than in their insulated suburban bedroom.

Owen's lips curl into a corkscrew. "I don't often 'clean up your mess'? All I do at home is clean up your mess. And Penelope's. And Mason's!"

Catherine is surprised that he challenges her, and this lights her short fuse. "We have a housekeeper! How much mess can there possibly be? Surely you do *not* spend your days cleaning up *our* mess!" She uses air quotes for "our."

"True," he says, his puffy eyes narrowing to slits. "Not 'ours,' because you're never home."

"I'm never home because I'm working!" Catherine cannot believe he's bringing this up again, like they haven't discussed this to death, like he hasn't gotten the same answer he's always going to get. She works; she's the breadwinner; what else does he expect?

"Well, then, that's why I'm at home always cleaning up the mess!"

"But you're *not* cleaning up the mess! You're not!" Catherine wants to calm herself, she does. She despises losing her cool, her grip, her stoic sense of order. But even as she tells herself to stop, to bite her tongue, she also feels her anger roiling through her, like a tsunami cresting from the deepest pit of the ocean, and once it's begun, there's no way to clamp it down. They've been building to this for months, maybe even a year. And now here, surely haunted by their fractured happiness, they can no longer simply contain things. "Last week, every single night, the dishes were disgusting in the sink. What? Do you think that they'll magically move themselves to the dishwasher? Or do you think that *I'll* just do it when I get home? Because of course that's what you think!"

"I don't think anything," he says. "I think that's what the house-keeper is there for! Who gives a shit if they get moved in at night or she does it in the morning?"

"I give a shit!"

"Then you should be around to do it!"

"Well, that would be absolutely miraculous! If, you know, someone invented a machine in which human beings could be in two places at once, and thus, I could be all things to all people, including your personal maid service, even though I have plenty of other crap on my plate, and I'm pretty sure you *agreed* to handle said household crap five years ago!" Catherine is sweating down both the front and back of her shirt now; her eyebrows are darting, her cheeks are spasming into likely all sorts of unflattering angles.

"A time-space machine, perfect! I'm surprised you haven't invented it yourself! Put it out in six different pastel hues with a yellow bow on top! The only question is: where else would you be . . . because it wouldn't be at home!"

"Well . . . my *God!*" Catherine shouts, unable to properly compose the retort she wants to articulate. "Let's take out an award, a plaque for the world's biggest martyr! Screw you, Owen."

Owen shoves his hands into the enormous pockets on his cargo shorts and marches ahead, baseball cap lowered, but head held high, like nothing could have delighted him more than airing this awful, intimate laundry out in the open.

Annie stares at the crimson bricks of the walk, then fiddles with her phone, then suggests, "Maybe we should skip the Quad for now?"

And Colin answers, "I really have to pee anyway."

So Catherine just strides forward, far enough behind her husband so he can't mistake her as trying to catch up.

There's a box waiting on the front stoop of Bruiser when they wind their way down the narrow street to the door. They hunch over it in a huddle—Catherine on the periphery so she doesn't have to engage (or seemingly share air) with Owen. The return label reads: DAVID MONROE, ESQ. But it's a holiday, so it must have come via special delivery.

"What the hell?" Lindy says.

"Very weird," Colin mutters.

"A Pandora's box," Leon exclaims. "Supercool."

"There is nothing cool about a Pandora's box," Catherine chides. "Who would want a Pandora's box? All they bring are problems." *Why are you here?* is what she really wants to add. But she has enough issues right now; this guy can't be one of them.

"Jesus," Lindy groans.

"What?" Catherine snips.

"You are *seriously* in a terrible mood," Lindy replies.

"Takes one to know one," Catherine says, though it's not quite on the nose, so Lindy and the rest of them look puzzled until they realize Catherine is actually calling Lindy a bitch.

"Oof, I'm not crazy about surprises," Annie says. "Well, I did once throw Baxter a surprise birthday party for his thirty-sixth, so maybe I am! I don't know." She chews on a cuticle, worry spreading across her face, which she attempts to disguise with an off-kilter smile.

Colin hoists it inside while Leon, carrying in a four-foot-tall foam Liberty Bell from the prize booth, gropes beneath the mat with his free hand for the key and clicks the lock open.

Catherine waits for someone to stop him, to say, "Hey! Who gave you all-access?" but no one does, and it occurs to her that maybe they're so used to a six-some, they'll accept anyone who comes along now. She thinks of Bea, closes her eyes for a fraction of a moment, really thinks of her, and tells Bea, if she's watching, that she's irreplaceable.

Before anyone can pull back the tape that seals the box closed, Catherine's phone begins to bleat, and she punches it on before it can ring a second time.

She's silent as she listens to the voice on the other end, her forehead wrinkling, then wrinkling deeper, while Owen breaks their standoff, frantically whispering, "Mason? Penelope? The kids? What is it?!"

Catherine raises her pointer finger toward him, then turns to ignore him.

"Well, crap," she says five times, then four times more once she's hung up.

"Is it the kids? Is everything OK?"

"It was Sasha." She won't meet his eyes, barely even turns back to acknowledge him.

"Sasha?" Annie asks.

"Her assistant," Owen replies, because Catherine is typing into her phone.

She finds what she's looking for, her free hand floating to her mouth.

"Well, crap," she says again.

They hear it before they see it, an echo of what they were all witness to thirty minutes prior.

"Cathy! Recycling."

They gather around her phone at that.

There's video. Some stupid undergrad recognized Catherine from The Crafty Lady and thought it would be so totally awesome to film her! In the background she says to a friend, "Should we go get her autograph?"

"Thanks. It's not often you clean up my mess."

The friend says, "Oh my God, what a bitch!"

"We have a housekeeper. How much mess can there possibly be?"

And then they've spliced it with that goddamn dumb I'm-gonna-slit-your-throat gesture. Which was a joke! Obviously! Then, a freeze frame of her in perhaps the worst snippet of a frame she has ever viewed: her blazing, moist cheeks, swollen like a chipmunk's, her eyes bulging like a zombie, her hair smattered against her neck, sweaty and oily and frankly, all-around horrifying.

She was just kidding! It was stupid butter churning! Why doesn't anyone on the Internet have a sense of humor anymore?

It's on YouTube, already picked up by *TMZ*, and God knows who else. Someone has sent one version to Momma's Gonna Knock You Out, and put that throat-slit motion on a loop. She almost looks like she's break-dancing.

Catherine takes the stairs two by two, rushing away from the rest of them without glancing back, without seeking comfort in the way that maybe her old friends—or husband—could have provided. Her brain is full of static, like a television that's lost its signal. She slams her door and collapses into the corner of the closet, then reaches up and slams that door too. Her head drops beneath her knees and her hands cover her ears, as if this can block it all out.

Jesus.

The humiliation of looking like a fool is bad enough.

Then she remembers Target and HGTV and realizes that the disclosure that the domestic goddess of the blogging world isn't even a domestic goddess in her own house might actually be the thing that ruins her.

She'd known this secret—the rationale behind her notebook, the reason she worked twice as hard as anyone else—all along, her whole career, even when she toiled for the perfect French toast, even when Bea assured her otherwise.

She'd known all along she might be a fraud.

15

LINDY

Lindy didn't consciously realize that at some point on their stroll up Locust Walk, Leon had slung his arm around her, that her hand had slipped into his back pocket. How did that happen? That casual intimacy? Was she too busy lugging the embarrassingly huge Liberty Bell he'd won for her?

Lindy did casual. She did not do intimacy. If anything, Lindy did liberty.

She wouldn't have noticed or given it a second thought if she hadn't seen it on the video from Catherine's phone: how they're walking as if they're a *couple*, as if they belong to each other. And after she retreats to her old room—with Leon racing up the stairs behind her—and slams her old door, she can't decide which concerns her more: that she didn't detect this wily, stealthy romance, or that someone watching YouTube or *TMZ* or God knows what else, is going to recognize her (and it) too.

Lesbian Lindy No Longer!

Lindy texts her publicist, who is at P. Diddy's White Party in the Hamptons and isn't going to be happy to hear from her today, at least not to hear the news that she's still in Philly and not on the first flight back to LA—as Lindy may or may not have texted last night that she would be. (She considered it last night, she really did, but then Leon was there, at her doorstep, and she told herself she couldn't leave *just then*, and there were always flights to catch tomorrow.) And now, because she is not a woman of her word, she will certainly not be making the *Rock N Roll Dreammakers* appearance at the Fourth of July fireworks off the Santa Monica pier (hosted by Ryan Seacrest).

Leon bounces on her old bed a few times, its springs squeaking. He reaches for her belt loops to pull her closer, to try to ease her on top of him.

More intimacy! She bats his hand away.

"I knew you shouldn't have come here. I texted you five thousand times and said not to come here!"

"What?"

Lindy thinks of that Klonopin again and so very much wishes she weren't knocked up and/or that she were the type of person she thought she was: namely, a type of person who was knocked up but took Klonopin anyway.

She is depressed to realize she is not.

Which is why she needs the Klonopin so badly.

She is *not* the fuck-all rock 'n' roll badass she has morphed herself into being. A fuck-all rock 'n' roll badass would shoot a gulp of whiskey or pop a wee touch of Xanax because this shit is about to hit the fan, and fuck-all rock 'n' roll badasses think only of themselves when shit is about to hit the fan. Not of some teeny-tiny pea seed of an embryo who doesn't even have fingers yet or maybe has webbed fingers, but certainly does not have toes; but Lindy can't bring herself to Google it, not until she makes a decision about her intentions, so how is she expected to know? Maybe that stupid magazine—*Pregnancy and You!*—she'd bought at the airport could tell her, but she can't exactly go and reference it at the moment, now can she?

She did call for the appointment next week, to terminate, she reminds herself. She gave herself that out, the exit door, if she opts for it. She was sure she wanted to opt for it. Why is she even doubting this?

Leon groans, stands, and kisses her forehead.

"I'll go. I was just trying to have some fun."

It's because of him that she has this doubt, she realizes, her chest tightening like she might blow an artery. *He* is here, and now nothing is as easy as she expected it to be.

"Fine, go." She flings open her door but stares at her boots. Her palms feel clammy, her underarms sticky. This really might be the onset of a heart attack.

"No sweat. I get it. Bad idea. If I leave now, I can still hit a Fourth party in Tribeca."

Lindy stomps her right foot, then huffs and swings the door closed before he can leave. His nonchalance bothers her, pricks her like a mosquito. No one is nonchalant about Lindy Armstrong. He plops back onto the bed and tosses his hands up while she scowls and chalks her bruised ego up to the pregnancy hormones. After all, he's the father of her pea seed. Evolution must prove that she can't entirely spurn the father of her pea seed.

"I'm sorry," she mutters. "You can stay."

"I can stay? Because you texted me five thousand times telling me not to come in the first place." He rests his high-tops on the floor by the bed, his hands against his knees now, casual but ready to rise, to leave, at any moment.

"You *should* stay," she acquiesces.

She drags the toe of her boot along a crack in the floor near the window ledge. The fissure was there back then too. She'd discovered it in the early dawn hours when she couldn't sleep, so instead she'd pluck her guitar strings, sitting cross-legged underneath the window as the morning light slowly warmed the campus. After a while it became the only spot where she could really write. Something about the weathered, imperfect wood and the promise of a new day.

She laughs to herself now at the cliché.

"Something funny?"

"Do you ever think about who you were at twenty? Christ, we weren't even legal." Lindy eases onto the unmade bed, back against the headboard, wrapping her limbs into a knot, her dirty boots atop the duvet. Not too close to him, but not so far either.

"Honestly? Not really." He leans back on his elbows.

"Me either. I used to. I think I used to write about it a lot," she clarifies.

"What do you write about now?"

She shrugs like it's not important. "The label doesn't use my songs anyway; no one's interested."

"I am."

Her eyes find the ceiling, consciously avoiding his gaze. "I guess I outgrew all that stuff."

"What stuff?"

"Thinking about all the ways things could have been different. At twenty, didn't it seem like life could go anywhere?"

"Twenty was not my shining moment. I barely made it through USF alive."

"You're from San Francisco?"

Leon nods.

"I didn't know that about you," Lindy says. Though they only recently started screwing, they'd worked together at least a dozen times. "I'm from Berkeley."

"Never came up, I guess," Leon answers, kind enough not to point out that she'd actually never asked. "Anyway. It seems like life came out exactly how you wanted it. Lindy fucking Armstrong, man."

She rolls her neck across her shoulders, considering this for longer than she thought she would, how it penetrates. How really, it should be true.

"My dead friend. Bea. She would have been forty today."

"Born on the Fourth of July," Leon says. He reaches across the bed to cup her chin in his hand. Lindy feels the burn behind her eyes, then the dampness on her cheeks.

"Hey, now," Leon says, which snaps Lindy to.

She hides her face in her palms, wiping away the tears, wiping away her weakness.

"Forget it," she says, already standing, already pulling her phone from her pocket, seeking protection behind its glow. Tatiana has texted her three times.

Shit.

"Ignore me. I'm acting like a fucking baby."

She hates that she used that word, hopes she didn't flinch when she said it.

Baby.

Leon shrugs like he doesn't mind. Doesn't mind taking care of her one bit.

There's a crash downstairs, and then a high-pitched squeal from Annie.

"We should get out of here. This is ridiculous: it's a goddamn circus here. How did I ever live here? These people are animals."

"We're not getting out of here," Leon says. "It's Bea's birthday."

Lindy chews the bottom corner of her lip.

She says, "Why is it that we casually had sex and now you're my spiritual guidepost?"

He looks at her plainly, like how should he know? So he offers: "I smoke a lot of weed?"

Lindy stares at that crack in the floorboard and wishes she could seal it up. Call a carpenter who would plug it and secure it together until every last ounce of the vulnerability that she left here, that she wept here, that she exposed on this floor, in this room, in this place, could be cordoned off and forgotten. She knows this isn't possible. She knows that she should lean in, not away, from this spot on the floor, which maybe helped shape her into the artist she was once (but isn't now).

But Lindy has never been one to listen to everything she knows. So she kisses Leon perfunctorily and pulls away when his hands reach for more.

16

ANNIE

Annie, Colin, and Owen hover over the box, peering at it. The banister rattles, and then Lindy is there too. Then Leon.

"This is it," Colin says. "This is what she had for us."

No one moves; no one is particularly inclined to delve into the unknown, a time capsule that's akin to a time bomb, really.

"Let's wait for Catherine," Annie suggests, her pulse racing. *Let's just wait forever.*

"No, she might be a while." Owen looks like he's used to waiting for Catherine, looks like he's not particularly interested in waiting another second for her.

Colin spears a knife from the kitchen into the packing tape and peels back the wrapping, gently opening the flaps of the box, making Annie wonder what he must look like in surgery. He plunges his surgical hands inside, beneath the packing peanuts, and pulls out his first, then Lindy's. Their letters to their younger selves. Framed, preserved forever.

"Oh my God!" he says. "I'd forgotten!" He looks closer. "They're all here. Wow."

Annie had forgotten too, and now her stomach plunges, like an elevator dropping from a penthouse, straight into her guts.

"But it hasn't been twenty years," Annie protests. "She said twenty."

"Close enough," Lindy scoffs. "Don't be such a stickler."

Annie barely hears her. Instead, her guts rumble, and she swallows hard and excuses herself to go to the second-floor bathroom.

Her hands are clammy, her breathing too fast. She lowers the cover on the toilet, then sits and drops her head between her knees.

She's certain that she threw hers out. She has no idea how Bea got ahold of her copy, and why she encased it behind glass and sterling silver. And further, why Bea now (or then) packaged it into this messengered box and delivered it smack in the middle of the afternoon of what would have been her fortieth birthday.

Bea had made them do it. The last night of senior year before they all journeyed to different corners of the country (though Lindy and Annie pushed off to the same tiny corner apartment in New York City), the last night before they would have to juggle schedules and new friends and random lovers and career commitments and, well, *more important* priorities. The last night they'd all slept under the same roof.

Write down what you hope for your life in twenty years.

Colin laughed like this was the most ridiculous thing, and he was also probably already drunk in preparation for the evening's pregraduation revelry. But Bea shot him a look that said, *This matters,* and he abruptly stopped laughing and picked up one of the pens she'd set out on the table. Annie still remembers this obedience, this understood language between the two of them. Annie also still remembers how much that moment gutted her. How Bea had something she wanted—*his dutiful attention*—and for a moment, it felt like she had *everything* Annie wanted. Colin. A trust fund. An adventurous spirit. A full heart. Lots of things, really.

Annie didn't covet much, wasn't the envious type. She'd made do with not a whole heck of a lot back in Texas, and when you make do without a whole heck of a lot, you tend to be more grateful for the good fortune you stumble into. But still, though she'd never tell the others, sometimes Annie loathed Bea. Just for slivers of seconds. Just quickly enough that she wasn't even entirely aware of the odious seeds of hatred. Because Annie could never actually *hate* Bea! Bea, who was so good to her; Bea, who never treated her like she was any less than the rest of them. But sometimes Annie hated Bea just for homing in on the one thing Annie wanted to hide: who she really was.

Write down your hopes for the next twenty years. Where you think you'll be. Where you want to be.

"Go on, Annie. This isn't that hard!" Bea had urged her. "Think about what's next. And what's next after that."

"I can't do that." All Annie had really thought about was the day-to-day, getting through *this*, about who she could be *today*, and how far that was from the person she was yesterday.

Bea sighed. "You can do anything."

Annie's cheeks blazed, and she'd wished the whole stupid idea away.

The others scribbled easily, as if each of them already had the foresight to know exactly where they'd be, who they'd be, two decades from now. Annie clicked the top of her pen over and over and over again and wrote in fits and starts, snippets of generic dreams—*a handsome husband, a happy marriage*, fragments of nothing that would ever come true—*a life that makes a difference!* When she finished, while Bea collected the other papers, Annie balled hers up and stuck it at the bottom of the trash in the kitchen.

Bea must have seen this, and must have fished it out, smoothed over the wrinkles, and one day, when they had cast their wings out into the wicked postgraduation world, she must have had them all framed for posterity.

A crash echoes from the living room, and Annie rights her head from between her knees, finds stability in her feet, then unlocks the bathroom door and stumbles back downstairs. A clutter of glass and packing peanuts are littered across the floor.

"I was trying to move it off the table." Owen shrugs. "The box slipped." He grimaces like he's expecting to be chastised. He's on his knees, gingerly setting the broken frames back inside.

"It's all right," she says, hoping he can't detect her relief, that maybe she won't have to read this thing just yet.

Lindy is already poring over hers, of course. She is sprawled on the couch with Leon, and she is cackling—*cackling!*—at whatever wisdom her younger self left for her current self.

Typical, Annie thinks. How cavalier she is. How this old box of skeletons wouldn't rattle her one bit. Leon is nibbling on Lindy's neck while Lindy laughs and laughs, and Annie finally looks away—uncomfortable at their open affection. Baxter never does PDA. Sometimes he holds her hand when they're entering a cocktail party, or places his palm on the small of her back, and she never knows if his touch makes her more or less lonely: more because it doesn't quite feel natural anymore, less because he's doing it all the same. Usually she'll clutch his hand, their fingers intertwined so tightly that eventually he'll say, "Babe, let go, I have to go say hi to so-and-so." And Annie bats her eyelashes and kisses him on the cheek and says, "Of course," trailing him to so-and-so, tuning out of Baxter's conversation with so-and-so as soon as it begins. She never has much to contribute anyway.

She thinks of that stupid *xo* and realizes that maybe he's entirely comfortable with PDA with someone else.

Cici.

Bile rises in the back of Annie's throat.

She unlocks her phone and checks her texts. Nothing from Baxter. *Maybe he's working. Maybe he's out with Gus. Maybe he's sleeping on the hammock in the Hampton's rental or at the farm stand buying ears of corn for a barbecue.*

Or maybe he's fucking Cici-whoever-she-is.

Lindy starts reciting her letter aloud, reading with an overdramatic flair. Colin and Owen grin moronically at her theatrics. Then Lindy has a better idea. Set it to music! She sings her letter like this is some sort of hip open-mic night, but stops abruptly in the middle of a sentence about playing at the Grand Ole Opry when she spots Annie, arms crossed, lips askew, eyes narrow.

"What?"

"Nothing."

"What, Annie, *what?*"

"I just don't think that, you know, Bea would want you treating this like a joke."

Lindy laughs. "Bea would want me to treat it exactly how I wanted to treat it. Stop trying to make something out of nothing."

Annie thinks the problem might be that she *never* makes something out of anything. That this *Cici* and her *xo* are exactly the sort of nothing that maybe should be turned into *something.*

"I just think you're acting like a *jerk,*" Annie goes on. "I don't think you *not* acting like a huge *jerk* is too much to ask."

Lindy laughs, actually laughs at this. "Don't be so uptight. They're just words. No one said they had to be taken as holy."

A handsome husband. A happy marriage.

Annie didn't think *these* things were too much to ask. In the scheme of a life, those weren't big reaches, aim-for-the-stars requests. But maybe for her they were. Annie was never the type to ask for much, and this is exactly why. Her mom always used to say, when she would catch her daydreaming up at the expansive Texas sky, "Stop wishing on a star, silly girl. Dreams are nothing but make-believe."

Lindy starts up again with her stupid singing, flooding Annie's brain with white-hot anger. She stomps up the stairs to her room and flops on her old bed, never stopping to reciprocate Lindy's gaze, which, if Annie had, she might recognize as tender, as something someone might even call love.

17

OWEN

When Lindy is done with her performance art—which actually takes a while, because once Annie disappears upstairs, Lindy becomes particularly manic, and then that dude she's with starts beat-boxing, then videotaping so they can upload it to some site that Mason and Penelope probably use but that Owen has never heard of . . . but when all of this subsides, Owen rises wearily to his feet. He stays there for a few seconds, just standing, immobile, because he realizes he has nowhere to go.

"You OK, guy?" Leon says.

"I should go check on Catherine." He doesn't move.

"Maybe Catherine should come check on *you*," Lindy says.

"Stop stirring the pot, Lindy." Leon elbows her and checks the upload on his phone.

"Yeah," Owen says. "Yeah, maybe she should come check on *me*. For all she knows, I hurt myself down here." Lindy cocks her head. "From the broken glass. It's not like she didn't hear that."

"I meant for how she treated you on the walk. With that emasculating bullshit," Lindy says.

Owen considers this. It was pretty emasculating bullshit.

"I just thought it would be fun! The butter churning. Jesus, who is she to treat it like the goddamn Olympics?"

"She's Catherine," Lindy says. "Of course she treated it like the goddamn Olympics."

Owen digs into a jagged cuticle on his index finger.

"Linds," Leon says. "Stop."

"No, she's right, dude. You should see it in my house: I didn't unload the dishwasher, I didn't *load* the dishwasher, I order pizza too much, I—"

Lindy interrupts. "See? I'm not stirring the pot. The pot is already boiling." She shakes her head. "But you two, man. If you can't make it . . ."

Owen doesn't hear her. Instead, he only hears his rage filling him up to his ears. So what if he orders pizza three times a week? So what if he promised, like, homemade lasagna when they agreed he should stay at home. Homemade lasagna sounded thrilling, like a goddamn vacation, when he first resigned from the law office. But then there was the kids' homework and their schedules, and he's practically a goddamn taxi service now! Homemaking proved much less enchanting than he realized: monotonous, dull, lonely. There weren't a lot of stay-at-home dads, not a lot of opportunities to make friends. So he does what he wants now to make himself happy. Does Catherine ever stop to ask what it is that makes him happy?

He marches up the steps two by two, a little winded by the time he reaches the third floor, near the ladder to the trapdoor to the roof. He loiters outside their bedroom, and he can hear Catherine's voice—clipped, officious—through the door. He scales the ladder upward.

No, he thinks as he heaves the trapdoor open, his already sore shoulders shaking under the weight. *She never stops to ask me.*

She didn't used to be this way. She used to love the entirety of him. He used to love the entirety of her too. Now, if he's being honest, who knows? You wake up every day and you're still married, and so you assume that because you're both still there, that it's still love. Is it? Owen doesn't consider himself an expert.

The afternoon sun hammers down on the roof, and Owen adjusts his baseball cap lower to shield his eyes. He's hungover, man, *really* hungover, though he did his best acting job this afternoon because he didn't want to hear it from Catherine. So he pretended he was *just fine*, basically pretended he was astonished that they thought he was so completely obliterated last night that he wouldn't be *just fine* today. Pretended he wasn't a little concerned that he might literally die out there, churning butter. Owen wonders if there's anything sadder than keeling over dead in a mock–colonial times butter-churning contest.

Then he thinks of Bea and realizes, in fact, there is.

He eases his way onto a sun chair that abuts the roof wall.

Oh, he's feeling it. But he isn't going to give Catherine the pleasure of knowing.

The metal picture frame around his old letter is already hot to the touch, so he slides it under the shadow of the lounge chair. He closes his eyes, curious whether he can remember what he wrote, what he wished for himself, but that night was a blur. He's pretty sure he and Colin and a few buddies from Sigma Chi had started drinking at the bars downtown well before the sun started to dip below the horizon. He remembers being intent on making the evening "legendary"—he and Colin and the boys kept shouting, "Legendary!" and chest-bumping—which to him, back then, meant a shit ton of Amstel and . . . he remembers that they peeled their clothes off at about 3:00 a.m. and streaked Locust Walk. In hindsight, it wasn't as daring as it seemed: most of the campus had emptied by then—the freshmen back to their parents, the sophomores off to camp-counselor jobs, the juniors to New York City for some important internship they were sure would shape the rest of their lives.

A jaded security guard pulled up in a golf cart, shined a flashlight, and said, "All right, boys, it's not that I'm not impressed, but let's wrap it up now."

Legendary.

Like that was supposed to be the best night of their lives. Before everything changed.

That much was true, though. After college, everything did change, but it was supposed to—life got going after college! Owen knew that. Catherine knew it. In fact, they couldn't wait for it to change. To move in and play house together—real house, not this dormlike townhouse. To be grown up. To be *responsible*. To make trips to Ikea and stock up on pot holders and lamps and wineglasses for red wine and different wineglasses for white. Like they ever used wineglasses just for reds.

Well, now Catherine does. Now she has five different types of forks, and ten different types of wineglasses, and plates for this occasion and plates for that occasion.

Maybe Owen should have seen it coming, how much she'd grow up. It wasn't like back then she hadn't told him that she wanted to take over the domestic-goddess world. She had! He's not selfish enough to pretend that. Maybe he just wasn't smart enough to see how much being grown-ups would change them.

A million different kinds of plates, none of them paper—which is all he asks for every once in a while.

When was the last time Catherine asked him what he wanted? He doesn't know. When was the last time Catherine asked him for advice? He doesn't know that either. Who does she listen to now? Who does she trust when she can't trust herself?

Owen has no idea.

He tugs his baseball cap even lower and thinks he might like to go streaking later.

Though he can't, of course.

Because now he has to be *prudent*, now he has to be *mature*, now he's a husband and a father, and the owner of a Volvo SUV and a pretty decent-size mortgage.

Grown-ups don't do that sort of thing.

He tells himself this, but mostly, he hears Catherine's voice saying it.

Owen groans aloud. His head is pounding, his stomach churning from that earlier burrito and the leftover vestiges of alcohol from last night.

His tongue is sandy, sticky against the roof of his mouth, and his eyes droop with heavy hangover fatigue.

He'll read the letter later. It can't tell him anything he doesn't already know.

18

CATHERINE

The house is quiet by the time Catherine wraps up with her publicity and marketing teams. No one was happy to teleconference in on the Fourth, but tough toodles, Catherine told them. She apologized immediately afterward, then hated that she felt compelled to apologize.

Male CEOs don't apologize when they call their staff with a crisis!

But it was indeed her fault, and her fault alone that their long weekend was now not their own, so whether or not Rupert Murdoch would apologize, Catherine felt compelled to do so.

She apologized four more times over the hour in which they drafted a statement for the press. Odette, her publicist, said that most of the online chatter is laser focused on the tiny detail that the queen of domesticity is not, in fact, all that domestic in her own home. She texted Catherine during the call to confidentially say, because she didn't want to declare this in front of the team, that this could torpedo Target, not to mention HGTV.

"So what we need to do," her publicist suggested to the team, half of whom were only vaguely listening because they were probably savoring grilled hot dogs or watching their toddlers splash in the kiddie pool, "is deflect."

"Deflect?" Catherine asked. "To what?"

"To you and Owen."

"To me and Owen?"

"Yes. We need to make this about you and Owen, not about your skills, or lack thereof, at home."

In the silence that followed, Catherine was pretty sure she could hear one of her employees trying to inconspicuously crunch on corn on the cob, or maybe that salted-caramel popcorn recipe her new test chef concocted in April.

Finally, she said, "So what you mean is, I have to choose—Owen or me."

"I wouldn't say it like that," Odette tutted. "I would say that relationship problems make you relatable. You were having a bad day. You took it out on your husband. Your audience understands that; your audience *wants* that."

"And the other option?" Catherine's voice echoed in the emptiness of the closet.

"The other option makes you look like a fraud. Which, frankly, is the only thing your audience won't tolerate."

Catherine hoped her team didn't hear her inhale, didn't hear her voice quavering. Her hands shook as she gave the OK, and she literally tucked them underneath her to control the trembling. She hadn't crossed this line yet, at least not publicly, but what choice did she have? It was Owen or her.

I'm deeply embarrassed that my foul mood was caught on tape. We are mourning the loss of a friend (which is why we are regretfully not with our children on this wonderful day in celebration of our nation's birthday), and after a heated (and fun!) butter-churning contest which reminded me of how grateful I am for the dairy section at Target, my emotions got the better of me. I took out these emotions on my husband, Owen, who has been nothing but a bedrock of support for me at The Crafty Lady. So much so that he is considering joining our in-house legal team. He has accepted my apology, and I hope that you can too.

"And this will stop the message boards? The things they're posting?" Catherine asked.

"They'll feel like they heard this from a friend. They'll want you to be humble, then they'll want to support you."

Rupert Murdoch never worried about being humble.

Rupert Murdoch never cared about making friends, Catherine thought while her publicist rattled on. Though she could use a few friends, actually. Not just her agent. Not just her assistant.

"OK, send it out," Catherine said finally. "Let's put this behind us," she added, already wondering what Owen would think, which is more consideration than she's given his opinion in a long time.

She flips on the closet light and stares up at the ceiling, the etching no more visible now than it was last night. Twenty years ago she'd never have imagined she'd sacrifice her relationship for her career. Twenty years ago, her relationship was what everyone envied about her. Twenty years ago, it was what she envied about herself. And yet, here, now, she just served her marriage up for public sacrifice, or at least public scrutiny, which is just about the same thing these days.

She sighs and drops her head into her hands, squeezing her temples like this will help assuage her guilt.

She owes him an apology for her behavior today. And now for so much more, though she's not ready to acknowledge that yet. Maybe he won't even hear about it, maybe it won't filter down to his little corner of the Internet, which is filled with . . . she doesn't know, ESPN and Barstool and Politico?

She should apologize. She should get up right now and go downstairs and find him and kiss him and say, *I'm sorry. Sometimes I'm a bitch and I don't mean to be. And sometimes you're a jerk, and I use that against you for longer than is fair. I shouldn't. I shouldn't have. I'm sorry.*

She tells herself three times to do this. It shouldn't be so hard. It really *isn't* that hard. No one ever regrets apologizing to their spouse, do they? Catherine remembers their last fight from a few months ago, well, their last spoken fight. It feels like they're fighting all the time now, just not out loud.

Catherine was sitting on the island in their kitchen, eating peanut butter ice cream out of the carton as a makeshift late-night dinner after an epic board meeting when he startled her; she'd thought he was asleep. He was wearing his boxers and an undershirt, and she knew immediately that he wanted something. He never roused himself anymore when she tiptoed in so late. She thought maybe he wanted sex, and she cringed a little because she was so bone-weary, but she vowed to smile and sound enthusiastic at the notion.

But then he scratched the back of his head and said, "Maybe I could come aboard the company as counsel."

(So it wasn't totally made up: the mention of possible employment in her statement to the press. Though it wasn't totally honest either.)

"Come aboard my company?" Her spoon lingered over the ice cream pint. She genuinely wasn't sure what he meant.

"Well, yeah. Why not?"

She dropped the spoon into the container.

"Because, well . . . why would you?"

"I'm restless here. I want to do something."

"You are doing something. You're taking care of the kids."

He shrugged like this wasn't enough.

Owen said he was bored at home. (But evidently not bored enough to make the interview rounds, tap-dance for kids who were younger but now more senior than he was.) He'd been unemployed for five years; he couldn't expect to just coast back into the corporate world, he said. Also, he admitted, he didn't exactly *want* to dive back into the corporate world. He wanted, he said, to juggle both: a few days at the office, a few with the kids, some time to maybe train for a half marathon or take more spinning classes. (Catherine had no idea that he'd even taken one spinning class, and he said, "Yes, all of the other parents go to SoulCycle, so I go to SoulCycle too now!")

Catherine said, "Well, who wouldn't want to work a few days and then have a few days off with the kids and then a few days more to go to SoulCycle?"

And Owen looked at her like his suggestion wasn't ludicrous. So he said, "I don't know?"

And she replied, "Everyone would like that, O!"

"Jeez, it was just an idea," he said. "You have all these lawyers working for you. I thought I could help."

Exasperated, she explained to him, "This is not a side project where you get to come in for a day when you don't have lacrosse pickup!"

Owen, more exasperated, said, "Jesus Christ! I never said it was!"

Cutting him off, she yelled, "It seems to me that's what you're saying!"

And he shouted back, "If you listened to me, you'd know that's not what I'm saying at all!"

Then they each swapped a bunch of words that Catherine really can't remember now but knows weren't particularly nice. Owen eventually retreated to the den and blared the television, watching who-knows-what, and she retreated to her laptop and work e-mails and the rest of the peanut butter ice cream, followed by a nearly full glass of Scotch.

Eventually, she heard the den door open and felt his presence standing there, in the kitchen archway, watching her, wondering who was going to forge a truce first. When she refused to make eye contact, she heard him exhale. Long and slow and frustrated.

"Look, I'm sorry, OK? It was a stupid idea."

"Fine. Let's move on." And she sipped deeply.

She didn't apologize then either.

She tilts her head back against the closet door and sighs again. It wasn't that ludicrous a request—that he wanted a life outside of their home. It's not like she doesn't think he's smart, doesn't know he's competent. She used to ask his advice all the time, look forward to hearing his insights, was open to his ideas and counsel. So maybe it was the casualness of his assumption that lit her fuse: that she'd built the empire and he could now ride her coattails. But that wasn't fair either. Owen had done plenty at home, at least for a while when he first left his job, to keep their family sane. Maybe it was that she needed him to have his own purpose outside of hers. They'd always been one entity, all the way back to freshman year, and while she had the opportunity to break out of their oneness at work, Owen hadn't. She'd been the one—and she knows this—who started seeking independence, relying on her own staff rather than him, relying ultimately on her own gut (and occasionally that shameful notebook of other people's ideas) rather than anyone else's. And now The Crafty Lady was *hers*. Just hers. She didn't know how to share it anymore. Maybe she didn't *want* to share it either. Independence, she's discovered, feels just as good as codependence once did. She's as surprised as anyone to realize this.

Also, there's that small voice that murmurs to her these days, about how much Owen has disappointed her by failing to live up to his domestic promises. How much would she disappoint him if he unearthed her own messes, her own fraudulent shortcomings?

Still, though. That doesn't forgive her behavior today. Her own childish behavior at the butter churning. The unkindness of her words afterward. The rest of it—the stuff with her publicist—well, that's self-preservation, a necessary evil to save the Target partnership. She'll tell him this eventually, and surely he'll understand.

Get up. Go find him. Meet his eyes and make amends. It's not too late to do that.

She knows the Catherine from college would be ashamed of her immobility. The Catherine who shared this room with the then-love-of-her-life;

who brought him Corn Nuts for all-nighters; who planned her senior-year schedule around his senior-year schedule; who would iron his shirts (not that he cared, but it was sweet all the same); who sewed him cute little parakeet boxers; who once dressed as Daisy Duke for Halloween because Daisy was Owen's childhood crush. Then she thinks of Bea and how she'd be ashamed too.

She plants her palms on the floor and pushes herself up.

Enough. It's Owen, for God sake! Go fix it.

∾

Annie is the only one downstairs, which already deflates Catherine's determination. She dawdles against the railing, spying the open box from their front stoop on the dining table, and Annie sitting next to it, her knees curled up to her chest, scrolling through her phone.

"Where is everyone?"

"Oh!" Annie starts, her eyes round as orbs. "Sorry, sorry. I forgot I wasn't here alone. They went to Smoke's for Fourth of July happy hour."

It's not even four o'clock, and after last night, Owen is already back at it.

The rest of Catherine's apology deflates out of her entirely.

"What's that?" She points to the box.

"A box of horrors."

"What?"

"No," Annie laughs. "Just kidding." Catherine doesn't think that Annie looks like she's kidding. "No, it's that time capsule Bea made for us, remember? With our letters? I guess that's what she wanted us here for, together, I mean. What she wanted to give us."

"Huh." Catherine pads down the steps and cranes her neck over the top of the box. "Weird. What does yours say?"

"Oh." More nervous giggling. "I haven't read mine yet. I just . . ." Annie runs out of words. She sets her phone on the table, screen down.

"I hear you—why get stuck in the past?"

"Yes, something like that," Annie agrees.

"Looking back can be complicated."

"I just prefer to look forward," Annie chirps. "Isn't that something you'd say on your site? Be present. Enjoy the sunrise!"

"That does sound like something I'd say on my site."

Annie's phone buzzes, and she flips it upward, glances at it quickly, then flips it back.

"Just waiting to hear from Baxter," she says. "I've been trying to reach him all day."

"Everything OK?"

Annie waves a hand. "Oh, I'm sure. Just . . . you know. Well, I don't go away very often. I mean . . . pretty much . . . practically never."

"You think he may have burned down the house accidentally?"

"Oh, Baxter? Never!"

Catherine wonders what that would be like, the total assuredness that comes from having a reliable partner. Not that Owen would burn down the house. But following through with his promises, keeping up his end of the bargain . . . ? They used to have this, of course. But once it fades, it feels like it was never there to begin with, like rain through your fingers, a mirage you wonder if you didn't imagine completely. She fiddles with her gold wedding band.

"Do you know that I made out with Jason Cohen two nights before Owen and I hooked up?" Catherine narrows her eyes, re-creating the memory. "Do you remember him? Jason Cohen? He lived on the floor below us. Played acoustic guitar. That's what did it for me."

Annie's pale skin reddens, camouflaging her freckles, and Catherine can see she's surprised at the admission. But Catherine doesn't have many girlfriends. Who else is she supposed to share this with?

"I remember him, sure." She nods. "But he wasn't nearly as cute as Owen!"

Catherine frowns, reconciling her memory with Annie's declaration. Maybe he wasn't as cute as Owen. Maybe the years have distorted things, turned everything upside down.

"Anyway," Catherine continues, "I was a little bit obsessed with Jason Cohen those first few days of school. I think these days, I'd affectionately refer to it as *stalking*."

Annie knows from affectionate stalking (Google: Colin Radcliffe).

"So we made out and stayed up all night while he played, like, Cat Stevens for me, and I was convinced that he was the guy. You know, *the guy*. Why was I so hung up on finding *the guy* so quickly?"

Annie drums the table with her fingers. "Your guy *did* make you happy."

"Yeah." Catherine considers this for a moment. "But would you tell your daughter to be in such a rush to find *the guy*?"

"I don't have a daughter."

Catherine flops on a dining-room chair. "Well, anyway, the next night I knocked on his door, but his roommate told me he was having a jam session in some other guy's room I didn't know, and I was too embarrassed to go find him. I mean, it was the first week of school! I didn't want to seem desperate."

"I can't imagine you ever being desperate."

"When I saw him for breakfast at the dining hall, he said, 'What's up,' and told me I should drop by some off-campus party that night. And I was like . . . Annie, you don't even know. I was like: 'Oh. My. God!'"

They laugh then because they might be almost forty, but it's not hard to remember the giddy pit in your stomach, the accelerated heartbeat, the stammering for words, the sheer joy that accompanied youthful infatuation.

"Seriously, I died. I ran back to my room and picked out a bunch of different outfits and went over all of these things that I was going to say to him, cool music references, concerts I'd say I'd been to . . ." She shakes her head. "I was like, *insane*, Annie. *Insane* for Jason Cohen." Catherine's heart quickens from a rush of adrenaline of the memory, at the chance to revisit what was lost. "Anyway, I got food poisoning. From that stupid dining hall. From the eggs or the bacon or whatever I ate that morning. I was barfing into a trash can on the side of the bed all afternoon, and Owen heard me whimpering in my room and came in and checked on me. Eventually I stopped puking, and I guess he found something alluring in my greenish-hued face, but after we binged on crackers and ginger ale, he kissed me."

She pauses, biting her lower lip.

Her shoulders rise and fall.

"I guess I've been thinking about that recently: if I hadn't eaten those eggs, if I hadn't gotten sick, if I'd gone to the party, Owen wouldn't have kissed me that night."

"It can't be healthy to think about what-ifs." Annie frowns.

"You don't have to," Catherine says. "You had a chance to figure yourself out before you found Baxter." She hesitates. "That came out wrong. I guess . . . well, we were very young, that's all. People change."

"Oh, people don't change *that* much."

"I don't know." Catherine looks unconvinced. "Sometimes I think people change to the point where you barely recognize them." She spins her wedding band like a top on the hard wood surface of the kitchen table. "And sometimes I wonder which is better: who they were when you met them or who they're set to become now."

19

LINDY

Lindy is starving, but the sight of the congealing hot wings at Smoke's is turning her stomach. Or maybe it's the baby doing somersaults. She envisions a tiny peanut spinning over and over on itself, fists flying, face contorted with glee. Then she tries not to envision it. *So why is it so crystal clear?* Still, though, she's ravenous, and when some undergrads invite her back to their fraternity for a barbeque, she doesn't hesitate. She knows they're just doing it because they recognize her, and at least one of the guys referred to Owen, Colin, and Leon as the "old dudes with her," but so what.

She's traded on her fame for less, she's sure.

Owen tags along at the promise of a keg, Colin doesn't care what they do, and Leon seems amenable to just about anything—probably because he smoked a joint in the bathroom, which set off the fire alarm, but also because Lindy is realizing he's just that type of guy. Not looking for problems, not looking for trouble. Happy to be. Just be.

Lindy almost tells him he's interested in the wrong girl if "just being" is what he wants, but his company is growing on her. Besides, she's not promising him a rose garden. Or, to quote one of her recent top five hits: "Don't Ask Me If You Don't Want to Know."

She does have to return Tatiana's calls, though, so she promises herself she'll hide in the bathroom when they get to the Delta Tau house and do that. She's been dodging T since last night, when she sent a flurry of texts that Lindy ignored.

Where are you?

I thought we were doing the 4th?

Why are you in Philadelphia? Why haven't you called me to tell me you're in Philadelphia?

Don't you have an appearance tonight?

How can you just blow that off? How can you just blow ME off?

Damn, girl, Lindy thinks, *can't you just relax?* Leon is relaxed! Leon isn't badgering me about this and that and where are you and why are you there? If I wanted a husband (or wife), I'd have one!

Lindy knows that's not fair, that Tatiana isn't being completely unreasonable, but Tatiana wasn't oblivious to what she was getting into when she signed up to date her; Lindy hadn't been in a committed relationship in years, and she made no promises to T that this would change. Sometimes she regretted her peripatetic commitment issues. It would be nice, she'd think (on a quiet evening over a bottle of wine in her big house with her big yard with her fancy security system guarding her big wall with gold records and big walk-in closet and big screen TVs and big pool with a big Jacuzzi) to share this with someone; to hear about his (or her) day, to have him (or her) hear about her day. But she'd tried that once, nearly a decade ago.

After that mess with Annie, she actually resolved to change. She called her sister from her new rental in Nashville, which was so empty that her voice echoed over the phone, and said, "I need someone on my side."

And her sister, who listened silently as Lindy recounted how she'd planned to confess her feelings to Annie but that Annie was mooning over Colin, and so Lindy naturally slept with him, said, "Well, then, stop pushing everyone off a cliff."

And she was right. Her little sister was fucking right, of course, but that's why she wore pumps to work and worked in advertising and had a little suburban house with a 1.5-carat diamond ring on her finger and would be perfectly content driving her Subaru wagon, which she would fill with chubby-cheeked mini-mes for the rest of her life. Her sister had taken their parents' free-range Berkeley hippie philosophy, their unstructured, chaotic lifestyle (before their messy, messy split), and shed every last ounce of it. Lindy spun the other way, rebellious for no reason at all.

"Try it," her sister said. "It's not so hard. And you should call Annie and tell her anyway."

Lindy wasn't brave enough for that—telling her best friend that maybe she was a little bit gone for her. More than a little bit. Instead, she opted to try the *it* her sister recommended: commitment. A few months later, just before Christmas, when the silence from Annie made it clear that she was no longer Lindy's to love, she met a winsome *Rolling Stone* reporter, Simon, while playing a one-night gig in Austin. She liked him and he liked her, and he was down in Nashville often enough that they found a balance between never seeing each other and seeing each other so often that Lindy wanted to throttle him. And then they liked each other enough that after eight months, he asked her to marry him. She was visiting him in LA, meeting with producers, talking to labels, and Lindy brimmed with the closest thing she knew to optimism. They drove up to the top of Mulholland Drive at dusk on a late August evening, as the sun was setting in this spectacular way that turned the sky into a light show of blazing oranges and fierce magentas and hazy yellows. The heat rose up from the valley below, and Lindy and Simon sat on the hood of his Explorer, and just as she eased back onto the windshield, happy to close her eyes and appreciate this hushed moment in her life that had increasingly been filled with noise—white noise, loud noise, all noise—he shocked her by pulling out a ring.

Lindy was so jarred by it that she blurted out, *"No!"*

Up on the cliff by Mulholland, she may as well have just pushed him off.

But once she said it, once Simon recoiled, and once they drove the agonizingly windy road back to his house in the Hills, she convinced herself that she meant it, and she didn't allow herself to consider how much she loved him. Because she *did* love him. Maybe not enough, or at least not enough right then. Timing, and all that. She'd barely gotten over Annie, might still not have been over Annie. It had been only a year. And since there's no bouncing back from a spurned proposal, that was the end of Simon.

Lindy doesn't think about him much anymore. They wave hello at junkets, and sometimes she scans for his byline when she flips through *Rolling Stone*. But he's a ghost now, like Bea. Someone who once was and now isn't anymore, at least not to Lindy.

They step inside the Delta Tau house, which is beige and damp and emits a general lack of hygiene. Lindy tries to touch as little as possible (and from the look on Colin's face, he does too), and thinks, *You have to call Tatiana.* She tells herself a million times to call Tatiana. But she'd rather push her off a cliff. Leon is here, and he's stoned and easy, and also the father of her maybe-baby (that appointment next week is such a reassuring exit to this whole mess), so why get caught up in the messiness of babies and girlfriends and what-to-dos. A few weeks back, after four months of dating, Tatiana told her she thought she might be falling in love. *Love? Christ.* That's what Lindy thought to herself. *Nothing good ever comes from love.*

Regardless, she owes T a phone call. Love or not. Lifelong commitment or not. Pregnant or not. (Undeniably pregnant, but who has to know?) Lindy latches the bathroom door on the ground floor of the Delta Tau and inhales, then regrets it, as the air smells unmistakably of fraternity-house piss. She's surprised to find her fingers trembling.

"Why has it taken you a day to call me back?" This is how Tatiana answers from the speakerphone in her Mercedes.

"Hey, babe. Come on, don't be mad."

"Mad? I'm past mad, Lindy! Where the hell have you been?"

"Philadelphia?"

Tatiana exhales, and Lindy can picture her clutching her steering wheel, firming her (lovely) jaw, stuck at a light, squelching the itch to honk her horn, flip off the guy in front of her, and rev the engine, just to quell her irritation.

"I fucking know that you're in Philadelphia. Your whole team apparently does. A: Why didn't I know until you landed? And B: Why didn't I know, period?"

"It was last-minute. I wasn't sure if I was coming." This is at least partially true. Less of a lie than plenty of others that Lindy has told, and will tell, her.

"And C: Why did Twitter know before me?" She pauses. "You could have texted me."

"I should have texted you."

Lindy can hear her softening. She won't stay mad. No one ever stays mad at Lindy, which is the brilliance of how she can keep pulling this shit. Theoretically, she's a huge pain in the ass. No, not just theoretically.

She *is* a huge pain in the ass. But she's charming and sexy and beguiling and, goddamn it, she makes you want to work for it, so everyone does. If she weren't famous, she'd be cut off at the knees. Because she's famous, she's magnetic.

Maybe that's why she loved Annie, it occurs to her only now. Annie never worked for it. Annie just took her for what she was.

Tatiana sighs, just as there's a knock on the bathroom door, then Colin's voice behind it.

"Lindy! Open up!"

"Is someone there with you?" Tatiana asks.

Lindy unlatches the door, bugging her eyes at Colin to *shut up.* She presses a finger to her lips, and he nods, getting the message. He's massaging his jaw, raising a bag of frozen corn kernels to his lip.

"No, no one's here." She grimaces at Colin. LIE #1.

"Are you coming home soon?"

"Soon," Lindy says. "Maybe tomorrow." LIE #2.

Tatiana is silent.

"I'm sorry," Lindy offers. "I know we had plans tonight. But it's my dead friend's birthday today, and I have to be here."

"Your dead friend? Oh my God, did someone die?"

"It's a long story."

"Seriously, did someone die? Who? What happened?" A horn honks, probably Tatiana's own. She always had places to be, though she makes time for Lindy.

"No, no. It was a long time ago." *A decade. A lifetime.*

"So someone died a long time ago, and then it became an emergency?" Tatiana blows out her breath. "I'm trying to understand here, Linds. Why wouldn't you tell me?"

Lindy knows that she's not wrong, but Bea isn't the sort of story she talks about. Tatiana doesn't know much about Simon either, and that's worked out just fine. *Why do we need to go around sharing the sad stories of our past just because we're sleeping together?* Who says that anyone is any better off for doing so? What is so wrong with preserving something just for yourself? A gem to cling onto, a nugget you can tuck away and nurse and nurture that makes you *you*?

"I should have told you," Lindy purrs. "I regret it." LIE #3.

She only just notices that Colin's lip is oozing blood. He's peering in the mirror, gingerly pressing on it, grimacing.

"Will you tell me tomorrow?" Tatiana's done holding the grudge.

"I will." LIE #4.

"I'll get you at the airport."

"Sweetie, you're too good to me." TRUTH #1.

Tatiana seems to consider this for a moment, or maybe she's just changing lanes, focused on the road ahead.

"I want to hear this story, Lindy," she says firmly. "If it's important enough to fly to Philly for a day, it's important enough to tell me."

"Let's order in tomorrow night," Lindy says.

"Something for just the two of us," Tatiana coos.

Lindy's fingers are twitching again, ready to hang up, ready to put an end to the ruse.

"Something for just the two of us," she echoes. LIE #5.

After all, if you consider the web-fingered pea-size being inside her uterus, there are three of them now.

◈

"First of all, what happened to you? Second of all, what was so critical that you had to eavesdrop on my phone call?" Lindy asks. Colin has made himself comfortable on the shuttered toilet, the bag of frozen corn against his face, as if he has no place better to be than this grimy, piss-smelling bathroom.

"I wasn't eavesdropping. And even if I were, it wouldn't be the first time I'd listened to the great Lindy Armstrong pull some shit on her . . . girlfriend . . . or whomever."

"Fuck off, Colin."

"I love you, Lindy, but it's true."

"I seem to remember you had no problems sleeping with me. My 'shit' didn't bother you one bit back then."

"It still doesn't bother me. But then I'm not the one sleeping with you now." He eases the bag of corn from his face. "Though it seems like you're not quite sure who you're sleeping with now either."

Lindy huffs, tapping her foot. "So what happened to you anyway?"

"The girl I met last night."

"The teenager?"

Colin nods.

"The teenager punched you in the face?"

"She's eighteen. *Jesus.*" He pales. "And her boyfriend punched me in the face."

"Come on."

Colin winces. "It's true."

"So you're pretty much, as you like to say, no different than I am. Hiding out in a bathroom avoiding your shit."

"Touché," he says. "And I think Owen may be out there defending my honor."

"Well, that can't be good for anyone."

Colin's phone buzzes. He holds up the screen to show Lindy.

"The eighteen-year-old. Wants to know where I disappeared to. Swears that guy isn't her boyfriend."

Another buzz. Another text.

"She's apologizing. Wants me to come play beer pong."

"Does she know that you're practically a senior citizen?"

"I told her I was thirty-two."

Lindy howls.

"Hey! She told me she was twenty-one!"

"So twenty-one was cool, but eighteen is not?"

Colin pinches the bridge of his nose, his phone vibrating against his forehead.

"I don't want to be that creepy guy chasing around girls who could be his daughters."

"Like, *literally,* she could be your daughter." Lindy says this and thinks of her own potential daughter, spinning and growing and blooming inside of her. Her throat tightens, and she points herself toward the window so he can't see her come undone. *What a mess I've created,* she thinks. *What a fucking, fucking mess.*

But Lindy doesn't like feeling accountable; she lost track of accountability years ago. In her world, sacrificing parts of yourself is simply how it's done, the only way to success. You slice off a little and say: Yes, I can give that, I can expose myself to the audience, in my lyrics, in the way that I'll compromise my music and then abandon my writing and then agree to synthesize my voice and the melody and be totally cool with the watered-down sellout that I've become on *Rock N Roll Dreammakers.* Of course you can use last year's single "Independence Girl (Look Out)" in that tampon commercial.

"Hey," Colin says. "Hey." Like he can sense the approaching crest of tears.

She blinks them away before any glimmer of her accountability can penetrate her armor.

"It's nothing," she says, facing him.

"It can't be nothing."

"It's nothing worth discussing."

Colin nods, used to her hardened exterior by now, and exhales loudly—a punctured, deflating balloon. "God, I don't think I've ever felt older."

"Life sucks and then you die."

He shakes his head and smiles. "You used to say that all the time."

"It's true."

"It's not true," he says. "It's not even close." He drops the bag of corn into the trash. "Look at you, look at your life. It doesn't even come close to sucking."

Lindy shrugs.

"Fine, then, look at Bea's."

Lindy doesn't have a quippy reply to this—no snark, no bite, no sarcastic, undercutting retort. She sits on the windowpane, trying to find the unfamiliar space in her emotional landscape for honesty.

Finally, "You asked me, back at the house, why I came back," she says, then falters. She inhales and winds up her nerve. It's too exhausting to keep up the façade when he knows her so well, when he could sense, just moments ago, that she was on the brink of vulnerability, on the edge of holding it together. "So here's the truth, and it seems ridiculous because she's dead. I mean, *she's dead*, Colin." Colin glances away to the filmy floor. "But I came back because I didn't want to be the asshole who wouldn't show up for Bea."

He peers up at her, and now she's the one who has to look away.

But it's true. Maybe she initially wanted to show up to stick it to Annie, or maybe she wanted to seduce Colin again for sport, or maybe she just wanted to come and have them all fawn over whom she'd become and how far she'd left them behind, how she left them in the rearview mirror when they kicked her out, deemed her a pariah. Not all of them, but enough of them. Catherine. Annie. Even Bea in her own way, not leaping to her defense, not assuring her that sleeping with Colin didn't ruin her character irreparably.

Nothing about Lindy's life now connects with who they were then. And maybe she was a little resentful that when she left them—not just for Nashville, but *left them* behind—none of them tried to prevent her from going. That they chose sides, and not enough of them chose her.

But perhaps her deepest motivation was simply that she didn't want to let down her dead friend, even if she still nursed a sliver of a grudge.

She admits this to Colin now and feels a strange, confusing, foreign tug in the guts of her soul.

Reverence. Remembrance. Restitution.

She feels all of these things for Bea.

However they're so foreign that Lindy can't even recognize them, even if she truly tries (which, it should be noted, she does not).

Instead, she says, "Want to get a beer?"

Because one beer can't hurt. One beer won't kill her. One beer is just the antidote to wash this ridiculous sensation of nostalgia away.

20

OWEN

Owen is certain he *can take this guy.* He is sizing up this douchebag who clocked Colin and thinking, *I can totally take this guy.* Colin absorbed the hit and shrugged it off, but Owen is up for the fight. He really wouldn't mind punching someone right now, and lucky for him, this dude has marked himself as a douche.

Said douche, in a yellow Delta Tau tank top and backward Yankees hat, is refilling his plastic cup on the weathered patio out back while Owen assesses his strategy. He hasn't been in a fight, honest-to-God fisticuffs, in well, ever. In high school he played squash, which lent itself well to the lanky, late-puberty kids, but didn't lend itself nearly as well to developing mad street-fighting skills. In college he wasn't the meathead lug who spilled out of his fraternity door, wrestling some schmo to the ground over, say, a game of quarters. He did occasionally play Ultimate Street Fighter on his iPhone, and he's gotten pretty decent, but real life hand-to-hand combat? Well, no.

But so what? he thinks. *So fucking what?* He tackles those monster hills in spinning class; he used to take boxing classes at Equinox; he's in pretty ass-kicking shape for a forty-year-old! Hell, he's in pretty ass-kicking shape for a thirty-year-old!

Owen grabs a red Jell-O shot off the bar, then three blue ones just for good measure. They slide down the back of his throat like he'd spent the past two decades perfecting his Jell-O shot technique. Behind him, the overzealous bass of some hip-hop song is blaring, shaking the remaining Jell-O shots on the tray. He notices now that they've been arranged to look like an American flag.

How quaint. Catherine would totally dig that.

Except that he ruined the design when he grabbed four from the upper corner.

She would totally not dig that.

But no matter. Catherine isn't here to tell him what to do and what not to do, remind him how much he screws everything up when, *please*, are the kids fed and bathed? Do they make it to school on time? Are they reasonable, generally polite human beings who do not resemble Cro-Magnons? Yes? Yes? Well, then thankyouverymuch, what is the problem?

The bass reverberates in the floor, and some guy also in a tank top (peach) and baseball hat (Red Sox) shouts something about booty shaking, and Owen nods his head, pumping his fist, swaying his shoulders, attempting to pulse his hips to the beat.

Yeah, he's totally got this.

The douche has his back to him, waving his hands in the air, spilling his beer on his wrist, laughing like a tipsy hyena, completely oblivious, which bolsters Owen's misguided confidence. *By the way*—he looks around—*where is Colin anyway?* Maybe he could use him for backup. That dude, Leon, is over in the corner with his eyes shut, swaying to the same inescapable bounce from the stereo, but Owen's not sure he'll be of much help. He's not really sure how he's standing, honestly.

Oh well. What's that hashtag Penelope always uses?

YOLO.

Yeah. You only live once.

This gives him pause for a second, but not too long, certainly not long enough. He thinks of Bea, and how she only got to live once and it was too goddamn short. Why Bea? Why at twenty-seven? Catherine was better friends with her because they were girls. But he always admired her, both from afar and up close too.

He remembers their junior year: Catherine's parents were divorcing, and it wouldn't be an exaggeration to say that she and her brothers (and Owen) were in a state of shock that careened toward denial/emotional paralysis. Catherine's home had always been the cheeriest one imaginable, at least it appeared so whenever Owen trekked home with her. He'd spent two Christmases there in college. Theirs was the house in the neighborhood whose decorations went up the morning after Thanksgiving dinner, the strung-up white lights illuminating the windows, the mulled cider beckoning in neighbors, the stockings hovering in a perfect line over the fireplace mantel. Catherine and her brothers (and Owen) cherished their home, their family, and it was easy to see why: theirs was the Hallmark card wrapped in Catherine's Martha Stewart dream. Until her mom evidently grew weary of her dad and unceremoniously dumped him on an average Wednesday in October. No one was really sure what happened; if there had been long-simmering problems, her parents had masked them entirely.

"I don't even remember ever seeing them fight," Catherine said, shell-shocked and cried-dry. Owen, though he loved her, didn't have the words to offer comfort. What could he say? He wanted to fix it, and he tried: he attempted to come up with a bunch of ways it could be fixed: *Maybe she should plan an elaborate dinner for them both and lure them each there under false pretenses? Maybe she should suggest some therapists? Maybe she should stage an intervention with her brothers? Maybe she should put together a photo album of their happiest family moments and send it to her mom?* But Catherine cocked her head and looked at him like he was speaking cyborg.

He couldn't fix it, and maybe he was dumb to try. After all, he'd bought into their Hallmark life as much as Catherine had.

Late on one of those October nights, he overheard Bea and Catherine lingering on Bruiser's stairs, their voices filtering through the just-ajar door to their bedroom.

Owen peered out the sliver of door space with one eye and watched them. Bea rubbed her back, and Catherine rested her head on her shoulder, and for a long time, the silence was enough. He was struck by how Bea let her *just be*. It took a lot of guts, he thought, to *just be*. To intuit that the only thing she could offer was a strong arm and a warm shoulder, and that was OK. He was, he remembers now, even in his drunken, hazy state in the bass-thumping living room of Delta Tau, amazed that this was all Catherine needed, and all the more amazed that Bea understood this.

Eventually, Catherine said, "I don't know how my life will ever be the same."

Bea replied, "Who said it's supposed to stay the same?"

Catherine bounced her shoulders. "Me, I guess. I liked my life. My mom took that from me."

"No, she didn't, not really. It's still yours to live."

Catherine twisted her mouth. "But it's different now. I feel a little lost."

"Everyone feels a little lost, Cath. There's nothing wrong with that. You only lose if you let someone beat you."

Owen watched them from his perch by the door and felt his shame rise up, his cheeks burning, disappointment in himself lodging in the base of his throat. No wonder he couldn't rescue Catherine: he'd led a perfectly cushy middle-class life. No one had died! No one had betrayed him! He grew up with a mom and a dad and a golden retriever and made the varsity squash team and got a used Toyota 4runner for his sixteenth birthday. He was ashamed, just for a minute, about how easy he'd had it, and doubted that he and Catherine could ever be as close. Not because Catherine had become a little shattered, but because he never had. Then there was Bea, who was triumphant in the face of loss, who literally scaled mountains to prove she hadn't been defeated. No wonder Catherine turned to her, not him. No wonder she solved her problems, fixed them while Owen could not.

He thinks of Bea's indefatigable spirit and bobs his head. *You Only Live Once.*

You Only Lose If You Let Someone Beat You.

YOLIYLSBY. Too long for an anagram, but Owen wasn't above trying.

No, Owen was not going to let this jackass in his tank top and Yankees hat beat him today. He burps out a hiccup of air and steadies himself. *No one punches my friend on my watch!* In his peripheral vision, he spies Colin and Lindy emerging from the bathroom, which is the final snap of motivation he needs. They'll have his back! His old dear friends! Surely they will lift him up and carry him on their wings to victory.

Having never been in a street fight, Owen's not exactly sure what happens next. It's all a blur. He'll tell the doctors this when he comes to. But witnesses claim he emitted some sort of primeval roar and charged across the living room, throwing himself down the two steps to the patio, lunging toward Robbie (he would learn his name later, when charges were being considered), who was still loitering by the keg. He tackled Robbie at the waist, leveling them both, but he miscalculated the depth of the abutting patio wall, and thus momentum tugged them both smack into the stone ledge, which simultaneously rendered Owen unconscious and dislocated his shoulder.

Robbie, because he was nineteen, spry, on the football team, and therefore padded with muscle, bounced to his feet immediately, a cheek laceration his only battle mark. Owen, because he was forty (and surely for other reasons too) blacked out for at least ten minutes while the fraternity dudes gathered around, hovering over him like curious toddlers, wondering who the hell this lunatic was, and how the old guy got into their party.

21

ANNIE

Annie is concerned that Catherine might kill Owen. Not without good reason. Catherine is pacing the waiting room of the ER, muttering things like:

What the hell is wrong with him?
I might kill him.
I think I'm going to kill him.

Annie was the one Lindy called, because Catherine's phone was dead from her conference call, and Annie's was always charged, always lying in wait. Not that she'd heard from Baxter today. *Where the hell was Baxter?* She was starting to panic that something had gone horribly awry at the Hamptons: that he and Gus had accidentally left the gas burner on and were dead on the floor of their summer rental. Or some terrible accident involving, oh, she didn't know, a helicopter crashing into Scoop Du Jour on Main Street, just as the two of them were striding in for double-helping rainbow-sherbet cones. But she's scanned Facebook a bunch of times, and none of her friends have posted anything alarming, so she's trying to defuse her concerns (*xo*) and not go from justifiably a tad paranoid to completely shrill and crazy.

Still, though! Why hasn't Baxter texted her back? Or called! Would it be too much for him to pick up the phone and call?

What the hell is wrong with him?

Annie starts at the thought. Even through the thicket of their worst years, when she was drowning in her postpartum depression, then chasing that depression with pills (and then more pills), and when Baxter was finding comfort elsewhere, she hadn't considered that something was wrong with *him*. Baxter was the gold she'd been lucky enough to stumble upon. Never once did it occur to her that she might want to kill him.

She stares at her blank phone screen.

She kind of wants to kill him now.

But regardless, it was Lindy who buzzed her phone to say that they were on their way in an ambulance from Delta Tau, but not to panic because she'd seen worse before and that Owen would be fine, but he may or may not require shoulder surgery, and incidentally, he also knocked out his front tooth.

Annie and Catherine ran here when they couldn't find a cab (holiday hours). And now her hair is winging out behind her ears, her mascara is flaking, and her T-shirt is sticking to her stomach, the perspiration marks like a Rorschach imprint against her Pilates-flattened abs. She stands by an air-conditioning vent, but it's no help. Then Colin turns the corner from the hallway, and her heat rash rises in the crease of her elbows.

She glances around the waiting room in an attempt to avoid Colin and perhaps find an escape, but there's nowhere to seek refuge. The ruby-red chairs are littered with all sorts of misfits from the holiday: at least a dozen drunk kids with various broken-ish-looking limbs, several guys with unfortunate facial hair that appears to have been singed by fireworks.

Annie raises her phone and clicks on her camera app, finding her own refuge of sorts. She can already think of a million captions: *Slice of real, red-blooded American life! Fractured arms, not fractured spirits! Hospital (red) (white) (and) blues.*

She likes the last one the best but, just before posting, remembers how much she hates hospitals, how she begged Baxter for a home birth because no good ever comes from the inside of these walls. She knew it was illogical; she knew it made her sound like the redneck hick she was deep down, where you soothed your licks with Band-Aids and an ice pack, and even if you wanted to see a doctor, no one had insurance, and they weren't about to blow their weekly pay on a visit to the doctor no one trusted anyway. Annie thinks of Bea. They hadn't saved her after the car accident, and if they could have saved anyone, with her money and resources and tenacity, surely it should have been Bea.

And of course, the doctors hadn't exactly fixed Annie either, after Gus was born and she wasn't quite right. Gus was an angelic baby: he nursed easily, he slept through the night at two months, and he didn't even mind a wet diaper. And yet, Annie couldn't seem to appreciate it, couldn't appreciate *him*. She knew it wasn't normal, as she'd read enough of those mommy boards to understand postpartum depression, but that couldn't have been what she was suffering from. She was just exhausted, even though Baxter had hired a night nurse; she just needed her hormones to stabilize. Still, though, after four months, her crying jags never subsided; her adoration for Gus was not at all what she'd anticipated—she'd been prepared to be the mother of the century! All she wanted to do was pass him off to the newly hired nanny and hide.

She couldn't tell Baxter. She *didn't* tell Baxter. When he arrived home from work, she was showered and pulled together and sometimes, if it was early enough, she'd made something like a pot roast. She saved the breakdowns until the apartment was quiet, when the nanny took Gus to a music class or out to the park. Sometimes, if she was desperate and they were home, Annie locked herself in the bathroom and turned on the shower to conceal her cries.

At her six-month checkup, her OB-GYN recognized the symptoms—the lethargy, the deadened eyes, the way Annie appeared to be sinking, even just sitting there on the stirruped exam table.

"I do sometimes feel like I'm moving through quicksand," Annie confessed. "But I'm sure it's nothing."

Her OB-GYN was much less sure it was nothing, and promptly wrote her several prescriptions to ensure that the quicksand dried up. And it did. After just a few weeks, Annie felt almost like her old self. Almost, because her old self was a moving target, but close enough. The Xanax helped, and on bad days, like when the other moms were talking about milestones (none of which Gus had yet hit), a Klonopin too. And then, on other days, when the stretch of hours rose up and it was only her and Gus, and Baxter was barreling toward a partnership and made no promises about when he'd be home, and the swell of the empty apartment felt like it might drown her and she doubted all of her parenting instincts because she hadn't exactly had a wonderful mother, and when Gus outgrew his angelic newborn phase and morphed into a fussy infant Annie couldn't hope to understand: when she'd changed him and fed him and made a million silly faces, including eight rounds of peek-a-boo, and still he wouldn't stop crying . . . well, maybe she'd take another pill on top of that.

Annie grimaces. She hates that today has stirred all this up. She'd blocked out those hazy days with the pills, as if forgetting about them meant they never happened. She thinks of Bea, of when she was sick. She wishes she'd known Bea back then, in her youth, isolated with her illness, isolated with her frigid grandparents in their lonely, grand apartment. Bea didn't like to talk about her illness much, said she never wanted to burden them with sad tales, with images of a girl who was so different back then from who she was now: vibrant, ready to scale a mountain. She already felt like a burden to her frigid grandparents, who never wanted to raise more children, who certainly didn't have the emotional space to raise a sick girl.

Annie surveys the waiting room: the buzz of the fluorescent lights, the click-clacking of clipboards and pens, the downcast faces and the groans of discomfort. If she'd known Bea back then, she would have taken her to chemo, if that's what she needed. She would have brought her clear broth and ice chips and trashy novels and wacky nail polish to make her laugh. She would have picked up prescriptions, scheduled her next appointments. How could Bea perceive anything about that to be a burden? None of it would be burdensome; all of it is the beautiful weight of friendship, and Annie would have been honored to carry it on her back. Then she realizes something else: if Bea had misperceived her burdens, maybe Annie had misperceived her own trials. Maybe Baxter could have carried her on his back too.

"I wish Bea were here," she says to no one and all of them too.

Catherine is chiding Colin for something like he's a little kid, and he looks appropriately apologetic. Lindy is tucked into a corner, her back to both Annie and the waiting room, with Leon's hands firmly grabbing her ass. The PDA makes Annie sick. Actually, it makes her think of Baxter, which subsequently makes her even sicker.

"I wish Bea were here!" she says louder, but still, they're all wrapped up in their little enclaves. Before she can implore them again, to pay attention to why they're here and what matters, her cell buzzes.

Finally! Baxter!

"Hello?" She is breathless. There's nothing wrong, nothing wrong in the world at all.

"Hello?" A female voice. Annie scowls.

"Hello?"

Silence. Annie hears the beeping of an open car door, then a loud bang as it slams shut.

Oh my God, Annie thinks. This is the call, the one you never hope to get. There has been a disaster, an emergency of epic proportions, and the police are calling to tell her that she never should have left Baxter and Gus, and this is her fault, and she should have known better, and why would she ever deserve to think she had a right to be happy? Or . . . maybe it's Cici. *Cici!*

"Are you sleeping with Lindy?" the voice says.

"I'm-I'm sorry?" Annie stammers.

"Are you sleeping with Lindy Armstrong?" The voice has gone from not particularly kind to cuts-like-a-knife sharp.

"What? What on earth are you talking about?" Annie presses her finger to her ear. "I think you have the wrong number!"

"I saw her on your Instagram, so tell me the truth: *Are you fucking Lindy?*"

"I am not fucking Lindy!" Annie says too loudly, and two nurses turn and stare. "Why on earth would I be fucking Lindy? I am very happily married, thank you very much. So I do not appreciate the phone call! If this is some stupid reporter, please know that you have your facts wrong. Lindy is here with Leon, so leave me the hell alone!"

Annie can't believe she said that, but it felt pretty exciting, pretty goddamn thrilling, to stand on bravado—partially false bravado, but bravado all the same.

She waits for a response, but the line has gone dead. Annie checks her phone to see if she missed a text or a "call waiting," but it's as empty as it's been all day, so she watches Leon grope Lindy's butt. But then Annie figures whatever happens next, she'll stay out of it.

Life is easier, after all, when Lindy's not involved.

$\sim$

"What the hell is wrong with you?"

Annie has hit the hospital cafeteria on a coffee run. She'd like to be the type of person who's useful in a crisis, so coffee seems like the right gesture, even though it's shortly after five o'clock, and no one is in dire need of coffee. She's not going to stand idly by and solely consider which filter would best illuminate Owen's crises in her Facebook feed. (She already knows it would be X-Pro to better contrast the horrid hospital lighting.) In fact, she practically vows to go on an anti–social media kick for the rest of the day! Well, maybe not the *whole* rest of the day. She has to document the fireworks, after all. Maybe until this crisis is wrapped.

She is tenuously balancing four coffees on a tray in one hand and cradling her phone in the other when she's assaulted by Lindy's vitriol.

"What the hell is wrong with you?" Lindy repeats.

"What is wrong with me? I went and got coffee."

Lindy swipes Annie's phone from her hand.

"Seriously, what the hell is wrong with you?"

At least five drunk/bruised/facial-hair-torched patients have fallen quiet and are staring. Annie doesn't know why Lindy hates her so much. Annie is the one who should hate Lindy. Annie *is* the one who hates Lindy!

"I was just getting lattes. Here."

She offers the tray forward, which Lindy dismisses with a wave of her hand, nudging the tray off-kilter. Foam tumbles out of the little baby opening on all four lids.

Leon slides next to Lindy, easing her back, guiding her by the elbow. "Babe, come on now."

"Oh, stop it, goddamn it, Leon! You don't know anything about this. And don't call me babe!"

Leon looks rattled, his eyebrows raised, his jaw lowered. He turns to his right, which points him toward Catherine, who is still fully, heatedly engaged with Colin, who himself is staring at the too-bright lights on the ceiling and appears to be counting to five hundred in his head rather than absorb her diatribe. Leon makes another abrupt turn again—completing a full 360 degrees, then readjusts to the left and shuffles down the hallway toward the bathrooms.

"Can I have my phone back, please?" Annie says.

Her palm feels empty without its comforting weight. Also, Baxter may call at any second.

"You are a goddamn idiot," Lindy snaps, then slaps her own phone into Annie's open hand. "Look. Look at what you've done."

Before Annie can even curl her fingers around it, Lindy's phone buzzes, then buzzes, then buzzes again, the screen illuminating like bomb explosions, one after the other. Texts, a dozen of them, maybe more.

Annie thrusts it back at Lindy.

"Congratulations! You're more important than I am. Do you feel better about yourself now? Let's all bow at the feet of the great Lindy Armstrong!"

"You're still not getting it." Lindy sighs like Annie truly is the biggest idiot she has ever encountered, and Lindy surely has seen her fair share of idiots. "You're responsible for this!"

"I'm responsible for . . . people texting you? What is wrong with people texting you? Isn't that what you always wanted: popularity, people falling at your feet?" A little spittle flies out of her mouth and land's on Lindy's shoulder.

"Do you not understand what happens when you push that little button that you like to push so much, the one that says, 'POST'? You know what 'POST' means, correct?"

Annie's neck throbs, her heat rash spreading up across her collarbone. She doesn't need Lindy to patronize her!

"Of course I know what 'POST' means!"

It occurs to her, the phone call, the conversation.

"Then that is exactly how I—and the rest of the free world, and probably part of the unfree world—got it! Have you not heard of privacy settings? Actually, have you not heard of privacy at all?"

Privacy settings. Oh.

Annie had changed hers a few months back because she discovered that she got so many more "likes" when her Instagram was open to anyone. Also, what a thrill when a perfect stranger discovered something fascinating enough about *her* life to want to "like" it. So, yes, she had heard of privacy settings and chose to be utterly un-private.

"I have heard of privacy settings," she says flatly.

Lindy mutters to herself as lights from her phone bounce off her face. "What on God's great goddamn earth would compel you to tell Tatiana about Leon?"

"Tatiana? Who? Wait, what?" Honestly, Annie had spoken so quickly, so roused in the moment, she hadn't really remembered exactly what she'd said.

"Obviously, you wanted to screw me! Thanks, well, you did it. Tatiana will officially probably never forgive me."

"Tatiana is a reporter?"

"Stop acting like a total moron," Lindy snaps. "Tatiana is my girlfriend."

Annie's chin juts out. *Oh.* She'd read about the girlfriend in *US Weekly*, but figured it must have been a ruse, since she was witnessing the very real boyfriend in the flesh. And it's not as if Lindy wasn't known for ruses. Wasn't known for bullshit. Also, since when did Lindy start dating women?

"Since when do you like women?" Annie asks.

"Give me a fucking break, Annie!" Lindy's face turns the exact hue of decadent apple-red, and for a second, with her wild hair and worse temper, she reminds Annie of Ursula from *The Little Mermaid*. (Gus went through an endless *Little Mermaid* phase. Annie didn't judge.)

"I don't think this is her fault," says Colin.

"*She* called *me*," Annie squeals, her humiliation rounding the bend to tears. "And how did she get my number?"

"She's a goddamn celebrity publicist! Getting your number is probably the easiest thing she's done all day!"

"Honestly, Lindy, you can't blame Annie here." Colin again.

"This was dumb," Lindy says. "This was a dumb fucking idea. To come back here and think that we could all get along. Pretend like we actually like each other."

"I do like everyone," Colin interjects. "Even when you act like a bitch."

"Oh, Colin," Lindy steps close, too close, and Annie loses her breath, worried she's going to kiss him and spark things up all over again. "Go fuck your beautiful fucking self."

Her motorcycle boots echo on the linoleum floor as she strides toward the exit.

"Lindy really has a girlfriend? I thought . . . genuinely, I mean . . . I read about it but . . ." Annie says to Colin, who sighs deeply and drops his head like an anchor that's simply too much to hold afloat for one second more. Then Annie remembers: "Lindy! You have my phone!"

But Lindy is past the sliding glass doors now, so Annie chases after her, the doors whooshing to open, then easing closed behind her. She can hear Colin on her heels, then Catherine's voice trailing them— *"Hey, where is everyone going? What's going on?"*

She catches Lindy on the sidewalk.

"My phone. Can I please have it?"

Lindy narrows her eyes, considering. Then she grabs it from her back pocket, holding it high, prepared to chuck it through the dusk air like a football. But then it buzzes, and Lindy, surprised, instinctively lowers it to eye level.

"Incoming text from Hubs."

That was Annie's screen name for Baxter.

"I've been waiting on that! Give it to me."

Lindy holds up a finger. "Pause, please."

Then her eyes broaden like an open window, and even though the late-day sun casts shadows underneath the hovering trees, Annie and Colin (and Catherine too, as she's dashed out to join them) can see the color drain from her face.

"Is it Gus? Oh my God, is it Gus?"

Annie thinks of all the things that could go wrong. She should have never left them! She took Baxter to be responsible, but anyone can make a mistake! Annie knows this! Annie knows this so well! Fires! Gas leaks! Car accidents! Locusts! Who knows? The list is long!

"It's not Gus," Lindy says.

She averts her eyes and limply passes the phone to Annie.

No, it's not Gus. It's Baxter.

Naked Baxter.

Naked, full-frontal Baxter.

Even without his face, she'd know it anywhere. He has three moles just below his belly button, aligned just so, a perfect arrow shooting south. On their honeymoon, Baxter joked that they were like Orion's Belt—a gateway to all the stars in the galaxy.

Underneath his Orion's Belt, a message:

We shouldn't have. But . . . tonight again after the fireworks?

22

LINDY

Well, fuck.

Lindy is at a total loss. Which is at least the second time she's been rendered emotionally incapacitated in the span of twenty-four hours.

"Is that . . . is that . . ." Catherine is peering over Annie's shoulder, trying to make sense of just what exactly she (and they) are staring at.

No one answers.

Did I just see a dick pic from Annie's so-called perfect husband, who is clearly much less than perfect?

Lindy tries to catch Colin's eye, as if to share a collective *WTF?!*, but Colin is rubbing his chin, furrowing his brow, looking a little panicked himself.

Annie palms the screen and clutches the phone against her chest.

"Give me that." Lindy reaches for Annie's phone, swiping it from her limp hand. "No one should have to see that. Like . . . no thanks."

"Lindy," Colin says, then stops.

"Seriously, when did men decide that women want to see pictures of their dicks up close and personal?"

"Be quiet, Lindy," he says.

"Why? I'm not wrong. You're a guy, so you have no—"

"Shut up, Lindy!"

Shut up, Lindy! As if she's responsible for this!

"I'm trying to lighten the mood."

"It wasn't funny."

"I'm trying to distract her." She tuts. "She's not the first person whose husband has sent a junk shot to another woman."

Well. There. She hadn't meant to say it so succinctly, but she did. Now it's out in the open. No pretending it's anything else than what it is. She says to Annie, "If it makes you feel any better, it's happened to me."

It doesn't appear to make Annie feel any better, who's currently walking in a teeny circle over and over and over again, as if she's entered some sort of fugue state.

"Seriously. It happened to me! Does anyone remember that time when I was dating the guitarist from the Strokes?"

Colin and Catherine stare at her like they've been lobotomized. Or maybe like *she* has been lobotomized.

Lindy shrugs. "Well, anyway, he did it. And I was just trying to be helpful."

"Shut up, Lindy!" Annie whispers, as close to seething as any of them have ever witnessed. She stops circling long enough to march over and snatch her phone back. Then it's right back to perfectly round orbits on the sidewalk.

Shut up, Lindy! From Annie? Lindy blows air in and out of her nostrils and clenches her fists into tiny, tight balls. *Shut up, Lindy!* How about you, Annie! How about you shut up? In fact, shouldn't Lindy still be angry at Annie for unleashing this shit storm on her? Shouldn't Lindy be the one telling Annie to piss the hell off? If memory serves, that's exactly what she was doing—and still intends to do!—when her depraved husband accidentally blasted out a shot of his penis right into Lindy's unsuspecting eyeballs! Lindy is the one who should be furious!

"Listen! Don't shoot the messenger here," Lindy snaps. "Like I had any interest in seeing that disgusting close-up of your husband's genitalia. I'm just trying to be nice!"

"Well, you are *terrible* at nice," Annie says.

Lindy opens her mouth, because oh, does she have a million things to say to *that*, like: *All I used to be was nice, kind, generous, loving to you, and a lot of good that did me, a lot of notice you paid to that!* But suddenly Leon appears, having apparently stumbled out of the waiting room and into their dysfunctional huddle.

Leon. What is Leon doing here?

"Why are you here anyway?" she asks. Something wicked is rising up from her stomach, and it gurgles loudly. Lindy squashes it down, and then it occurs to her that this bubble of queasiness may be the baby, and that baby is saying that Leon is here because he's the goddamn father.

"Are we starting this again?" Leon sighs. "I can go. God knows, I *will* go. But you told me to stay."

Then Annie stops circling the pavement and starts weeping, so quietly at first that none of them notice, but then her shoulders are quivering, and then her body is shaking, and Lindy regrets her stupid anecdote about the Strokes' guitarist.

Lindy contemplates her own infidelity, her own broken promises, and knows she should check her cell to see how many of Tatiana's calls she's now missed; in other words, how many furious voice mails Tatiana has now left her. But even tone-deaf (not literally), Lindy recognizes that when your former best friend has been sent an inadvertent dick pic from her husband, which was clearly meant for someone else, now is not the exact moment to focus on all the ways your own personal life is going to hell.

Annie's phone hums to life just then. She has it set on this cutesy ringtone that Lindy pinpoints as an electronic version of Pharrell's "Happy."

"It's Baxter," Annie whispers.

"Give me that." Lindy grabs the phone and presses it to her ear. "Hello? HELLO? HELLO? No, wrong number, douchebag!"

She returns the phone to Annie, who's breathing in and out through her mouth in what Lindy envisions to be the Lamaze technique (she read about it on Babycenter), and who then steps to the curb and vomits. Catherine holds her hair at the nape of her neck and rubs her back, and Lindy is reminded of how often they all did this for one another back then. Twenty years ago and then today. Well, back then, no one held Annie's hair back because she was too busy holding theirs.

Lindy chews her lip and looks away—*she should be the one holding back Annie's hair!*—while Annie has another go at purging her insides. Still, though, she doesn't move.

She remembers that night when she made Annie swear they'd always be sisters. That was the night Lindy thought she might tell her, come clean about her feelings, about her confusion as to where she drew the line with Annie, between friendship and love. But once she kissed her, once she leaned in and put every ounce of herself, stripped bare and completely vulnerable, into that kiss, and once she pulled away from her, Lindy realized Annie didn't have a clue. That she'd be so blindsided, sweet innocent Annie, that Lindy would lose her entirely. So instead she cast it aside, like a silly prank, like something you'd do late at night at sleepaway camp because your bunkmate dared you to. She told herself that maybe she'd finally tell her at Catherine and Owen's wedding. That went about as well as most things Lindy told herself she'd do . . . but didn't.

Lindy wonders if Annie remembers that night, remembers that she kissed her.

"Should I call him back?" Annie asks, when she's done vomiting. She's squatting on the curb outside the university hospital, the rest of them in a horseshoe around her. "Maybe I should call him back. Hear what he has to say."

"You're not calling him back, for God's sake," Lindy barks. She doesn't know why she's being so protective, even though she *does* know; she just wishes she no longer cared.

"He's my husband."

"He's a lousy husband. You settled."

"You don't know anything about him!"

"No," Lindy concedes. "But I still know a lot about you."

"Ha! Like you're an expert on me? Like you're the expert on men all of a sudden?" Annie yelps.

"I *am* a bit of an expert, actually!"

"Well, that is just absolutely laughable!" Annie ekes out some sort of weird pseudo-laugh that reminds Lindy of *American Psycho* or *The Shining*. A crowd of onlookers have gathered, trying (and failing) to inconspicuously record a public meltdown of the great Lindy Armstrong. Annie's fake cackling echoes across the street onto their devices.

"Listen," Lindy seethes, fully cognizant that they're being watched, that they're being judged, that everything that's being said and done right now is being recorded and will likely air on *Access Hollywood*, on *Extra*, on *TMZ*. Why did she ever want this for her life? To live like a mouse in a lab? Fame seems alluring from the outside, but once you're inside the bubble, you discover that there's so little room to breathe, so few chances to get fresh oxygen. She'd been naive, she realizes, to even consider that this weekend could have been an escape from it, that for a wee second she could simply pretend to be who she was before her life blew up into something she couldn't control on her own.

"Listen," she hisses, "I am trying to *help* you here! Don't want my help? Don't take it!"

"*You* are trying to help *me*?" Annie shouts. "Well, that is absolutely ridiculous! An absolute first in the history of firsts!"

"You are so clueless that it's no surprise your husband is cheating on you!" Lindy regrets it from the moment the words fly out, even before she sees Annie's face crumbling like an avalanche, but there's no taking them back now. Lindy Armstrong does not retreat. She spins toward the crowd because it's not like they're not watching, not like they're not voyeurs into their family dysfunction. "Her husband sexted her a dick shot that wasn't meant for her! Should she call him back?"

"*SHUT UP, Lindy!*" Colin now. "Jesus Christ. What is wrong with you?"

"Fuck you guys. Seriously. Fuck you."

Lindy salutes the three of them (plus Leon), as Annie's phone sings out again—*"clap along if you feel like a room without a roof!"*—and then she takes a bow and strides out of the parking lot.

"Lindy!" she hears Leon call after her. She doesn't slow, doesn't stop. She doesn't need him; she doesn't need any of them. She pretends they're sorry she's gone, that they're sorry it came to this.

But she suspects what they're really thinking is: *Lindy's always running from something.* This is nothing new. This isn't any grand surprise.

23

CATHERINE

The doctors have given Owen a hit of Vicodin for his pain and have sent him on his way. Maybe if it weren't a holiday, and there wasn't a line of boozy idiots winding out the door to the ER, they would have kept him overnight. But it's only a missing front tooth, and really, just a veneer that popped off from when he was struck in the mouth with a squash ball in high school. He'll be fine once the swelling subsides and his dentist back home slaps on a new one. They managed to pop his shoulder back in with little fanfare, so other than his drowsy eyes and pronounced lisp, Owen is mostly in one piece.

After Lindy stomps off, Catherine and Owen taxi it the few short blocks back to Bruiser, awash in silence, each pressed to their respective sides of the backseat. The campus, adorned in American flags for the evening's festivities, whizzes by in a red-white-and-blue blur, and Catherine can't help but feel like that's how time has gone too—how it sped up all at once, and now twenty years have passed and suddenly you're here, staring out the window wondering where you've been the whole time. They stop at a light in front of the Quad, and some kids with Bud Light cans walk by, laughing, howling, hooting—too loud but also exactly the right level of loud for where they are in this moment of time.

Forty. This age, this decade, the complications present—a fractured marriage and a pressure-cooker career and two children who both fill you up but also sometimes drain the last vestiges that you wanted to save for yourself—no, they're not even a blip to those kids. Back then they weren't even a blip to Catherine.

The light changes, the taxi driver accelerates too quickly, and the Quad is a blur now too.

Speeding up, slowing down, speeding up again.

This is pretty much life until we die, Catherine thinks. *Why don't we stop moving for a minute to appreciate it? Why don't I stop moving for a minute to appreciate it?*

Bea did. Bea appreciated all of it, which is probably why they all loved her. Even without recognizing this back then. At eighteen or twenty, Catherine couldn't have known how precious this was: Bea's reverence for the path in front of her, Bea's gratitude for the path behind her. When was the last time she'd felt gratitude? She snips at her kids all the time: *Be grateful for what you have! Stop asking for a new iPhone, another app! Do you know what kids in Africa get by with?* But it's not as if she doesn't want, want, want, herself. She wants more spots on *Good Morning America*; she wants that HGTV pilot; she wants more spots on the Top Ten Best Designer lists; she wants more website traffic and more staff support. Right now, she very much wants Target, and after today's outburst, it may be the one thing she can't have, regardless of how deeply she covets it.

Also, of course, she wants more of everything from Owen.

Owen has closed his eyes, tilting his head back, missing everything.

Catherine is waiting for him to apologize for this mess, but his lip is stuffed with gauze, and she's not even sure he would if it weren't. No, that's not fair. If they were home in Highland Park—safe in their ways and patterns and balances—he'd apologize. He might not mean it, but he'd say it all the same, and Catherine would pretend that the words were enough, even without the right intention behind them. That's what encompasses at least half of their conversations anyway: they speak, they converse, they've braided themselves into each other's lives, but that's different than meaning it. A few years ago, Owen would have apologized without hesitation; a few years ago, Owen would never have found himself in this position in the first place: behaving like a misguided freshman, picking ridiculous fights, going on a twenty-four-hour bender. Now? Who knows. This isn't the Owen she loved for her four years here; he's not the Owen she loved in Highland Park before they started going sideways, with his time at home and hers always in her office. He's listless, he admitted as much. And it occurs to her—and truly resonates for the first time—he's unhappy. She glances at him as the cab turns down the narrow, cherry blossom–lined alley toward their old row house and wonders, *How have I missed how much you've changed?*

With the swelling of his front lip and the cotton packed in there too, he doesn't even look like himself. She taps his elbow, and his eyes flutter open.

"We're here."

"Where?"

"Our house."

"We're back in Chicago?" He's highly drugged, but even Catherine can hear his disappointment, which sounds surprisingly sober. Owen doesn't want to go home.

"No. Walnut Street. We're home at Walnut Street."

"OK," he says, closing his eyes again. He sighs and tries to steady his head upright.

Catherine wonders what he's thinking, with his eyes shut tight, his hand clenching the taxi cushion. She wonders, but still, she doesn't ask.

Leon has used the spare key left under the mat to let himself in. He's watching the local news—coverage of the parade near the Liberty Bell—when Catherine unlatches the door. There's no sign of Annie and Colin, who were winding their way back here through campus. Annie needed air, but when she announced this, she kind of looked like she just needed Colin. Maybe things haven't changed as much as Catherine thought they had.

"Hey," Leon says, then shifts back to the TV.

"Hey," Catherine says, as if it's totally normal that he's now crashing at their old house. She was hoping for some quiet; she was hoping Owen might nap, and that she could simply be left alone. Catherine is never left alone anymore, and would it be too much to ask for a few minutes without Sasha ringing her, without her team needing her, without her kids asking one thing or the other from her, without her husband knocking out his front tooth because he clocked a nineteen-year-old college football player after emptying out half the contents of a keg? (Catherine is unaware that it was actually *numerous* Jell-O shots that ultimately did Owen in.) Everything in this house, their six-some, was always about togetherness, about inclusiveness. What is so goddamn wrong with wanting to go at it on your own?

Also, who does this guy think he is, insulting her French toast, creaming her in butter churning?

Owen shuffles in and plops on the couch next to Leon.

"Whars Windy?"

Leon shrugs. "I didn't catch up to her. But I have her wallet." He pulls it from his pocket. "So she'll be back. She couldn't have gone far."

Catherine wants to say, *Lindy can run farther than you could imagine, and even if she doesn't, why would you want her back anyway?* But Leon's not her problem, so she says nothing. Lindy's not her problem either. She has enough problems. Those two can figure out their dysfunction on their own. She's sick of people getting bogged down in their own crap, refusing to take responsibility for sticking their own two feet firmly in the pigsty in the first place.

Her temples pinch as she considers her own set of problems: the earlier video on *TMZ* (was that just today?—it feels like a month ago), and her displeasure at the details she overlooked for today's Fourth of July spread, and she thus clods up the stairs to retrieve her phone from its charger. She should also probably check in with her mom, who's watching the kids for the weekend, but if there had been an emergency, surely someone would have called. Then she regrets her passivity; these are *her* kids, for God's sake, and they already see too little of her to begin with.

Not that they'd want her home all the time. Catherine knows she's not that type of mom. As it is, on the rare free weekend when Catherine has no event to attend, no copy to edit, no photos to approve, no competitor websites to browse, and she attempts to corral the two of them in to bake banana bread or play Monopoly, Penelope usually leaves the room, and Mason, sweet boy, still attempts to appear interested. But he's lanky and reedy and growing, and Catherine knows that soon enough he'll itch to scamper away when she tries to pin him down for those free hours.

She calls her mom's phone but gets no answer, so she tries the home phone and leaves a cheery message on the machine, detailing how much she misses them. She thinks to tell them to call back, but she's so very tired and doesn't want to have to put Owen on with his lisp, so promises a vague return call later.

She belly flops onto the bed, which squeaks loudly, then quiets. She doesn't want to scroll through the forty-two new e-mails or the thirty-seven texts. This flurry of incoming communication can't be good news. She drags a pillow over her head and mentally rewinds the scene from earlier today, wishing she'd done it all differently. She flings the pillow off and reminds herself to stop being a baby. She's a goddamn CEO. She needs to man-up in a crisis. (She hates that term "man-up," but it's what she thinks all the same.)

The coverage on *TMZ* has gotten no kinder, despite her publicist's assurances that Catherine's apology—and finger pointing toward her marriage—will change the narrative. True, no one is buzzing about her faulty homemaking skills, but that hasn't stopped other rumors from spreading like hives. The slit-your-throat meme has gone viral, hashtagged, a sensation. Now that the reporters have made the connection between her and Lindy, they've uploaded one of Lindy's songs as background music to a three-minute video comprised of clips of Catherine using various steak knives on her *Today Show* segments. They've tracked down alleged members of her staff who offer anonymous quotes about their suspicions about her dissolving marriage, and potential affair with the pastry chef at the Ritz Carlton.

The pastry chef at the Ritz Carlton!

Catherine is used to her competition attempting to outdo her—with more succulent stew recipes or more folksy but still hipster homemade laundry-detergent ideas—but this? Oh God. She hadn't even considered that this would be the fallout. She'd simply been trying to salvage her brand, deflect attention, and save the Target deal, because the Target deal meant saving The Crafty Lady. Her hand rises to her mouth and stays there. She hadn't meant to betray the loyalty that, despite their spiraling few years, they'd spent half their lives building.

Bea used to say that there couldn't be secrets between them. That secrets were like walls: you started erecting them and before you knew it, you'd built yourself a moat—you couldn't jump over it, you couldn't knock it down. You were stranded on the island without anyone to come to your rescue.

Catherine wishes so very much that she weren't on her island, but she's been here for so long, what can she do about it now? Besides, it occurs to her suddenly, angrily, that Bea had plenty of secrets of her own. The hypocrisy! The standing on ceremony. *Who is she to judge?*

She opens her e-mails, which bring no better news than the *TMZ* videos. Her CFO writes from Martha's Vineyard that Target has demanded a conference call on Monday. He expresses his concerns that this unexpected request means a dead deal. He doesn't need to express what a dead deal means. There's no word from HGTV, but Catherine doesn't need word to know she can kiss that stint good-bye too.

Catherine furiously punches her publicist Odette's e-mail address into her phone, determined to rectify this, to clean up this mess before it gets any worse. She rage-types and thinks of how coming back here could have potentially cost her the past decade of hard work, of the company with her name on it, of the proudest thing she's ever done. (Of course, she's proud of her kids too.) How Owen ruined that because he was drunk and hungover and embarrassed her and she snapped. How stupid Lindy and her pretense that consequences don't matter ruined that too.

Also, who is this person in her office who suspects her marriage is on the rocks because of a pastry chef? Her marriage isn't on the rocks because of a pastry chef! People can say a lot of things about her (evidently people *do* say a lot of things about her, which, naively, Catherine had never considered; she'd just merely shut her office door and assumed that, at the risk of sounding like a silly high school girl, people *liked* her), but it's never even occurred to Catherine to entertain the notion of finding someone else to fill the pocket of emptiness that occupied the space that Owen once did.

There's a knock on the bedroom door, and Catherine, surprisingly, hopes it's Owen. That maybe she can say something to make this all go away—not the *TMZ* stuff (though that too), but the rumors and the truths between them too. But then Leon opens the door just a crack, and she regrets her instinct that he could come repair her.

"Sorry to bother." He casts his gaze downward. "Uh, your husband needs you."

Catherine sighs, blowing out her breath like it's her last.

"Uh, he has something oozing from his mouth, and I'm pretty cool with bodily fluids, but I think I'm gonna step aside on this."

Catherine throws her phone against the pillows and sits up straighter, clasping her hands behind her back, stretching her shoulders, coaxing out the knots.

"I guess I owe you an apology?"

"Sorry?" Leon appears genuinely confused.

"For my behavior at the butter churning. I should apologize for how I behaved."

"Oh." He hesitates.

"I'm used to being the best."

"OK."

"And I don't like losing."

"That's cool."

"So . . . that's what happened."

"Well, all right." Leon nods, ready to be done with it.

Catherine is a little miffed that he's not more gracious. Or maybe she's more miffed that he's not Owen. Or that she wanted, hoped, for him to be Owen.

"I mean, it wasn't that big a deal," she adds.

"It wasn't."

The front door slams downstairs, and Annie yells something unintelligible.

Leon lingers on the landing, poised to rejoin the fray on the ground floor, but then turns back toward Catherine.

"What else?" She sighs.

He gazes at her for a moment too long, and Catherine can't decide if he dislikes her (add him to the list!) or pities her. What happened to the reverence of just a few hours ago, in the kitchen, over the French toast, when he realized she was *Catherine* from The Crafty Lady?

"Look." She juts out her jaw. "I'm sorry! OK? I'm having a pretty spectacularly bad day." He nods. Then she adds, more quietly: "I'm not usually like this. I mean, I don't think I am." Her hands sweep from behind her back into her lap. "Well, I don't know."

He hesitates, then steps nearer. "I work with a lot of artists who lose track of their A game."

"Like Lindy?"

Leon smiles but shakes his head. "No, not like Lindy. She knows who she is; she just doesn't like you to see it. That's actually why I like her. It's both the best and worst thing about her."

Catherine says nothing.

"I guess, listen, it's none of my business . . ." he starts.

"No, it's fine. Say what you want. I mean, tell me the truth. People don't do that often anymore. Or maybe I've gotten used to not listening."

Catherine thinks of Bea, how if she were here, she'd set Catherine right.

Leon twists his wooden prayer beads on his wrist.

"You're different from who I thought you would be," he says. "I know, it's lame, I'm a closet obsessive crafter . . . what can I say? It helps me de-stress." He laughs at this, and Catherine manages a smile. "But what I mean to say is that what I thought of you . . . well . . . I thought there would be more joy."

"More joy?"

"Yeah, like, you bring so much happiness to people, so I figured your own life would be full of the same thing."

"Oh." She stares at the comforter.

"It happens a lot," he says. "Mistaking people you don't know, like, famous people, for who you think they should be."

"I'm really that far off?"

"Well, I guess I have to believe, because I'm used to drawing out authenticity in someone in the studio—even if it takes staying there all night or scrapping a track if they can't find honesty—but I guess what I'm trying to say is that it seems to me like there has to be joy left in you too."

"You don't even know me."

"That's true."

Then Catherine says, "You remind me of Bea. If she were here, I think she'd tell me the same thing." Catherine feels the pinch of tears behind her eyes. "My company is struggling, having some problems. Owen doesn't know." The words come out before she can think about all the reasons she should stay quiet. She waits to regret it, but instead she feels a slight glimmer of relief to have shared her burden and eased it off her solitary shoulders. "Today made things worse."

"I'm sorry," he says. And he seems genuinely so. "Maybe you should tell Owen?"

She shakes her head. "It's complicated now."

He nods, and they both realize this is about as far as he can take her. He's a producer; he's not the one behind the microphone, not the one who has to turn a simple melody into magic. Also, he's not really Bea.

"Anyway." His boots echo closer. "This was downstairs. The rest of them took theirs, so I thought you might want it."

He holds out her frame, her old letter to herself. Catherine's not sure if she wants it, but he takes her silence as a tacit yes, and so rests it on her bed and then slips out. She hears his *thwomping* down the steps, taking them two by two. She recognizes the pattern—*thwomp, thwomp, thwomp*—from years back, when one of them was late to a midterm or racing off to a party that felt like the party that might change their lives, or just scurrying off to wherever because wherever couldn't wait. There was always an urgency about everything, even though there was also an urgency about nothing.

Where will you be in twenty years? Write down your wildest dreams!

Unlike the rest of them, Catherine remembers what she wrote. She doesn't need to read it, to prop the frame up on her nightstand or a mantel or wherever else you'd rest a framed letter to your old self, like you might a piece of artwork. Like a letter to your old self merits a place on your wall, merits homage or nostalgia or even a second thought. At twenty-two, you had no clue about anything!

Catherine's phone buzzes a million times more, and she listlessly scrolls through more Google alerts on her, none of them kind. New rumors of divorce lawyers being retained, a quote from the pastry chef citing "No comment."

She pulls the framed letter closer, her fingers fluttering over the glass, fanning an old memory. She wasn't an idiot back then. She knows this. She was wise and hopeful and naive, perhaps, but she wasn't an idiot. Catherine has been many things, but she always kept her head down, focused on the road before her, aware of the potholes ahead and behind.

In twenty years, this is what I hope for you, this is
what I want you to be:
Be inspired.
    Be your best.
    Don't hesitate to fail.
    Don't hesitate not to.
    Undercook your bread. Enjoy the goo.
    Overcook your bread. Enjoy the crust.
    Love Owen forever.
    Let him love you forever back.
    Build a big white kitchen.
    Make cookies with your children there often.
    Be honest. Never less.
    Don't lose track of everything because you think
something else is your everything. It's not.
    Your wildest dreams? Don't limit yourself to
those.

Catherine's phone beeps again. She curls her knees in tight and starts to cry for real.

24

COLIN

Colin is rubbing Annie's back in concentric circles as she mutters over and over again about how she should have *known*. He finds this calming almost, being here, comforting her, playing hero. That's why he got into medicine in the first place, though plastic surgery isn't exactly saving lives, and that's also why he didn't say no to Bea when she called and said, *Please help.*

"I should have known," she moans for at least the hundredth time, and Colin shushes her for at least the ninety-ninth time and assures her that she couldn't have. "How did I not know this? Am I the dumbest wife in the history of marriage?"

Colin's hands falter on her shoulders, and he tries to pry the tequila bottle out of her clenched hands. But she lifts it to her lips and cringes as it burns down her throat. Leon, who's parked on the sofa with worried (half-mast) eyes, silently indicates that Colin should just let her drink. Owen, who's parked next to Leon, slouches into the couch pillows and offers nothing.

"Men are assholes," Colin says, which makes Annie cry harder, so he apologizes for the comment. He tries not to think of the various ways *he's* been an asshole, including but not limited to the lies he told them all just yesterday. He regrets how easily those lies come to him, how quickly he rattled them off, even after all these years. Isn't the whole point of being here, of this exercise, to peel back the layers and get at the truth?

He wonders what Bea wants of him now. If she finally wants him to deliver the truth.

"You're not the problem," Annie says, wiping snot on her sleeve and gazing at him in much the same way most women gaze at Colin. "I mean, you were, once. But not today." She nods, as if she's given this quite a hearty dose of thought. She cups his cheeks with both hands and stares for a beat that makes Leon fidget. Colin does not fidget. "I should have slept with you freshman year. I deeply, deeply regret not sleeping with you freshman year."

Now they're all a little uncomfortable, but that's really the least of their problems.

Annie sighs. "What was my virginity? What was it, really? But I guess there was Bea. I mean, you always loved Bea. After the fire any-way. And I always loved you." She hiccups into her hand, so casual in her admission that Colin's not sure he heard her correctly. He knows he did. Part of him always knew she loved him just a tiny bit, but not *love* love. Just . . . you know. Well, he always knew that Annie was a tiny bit hung up, but so were a lot of women. And then there was that atomic bomb at Catherine and Owen's wedding, but he'd chalked most of that up to drama between Lindy and Annie—*girl drama*—so he hadn't given Annie's actual feelings for him too much thought. But then Bea told him, of course, how Lindy—well, both of them, he wasn't absolved from it—crossed the line that Bea said was understood they shouldn't cross.

So when she says this tonight, and he thinks about it more honestly, he realizes that he did know, and he *did* cross a line, and her admission is only surprising in its bare honesty.

He doesn't know a lot of women who are honest. He doesn't know a lot of women like Annie, actually. She is kind; she is sincere; she does not have inflated, bee-stung lips; she isn't at all interested in him because he's the Boob King of Hollywood. She knew who he was when he wanted to get into neurosurgery. He liked that guy. He still likes that guy. If Bea were here, she'd remind him of that guy; she would have reminded him for years how far he'd strayed from him too. But after Bea . . . well, after that whole mess and what it took out of him, he buried that guy. Rightly or not. But that Annie can do this now, remind him of who he thought he could be, so effortlessly, without trying, spins his brain a bit, muddies his usually simplistic thoughts.

"Baxter doesn't deserve you," Colin says, more sure of this than ever. "What sort of shithead would do this to a woman he loved?"

"Love," Annie whimpers. "Who knows anything about love?"

Love, to Colin, meant end-of-the-earth-level devotion, flying to the stars. He went to the end of the world for Bea, but it was too late, and it shattered him so completely that he never dared come close to it again.

Baxter has called seventeen times, but Colin has seized the phone at Annie's halfhearted request, though she keeps asking for it back, then keeps changing her mind. Colin makes the executive decision to tuck it into his pocket until she's at least breathing properly.

"Just for a while," he says. "A little break won't change anything."

So Baxter has taken to texting.

"What a pussy," Leon says, though no one has asked him. "Texting your wife to explain your dick shot? Like, is romance officially dead or what?"

"Romance is officially dead," Annie echoes.

Then she gazes at Colin, who gazes back, blood flushing his cheeks. He knows he shouldn't, shouldn't enjoy playing the hero so much. Just look where it got him with Bea. But he can't help himself. He feels something new rising within him for Annie, and damn if Bea wouldn't support that, wouldn't endorse it. *That's why we're here!* she'd say. *I want you to be happy!* In fact, she did say this, nearly exactly, when he logged a few vacation days and flew back to see her after she beckoned. She was so frail already, the leukemia having wormed its way into every part of her. Well, not her heart. Her heart, the thing Colin had cherished most about her, was still clear, pure, generous. He linked his fingers into hers and noticed her tiny wrists, then her damp, downcast eyes, and he knew he'd do it, knew she couldn't suffer through one more moment of agony, one more moment of the horrors that come with losing sight of your life, your sense of self that cancer destroys. She said it felt like her bones could snap when she shifted in bed.

It wasn't even a choice, what they did.

It was an understanding that he loved her enough to grant this for her. Before he did it, before he gave her the pills and then sat with her as her breath slowed and her eyelids fluttered then dropped, they talked for hours. About how she *wanted him to be happy*, about *how she didn't want the others to know* (not about this anyway), about *how the only thing that mattered in life was family*, and he was hers, and so were the rest of them, even if they'd lost track.

He'd get booted from his residency if he were ever caught, and Bea made him promise that he'd slip out of the apartment and disappear before the nurse came for her shift. It would look natural, like it had been the leukemia all along. And since that's how she wanted it, Colin obeyed. His fingers finally unwound from hers, only to wipe his unremitting tears, and only once he'd found a way to steady both his feet and his breath did he dare stand. He couldn't leave her. He knew the nurse was due any moment, and yet he couldn't leave her all alone, dead now, almost as if she were merely sleeping. Finally, he willed his legs to move, just a minute before he'd be caught, and took the apartment's service stairs, two by two, vomiting in the alley between Park and Madison.

That's love, Colin thinks today. *Annie deserves that kind of devotion. Not this asshole shit of a husband who won't stop texting, contrite only because he's been caught.*

Colin kept his end of the bargain and never told a soul, certainly never told any of the four others. Some mornings he woke up and couldn't believe that he'd done it, like it was a mirage, like someone else's life. Other mornings he woke up and made his peace with it, knowing she would have died either way, knowing that he granted her a bit of peace before she did. Bea always did things on her terms. That wasn't any different. And still other mornings, he woke up and hated himself for not fighting harder to find a cure, to heal her, even though, of course, this was impossible.

But back then, they still believed in impossible things.

"I need something!" Annie announces, standing abruptly. "Who has something they can give me?"

"Anything," Colin says, without thinking. Yes, that's what he does for people he loves, *anything*. He was born to play hero; there's nothing he does better than that.

Catherine, who has joined them from upstairs, coos, "I can make you some tea from the spice rack."

"Tea," says Colin. "Yes, let's get her some tea. What else? Ann, what else do you need?"

"*Something to kill Baxter with!*" Annie screeches. Then she adds, "I need another drink!"

Colin grants her the tequila bottle, because if there was ever a time for balls-out liquor, this is it, and if it's really what she *needs*, then Colin, with his new figurative superhero cape tied firmly around his neck, will be her savior. "No! Something stronger! Who has something stronger? Give me something stronger!"

Colin reaches for her arm, to tug her back to the couch, to massage her shoulders, to placate her, to make this all better, maybe make it evaporate for a flicker of a second. But her arm slips through his hand. She's already marching forward, on her way up the stairs like a thunderbolt to Lindy's room. *Thwomp, thwomp, thwomp.* Taking them double-time.

The door creaks open above them, then slams so loudly the banister shakes. Colin rises to go rescue her, but Leon says, "Dude, let her be."

And Catherine shrugs and says, "Yeah, I don't know. This is a complete mess." Owen appears to have drifted off to sleep. Colin flops back next to them.

He'll save her later. This time, he'll be sure the hero saves the damsel in distress.

25

LINDY

Lindy is clutching a beer on the steps in front of Van Pelt Library, which offers her a view of the main hub of campus: the gothic brick buildings that have stood for a century and a half; the kelly-green lawns on which she used to sunbathe; the narrow, winding pathways that lead to all the nooks and crannies where students could scamper to hide from whatever they needed to hide from.

The Road to Freedom festival booths are still thriving, pulsing in full force. The butter-churning event is just up the walk. In front of her, an ironsmith teaches a set of siblings how to put on a horseshoe. To his right, women in rocking chairs needlepoint what appears to be the colonial flag. Down from there, there's a mock signing of the Constitution. She overhears a mom attempting to explain the Boston Tea Party to her daughters, but one of the girls just keeps screaming, *I don't want tea, I want lemonade!* She watches as the mom's nerves wind their way up from bemused to exasperated, and as she grabs her daughters by their wrists and marches them off toward Ben Franklin's booth, where he's feigning being struck by a lightning bolt.

Lindy wonders how the mother can bear it. If her brattish little kids are worth it. Would Lindy's brattish little kid be worth it?

She raises the lager to her nose and inhales, debating guzzling it all in one chug. She tests it with her tongue, savoring it, then concedes herself a gentle, tiny sip.

She'd bought the beer with a twenty she'd found stuffed in her back pocket. But she'd given Leon her wallet to hold at that stupid fraternity party, and therefore finds herself stuck on this godforsaken campus with these godforsaken memories. She could Uber to the airport, but then what? No ID, no nowhere. She swiped a Phillies hat from the Wawa, along with the beer, and it's tugged low, casting shadows over her always-recognizable face. Now, for once, she's anonymous again.

There are throngs of students and families milling about now, hordes of them moving in packs down Locust Walk. The July heat has started to turn, the humidity falling and leaving a bit of breathing room in its wake. Lindy inhales, as if she can taste the oncoming sunset, and feels the freedom course through her. She could be one of them, one of those kids, wandering freely toward whatever path, party, parallel she chose. Now, without her ID, with the ball cap disguising her face, she could be anyone.

Who would she want to be?

Lindy swigs another sip—her last one, she swears to herself—and considers it. *If you could be anyone, who would you be?* She and Annie used to play this game sometimes in their New York apartment. The radiator would be clattering too loudly, steaming up their windows on a frozen city night, or the windows would be open too wide because of a sweltering heat wave and the noise from below—taxis honking, trucks screeching, happy people filling the air with happy laughter—would filter upward, keeping them awake much too late, or too late for Annie anyway. She had a job the next morning. Lindy—this was in the early years when the gigs were few and far between—usually didn't have anywhere to be the next morning. She loved those late nights, secretly, selfishly, because she had Annie by her side. Even though she knew it wasn't right—to keep her awake when her alarm beckoned so soon. But Annie never seemed to mind.

Lindy thinks of that unfortunate dick pic and wonders if maybe Baxter isn't a bit like Lindy was back then—taking, taking, taking, even though she knew that with each extended palm, she drained a little more from Annie. Not on purpose. Lindy got a little drunk on Annie, and well, Annie didn't stop her. Lindy knows now, today, it's because Annie had no fucking idea how deep Lindy was in, but back then Lindy didn't have this perspective, this clarity that comes from hindsight. Back then she deluded herself into thinking maybe Annie would reciprocate, and that's why she asked so little in return from Lindy; Lindy figured that's how Annie liked it, that's what Annie wanted. Actually, she'd never really considered it until right then, until this very moment on the front steps of Van Pelt. Her cheeks burn, and she's certain it's not from the beer, though this is the first drop she's touched in the ten weeks since she found out.

If you could be anyone, who would you be?

Their apartment was miniature, so they shared a bedroom with a sheet hung across the center to give them each their privacy. They'd lie on either side of that sheet—Lindy remembers it was sort of this putrid green, and Annie had bought them half off at TJ Maxx—and talk through the night as if the sheet were the only thing that divided them. Like Lindy couldn't call her dad and ask for a fat check to upgrade from this hovel. Like Annie wasn't chased by wolves that she mentioned only in passing, that she skirted around the edges of.

On those serene evenings, Lindy would fold her arms behind her head and dream of playing the Opry, of stadium tours, of *The Tonight Show*.

"If I could be anyone, I'd be Shania Twain! Trisha Yearwood!"

Once she said Dolly Parton, and Annie laughed for a good five minutes straight.

"Because of the boobs? Are you laughing because of the boobs? I didn't mean the boobs!" Lindy said, but pretty soon, she was howling too, tears staining both of their pillows.

Annie would always say Princess Di. Even though Lindy would poke her (literally, she'd poke the sheet because she was close enough to reach it) to choose someone else. But she never did. Once, not long before everything imploded and Lindy packed up and jetted off to Nashville, Annie said, "That girl who's dating JFK, Jr. She has perfect hair and skinny legs, and oh my God, her wardrobe. Have you seen the way he looks at her?"

"I don't think I'd want to be as famous as JFK, Jr.," Lindy had said.

"But you'd want to be Dolly Parton?"

Lindy thought about it for so long that she asked Annie if she were still awake. Finally she said, "I guess it's not the fame I want, but the acknowledgment. Of my talent, I guess. Or that I'm good. JFK, Jr. only has fame. Dolly is famous for *something*."

From behind the putrid green sheet, Annie answered, "Maybe you want a bit of both."

It wasn't lost on Lindy that both of Annie's aspirations ended up as tragedies, as brilliant, shining stars who never got to reach their potential. And sitting on the steps, remembering it all, it's also not lost on Lindy that while she started out with acknowledgment—there was that Grammy nod and a few CMA nominations early on—mostly what she has now is the fame. The JFK, Jr. fame. Is that what she wanted all along? She insisted otherwise that night to Annie, but she didn't put up too much of a fight when the label started sending songs written by younger scribes because they told her they'd sell more singles; she hadn't exactly dedicated herself to mentoring her young upstarts on *Rock N Roll Dreammakers*. She has enough money to tell her label to fuck off. To make the music she wants. But she doesn't. She hasn't. She won't.

Even with her Phillies cap tugged low, someone has spotted her. A camera flashes, and she squints toward the intrusion. Whoever it was is already on his way, though. Just another stranger crafting her into whatever he wants her to be for himself.

Rock goddess.

Sex bomb.

Reality judge.

Sellout.

Lindy tosses the beer bottle toward the trash at the bottom of the steps, the beer spraying a glorious arc, like a fountain, as it careens into the bin. It clangs on the metal side, shattering on impact when it hits the bottom.

If you could be anyone, who would you be?

That's what they didn't get back then, Lindy thinks, pushing herself to her feet. Bea didn't get that either.

You *can't* be anyone.

Like life is that easy!

There's only you.

Too bad.

She stomps down the steps, furious at herself for even entertaining a notion otherwise.

⌒♡

She follows the crowd south toward the river, past the food court where they used to get salads in bowls the size of wheelbarrows, past the music lab where Lindy took her first and only class in songwriting. Ironically, she got a C, frustrating her teacher at every turn, refusing to color within the metaphorical lines. She smiles now, wondering what the hell ever happened to *him*. Little prick. Though as soon as she thinks this, she can hear Bea in her ear, chiding her for the vengefulness, for her immaturity. Isn't it enough that she's the one who hit it big? Left that professor so far in the taillights that she can't even remember his name? Lindy wonders if he watched her at the Grammys and felt bad for implying that she had no talent, or if not no talent, then not enough of it. Then she hears Bea again suggesting that if Lindy can't remember the professor, who's to say he remembers her?

She stops on a corner near the football stadium, startled by this notion.

What if he didn't remember her?

She turns and heads back in the direction of the music lab.

It's futile, she already knows. It's summer break, and it's edging toward sunset on July 4th, and she can't even remember his name! The odds that he's *here* right now—frankly, the odds that he even still works at Penn—are slim to none. Lindy tries to envision him. Was he young? Was he old? Is he still even alive?

Her feet stumble, and she trips over the curb. A wave of feet rush past her, but then someone extends an arm, pulling her up by the elbow. He shoves a flyer into her hand. "A battle of the bands later at the fireworks," he says. "You should come."

Lindy starts to protest, "Oh no, I'm here on vacation, not working," until she realizes that he's already walked past, pushed himself into the wave of the crowd. He wasn't inviting her to come because she's Lindy Armstrong; he was inviting her to come because he was inviting everyone. *Everyone. Anyone.*

Anonymity. Lindy hadn't realized how much she missed it. If she hadn't gotten famous, would she consider herself a failure? If she hadn't been famous, would she be happy? Or would she be happier? Would she be a mother? A wife? Do either of these things add up to more than she is now?

She buys a Diet Coke and oversize pretzel from the hot-dog guy on the corner and thinks about Annie, about Catherine. They're wives. They're mothers. Lindy doesn't think *they* necessarily add up to more than she is now. But she can't be sure.

She wrestles the pretzel in half, downing the center knot in one mouthful. Inelegant, sure, but she blames it on the baby. She's feeding two these days, you know. By now, she's in front of the music lab, the battle-of-the-bands flyer crumpled in her back pocket, the brass doorknob hot in her free hand.

If she hadn't slept with Colin, would they all have combusted anyway?

If she hadn't slept with Colin, would she have run to Nashville, where she found her fame? If she hadn't gotten famous, would they all still be friends? Would she have told Annie the truth? Forgiven herself for loving her, forgiven Annie for not loving her back?

Fame or acknowledgment. Lindy can't stop considering it.

The knob turns easily in her hand, the latch unlocked and welcoming. She's not sure she wants to step back, almost literally but certainly metaphorically, to who she was back then: a maybe not-so-talented, definitely listless and disrespectful C student who was defiant about coloring outside the lines for the sake of being defiant. Also, she wasn't famous then. And maybe her fame now arms her with false bravado, or maybe she just wants to see her old professor's face and hear him say, *I was wrong about you.*

Her boots echo on the marble floors of the long hallway leading to the lab. Mr. Pearson. That was his name.

She wasn't famous back then. So maybe now she just needs the acknowledgment.

26

ANNIE

Annie is surprised about two things. Well, plenty more than two things with the way that the past twenty-four hours have gone down. She flips her hand into her back pocket for her phone but then remembers that Colin—sweet, dear, sexy Colin—refused to relinquish it. Better for her mental health, he said, which is *laughable—ha ha ha ha ha!*—but she knew what he meant. She understood his intention, and it was all she could do not to pin him down on the couch and strip him down to his underwear right there, while he was reading Baxter's frantic texts aloud to her, his free hand coaxing the knots out of her shoulders.

In his series of unending texts, Baxter repents like a schoolboy in confession. As if he couldn't wait to heave his remorse off his chest, as if repenting would somehow cleanse him of the damage he'd done. The affair was over, he said. Or it had been. He knew it was wrong! Broke it off when his dad died! He loved her. It was a mistake! They'd run into each other at the farm stand. (There had been a typo here, thus it read, "fart stand," but Annie clarified through her sniffling. Owen giggled, but Catherine shot him a look as if to say, *One more laugh and you die,* and he subsequently got ahold of himself.) And it had happened only this one time (recently), he promised, with a particularly egregious use of exclamation marks. He didn't know what to do, he was distraught, horrified! Please call him! Please text him! Then his final text was chock full of emojis, which Colin did his best to decipher.

("I think that's the one that means sobbing? And I think that's the one that means embarrassed? And maybe this one means broken-hearted? Yes, that's definitely a broken heart.")

But now, without her phone and with a gut full of tequila, she's trying to focus, trying to marginalize all of *that*, because if she doesn't marginalize all of *that*, she's going to have a mental breakdown. Colin wasn't so wrong. If she sat here, on the braided rug of Lindy's room, and pored over his texts, reading them again and again, it's possible that her hysteria might literally implode her brain, lighting her cerebral cortex up like a nuclear explosion. It's not like she hasn't come close to this point before.

She crosses her legs in front of her, her hand flying to her mouth at the two surprises in front of her.

1. Lindy does not have any goddamn pills. Why does she not have any goddamn pills? Lindy always had something, Annie was sure of this. In college, it was alcohol; postcollege, Annie wasn't naive enough not to recognize that Lindy occasionally stumbled home with dilated pupils, with chemically induced energy that practically radiated off her fingertips. She'd even offered something to Annie from time to time—little white pills or oval-shaped pink ones. Annie always declined, though later could identify each pill simply by touch. *Ah, that's the Xanax. There's a Klonopin.* The better to pop one late at night in the blackness of her bathroom. But now, Lindy does not have any of these goddamn pills, which Annie

has never needed more in her life. She knows that it's a slippery slope for her—one, then three, then five—but she rationalizes it. Tells herself this is an honest-to-God emotional *crisis*; and even though those pills generally lead nowhere good for her, without them, she is surely headed to a dead end too.

2.   But while Lindy does not have any of those precious pills, she does have a copy of *Pregnancy and You* magazine tucked underneath her lingerie. (Why did Lindy bring lingerie for the weekend? This opens up an entire line of questions for Annie that sends her on a momentary mental tangent until she swigs the tequila bottle she toted upstairs.) Annie fingers the glossy pages of the magazine, which appears to be unread. She used to read these magazines . . . she used to read *all* these magazines. Like they made her a better mother! Like some stupid advice column on page fifty-five gave her any true insights on taming her insecurities, trusting her maternal instincts.

Ha!

That's what the Xanax was for.

She rests the magazine back in Lindy's bag, connecting the dots. The tequila has blunted reality, but it hasn't blunted everything, and as she slips the pieces into place, she imagines a lightbulb illuminating above her.

"Ding!" she says aloud. Followed by, "Oh my God, oh my God, oh my God."

She's been watching Lindy, after all. And even after all this time, Annie knows—probably better than any of them—that a leopard doesn't change its spots. Because deep down, Annie hasn't changed hers: she might have better highlights and a fancy Bergdorf's wardrobe, but she's not so far removed from that girl in sixth grade who brought Twinkies to the bake sale, who knew she was trailer trash compared to the rest of them.

The way Lindy has dodged any alcohol; the way she pulls, then pushes Leon away; the way she lied to her girlfriend and has avoided her calls. Annie knew that Lindy wasn't a lesbian, could never be faithful to any gender, regardless. Give her a break! And to think that Lindy was pissed at her. *Her!* She knew that tabloid lesbian stuff was ridiculous. She knew it!

That poor kid of hers, she thinks, though she hates her unkindness. When did she start being unkind? *Well, Lindy started it, put me here in the first place.* She tries to remember their early days, back in the dorm at the Quad or back in that dump of a New York apartment when she considered Lindy a sister, but it's all so colored now; it's all so skewed.

Annie abruptly laughs out loud—a staccato sound that echoes in Lindy's old room, bouncing around, then evaporating. None of them gave her any credit. Baxter never gave her any credit. Maybe she never gives herself any credit either.

Screw you, Lindy. Screw you too, Baxter.

"Text my husband back and tell him to screw himself!" she shouts down to Colin, and to Leon, who's sitting beside him, pretending that he doesn't stick out like a square peg in the round hole of the current mess.

It dawns on her that Leon doesn't know. Her jaw slackens. It further dawns on her that she might be the only one who does.

She giggles into both hands, like a kid at Christmas who just got exactly what she always wanted.

Yes, she knows Lindy's secret now. She's just not drunk enough yet to know what to do with it.

◦◦◦

Colin coaxes Annie out of Lindy's room by promising her phone back.

"Also, Owen is thinking of streaking again. Maybe I'll join him. Just imagine how many 'likes' you'll get if you post that to Instagram!"

She unlocks the door, and there he is, grinning and beautiful, and she knows that he's not going to go streaking, much less let her video it, but she can't help but smile back at him. Partially because she's definitely tipsy now, the floorboards swaying just a touch, not enough to throw her off balance, but enough for her knees to wobble. And partially because it is Colin, rescuing her, and his smile, with a wayward dimple and two years of braces, is akin to staring at the sun. It's golden and mesmerizing and warms you to the core.

"OK," he says. "We're not going streaking."

Instead, he proposes that they break into the stadium, weave their way through the bleachers, and drink more tequila on the fifty-yard line. Get back to visiting all of Bea's favorite places. In the mayhem of, well, *everything*, they'd forgotten.

Bea once made them break in during their junior year when the campus had shut down due to an epic snowstorm. Annie was terrified they were going to get caught; she spent the duration of the afternoon casting about for security guards while the rest of them—after Bea cut a lock on the east gate with metal shears that she naturally had stowed in her room—rolled smaller snowballs into larger ones for snowmen, flapped their arms to create beautiful snow angels, and tumbled atop one another in a snowball fight that left them giddy and breathless.

"Yes!" Annie says, the tequila as her armor. "YES! Let's break into the stadium! There is nothing I want to do more than THAT!"

"I think she needs some food," Catherine calls from downstairs.

"She is such a downer," Colin whispers.

"Seriously." Annie burps into her hand.

The fresh air on Walnut Street feels good against Annie's skin. She has stripped down to a tank top, her bra straps askew, her hair knotted into a messy bun. She never looked so unkempt for Baxter. Well, unless he caught her just after the gym, but she usually scampered into the shower immediately, so she'd have time to blush her cheeks, perfume her collarbone. Not that he ever appreciated her perfumed collarbone!

The five of them (Catherine had nudged Leon into coming) point themselves south, toward the stadium, wandering past the fraternities that Annie so diligently avoided her freshman year so she wouldn't be taken advantage of by a predatory senior, past the bagel shop where Lindy's bike was once stolen, past the bench where "Quarter Joe" resided (he sat there day and night and simply asked for quarters). Bea always stuffed her pockets with extra quarters, just for him. He died a few years back, and the college paper wrote a kind obituary. Annie read it online and thought about how the last vestiges of their friendships really were gone. She sent a hundred dollars in for the memorial fund.

She runs her hand over her delicate collarbone, sweaty and exposed now, wondering when the last time was that Baxter noticed it, when the last time was that he kissed Cici's collarbone. Or all of the other collarbones that came before hers.

xo

How long?

Why?

How many?

Why?

How could this happen?

"I think I need to call Baxter. Ask him exactly how many collarbones he's rubbed up against lately." She jabs Colin. "My phone, please."

"Annie, let's let this settle in," Catherine says before Colin can retrieve her phone from his pocket. "It's hard, I know."

"You don't know at all!" Annie gestures toward Owen. "You've never had to know."

"I'm sorry? I'm just trying to help."

"Stop helfing," Owen manages, through his gauze.

"Spit that out!" Catherine holds out her palm. "You're done bleeding by now, for God's sake."

Owen spits the bloody gauze into her palm like Gus would spit a wad of gum into Annie's. *Spit that out, Gussy! You have to be proper! Don't look like disgusting trash by chomping on that gum!*

"No! You don't get it! You wouldn't get it!" Annie's voice is rising like a whistle on a slow-moving locomotive. "You two . . . my God . . ." Tears crest again with no fanfare. "Like either of you has ever had to fight for someone, like either of you would ever feel betrayed like this! Please! You've been together forever!"

Annie strides ahead, wishing so much that she hadn't listened to stupid Catherine, who insisted she leave the tequila at home. Not that it hasn't done its damage. Her feet are weighted, her hands tingly, her brain an endless buzz of static like the black-and-white fuzz that would fill the TV screen late at night in their tract house in Texas, her mom out too late, Annie home keeping watch, drowsy but hopeful, illuminated by the glow of the screen.

"This is my mother's fault!" Annie shouts. She pumps a fist into the air, a non sequitur, but she does it all the same. *Yes! Her goddamn mother!* How was Annie expected to hold on to a man when her mother ran through them like water? How was she expected to know what a happy marriage looked like when she never had an example from which to learn?

"This isn't anyone's fault," Leon offers.

"This is Baxter's fault," Colin states, speaking over him. He reaches for Annie, protectively, instinctively.

"Yes!" Annie's fist has morphed into a pointed finger. She pokes the air, then Colin's chest. "Yes! This is Baxter's fault! *And* my mom's fault!"

Two guys in Penn Crew T-shirts loiter in their path, just in front of the Road to Freedom tents, as a few of the proprietors pack up for the early evening. Each crew guy has a buzz cut and scraggly facial hair. The towering blond one, whose muscles swell through his shirt, offers them a flyer. "Battle of the bands later. Yo, you should come."

"I would very much like to come!" Annie replies, still too loud.

"You should!" He grins. "Totally."

Back in college, the crew guys would never have invited Annie to a battle of the bands. Unless she was with Lindy or Bea, then maybe. It's not that she wasn't attractive; she was. It's just that they wouldn't have noticed her to invite her in the first place. She was so busy trying to blend in that she became like every other face in the crowd.

"I totally will!" Annie says. "I will *totally* come! I've never *been* to a battle of the bands! What bands?"

The crew guy shrugs. "Not sure. Some dudes on campus."

"Well, who cares anyway? I don't care at all! First, we're breaking into the stadium, though!"

"I'm not sure that we'll come," Catherine tuts. "And we're not breaking into the stadium."

"We will absolutely come!"

"Well, all right." The crew guy winks. "See ya there! Find me. I'll be waiting."

Annie raises her eyebrows and twirls around, snapping her fingers, gyrating her hips.

"Annie!" Catherine hisses, but Annie's brain is spinning too quickly to hear her. When was the last time she felt coveted? When was the last time Baxter lay in wait for her? Annie doesn't know, not that she's giving it a heck of a lot of thought, but she does know that her Pilates and her spin classes and her personal shopper at Barneys have kept her in pretty damn fine shape. She might be (almost) forty, but she's pretty sure this kid would do her. *This kid would do her!*

Colin steadies Annie by her shoulders, then yanks her elbow and guides her onward.

"What?" Annie says, swiveling her head, waving back toward the oarsman. "Ouch! Stop! Why are you doing that?"

"I'm just looking out for you. It's been a long day."

"I don't need anyone looking out for me!"

"Annie," Catherine interjects, "it's . . . a lot. This news."

"Fuck this news!" she yells. "I will not dignify this news today! I do not want to speak of *this news* for twenty-four hours! *Do not speak of this news!"*

"OK!" Catherine's palms face up, surrendering.

"Say it," Annie says to the rest of them. *"Say it."*

So they do. They swear they will not mention the news for a whole day. How that will happen, in the midst of this atomic meltdown, is anyone's guess, but for Annie to use the F-word, she really must mean it. The others aren't fools. They may not know her like they used to, but they know her well enough to know that she's not like Lindy—rough around the edges, crass just to be crass, unladylike for the sake of making a point. Maybe she used to be rough around the edges, back in Texas, but no longer. My God, she has almost turned herself inside out to escape who she used to be.

And why bother? Baxter didn't care! Baxter didn't notice that she'd practically killed herself to make herself over entirely, to leave behind the winds of South Texas and be someone. Really be someone. Not someone who anyone felt sorry for; not someone who still wore boot-straps on which to tug; not someone who in any way rocked the boat, demanded attention, or in any other form insisted on being different. Leave *different* to Lindy. Leave *showstopping* to Catherine. All Annie ever wanted to be was accepted, loved. Baxter was going to save her, and she never once, not for one second, did anything less than redo herself completely to give him everything he wanted.

She stops short on the red brick walkway, next to a statue of Ben Franklin.

"Ben Franklin seems like such a good guy," she says. "Ben Franklin would never cheat on his wife."

But then she remembers that back then they all died of an STD of some sort, so maybe he would. Gus read a book about it once; George Washington died of syphilis, though Annie had no idea why they'd include that in a children's book! But you learn new things every day, so on that day, Gus learned that George Washington would have benefited from the invention of condoms, and since Annie is feeling ungenerous right now, she'll go ahead and lump Ben Franklin alongside George Washington.

Screw you, Ben Franklin! You probably had syphilis! You probably did screw around on your wife too!

Is it too much to ask for a little loyalty? For fewer secrets? Why must they all carry the weight of these secrets? Why can't they—Lindy, Baxter, Bea—all unburden themselves, or maybe never opt for the lies in the first place?

She sinks onto the pedestal of the statue, dropping her head between her knees. She really shouldn't have had so much tequila. She doesn't drink much anymore, so the waterfall of liquor that she carelessly poured down her throat has done its damage. Her eyes droop; her tongue feels like sandpaper.

But she has secrets too: the pills, the blame for the miscarriage. Further back too, obviously. Plenty. And maybe that's what chased Baxter away, into the arms of some woman who likes receiving text messages of his penis.

"Gus wasn't supposed to be an only child," she announces to no one, and yet to all of them. "I miscarried a few years ago. It was my fault."

Colin sits next to her, resting his hand on her knee, the ledge of the statue not quite big enough to accommodate his rear. "Ann, it couldn't have been your fault."

Annie suddenly looks aghast. "Oh my God, what if I have syphilis?"

"No one has syphilis," Colin says.

"George Washington had syphilis! Ben Franklin probably did too! Who knows who Baxter was sleeping with!"

Her bravado from just five minutes earlier is fading. Annie can feel it seeping out of her like blood from a punctured artery: slowly, but urgently too. Who did she think she was? Like she could pretend, even for twenty-four hours, that this didn't mean the end of her marriage, her life up till now. She might be excellent at kickboxing, but she's not really a fighter, she's not the brave one. She's just the poor kid who never belonged here in the first place.

"Well, we can be certain that Baxter was *not* sleeping with George Washington, so we know that you're safe there," Catherine says, in that tone she usually reserves for the kids, and sometimes her staff too.

Annie is crying again, and Colin leans in, one arm around her shoulder, one arm slung over her chest. She wipes her nose on his upper sleeve and inhales and tries to slow her breath.

Colin smells good, like the first few days of autumn. Or an overpriced vanilla/sage candle that Annie would buy for their living room. She inhales again, and then again, and then one more time.

Yes, Colin smells so very good.

"I don't want to talk about this for the rest of the night," she says. He rubs her back in reply. Indeed, Annie wants to have one night when she can pretend that everything and nothing has changed. That she might not have syphilis, and that her husband really had saved her, and even if he didn't save her, he was at least decent enough to honor his promise.

"No one keeps promises anymore." She runs through her mental list: not Baxter, not Lindy. Probably none of the rest of them either.

"That's not true," Colin says.

"Please," Catherine says. "Like you're a shining example."

"I don't make promises. That's why I don't break them."

"Well, I'm not sure that's really any better," Catherine replies.

"I think it's perfect," Owen says, air whistling in the crater where his front tooth once lay.

Leon says, "Men can be real dicks."

Colin replies, "Hey, man, don't get personal!"

And Leon waves his hand in apology. "No, man, not you. Her husband."

Colin nods and says, "Oh, yeah. Cool. True." He untangles himself from Annie and rises, his knee cracking as he stands.

"Shit, I'm getting old."

"I wish I were still twenty." Annie's face sags.

"No, you don't." Colin offers her a hand, and she links her fingers into his, braiding them, intertwining them, sealing them together. "I promise."

27

CATHERINE

They've detoured toward the Quad, Catherine having convinced Colin that Annie is too drunk to break into the stadium, and besides, none of them have tools to crack the lock. If she were in her test kitchen, well, she would have a blowtorch and a crowbar and maybe even some shears for heavy-duty sunflower stalks that could do the trick on metal, but she is not there, she is here, and thus, the Quad it is. Besides, though she blames Annie's intoxication, Catherine knows that if they were to get nabbed, even by some innocuous campus police officer, *TMZ* would have all the ammunition they need to nearly literally drive the final nail into her professional coffin. No, thank you. She's not Owen, she's not a streaker, she's not reckless, and damn it if she's not going to try to salvage what she can.

She glances at Owen. His upper lip has swelled to the size of a Meyer lemon.

"Does it hurt?"

"I've felt better."

She nods. He winces.

She remembers that time in Florida when they discovered that Penelope was allergic to bees. She'd been so fearless back then as a toddler. She was chasing one around the kiddie pool, happily clapping her hands together, trying to squash it in her palms. She was singing "Itsy Bitsy Spider," and everyone at the pool thought it was perfectly adorable; no one really thought she was going to catch that thing. Catherine had been preoccupied changing Mason's diaper and examining his diaper rash, and Owen was on the phone with a client who was having some legal crisis or whatnot. She remembers that he kept rolling his eyes and making the "blabbermouth" signal to her with his fingers. She probably knew back then how much he hated it—the law, his job, all of it—but one of them had to work, and she was just a start-up blogger. They never discussed it, really. She listened to his occasional complaints, accepting the intrusions on their vacation, and frankly, figured that this was life. Real, grown-up life. You're not always happy; you don't always get what you want. Catherine would have liked a kid who wasn't colicky, whose butt didn't look like raspberry jam, and a website that got more than 120 hits a day, but so what?

Anyway, neither of them was paying attention when Penelope finally got close enough to make her kill, only the bumblebee took aim first, like a kamikaze pilot: stinging her squarely above the eye. Owen saw it before Catherine did, Pen screaming by the kiddie pool, and even when Catherine did see it, she didn't leap to her feet the way she should have. She was tired, and she was wipes-deep in a dirty diaper, and frankly, she figured Penelope was hysterical because one of the other kids had taken her plastic fishing rod that they'd bought at the overpriced gift shop. But Owen hung up on his client right there and then, and dashed to their three-year-old daughter whose eye was already the size of a walnut and growing.

Why do I always compare injuries to foodstuff? Catherine wonders now, mulling Owen's upper lip, a little lost in the memory of that day. How well he calmed Penelope, how he coaxed her into swallowing some Benadryl, how he turned his phone off for the rest of the day and bought her ice cream and somehow miraculously cajoled her into taking a nap (she had given up naps at sixteen months).

He's been a better husband than she's given him credit for, she thinks. Or maybe it's just that he's been a better husband compared to Annie's. Maybe neither of them—she or Owen—has been particularly good to the other recently. But perspective is everything today. Owen's not screwing around; Owen's not sending pictures of his dick to faceless women. Annie was right about promises, though, even if she hadn't been referring to them, to him, to Catherine. No one tries to live up to them anymore, like the vows they took fell away when a sliver of space, of independence, squeezed into their union. When he left his job. When she discovered that she could do hers without him. But maybe Annie knew long before any of them that you don't hold grudges for broken promises, because no one ever keeps them anyway. Maybe that's what a happy marriage is: forgiving small lapses in the face of the bigger picture.

It's not what she thought at twenty, and it's not really what she'd like to believe at forty, but refusing to accept the difference between idealism and reality is really just naïveté. Catherine hasn't made it this far in the surprisingly cutthroat world of domestic blogging on naïveté. *TMZ* could now tell you that. Her staff could now tell you that. Catherine, if she were being honest enough with herself to expose her own set of secrets, with her failing bottom line and desperation for a buyout, could tell you that.

She wonders who she'll be if the company goes bust. Sure, she'll scramble and find something new—an advisor at Martha Stewart, an occasional expert on *Good Morning America*. But it won't be *her* empire; it won't have been built with her steady hands from the ground up; she won't have the pride of ownership that made her willing—eager, almost—to make sacrifices in other aspects of her life that were inevitable. She watches Owen, with his easy demeanor, even when his lip is swollen like a potato, and he's slapping Colin on the back, musing over something that is lost to her. Maybe she'd just return to being his wife, Penelope and Mason's mom. She was "just" that for a while, and though it made her antsy, like she had an itch she couldn't scratch, she knows too that there's fulfillment to be found in all sorts of corners. Not forever. She wouldn't want to do that forever. But reinvention isn't always the worst thing in the world. She watches Annie, stumbling in her stride for a step, then grasping Colin for support. Annie knows all about reinvention; she's managed to keep her head high.

She thinks of Bea, who was always dodging a jab, shadowboxing against the punches thrown her way. But Bea would be the first one to tell her that she couldn't have gotten into the ring alone, that she needed the five of them alongside her. Catherine shouldn't be standing in the ring alone either. She didn't mean to, didn't expect to. Perhaps she should invite Owen into her corner too.

The campus is full of shadows now, the last rays of the orange sun bouncing off the trees, casting unexpected glares that come and go, rise and fall. The colonial festival is nearly over; one of the men has changed out of his culottes but still dons his gray wig and topcoat; Betsy Ross complains loudly about the blisters on her fingers from all the sewing.

Tomorrow they'll be packed up, gone. Tomorrow Bea's birthday will have shifted to the last day of the yearly cycle, another 364 more until they all stop to remember her.

The guy in the topcoat hands her a printout. "Had extras of these. Throw it out if you don't want it." He shrugs and continues disrobing.

It's the Map to Freedom—the trail where the settlers came in with their aspirations for a new life, how they built the city, where they planted their roots to stake their claim toward independence. There's Franklin Square, there's the Liberty Bell, there's Independence Hall, where they signed the Declaration of Independence.

Catherine squeezes the bridge of her nose, presses her eyes tight. How far would she walk for her own aspirations, her own slice of independence?

Too far, she worries. Too far.

28

COLIN

Colin is staring up at the brick facade of the Quad, thinking about all the nights he spent stretched out on Bea's bed, talking until their eyes drooped and they scrambled awake a few hours later, late to whatever 9:00 a.m. seminar they'd foolishly enrolled in. Then he thinks about that first time he met Annie, in the unisex bathroom. How he could tell she was mortified to find him standing there in nothing but a towel; how he tried to make small talk to ease her mortification; how he thought it was pretty dang adorable that she was so mortified in the first place. It's funny, he thinks, how breaking up with Annie that night had led him to Bea, and now maybe Bea is leading him back to Annie.

"Let us in!" Annie shouts, shaking the locked metal gate under the arched entrance, covered in shadows. "Let us in, you fuckers!"

You'd think she'd been imprisoned and was clawing her way out, not the reverse. Colin gazes at her. He can see she needs something, needs someone. He thinks to himself, *She needs me.* It's been a long time since someone's needed Colin. Since Bea. His patients need him, he supposes, but that's work. That's different.

"These weren't here when we went here," Catherine refers to the bars and gates. "Also, I obviously can't break in. After the day I've had."

"Yes, they were here," Owen replies.

"No, they definitely were not."

Owen sighs and kicks his toe against the sidewalk.

Colin has a vague recollection of a security booth of sorts and maybe an ID detector, but he's not so sure he's willing to take sides. Metal bars? He can't say. He wouldn't lay down his life on it. Besides, what's the difference? Things changed. They can't expect that they can come back here and everything will be as it was.

Annie is still braying into the open courtyard denied to her by these jailhouse bars, her voice echoing around the empty humid air. Colin watches her and wonders if she'd been this brazen, this unfettered back then, freshman year, if he'd have slept with her, if he'd ever have broken up with her. It's almost as if he's seeing her—the one who'd been lurking underneath all the other bullshit—for the first time. She steps onto a bar and propels herself a foot higher.

"Let us in! I know you're in there! I know you can hear me!"

"Who are you screaming at?" Catherine asks, edgy, glancing around for amateur videographers. "Also, can we leave?"

"Everyone," Colin says. "She's screaming at everyone. Let her."

"Fuck you, security guards! Fuck you very much!"

Colin cocks his head as Annie roars; he's a little turned on right now. She dismounts from her perch, her voice growing weary and cracking, and resigns herself to defeat. She slides down onto the grimy sidewalk, and Colin is beside her in an instant, rubbing her lower back, the space between her jeans and her pink tank top, which is damp from her efforts. He tries not to notice the stains of dog urine folded into the sidewalk cracks, the years-old chewing gum embedded into the concrete.

Annie rests her head on his shoulder, the warmth from her body spreading onto his like an aura cast over them both. Maybe he should tell her about Bea, about what he did. He wonders if she'd still find him heroic, if she'd still let him guide her through the wreckage of this day, if she'd still link her elegant fingers into his.

He suspects that she would not. He killed her, goddamn it! How do you go about spilling that secret to her dearest friends, the ones who loved her best? She asked for it, sure, and it was only a way to ease her suffering, but he didn't have to; he could have drawn the line. Still, though, he would like to tell *someone*, ease his own burden, release himself from the prison of that secret.

Annie groans and drops her head into her hands. He gazes over and wants so badly to fix her, to fix this. He's never noticed her ears before, how small they are, how delicate. She's wearing huge solitaire diamonds, which tug her earlobes low—probably a gift from her husband, who felt guilty about one thing or another. Colin has never bought a woman diamonds. Once, he considered a little necklace for Bea, but it felt like too much of an admission, an open gesture or proclamation, and they didn't do open proclamations. And anyway, he didn't buy them back then. That's what matters now.

No, Annie wouldn't forgive him, wouldn't understand that he would have walked to the end of the earth for Bea, so that's what he did. Bea hated secrets, and yet because of her, he bore a nearly unimaginable one. He bristles, fidgeting on the sidewalk, uncomfortable with this new irritation with Bea. He gazes again toward Annie, who's biting her thumbnail, pensive, silent.

Annie must feel his stare and turns to meet his eyes.

"I can't remember why I needed to get in there so badly." She shrugs. "It's stupid. I'm tired."

Colin offers her a kind smile, the one Annie fell in love with eighteen years before. "I can't remember a lot of things. Sometimes it's better that way."

29
LINDY

Of course he wasn't there. Her old professor, Mr. Pearson. What did she expect anyway?

Well, she expected him to be there, to grovel, to apologize. To say, *I was wrong about you.* That's what Lindy Armstrong is used to now, and damned if she didn't actually believe she'd get the same from Mr. Pearson that she does from everyone else. Not everyone. Not Leon. Maybe not Tatiana, but usually her too.

Not now, though. Tatiana is onto her, aware of the ruse, even if she's not exactly sure how deep the ruse runs. She doesn't know about the baby. Maybe she'd forgive her for Leon, but certainly not for the baby.

Lindy runs her fingers over the shiny black grand piano in one of the music rooms she found unlocked, a disharmonious melody echoing around her. She slides out the bench and steps around it, sitting on the worn leather, straightening her spine, arching her fingers above the keys. She holds them there, then falters. She doesn't know what to play. She eases her hands back into her lap.

She's lying to Leon too. And that lie is much more complicated. What's she supposed to do? Just blurt it out? *Surprise! I barely know you! I'm carrying your kid!*

She lies so easily to him, just like to Tatiana. Like she's not even trying. That's how easily she manipulates them, *like butter.* She and her sister used to do that *Saturday Night Live* routine—*like buttah.* She lies so easily it's like sliding a knife through warm butter. It's all so second nature to her that she can't even differentiate between all the untruths: which are worse, which aren't so bad.

Lindy sighs. She should call her sister, but they're not on the best of terms this week. Who knows why? Actually, she does; she forgot to FaceTime for her niece's birthday, even though she promised, and then she subsequently ignored her sister's passive-aggressive texts suggesting that five minutes out of her very important life shouldn't be too much to ask. It wasn't. Of course it wasn't too much to ask. Why did Lindy make everything such a struggle?

Like buttah.

It's not like she can call Tatiana for advice. And it's not like she can ask Bea. Who else is left? Her manager? Her publicist? Is there anyone she can trust who isn't on her payroll? She squeezes her temples, a headache worming its way in.

Annie. Of course Annie is left, but that bond has been blown to smithereens. For the first time in years, though, Lindy wonders if maybe she couldn't try to glue it back together. Begin with apologizing for that moronic wedding weekend. End by telling her the truth, or some version of the truth. She doesn't have to, like, pour her heart out about unrequited love or anything. Just say, *Hey, I adored you, and I fucked it up, and I'm sorry.*

Her fingers find their way back to the keys, and she begins to play by instinct, by memory, but also by nostalgia, which she was certain she'd run out of years ago.

It's an old song, one of her first. She wrote it three months after moving to Nashville, and for the first time in as long as she could remember, she was alone. And alone not because she was being an asshole, but because she'd been brave enough to leave New York and Annie—though under unpleasant circumstances, it's true. But semi-brave all the same. To leave what you loved behind because it was self-preservation.

But this song, it isn't a song about loneliness; it isn't a sad-sack love song. It's a song about the courage you need to will yourself to fly, even if you aren't sure you'd ever catch air. A song about courage and faith and generosity of spirit. A song about just about everything Lindy lost after the wedding and after Bea, in the years that followed in Nashville, then LA. She sat beneath her windowpane long after sunset, cross-legged, in torn long underwear and a floppy, fraying sweatshirt, as time faded into itself, just like she had at Bruiser; and she wrote every last stanza, every last note. It got her a CMA nod, but that's not why Lindy loves it now, though for many years, maybe up until today, it was. The acknowledgment *and* the fame. That's why she loved it.

Now, her fingers glide over the keys, and she shuts her eyes and the music reverberates deep down, all the way to her soul.

No, now she loves it because it's hers.

∽

A funky-ish looking dude kicks her out. He's lanky and smug and wears Elvis Costello–like glasses and has a wiry goatee that isn't filled in enough.

"You can't be doing that," he says, beckoned by her noise. "This room is supposed to be locked."

"Is it bothering you?" Lindy asks.

"I'm writing next door, so yeah, it is."

She almost lashes out, telling him that whatever he's writing can't be as important as *her*, but she stops herself. Maybe without the Phillies hat he'd recognize her, be more deferential, let her stay. Maybe even beg her to play, beg her to teach him. But she's wearing the cap low over her face, and he doesn't appear to consider her special or famous or anything other than a nuisance.

Anonymous. That's what she is.

She rises, pushing the bench back with her legs, its feet squeaking on the floor.

"Sorry," she says. "I was just revisiting. I used to go here."

He softens a bit, his shoulders relaxing.

"Oh, that's cool. An alum. Did you learn anything? Did Pearson make you any good?"

"*Mr.* Pearson?"

"Yeah," he says, like he'd be speaking of anyone else. "Professor Pearson." He waves an arm like Pearson owns the place. "He's been here forever."

Lindy smiles. That's right. She'd refused to call him "Professor" because he had, like, seven years on her. Ten at best.

"He told me I was total shit." She laughs.

"Ouch! But . . . were you?"

She shakes her head. "I don't know . . . but I don't think so." Her hands find her pockets, her shoulders rounding downward.

"Hell if any of us know," he says, biting his thumbnail. "You do music afterward? Because, like, my parents think this is the dumbest major ever. They want me to be a banker."

"I think most parents want their kid to be a banker. At least, instead of a musician."

"Yeah." His face turns to shadows. "I mean, I guess I'll go on the interviews. Internships and all of that shit."

"Well, don't tell your parents that just yet. You haven't even gotten out there, haven't even tried."

"So you'd do it the same way all over again? Really?"

Lindy can see now that he's maybe nineteen—twenty, tops. Unsure, full of questions, just looking for a little hope.

"Oh, I wouldn't say that. I've screwed up plenty."

"Huh," he says. "So . . ."

Lindy tugs her cap lower, considering it.

"I guess I'd do it all over again, sure. But maybe not the exact same way."

"Hindsight," he says. "They say it's everything."

"Nah, not everything. There's foresight too."

"If I had foresight, I'd probably never do this in the first place."

"Maybe." Lindy thinks of everything that lay on her own horizon, of all the havoc—both beautiful and awful—her choices up until now are about to wreak, all the people she's lied to, all the hearts (mostly Tatiana's) she's about to break. "But maybe you'd know, and you'd do it anyway."

30

ANNIE

Annie has never been to a battle of the bands. In fact, she hasn't been out dancing or to a club or lost herself in the beat of live music since just after Lindy moved out. Sure, she digs it when her instructor turns up the speakers superloud in her spinning classes—she puts her head down and bobs her shoulders and *feels the music, feels alive*, but it's not quite the same, is it?

They've made their way through campus, down past the graffiti-covered bridge over the freeway, and onto the banks of the Schuylkill River, near the crew house, where those rower boys must spend half their days in and out of the water, coasting atop it for miles and miles. There are hundreds of others there now too: on blankets, with six-packs (or twelve-packs), sprawled on top of or next to or wedged near one another. It's dark by now, the lights of the river walkway illuminating the lawn, along with iPhone screens lit up like electronic fireflies.

Annie thinks this might be what Woodstock felt like.

Maybe not exactly.

But something. Maybe it felt something like this. Like community.

Annie can't remember the last time she felt a sense of *community*. That stupid PTA doesn't make her feel like she's part of any *community*! Her goddamn Facebook feed doesn't make her feel like she *belongs*! She thinks of Bea, and how maybe that was the last time she felt it, back then. Maybe, possibly, when she first met Baxter, but she lost herself so quickly with him, the constant swirl of pretending to be better than she was . . . God, how long has it been since she was at peace, since she felt comfortable in her own skin? Lindy challenged her once, to stop apologizing just for a day—don't say "I'm sorry" for her complicated coffee order, don't offer "I'm sorry," when some guy jostles her on the subway. "Stand tall," Lindy said. "You can do it. Then you'll start to stand taller on your own."

Well. *Look how well that worked out! Screw you, Lindy!*

She wants to text this exactly to Lindy—*Hey, fuck you for everything!*—but it occurs to her, very briefly and fairly hazily, that Lindy has made her bed (along with a fetus), so Annie will just let her lie in it.

Annie finds an open pocket on the lawn and tumbles onto the grass, the others following suit, Owen and Catherine flanking Annie and Colin like awkward bookends. Leon stands behind them, casting about, maybe searching for Lindy, maybe just feeling a little lost. Maybe stoned. Hell, Annie doesn't know. He's not her problem; she's not his babysitter. She's tired of being some man's goddamn babysitter!

Colin grabbed some Amstels at Wawa along the way, so he twists off a cap and passes one her way. She probably shouldn't have another—she's still a little glassy from the tequila at the house, but so what? *So what?* What's the worst that can happen? She'll ruin her marriage? Her husband will text her a picture of his disgusting penis that was intended for someone else and—*Oopsie!*—send it to her?

Annie has watched enough cop shows to narrow it down to one suspect. It's not difficult to figure out that "Cici" is probably Cecilia Kirkpatrick, whose daughter is in Gus's grade and who managed a deal or two with Baxter a few years ago. She and Baxter had gone to high school together. She remembers him telling her that—that they hadn't really been friends, but they hadn't not been friends either. At the time, Annie was impressed with Cecilia's ability to juggle a high-powered job, three kids, a Labrador, and a cushy position on the PTA (auction cochair!). Not to mention the upkeep at the Hamptons house. (They owned, didn't rent, like Annie and Baxter.) But now she wonders if Cici's life weren't just another Instagram shot, like so many Annie uploaded herself lately: all filter, no substance.

Well, shit. Does this mean she has to stop posting on Facebook? Does everyone know about this except her? Is she the laughingstock of the PTA? Does Cici swirl into meetings with her freshly made blueberry muffins and whisper to Rue McLaughlin (current PTA president): *Oh, that Baxter, he is just such a naughty little boy!*

Annie resolves to unfriend Cici on Facebook immediately.

"Hey," Colin says, leaning over, whispering in her ear. Annie feels his breath against her skin and thinks it feels like heaven. "Cheers."

"Cheers." They clink the necks of their bottles together, then Annie chugs half immediately. She hiccups. "Please don't tell me to slow down."

"I would never tell you to slow down."

Annie tilts her head back, peering at Leon upside down, like Gus used to when he was little.

"Why are you trying to find her? Don't you think she'd find you if she wanted to?"

"I'm just hanging," Leon says. "Don't worry about me."

"Maybe *you* should worry about you. *I'm* not worried about you."

"OK."

Annie rights her head, then scrambles to her feet. "Maybe we should all stop worrying about one another and worry about how *fucked* we are ourselves!"

"Annie!" Catherine yelps, her tone a little too pierced, a little too cutting. She glances around, eyes darting.

"What?" she yelps back.

Colin stretches his hand up to her thigh and guides her back toward the grass. His fingers linger for a moment too long, and Annie's not too drunk to notice.

"That's nice," she slurs, right up against his shoulder. "You're nice. You smell nice."

"Oh my God." Catherine sighs.

"Give her a break," Owen says.

"Give *me* a break," she replies.

"You two! *Just shut up!*" Annie says. "What is wrong with you?"

"Nothing is wrong with us!"

"Well, that's what I can't figure out," Annie says too loudly, her arms spanned into a *V*, like wings. "If nothing is wrong with you, why the hell are you so unhappy?"

"I'm not unhappy!" Catherine says, then catches Leon's gaze. "What? You don't know me! You don't know *us*. You don't even know *her*." She pokes the air, a breeze floating through, as if she were poking Lindy.

"No one knows anyone!" Annie shouts, and the rest of them clench their jaws, steel their eyes away from one another. But then Colin massages her neck, hard, deep into knots she didn't even know had, and she quiets. Thirty-six hours ago, Annie couldn't have imagined that Colin would be massaging her neck or that she wouldn't be basically having an aneurysm that Colin is massaging her neck. But now, she *deserves* this. She *deserves* the tequila and the beer and the massage and how good he smells and the fact that for once, maybe someone really is going to rescue her like she deserves to be rescued.

Oh God, yes.

Colin.

She'd wanted him to be her prince all along.

31

LINDY

Lindy knew the Phillies cap would work for only so long. She kept it low the whole walk down to the river, taking her time, slowing her pace, just enjoying the sun setting behind her, the rays bouncing off the downtown buildings, then the water, then gone.

She unplugs her headphones, turns off her phone.

She tries to remember what it felt like when she was here and twenty and anonymous and maybe nothing special. But she had her friends, the crew of them, and she had her integrity. And as she wanders down to the Schuylkill, she realizes, as one often does in *hindsight*, that this had been enough for her then.

And she had Annie. Even if she never had her in the way she wanted. It's probably time to accept that it was never Annie's fault in the first place. One of the first of a few small steps down the road to who she was then, closer to who she'd like to be now.

She has to tell Leon about the baby. If she is ever going to even attempt to reclaim an ounce of her integrity, she has to tell him. And if she tells him, this makes it real, and if it's real, she will keep it.

She slows her stride, her breath deepening. She knows she can't feel the baby kick this early, but she feels *something* in her belly. Maybe it's just her nerves fluttering. Hell, maybe it's that pretzel settling in. But Lindy steps forward and chooses to believe it's the baby. She's keeping it, of course. She almost laughs to herself at how deluded she was to convince herself otherwise. Well, she convinces herself of a lot of things. She won't beat herself up for trying.

She settles into her pace again. She'll now also have to tell Tatiana. Although she may have burned down that bridge, it may be irreparable. She'll miss T, of course, but she'll recover. That's who Lindy is. Or has become. After Bea, after Annie. Lindy could probably weasel her way out of it, but she finds that she has no energy to keep digging herself in deeper. No. It's time to stop trying to outrun it, time to call Tatiana and explain. Apologize. Accept the consequences that accompany a royal fuckup. Which is quite possibly the last thing in the world she wants to do. But when was the last time she did something she truly, utterly didn't want to do? She'd fled to Nashville rather than tell Annie the truth. Recording an album that she didn't cowrite didn't count. Sitting in a judge's chair for $4 million didn't count either.

No. Something painful, something terrifying, something that she could write a song about because it unearthed a wound inside of her that might never heal.

Bea's funeral. That was the last time she'd done anything she truly couldn't stomach. She hadn't wanted to face the four of them; she hadn't wanted to accept that Bea was really dead. But she went, she tried to forge peace, and when that went to shit, she resolved to never do such a thing again.

Oh, Bea.

She stops on the graffiti-covered bridge over the freeway, the traffic shooting back and forth below. People going on with their lives, to and fro, on to wherever, to whoever awaits them. She grasps the sides of the overpass, doubling over, a sudden cramp in her side, the ache of an old memory that she'd long ago erased. *Bea.* Lindy's startled at her stream of tears, which come immediately, angrily, without warning. She mourned her friend a decade back and put all that to rest. So maybe that's not what she mourns now. Maybe this isn't just about Bea. It can't be just about Bea; that would be the easy way to grieve. No, perhaps what she's mourning is her old self, the younger her who lost so much along the way from then to now.

No one would say that about her, of course. No one would ever think she had anything to grieve. You could read a million articles on Wikipedia, or Google her until the end of days, and no one would say that Lindy Armstrong didn't have everything she ever dreamed of.

But none of them would know what Lindy dreamed of.

∽

She thinks there's a chance Leon and her friends might be here, at the battle of the bands—that if Leon wanted to find her, he'd know she'd gravitate toward a melody. It's a small chance, sure, and if they're not, she'll hurry back to the house and tell him. Maybe she's still biding her time—opting for a few more moments before she shifts the axis of everything. Because keeping the baby will, of course, turn her world upside down. Tatiana might roll over and play dead for most of their battles, but this humiliation will be too much. And Lindy knows it is indeed a humiliation. A terrible one. An unforgivable one. The tabloids will go bananas; Lindy's publicist will go bananas. She'll take it on the chin, she will. Because it won't be as awful as what Tatiana will be taking on her chin. Lindy's wronged a lot of people in small ways, she realizes this now to be true. But maybe no one as egregiously as this.

She thinks of fucking Colin that night at the W after too much champagne and a plate full of marzipan-vanilla wedding cake. Maybe that one was just as awful too; it's not like she didn't know she was breaking Annie's heart. She did. She slept with him anyway.

Lindy squints across the lawn and tries to make out her old friends in the sea of the crowd. She'll tell Tatiana to blame *her*, not Leon. The same she'd say to Annie if she'd ever had the gumption: *This was on me. I wanted to wound you so you knew how it felt. I should have considered that we're all wounded enough already.*

Yes, she'll say the same to Tatiana, whom she'll mourn because part of her loved T, but perhaps the whole of her didn't. Lindy doesn't know if she's capable of loving the whole of anyone anymore. Maybe the baby. The little pea. She'll start with that. She'll say this to Tatiana too.

But in a few minutes. She'll say this to Tatiana in a few minutes. For now, she'd like to see an honest-to-God battle of the college bands, to remember what it felt like to play for the hell of playing—to be the best you could on that stage, on that night, in front of that crowd. And she wouldn't mind seeing the fireworks afterward. She hasn't enjoyed July 4th fireworks in years; she's always working, always busting her ass for a show, always shaking hands or speaking into a microphone or (most often) tossing back a shot or three to celebrate.

But the lawn is dark, other than some cell phones and the dim light from the river lamps. More anonymous faces. Strangers. She can't see any of them. Who knows if this is a wild-goose chase? Still, she feels like Leon could be here, that maybe he came to find her too. So she tilts up the Phillies cap and stands on her toes, hoping for a better view.

∽

Somehow, the hipster guy from the music room beat her down here and is at present inexplicably standing directly beside her. Unlike in the hallways of her old haunting grounds, he recognizes her immediately.

"Holy shit!" He literally slaps his hands together. "Why didn't you say who you were?"

"Oh no. Shhhh. Please."

He has no regard for this at all. "Lindy Armstrong! Holy fuck! I didn't know you went here. Why aren't you, like, up on the wall at the studio? Now I can tell my parents, *I can be Lindy goddamn Armstrong*, and they can lay off my case!"

"Shhhh, please. I'm really just looking for my friends. Please, I don't want any attention."

"Pearson!" The dude is shouting at the direction of the stage perched by the water. *"Professor Pearson!"*

"What?" Lindy whispers. "He's here?"

She's suddenly mortified that he'll think she came here for him, even though, of course, an hour or so she *had* gone in search of him.

"Hell, yeah!" Hipster dude is easily excitable. "He organized this whole thing!"

"Shit." Lindy stubs the grass with her motorcycle boot and slams the Phillies hat back on her head. "Shit, shit, shit."

She swivels around to hightail it back toward campus, but hipster dude has a hand on her wrist, unafraid of personal space boundaries, and is tugging her toward the river, tugging her toward her past.

"No, no, no," she protests, literally digging in her heels. "I'm good. I'm OK."

"Are you shitting me? You gotta get up there! People will die to know that Lindy Armstrong is making a surprise appearance."

"No, I couldn't. It's not why—"

He cuts her off. "Of course you can! Isn't that the point you were trying to make back there? Of course you can! If you can, we all can. Lindy goddamn Armstrong! Holy crap!"

Lindy sighs and acquiesces because, after all, this is what she does, this is who she is; this is why people value her. She's Lindy goddamn Armstrong.

Time to put on a show.

32

OWEN

Owen feels a little guilty about how badly he screwed up the day. Maybe last night's inebriation was forgivable—who doesn't want to get a little hammered after years of politely sipping wine at an occasional stuffy dinner party?—but today, well, he royally tanked it. With the fight at the frat house. With the Jell-O shots. With everything. He's not quite sure what he was thinking other than he wasn't. Maybe he just wanted to touch the sun one last time like he thought he could back then.

He thinks Catherine will forgive him for his mess, because he can't imagine the alternative. He wants to, *has* to, *needs* to forge a bit of peace right now, sitting on the riverbank lawn. He says, "Cath, *Cath*," trying to get her attention, but some guy keeps tapping the mic onstage, saying, "Testing, testing," and then everyone shouts: *"It's working!"* and Owen's words float out into the air, swallowed up by the other noise. Owen wonders how much of a disaster this show is about to be; it doesn't exactly seem like U2 at Soldier Field or even Lindy Armstrong at the United Center. He tries to catch Catherine's eye again, to remind her of that U2 show, to make a joke about the couple they went with, a work colleague and his wife, who argued so much the entire night that he and Catherine later giggled that their theme song must have been "With or Without You." Those two, they hated each other. Owen later heard that they'd split, but he'd left the firm by then, and maybe he should have reached out to see if his old friend was OK, but he didn't. It felt like ancient history, like a different life.

Catherine is focused on her phone, which chaps him. Goddamn it, why can't she ever just enjoy herself, sink into the grass and be still and listen to the chatter and hum and buzz of *life* around her? When did she make the choice that work was more important than the rest of it?

"Cathy," he says. She doesn't look up. Of course, maybe it's not just work. It's also possible that she's just ignoring him, giving him the cold shoulder, something he's grown used to recently. Neither of these two options brings him comfort.

"Cathy!" he calls louder. He sees her eyes grow a little wider, her muscles clenching in her grip around the phone. She heard him. "Come on, stop working for one goddamn minute."

Annie lifts her head from Colin's neck, her eyes a little unfocused, her cheeks a little flushed. "Yeah, come on, Catherine! Stop working for one goddamn minute." She wiggles closer to Colin, then jolts up again. "There's more to life than work!"

"Like Facebook?" Catherine says, her fingers still tap-tap-tapping away. "Like Instagram?"

Annie furrows her brow and juts her lower lip. Colin runs his thumb in figure eights over her hand and whispers something in her ear that Owen can't detect but which must be pretty wonderful, because the lines across her forehead ease, the delight in the corners of her mouth returns, and she points her smile upward.

"She's right," Owen says, facing toward the stage, a little irritated now at Catherine. "Annie's right." He clarifies because his mind is slippery from the painkillers and the beer, and he wants to be sure that he's clear. "There's more to life than work, Cathy. She took the words right out of my mouth."

He's pretty sure he hears her snort. Why is he rehashing this again, here, now? Like she's suddenly going to be entirely different from who she is, like this argument is going to end any differently than it always does?

He winces and wishes the guy onstage banging on the mic would shut the hell up. His head hurts and his tooth hurts and frankly, everything about his being hurts right now. He stares toward the night sky and wonders what happened to his old office buddy, whose wife left him shortly after the U2 concert.

Owen realizes you might think that back then, back whenever, it might feel like a different life, but it's not, really. It's all connected. U2 and this battle of the bands, then and now, twenty years ago and today. You might want to pretend you can reinvent yourself; you might want to give yourself that chance to wash it away into blank space, but you can't. The past doesn't change. That history doesn't change. You don't change unless you swim so hard upstream that you're lucky not to exhaust yourself into drowning. It's no surprise that no one else changes either.

Maybe that's why Bea brought them here. Maybe that's what she's trying to say.

The past is who you are. The future is what you do with that.

33

CATHERINE

Catherine can see that Owen is trying to get her attention. Annie and Colin are neck-deep in each other, googly-eyed and intoxicated, which irritates Catherine for no reason at all, and Owen keeps twisting his head around them, trying to catch her eye, murmuring her name, imploring her to *stop working*, and like, she doesn't know, what? Party? Is that his way of apologizing?

This is so Owen! Minimal effort, maximum expected reward.

She gazes, instead, at her phone. Her team is keeping her abreast of the continued fallout from her outburst today: the memes are still coming, the YouTube hits growing by the hour. Her apology is the top story on People.com, but there's no further word from Target. Most likely they're strategizing on how to distance themselves from the absolutely catastrophic implosion of the nondomestic domestic goddess, Catherine Grant.

Stop working. He wants her to stop working when what she really needs to do is scramble harder, faster, to try to fix this.

My God, her husband has no clue about the complexities of her life, about how hard she's tap dancing to salvage the company she's sacrificed the past five years for. That might be the most insulting part of this whole mess—that she once loved all the things her company stood for. Loved testing homemade baby-food recipes for the kids. Loved inventing a toxin-free lemon cleanser. Loved mixing and melting a rainbow of hot waxes and molding them into lavender-scented candles for teacher gifts. That she might be thought of as a fraud, an interloper? Surely, yes, that is the most wretched part. Her mistake, she realizes, is that she had to be the *best* at all this, rather than simply enjoy it. In her quest to be on top, she turned into the biggest fraud of them all: someone who didn't revel in the joy of it, someone who didn't practice what she preached. That, she thinks, is the worst fraud of all.

Her chin quivers, but she holds it steady. It's hardly the most difficult thing she's done today.

Owen glances over one more time, and that's it. She's on her feet, sending him a clear signal. (She thinks.) She digs her heels in next to Leon.

Try harder.

She tries hard, for God's sake! Maybe not with Owen, she realizes. But with everything else! Wouldn't it be nice if he could carry her this one time, with this one thing?

"Something you want to talk about?" Leon leans in.

She folds her arms. "Does it look like there's something I want to talk about?"

He shrugs, then rises to his tiptoes in his unending search for Lindy.

"It seems to me, since you're out here chasing *her*, that you're not the best one to give advice." Catherine's phone buzzes in her palm, and she can't bring herself to look at it.

"I never said I was the *best* one. Just one."

Catherine considers this and hates, then loves, then hates, that it makes so much sense.

"I like being the best one, the most perfect."

"That much is obvious." Leon smiles.

"I don't know how to do it any other way."

"Listen, I admire my artists who are balls-out a hundred percent of the time."

"But?"

"But what?" Leon looks at her, genuinely curious.

"There's a 'but' coming."

"No buts."

"But 'perfect' is a moving target."

Leon smiles, and Catherine can see why Lindy is drawn to him. The way his whole face opens up into kindness in the folds around his eyes. She thinks again of Bea, that maybe she sent him because she couldn't be here herself. She knows this is crazy—Catherine doesn't do spiritual juju—but she thinks it all the same.

"I mean, I'm just saying that sometimes the bar keeps getting higher, and that's enough to make the hurdles impossible for anyone."

"I don't know how to do it any other way." She's ashamed of this admission. Not because working balls-out is anything to be ashamed of, but because if she were truly the best, she wouldn't have to find another way in the first place. That's why she keeps that notebook full of other people's ideas; that's why it was almost inevitable that she'd be exposed eventually. *She is a fraud!* In more ways than just one. How long did she think she could keep it secret?

The emcee steps onto the stage, asking the crowd to hush. They're about to begin.

"I don't know how to change," Catherine says quietly. Then she remembers who she was twenty years ago, how far she's come since then, and considers that it's not that she doesn't know how, it's that she's choosing not to.

34

LINDY

Lindy can't decide if she's relieved or not that Mr. Pearson remembers her.

"Of course I remember you," he says, distracted by the first band's opening number, an off-kilter headbanger, which ensures that they certainly will *not* be winning this battle. "I didn't think you'd become anything other than a waitress who sang at bad open-mic nights."

"Yeah, I think that's pretty much a direct quote." Lindy presses her lips into a thin line and falls quiet while the lead guitar plays a particularly disharmonious chord arrangement. "I couldn't have been worse than these guys."

"Works in progress." Pearson grimaces. "Works in progress. And obviously I was wrong about you. I'm not too proud to admit it."

"Well, I appreciate that," Lindy says, because she does. Because it's the acknowledgment she seeks, after all.

"I'm not above admitting I was a bit of a dick. But it's not like you weren't a pain in the ass too."

Lindy nods, conceding. She was. She still is. She'd like to be less of one, though.

A kid who looks like a skinny freshman and who should seriously rethink the mustache he's growing thrusts a clipboard at Pearson.

"The full lineup," he says, then notices Lindy. "Like, whoa."

Will, the hipster dude from before (full name: Will Overland—he tells Lindy this three times), waves him away. "Give her space, Brandon, give her space!"

"I don't need space. It's fine."

"She certainly doesn't need space," Pearson agrees.

"So you're still keeping me in line?"

"If I didn't, who would?" He grins, and Lindy can see that maybe he was never the enemy, that with his calloused guitar hands and slightly graying temples, and his Sex Pistols shirt that somehow doesn't look too trying-too-hard, maybe they could have been friends back then. She'd been too busy trying to buck the system, stick it to the man, to realize it.

"I'm trying to be less of a pain in the ass," she says.

The lead singer introduces the band as Strange Fiction, and a smattering of applause spreads throughout the lawn. The singer looks mildly embarrassed to be there, but gamely continues, counting down—*three, two, one*—he jumps into a semisplit and lands on his feet—to the next disaster.

"I put them on first so that no one could compare them to any of the better guys," Pearson says. "God bless them, they want it so badly. Maybe with some time . . ."

"You'd never have even put me on," Lindy says. "I mean, if you'd done something like this. Which you never did. I firmly remember you being absolutely no fun."

"Oh God." He rolls his eyes. "I was young and inexperienced and wanted to 'prove myself.' You guys had to take me seriously." He hesitates. "But you're right. I probably wouldn't have put you on anyway."

"Twenty years later and you still suck."

Pearson laughs easily. "Not as much."

"So you really didn't think I'd make it?" Lindy's not sure why his answer matters so much to her, but it does.

"It wasn't my job to tell you that you'd make it. It was my job to teach you enough so you could."

"So you take credit for my success?"

He smiles. "I take credit for nothing." He gestures to Will, who pops over like a lapdog. Pearson tells him to cut the band's third song. Will trots toward the stage to deliver the message: *Sorry, you suck.* "But, listen, you *were* a pain in the ass. Just to be one. Maybe I was a dick just to be one back. But you weren't standing on principle; you just wanted to get under my skin for the sake of it. You were a pain in the ass for the sake of it."

"But that's what made me successful."

He checks something off on the clipboard. "I doubt that's what made you successful. That might just be what you *think* made you successful."

"Well, you already told me it's not my talent."

"I didn't say that." He looks at her now, and she can tell it's not because she's Lindy Armstrong, but because she's some kid he used to know, some kid who maybe had potential but who was too pigheaded to recognize that artistic integrity and asshole-like behavior were not synonymous.

"I could have sworn I heard you say that," Lindy mutters, the levity of the conversation gone.

"That was the problem with you, Armstrong. You always heard what you thought people were saying, and never paid close enough attention to actually hear the truth."

∽♫

Will has taken to the spotlight like a cat does to milk. He's lingering too long up there, soaking it in, bantering with the crowd.

"He's just supposed to introduce the next band," Pearson says. "He's become a bit of a stage whore."

"All right," Will says, his voice echoing over the lawn. "Before we bring out the next band, I have a *huge* surprise for you."

Some guy shouts, "I hope it's not that they suck dog shit like the last band!" And then a few people clap and holler.

"Quiet down, quiet down. I want everyone on their feet for this." No one moves except for three drunk girls down front. "Come on, everyone up!" Reluctantly, like a slow wave, people slink upward.

Lindy looks at Pearson, who appears befuddled.

"Ugh," she says. "Shit." She had hoped Pearson had quietly nixed Will's unbridled enthusiasm for a performance when her back was turned.

"We have a grade-A superstar here tonight!" Will yells, too loudly, the mic too close to his mouth.

"Shut up!" the same heckler bellows.

Will ignores him. "Seriously, folks! Who watches *Rock N Roll Dreammakers*? Come on, don't be embarrassed to admit it!"

At least half the crowd claps now, a buzz building, a rumbling like an oncoming train.

"OK, who owns her last album, *Don't Make Me*?"

The screaming starts in the back and begins to build to a fever pitch.

"Jesus," Lindy says. "I'm not here for this! Did you approve this?"

"Do you seriously think I approved this?" Pearson replies.

"Well, shit." She chews her lip, blows air out of her nose. *Shit.* She wanted to find Leon, have a private moment to tell him the truth.

"I don't remember you ever wanting to be inconspicuous."

Everyone is on their feet now, clapping and hooting, and Will, to his damn credit, has handled the crescendo perfectly.

"Well, *all right*! That's what I thought! Because we have *Lindy god-damn Armstrong* here tonight!"

The three drunk girls down front start shrieking—real, honest-to-God shrieking.

"I don't want to go up there," Lindy whispers. "This isn't what I came here for!"

"Really?" Pearson raises an eyebrow.

"Welcome her, everyone! She's a good old alumna, and she's back to show us how it's done!" Then he adds, shaking his free fist toward the blinding stage lights: "Screw you, Mom and Dad! I'm not applying for that internship! Yeeeeeeeeeaaaaaaaaahhhhh!"

The lawn has ignited now, yelling and howling and exploding with applause that until maybe yesterday, Lindy thought was everything. Validation, triumph, acceptance, happiness. Somehow happiness had gotten tangled up with all the rest, so skewed and jumbled in the mix that she wasn't able to parse it out, distinguish it all on its own.

Lindy stands immobile on the side stage, paralyzed, her legs unwilling to surrender, torn between what she *thought* mattered since she lost track of her old friends, and what she realized actually *does* matter in the hours since they've been reunited.

"You'd better get out there," Pearson says. "Do what you do best."

"What's that?"

"I've kept tabs," he says. "Even caught a show two years ago."

"Really?" Her stomach spins. "So, then what? What is it that I do best?"

"Fake it." He shrugs. "I have no idea how you didn't know that until today."

35

ANNIE

"Oh my God!" Annie shouts, covering her ears like Gus used to when he didn't want to be told it was bedtime. "Oh my God, does it always have to be about her?" She looks at Colin. "Seriously? Why is it always about her? Why am I sitting here listening to a Lindy Armstrong concert instead of enjoying my perfectly fine evening with crappy college bands?"

"Shhhh," the undergrad next to her hisses. "I'm videoing!" Her phone is held aloft, her face aglow with the bliss of stumbling on a real superstar in their midst.

"Oh, shut up!" Annie says. "She's not all that special." Then to Colin, she says, "Seriously, what is so great about Lindy goddamn Armstrong?"

Annie's on her feet quickly, marching down the lawn, weaving in and out of the throngs of fans who are pulsing to the beat of one of Lindy's new singles, something about female empowerment and girls' nights and no men allowed. (Annie recalls that might be the name of the song: "No Men Allowed," because she thinks Gus was singing along to it last week on his iPhone.) Annie finds this particularly ironic, not only because she's now downed several of those beers that Colin toted along, but also because Lindy knows *jackshit* about girls' nights and friendship and female empowerment.

"This is crap," she says to two girls who have their arms flung around each other's shoulders, nearly tearful with reverence.

"She's the worst," she says to another threesome, who gape at the stage with doe-eyed admiration.

"She didn't write a word of this!" she hisses, as she passes by those crew guys, the very ones who beckoned Annie here in the first place.

She wedges her way through the drunk girls up front.

"Excuse me. Excuse me. *Excuse me!*"

"Ann, Annie, stop!" Colin is two steps behind her, Leon, one step behind him. Catherine and Owen pull up the rear somewhere.

Colin reaches for her shoulder. "Come on, Ann. Come on. Whatever you need to say, don't say it here."

"Why are you so forgiving of her? Why are all of you so forgiving of her?" Annie cries. "You!" She points at Leon. "She stranded you with a group of strangers when you came all this way for her!"

Leon stares at his feet.

"And you!" She pokes Colin in the chest, hard enough that he winces. "She slept with you knowing it would break my heart!"

Annie can feel the blood rushing to her face, and even though she's well past tipsy and also pretty sure that Colin is into her tonight, she regrets the jealousy, the shrillness in her voice. She is not that woman! She lived with Baxter's infidelity for years, for God's sake. Why is she dragging this up now?

So she adds as a means of distraction, "Bea didn't like it either."

"You're right, Bea didn't like it, OK? I've felt guilty about it ever since. But she forgave me, and we moved on, and can we please stop keeping score, all of us? All of you? She just . . . she wanted us to be *happy*. She made me promise to be happy."

"When did she make you promise this?" Catherine asks.

"I don't know. Sometime!"

"I'm confused," Catherine says. "Like, this was part of a philosophical discussion that you guys had while she was in Honduras after the wedding? I thought she was barely reachable in Honduras?"

"No," Colin says.

"No, what? It was not part of a philosophical discussion that you guys had while she was in Honduras?"

Leon, who knows nothing about any of this, says, "Well, I'm sure they had some private conversations every now and again, right, dude?"

Catherine narrows her eyes. "When did she tell you this, Colin? I'm unclear on the timing."

"I don't know! Years ago. What are you, the Bea police?"

"Years ago, when?" Annie cries. "I tried to reach her for weeks before she . . . for weeks before we got the news, and she never called me back. Was she mad at me? Oh God, I shouldn't have thrown such a fit at the wedding." She eyes Catherine. "I'm sorry, I shouldn't have. I was so stupid!"

"She wasn't mad at you, Annie." Colin's voice has turned brittle. "My God! Will everyone just stop and shut up for a minute? It was when she was sick, OK? She told me this when she was sick. Her cancer came back. Quickly." He shakes his head like he still can't believe it. "She was too sick to call you all back after the wedding, with all of that crap, and then she was gone. OK? None of this is about you . . . or you . . . or you." He points to all of them. "It was about Bea. What she wanted, how she wanted it, so stop turning this into drama that it's not."

Lindy wails in the background. Annie's hand covers her mouth, her eyes wide and round and bright with shock.

"What?" she says.

"What?" Catherine says.

"Fuck," Colin says. "*Fuck*. This isn't . . . this wasn't how you were supposed to find out. You weren't supposed to find out."

"What?" Catherine's shoulders are curled up near her ears. "What are you talking about? Cancer? I don't . . ." She pauses, like the news is broadcast from Mars, taking a moment to catch up with her brain, with the reality. "Wait . . . you knew she was sick this whole time? You told us it was a car accident! It came from you—all of this! It started with you . . ." She spits out the words. "You let us sit around and wonder about the details. Wonder exactly what happened. Do you know how many times I've replayed Bea slamming into a tree or swerving off the road? Or . . . dying by herself, all alone?"

"I wasn't letting you sit around!" he says. "I just . . . she was dead, OK? She was already dead! Would it have been better to imagine her going through chemo?"

"That's bullshit! If we'd known, maybe we could have helped save her! Done . . . I don't know . . . but *something*. I cannot *believe* the lie started with you."

"We couldn't have saved her," Colin snaps. "You can't just go around saving people just because you want to! I'm a doctor. I know!"

"That's ridiculous!" Catherine yells. "I cannot *believe* this. What did she used to say? That we were her family. Well, we obviously weren't family. You don't do these sorts of things to family! Lie to them forever."

Lindy hits a high note.

"SHUT UP, LINDY ARMSTRONG!" Annie screeches toward the stage. "And by the way." She jabs Catherine. "That's exactly what I've been saying! Family! What crap. Look at her. *Look at her!*" She flaps her arms toward Lindy. "We're not family! She was the first to leave. She's always leaving us. She never wanted to be part of *us* for a second longer than she had to be!"

"God, Annie, will you please just let it go!" Catherine raises her hands in the air. "She's only acting this way because she was in love with you and doesn't know any better. Christ! It's been forever. Can we get it together already? Move on?"

Annie feels something run cold, then hot, then cold again, through her. But then she's marching once more—the others falling in line behind her like an army of ants, toward the stage, onward, with no idea what she's doing exactly, or why she's doing it, only that she's *had it up to here* with Lindy Armstrong. After she stormed off from the hospital, the rest of them were wondering whether Lindy was OK (well, they were half wondering whether she was OK, but it's easy to pretend they were swelling with concern), and here Lindy was, preparing for a surprise performance! Looking to boost her notoriety! Hoping to relive her glory days!

"This is just crap. Crap, crap, crap." Annie says. "That she made this weekend about *her*. This weekend was about *Bea*."

"I thought this weekend was about you guys," Leon interjects.

"Why are you even talking?" Annie shouts, mostly because Lindy is howling the chorus, and no one can really hear anything if they don't match their own voices to decibel level ten. "Why are you even here? Did Lindy invite you? Did Lindy call you and say, 'Baby daddy, come down and play house with me?' Did she? Did she do that?" Annie doesn't even realize what she's said until they're all frozen, heads tilted, jaws agape slightly more than they should be. Finally. One secret slithers out that's impossible to ignore. Annie doesn't dare breathe.

"Crap. Crap, crap, crap," Annie repeats.

Leon has gone pale; the rest of them hover with quiet alarm, doing the math, putting the pieces together that Annie did just hours ago. Catherine looks particularly put out, her face folded into a permanent scowl with the rapid-fire admissions of the last five minutes, like they'd all somehow decided to purge themselves of the shadows of the past decade.

Annie resolves not to apologize. The world owes *her* an apology, so too bad if she's screwed up someone else's day. Welcome to her life for a minute!

She nudges her chin higher, self-righteously aimed directly at Leon. "Well, now you know."

Lindy croons out the final trill, and the crowd explodes like early fireworks.

"Well, now I do," he says.

"You're welcome."

Catherine glares at Colin. "We're not done discussing this."

Before he can answer, Annie flips off Lindy's general presence, yanks Colin's elbow, and marches toward home.

ლ

There's so much to say between the two of them. Colin is angry, flustered; Annie can feel it in the heat emanating off his neck when he closes the door behind her, and she lingers too close. She should ask him about it, what really happened with Bea, but if she speaks, if she ruins this moment, she might lose her nerve. And the last thing Annie wants to lose is her nerve. So they say nothing. Colin latches the door, and Annie stretches out her arm to clasp his, and then together they descend the steps to his old room. Annie tries not to breathe. If she does, she might wake up from this; she might come to and discover that none of it is real.

ლ

Now Annie finally breathes.

Colin runs his fingers over her collarbone, down through the crease in her breasts to her belly button. His fingers feel nothing like Baxter's, even though they're just hands, limbs, extensions of one's body, and Baxter has probably felt her collarbone and belly button a thousand times.

He shifts on top of her, and his old bed squeaks, then lurches an inch lower. Colin laughs, low, deep in his throat, and Annie wonders if it always used to lurch like that, if he's laughing because of an old memory, or if it's because they're both a little awkward, even though sex is so much more casual now in middle age, now that it's not some sort of contract like it could have been back then.

He kisses her neck and she inhales, her chest rising, and refuses to think of Baxter and how he probably did this all weekend with Cici. Instead, she finds her mind drifting to Lindy. She tells herself to focus. *Focus, Annie, focus!* This is what she's dreamed of forever; she wants Colin to kiss her neck forever. She remembers all the moments she dawdled on this bed, sitting, feet flat on the floor, full of excuses to stay. *Have you studied for chem yet? Maybe we'll order in a late-night pizza?* Lingering another moment in his room, waiting for him to notice her. But she *had* heard Catherine back on the lawn, heard what she said about Lindy, and now she replays it: *"She's only acting this way because she was in love with you."* Even as Colin's fingers trail down her belly button and around her back and under the edge of her black lace underwear, sliding them lower, then off entirely.

Annie sighs, and he asks, "Is this OK? Should we not be doing this? Is this not OK?"

"It's OK; it's more than OK." She links her hands behind his neck and pulls him down to meet her lips so he won't ask again. She's still woozy from the booze; she doesn't want to stop and think about what they're doing. She doesn't want to stop and talk about it. If they do this right, if they do it well enough, she won't be thinking about Lindy or Baxter or Cici much longer.

But she does. She does think about Lindy at least for another moment or two. She plays back that kiss from way back in their dump of an apartment, when they lived together, separated only by that putrid green sheet. She plays back Lindy's loyalty for so many years, her sister-like possessiveness that went a step beyond kindhearted friendship; she plays back Lindy's betrayal too, in taking the one thing she knew Annie wanted. But then Annie considers that perhaps she also betrayed Lindy in her own way; she wasn't as naive as she pretended to be; she wasn't just some dumb poke from Texas. Maybe she knew, knew enough, noticed how Lindy sometimes sang toward her at her shows, how Lindy never thought any of Annie's suitors were good enough. (They usually weren't.) Maybe Lindy should have told her, but also, Annie didn't make it easy. She didn't want to know. Didn't want to lose the friendship when Lindy's feelings went unreciprocated, at least romantically. Annie loved Lindy, sure, but not in the way Lindy needed her to. So instead, Annie behaved as if Lindy's feelings were never there to begin with, imaginary, an apparition.

She considers that perhaps she treated Baxter and his infidelity in exactly the same manner: *close your eyes and act like it's not there.* Then maybe it never happened at all.

Colin kisses her again, his fingers tangling her hair, then flitting down her back, pressing on her hip bones.

"Hey," he says, pulling back, pushing his arms straight so he hovers above her, stares right at her. Her cheeks burn from his stubble, but she finds she doesn't mind.

"Hey," she says and bites her lip.

"Are you with me?"

She hesitates, examining the face above her, how she has loved it for two decades—the protruding cheekbones, the honest eyes, the flush of his tanned skin, the flicker of a scar over his top lip. She's not going to let Lindy ruin this for her. She's not going to let Baxter either. Her whole life, everyone has taken a tiny piece of something from her, etched out a sliver of her heart like she wouldn't feel the twinge, wouldn't notice it was missing.

But Annie's never taken anything she's wanted just for herself in as long as she can remember.

So if it's Colin, then for once, goddamn it, so be it.

She nods. "I'm here." Then she eases his head lower until he kisses her.

She is here with him, so very much *here* with him. She flushes the rest of it from her mind, until there's nothing to think about at all.

∾

Colin falls asleep almost immediately, tucked under the navy sheets, the duvet lumpy atop his heavy chest. Annie is cradled in the nook of his neck, right under his chin, listening to his breath. The front door opens and slams shut, the others trekking home, she supposes. No one stayed for the fireworks, after all.

She moves her hand over Colin's warm skin, her palm covering his heart. She lets it linger there for a moment, worried she might wake him, that he'll realize what they've done and bounce quickly to his feet, casting her off like any of the rest of the women who scurried up the steps, out of the house, and out of his mind.

She rolls back onto her own pillow, palming her own heart. She's a little more sober now; she has a little bit of clarity. And she can feel it there, beating to its own cadence, beating strong enough to echo all the way through her flesh and bone.

Thump, thump.

Thump, thump.

Annie stares at the ceiling, with Colin on her left and her heartbeat in her right.

She wonders if this is what it's like to feel alive.

36

COLIN

Colin wakes with a start, his throat parched, his neck sweaty. Annie is curled up into a C beside him, her spine a snaking line up her back, then disappearing under a mess of her hair. He climbs over her gingerly, careful not to wake her. She deserves this sleep, a chance to recover from all the blows of the day.

He hopes that what they just did doesn't add to her list of complications. He hadn't thought it through—what it would mean exactly, where they'd go from here. He tiptoes up the steps, desperate for water, like he's been stranded in a desert for days. He glances back through the dim light; she hasn't woken. He hesitates, torn between going back to her, under the warmth of the duvet, and indulging his more immediate need to quench his thirst.

His bare feet pad upward, the hardwood squeaking. He turns again. Still asleep. He can slip upstairs quickly and be back down to her before she realizes he's gone. This isn't a metaphor, he tells himself, no deeper meaning than that he's truly parched.

He reaches the living-room landing and flips on the light to get his bearings.

"You." Catherine is parked on the couch.

"Jesus Christ!" Colin jumps.

"Me."

"Were you just, like, sitting here in the dark? Trying to be creepy?"

"I was sitting here in the dark, trying to figure out why you knew she was sick and none of the rest of us did. What made you lie, how that lie spun out of control."

Colin scratches the back of his head. "Don't you have more important things to be dealing with right now?" He looks around. "Where's Owen?"

"Bathroom." She nudges her head toward the second floor.

"Well, maybe you should deal with your own business before nosing into mine."

"That's just it," she says, rising. "It wasn't just your business! It was all of ours."

"Not really."

"That wasn't your decision, your thing to decide! We were always a unit; who chose you to be special?"

"God, Catherine! Bea did, OK? Bea chose me. Bea called *me*. Not you, not any of the rest of them. So Bea decided."

"That's crap." Catherine sits back on the couch. The cushions bounce.

"I think it's crap that you're sitting here pretending that you care about the 'unit,' that you care about all of us." He waves an arm toward the upstairs bathroom. "When was the last time you included Owen in your 'unit'?"

Catherine glares at him.

"Owen texts me every once in a while, OK? He's not as oblivious as you think."

Catherine sits up straighter.

"Listen, I don't judge. I don't really even care that much. I'm not married, so before you point that out, don't bother. But you're not angry because Bea told me. You're angry because she *didn't* tell you. Because you have this martyr complex that maybe served you well once, but seems to me is not working too well for you now."

"Listen," Catherine interjects.

"No, *you* listen," he retorts. "Start *listening*, stop telling. Stop goddamn telling everyone what to do, like you always know best."

Catherine grows a little smaller, fidgeting with her bracelet.

"Fine. Fine. I don't always know best."

"Well, that's a small miracle."

"I just would have wanted to help her. Maybe try, you know?"

Colin steps closer, then sits on the arm of the couch.

"She was sick, Cathy. Really, really, sick." He pauses. "She . . . she didn't call me until it was almost the end."

"I don't . . ." Catherine's face twinges, and Colin rests a hand on her arm. He hopes he isn't miscalculating, reading her wrong after all these years. But she's a fixer, he realizes. She might be the only one of them who would get it, who would make the same choice that he did when Bea asked, when she begged.

"It came back furiously, Cath. We see it often, too often. I mean, doctors do. Not me, in plastic surgery. But remission one minute, terminal the next." He squeezes her arm and doesn't let go. "She just . . . she was in so much pain. She wasn't herself. Her eyes . . . they were cloudy, unfocused . . . you know how she always was. They weren't *Bea's*. She was breakable, so tiny, so thin. White and colorless. Her lips were cracking, her hair all but gone. And . . . she wanted to let go. Be done with it with dignity." He shrugs and doesn't dare look up. "So she called me. Not you. Not because she didn't love you. But . . . because you couldn't help."

Catherine's chest rises and falls. Colin can hear her breathing.

"She called you . . . because you're a doctor," she says finally.

"Yes."

"Because you were the only one she could ask."

"Yes."

Catherine's face twitches, and she bats her eyes quickly. She stares at the floor, and Colin stares with her.

Eventually, she asks, "At the wedding? Was she sick?"

Colin hesitates. "I . . . I don't know. Truly. I don't think so . . . or maybe she was sick and didn't know. She would have told us." He pauses. "Things probably would have gone differently if she had or if we'd known. But . . . no, I don't think so."

"Oh, Bea," Catherine says, her voice finally breaking, shrinking into the couch as if the enormity of this news is simply too much to carry. "Oh my God, Bea."

"She wanted it this way. She begged me, told me it made her happy. Or . . . made it easier." He falls silent. "I mean, none of it made her happy." He slides his hand off her arm and drops it back in his own lap. "Listen. I've never told anyone. That's how she wanted it. That's what she asked. It's why she also asked me to lie about how it all went down."

"OK," Catherine says. "OK."

"OK?"

"It must have been awful."

"For her? Or for me?"

Catherine's nose pinches. "I suppose for both of you . . . I'm sorry I got so angry with you. I guess I don't know everything about everything."

"Sometimes it's better not to."

She manages a halfhearted laugh. "I suppose I've never thought of it much like that."

Colin shivers and crosses his arms, then rises to close an open window near the dining table. He cranks the pane closed, locking it. He wishes he felt better, relieved at his admission, but his stomach churns like he's been cast out to sea.

"So, please." He turns toward her. "No one else knows. And I think that's how it should be."

"We all have secrets." Catherine narrows her eyes, and Colin senses her assessing him. Then her face falters, softening. She looks younger, almost the way she looked back then. "Bea's entitled to hers too."

Colin nods and exhales. Then he flips the light off again, heading back down the steps to Annie, forgetting his thirst, forgetting why he came upstairs in the first place.

37

CATHERINE

Catherine sits in the heavy darkness for what feels like forever—absorbing the brunt of Colin's confession, considering what she would have done if Bea had asked her, how she'd live with her choice either way. She's surprised to find herself totally devoid of anger at him, like she geared up for a war, and once she was on the front lines, discovered that, in fact, she was a pacifist. She doesn't think she could have done for Bea what Colin did, and part of her admires him for his selflessness, even if she's unsure how to feel about it. Catherine likes to think of herself as the type of person you call in a crisis, but the notion creeps up on her, slowly, like a tide ebbing, that acting strong and being strong aren't the same thing. Bea was strong when she asked for Colin's help. Colin was strong in breaking his own heart and granting it to her.

Finally, when her legs feel steady enough to bear her weight, she rises. She slips up the stairs. The bathroom light still creeps out underneath the door; Owen is still locked behind it. She doesn't know how long he'll be in there, so she scampers up the ladder to the trapdoor, the best she can do for an escape from the claustrophobia she feels inside the walls of this house.

He apologized on the walk home from the concert. Catherine had to give him that, even though she didn't want to give him that. But he did, and she said, "OK." Like words could just erase a day's worth of disaster. More than a day's worth. It had been months running into years. But she's culpable for that part too.

In marriage—one that manages to stay together—that's what happens: someone apologizes, and what are you going to do? Hold your resentment against him forever? Maybe for a night, maybe you're still pissed off when you click off the light for sleep. But the only other option, other than forgiveness, is letting your resentment seep down into you, into your pores, into your veins, eventually into the foundation that you built together, and that undoes everything.

Catherine doesn't know if they're that far gone. Have they undone everything? When they shared Bruiser twenty years ago, she couldn't have imagined they'd ever find a way to undo everything. Their foundation from back then, though, that's maybe all they have left. Like a demolition site, they've gutted nearly everything down to the studs. Now they have what they built here, *here*; they have who they were and how they loved each other, and Catherine doesn't know if that's enough.

The July heat still bounces off the roof deck, even at this evening hour. Catherine eases down her bun, her hair already clinging to the sweat on her neck. She leans over the brick ledge of the roof and spies Lindy sitting on their stoop—sullen, no doubt—sulking at the mess she's made. An SUV pulls up and Lindy's on her feet, suddenly alarmed, her raised voice echoing up to the roof deck. *Probably her publicist, someone to make excuses for her.* Catherine thinks to check her e-mail to see how many excuses her own publicist has made for her. She trembles, even in the heat, her hair on end, at the notion that she and Lindy aren't so different, might actually be peas in a pod. Then she thinks about Bea and how she'd like to not be someone whom other people had to make excuses for. Ever.

She peers over the ledge again, but rocks back quickly on her toes, a wave of vertigo overtaking her. It's only three stories down, but it's too far for her to look again.

Catherine sighs and folds herself in half, stretching down to her toes, her arms flopping. Rag doll. One of her exercise DVDs called this the "rag doll" pose. Her back spasms, and she rights herself.

She finds a deck chair toward the back edge of the roof and lies flat atop it. She imagines herself floating. Floating up into space, floating away from all her other problems—Owen and Target and *TMZ* and her moronic need to always be the best at everything. Why does she always have to be the best at everything? Would *anyone* care if she said, *I cannot keep up this pace without stumbling. I cannot compete with twenty-five-year-old bloggers who discover muses in every jam jar, in every garden, on every corner.* Then she considers that age isn't the problem. The walls that she—*she*—built around herself are. All she wanted was to make beautiful things, candles, scarfs, centerpieces. No one cared that the used pea-green dining table never quite got white. No one cared that her French toast took twenty-three tries to master. Owen never complained when those boxers she sewed him sagged in the rear, or if the fly wasn't quite big enough.

She forgot all of this, though. In her quest to prove she was the best, that she merited all the praise, she forgot why she did this in the first place. *Joy.*

She should have asked for more help; she should have told Owen she was drowning. She could have said, *Sometimes I worry that I'm terrible at this job. I barely keep up our own house. I have a notebook full of other people's ideas. Can you help? Can I lean on you? Can you prop me up?*

Bea asked. Colin helped. It seems simple when you think of it that way.

She floats and floats and floats. Her hands, heavy and weighted, skim the paved roof, her fingers grazing something glassy and smooth. She reaches underneath the chaise and finds it: Owen's old letter, preserved like an archaeological relic in its frame.

It feels like a betrayal to read it, but she does anyway. She needs it, *they* need it. Maybe it can rescue them, this reminder of who they used to be. Maybe it will be the map to lead them out of this road of ruin. Their own Road to Freedom, Catherine thinks.

> Dear old you:
> I don't know what Bea wants from this. I mean, I don't know what to say to my old man self! Jeez. I guess something like: I hope you're filthy rich, and I hope that you've popped out a few kids. Kids would be cool. I hope that tonight (last night of college!!!) is legendary!!! I dunno, man. I guess I hope that you're happy. That you and Catherine live happily ever after. Don't fuck it up, dude. She's pretty great.
> Your young you,
> Owen

Catherine laughs out loud, then slaps her hand over her mouth in surprise. But what was she expecting? Shakespeare? Still, though, it's so Owen, and she laughs again. He was just a kid—they both were, and if there's any hope for their happily ever after, they have to rejigger their expectations of who they were (to themselves, to each other) and who they're yet to be.

The fireworks begin their dance overhead: a pop, pop, pop, then meteors of reds, then whites, then blues. She closes her eyes, white lights still flaring behind her lids, the cacophony keeping her company.

She doesn't know how long she lies there; she doesn't know how long Owen has been standing beside her, gazing up at the sky, contemplating his own set of thoughts, his own laundry list of mistakes. She only notices him when he startles her by rattling the chaise when he lowers himself and sits beside her.

"Jesus!" she says, jolting up quickly.

"Sorry, I thought you knew I was here."

"No." She shakes her head. "No . . . Your mouth. You're not lisping. Is it better?"

He runs his tongue over his gap, over the missing veneer, and winces.

"It hurts. But it might be fine by tomorrow."

Catherine falls silent for a long time after that. She's not sure what else to say, or maybe she's waiting for him to say something else too. She doesn't know. She doesn't think he knows either.

"Do you miss this place?" she asks finally. The fireworks have slowed for the moment, waiting to build to their big finale.

"I didn't think I did. I mean, not when we're in Chicago—I don't miss it when we're there. But, yeah, maybe a little."

She nods.

"We were better then," he says.

"We were *simpler* then," she corrects.

He shrugs. "Maybe. I don't know."

"I don't want to be unhappy."

"I don't think anyone wants to be unhappy."

Catherine wants to reach for his hand, tell him they shouldn't be, that together they'll find a way to fix their unhappiness. But she doesn't have a recipe for that, a cutesy rubber stamp to compensate for five years of spiraling. Besides, if she and Owen are going to be OK, it's going to take more than romantic proclamations, more than sworn declarations on the roof of their old house with their old selves haunting them.

So, instead, she eases back into the chaise, and he sits beside her. And they watch the fireworks tap dance across the darkened sky, hoping to wake tomorrow to a brighter day, but knowing that the lights of tonight might be the brightest they'll shine for a while.

Then she reaches for his hand anyway.

38

ANNIE

Annie is floating in a state somewhere between dreaming and conscious-ness when the shouting brings her to. She raises her head from Colin's pillow, and beside her he does the same. Lindy. Lindy is screaming at someone—no surprise. The doorbell blares.

BEEEEEEEEEEEEEEP.

Lindy shouts again over the buzzer.

BEEEEEEEEEEEEEEEEEEEEEEEEEP.

"Ugh," Colin says, his hand worming its way over her stomach. "What the hell?"

"I don't know. More drama." Annie sighs, trying to relax back into his touch.

But then another voice. She sits up abruptly.

Oh no. Oh nooooooo.

Her hand floats across the floor, seeking her clothes. Instead, she finds Colin's shirt, crumpled beside the bed. Annie hesitates. Then she grabs it and tugs it over her head. She scampers barefoot up the steps. To her back, Colin says, "What? Hey. Hang on!" She hears him scurry to his feet.

Annie already knows who will be waiting for her when she flings open the door, but she's shocked all the same.

Baxter has his finger on the doorbell, like the president on the nuclear button, poised to blow it again at any moment. Behind him, Lindy is working herself into a fit.

"You have no right to show up here! How audacious can one person possibly be?"

"Annie." His voice craters. Annie barely recognizes him, this broken version of her husband. His polo is disheveled (and she thinks she sees a mustard stain), his shorts are unironed, his wild hair nudges north, and his skin is splotchy and pink.

She's so stunned, she says nothing. She and her husband stand in the doorway, eyeing each other, staring without words.

"You don't deserve to speak with her!" Lindy yells from the street.

"Lindy," Leon says, "this isn't about you."

"It's about me, Leon!"

"For Christ's sake, Lindy! You have a kid inside of you that you failed to mention. You have a girlfriend and you have me and you have a shitload of problems, so stop making *this* problem all about you!"

"So the kid *is* a problem," she says.

"Jesus," he says. "Do you ever hear what anyone else is saying?"

"Annie," Baxter tries again.

"Can you not take the hint?" Lindy says from behind him. "What do guys like you need to take a hint?"

"You don't know anything about me." Baxter swivels toward her, angry now. Annie can't remember the last time she saw him anything less than placid. Annoyed at her sometimes, yes, when she posts on Facebook or whatnot. But not angry. Not actually up in arms, prepared to fight. She wonders if he thinks that he's here to fight for her. If he thinks he can win.

"You don't know anything about her!" Lindy yells.

"Lindy, please," Annie says finally. "Stop screaming."

"I'm sorry." Baxter returns to Annie. "I'm so goddamn sorry!" He retrieves a bag resting at his feet. "Here, this . . . I got the owner of the store you love on Main Street to open up tonight. Just for you." He thrusts the bag forward.

Annie takes it as if she's in a dream, without glancing inside, without really registering exactly what is happening.

"I-I . . ." she stutters.

"It's that necklace you've wanted. With the three diamonds."

"Oh."

"Here, let me open it, put it on you." He takes the bag back.

"No." Annie shakes her head, feeling a bit like she's mired in quicksand. "No . . . I . . . a necklace won't fix it this time, Baxter."

A vein bulges in his forehead, the same one she sometimes sees when she pokes her head into his home office and he's mired in a deal that's going south. She watches the vein pulse, a light shade of purplish-blue, and Annie knows he understands. *This time.* She knew about the last time too. Last time he assuaged her with a bracelet and better behavior. This time, shiny jewelry isn't enough.

He shuffles his flip-flops. Baxter is wearing flip-flops! He must have rushed out of the Hamptons rental in a whirlwind. He recalibrates. "I was stupid. I was . . . I just . . . I miss you . . ."

"I've been gone for a day. *A day!*"

"No, no. *You.* You were gone for a long time."

Annie inhales sharply at the accusation. Not an accusation, actually. The truth. Her hand flies to her neck. After so many years, this is the moment they're finally going to start telling the truth? She swallows, her mouth suddenly dry. She's not sure they're ready to peel back everything, expose everything to each other. She's not sure *she's* ready.

"You're only here because you got caught," she says.

Before Baxter can reply, Annie hears Colin's footsteps behind her, then feels his presence next to her. Baxter's eyes shift from Annie to Colin to Annie's oversize gray V-neck to Colin once more. His face drops. She thinks she should cower, be ashamed of the obviousness of what has occurred, but Annie is tired of being ashamed. She is so very, very tired. If Baxter wants to air their dishonesties, their battle wounds, then let's start now.

She bites her lip and doesn't apologize, doesn't pretend it's anything other than exactly what it looks like.

Finally, Baxter says, "I screwed up." Plainly. Honestly.

She thinks he's going to add, *So did you*, but something stops him. She isn't sure what, because it's not as if he's wrong. Perhaps it's because he understands his penance. That you can't go around casting off responsibility for falling into a trench when you were the one who helped dig it. "I can't lose you now," he adds. "Please. There's Gus."

"Don't you dare. You should have thought about Gus before—"

"It's a midlife crisis," he interjects. "Like that Porsche or that stupid raw-food diet! Oh my God. No, you're right, I shouldn't have brought up Gus." He starts weeping then.

Annie hasn't seen him cry since his dad died, and a small part of her splinters. Not really for Baxter. Maybe a little bit for him, yes. But for both of them. How wrong they've gotten it, how wrong they've gotten each other.

"Jesus, you have never looked more beautiful than right now," Baxter manages.

Colin sighs, and Annie glances over at him, as if she's just remembering he's there.

"You have to forgive me," Baxter stammers. "I mean . . . you don't have to . . . I mean . . . please. I'll get you anything . . . necklaces, bracelets, rings. Anything." He sputters to a stop. "Sorry, sorry. I know you don't want that crap." He sighs. "I just . . . please tell me how to fix this."

"Annie," Lindy says from the sidewalk, "you don't have to settle."

Annie gazes over Baxter's shoulder to her old friend, and she feels herself soften. There is something in Lindy's tone, something about her sympathy, that reminds Annie of something else. Love.

Love.

"You just . . . don't." Lindy nods, as if she understands that it has come to this, that Annie finally sees it. "I told you that forever ago. It's still true."

"Annie, please," Baxter pleads. "She's right. I don't deserve you. But I'm asking anyway."

But Annie is still processing Lindy, struggling to focus on Baxter, struggling to grasp all this. She has never been good in a crisis, never been the sturdy one who keeps a cool head. It's why she started with the pills, why she loses herself in the distortion of the posed, filtered, reassuring images of her Instagram feed.

She breathes in, breathes out.

"Please," Baxter repeats.

She finds a reserve that she didn't know she possessed, refocusing on him, steadying her voice, her resolve.

"Not tonight," she says, hoarse. "You don't get to come here and do this tonight."

"But . . . I drove here straight from the beach . . ."

She doesn't budge. Another surprise to them both. Annie budged so often that she usually couldn't even sense when her footing was giving way.

"I'm staying downtown," he manages. "Please. Tomorrow?"

Annie considers this and then nods. Then she closes the door slowly, gently, as if it might shatter if she's too forceful. Her white knight arrived. But it turns out maybe she didn't need him to rescue her after all.

39

LINDY

Lindy wants to punch that asshole's lights out.

"I just want to clock him square in the nose!" she spits, once she's regained her composure and Baxter has fled in his Escalade. She's not even sure why she lost it in the first place. Actually, she is. She thought she was over it, this, *her*. She *is* over it, she tells herself. But she's still allowed to care. After two decades of not caring, it's OK to let that in again, just for a bit, just for a gasp.

She sits back on their front stoop. She beckons Leon to sit next to her, but he will not join her. He keeps his distance a few feet away, pacing in the street. The alley in front of their old house is wrapped in darkness again, the fireworks done for the night—all of the hoopla, the Fourth of July hubbub snuffed out for another year . . . the Maps to Freedom folded-up dead ends. She rolls the toe of her boot over an old cigarette butt, shredding it apart.

"Is her husband an asshole or what?" she mutters, and Leon throws his hands up and then slaps his thighs.

"Jesus Christ, Lindy, is there anyone you're not angry with? Other than yourself, of course."

"What the fuck does that mean?"

He stops short, every muscle clenched, and Lindy thinks he's about to scream to the sky. Instead, he blows out his breath slowly, like a deflating tire, until he has nothing else to give.

"I don't know what to say right now."

"Because I'm pregnant?"

"Not because you're pregnant!" He starts pacing again. "Well, sure, fuck, yeah. Maybe because you're pregnant."

"Well, this is exactly why I wasn't going to tell you."

"So you *weren't* going to tell me."

"I didn't mean it like that! God, I have a girlfriend, Leon. So don't absolve yourself. You knew I was with her!" She stands now, ready once again for a fight.

"Well, I regret it!"

Lindy drops back to the steps abruptly.

"So you regret this. Well, great. Fucking A. Gee, grand surprise that I wasn't like, signing up for a baby registry as soon as I took the test. Should I have sent you pink-and-blue balloons instead?"

"God, Lindy. Come on. I regret *my part* in it. I'm a grown-up, so I can admit when I fucked things up." He pauses. "I don't regret . . . this." He gestures toward her, but she's staring at the pavement and misses it. "You are just . . . you are such a pain in the ass. Why?"

Lindy thinks about Tatiana, how, finally, her actions will have absolutely irreparable consequences. There's the baby now. There's no hedging, no excuses, no manager or publicist who can clean up the mess she made of things. Pearson was right—she's a pain in the ass for no reason at all. Just because she can be.

"So this is how it feels to be a grown-up," she says.

"Yup."

"It sucks."

Leon's laugh cuts through the air.

Lindy drums her fingers on the stoop, a beat, a rhythm, to calm her. Grown-ups face regret; grown-ups own their culpability; grown-ups try to do better.

"I'm sorry. I should have told you sooner. That I was pregnant. I didn't know how. I didn't, if we're confessing things, know if I wanted to. I . . . I guess I'm not known for perfect etiquette."

"All true statements."

"I don't know what kind of mother I'll be." Her fingers slow, the beat now lost.

"None of us really knows who we'll be until we get there."

Lindy gazes upward. She thinks she hears Catherine and Owen on the roof. She wonders if Annie's OK inside, wonders if Annie finally understood what had simmered inside of Lindy for so long. She thinks she saw it in Annie's face over Baxter's shoulder: the recognition of the truth, of what really splintered them all those years ago. Lindy's surprised to discover that this calms her, that she no longer has to run from the secret or the rejection or the tiny hope that maybe Annie loved her too. Lindy wonders if Colin is comforting her now instead, or if Annie even needs to be comforted.

She eases back against their old stoop and realizes she's ready to let it go. It's been long enough, it's weighed her down long enough. She realizes this is a gift, and she realizes further that it's a gift from Bea.

"Happy birthday, lady," she says aloud.

And she smiles because it's fitting: that even on her birthday, Bea is the one who gave something back.

40

ANNIE

After the ruckus, Colin pours himself a glass of water, then climbs the
steps to Annie's old room and tumbles into her bed. They were always
doing this back then: waking in someone else's room after wandering
around at ungodly hours. She smiles at the memory but doesn't follow
him up the creaky wooden staircase. Instead, she retreats to the basement for a bit of cool air, a bit of space.

She wanted this night with him to last forever, but even as she
wished it, she knew it wasn't what she truly wanted. Wasn't how she
wanted it, anyway. Maybe it's what she needed, though, she considers,
after all those years, all that pining. But more than that too; maybe after
Baxter, after their carefully edited life that she was culpable in creating,
maybe she needed this with Colin to recognize that she'd spent twenty
years editing him too, choosing the good parts, filtering out the rest.

It was fun.

It was wonderful.

It was what she hoped for after so many years of loving him.

It was different, and he made her feel beautiful and coveted and cherished.

But it was also less than she expected too.

It didn't feel indelible; it didn't feel like something she couldn't rinse away if she tried. She never expected that: to both get what she wanted and also realize it wasn't what she thought it would be. She'll have to be OK with this uneasiness, with the gratification of the reward along with the discovery that it wasn't what she'd hoped. Annie has never quite been OK with this—she's always too busy chasing the carrot to contemplate whether or not she likes carrots to begin with. So now she'll have to accept the uncertainty that comes with unexplored territory, of sincere vulnerability, of all the things she ran away from while chasing her carrot.

She falls onto Colin's bed, the comforter puffing up around her.

She thinks of Lindy tonight, protective and pregnant, and wishes she'd confessed her feelings back then. Even though Annie had her suspicions, it would have been nice to have known the truth. Annie presses her eyes closed: she knows she shouldn't expect the truth from Lindy when she's concealed plenty of her own truths from just about everyone. Besides, what would she have done with it anyway? Run from it, probably. Annie ran from a lot of things, another reason she and Lindy probably felt secure with each other. They were both experts, of sorts, in escapism.

She thinks of how Gus went through a phase when he was three, when she was up to, she didn't know, five or six pills a day. Everything was a haze, her parenting to Gus no exception. She gave him her time, all of her time, but her eyes were glassy, her brain static-y, her attention short and hiccup-y. Seemingly overnight, Gus grew destructive: crayons on their linen wallpaper, food strewn across the walls, epic wailing tantrums in quiet museum observatories. At the time, Annie read posts on CitiMama and worried something might be psychologically wrong;

he was so stubborn and so angry and so intent on challenging her that it was almost unbearable. And then, when she finally flushed the pills, he came back to her, her old Gussy, and she realized that maybe he just wanted her attention, the entirety of her.

Annie folds her arms over her face. Maybe that's all Lindy wanted too. That's why she took Colin from her. It was the only way to get her attention completely.

She rolls to her side and tugs a pillow over her head. It smells like him, Colin, down here in the basement. It smells like it always did. Like it did twenty years ago. She breathes it in over and over again. She lets herself enjoy this, the easy nostalgia from so long ago, until it's time to stop.

She pulls her phone from her back pocket, its fake glow the only light in this old cave of love. She scrolls through her photos, all tweaked and highlighted and filtered such that, looking at them now, they're unrecognizable. Nothing like real life. Nothing like *her* real life anyway. Probably not anyone else's either: not Cici Fitzgerald's, not the PTA president's, not Lindy's, or even Catherine's.

She finds that shot of her and Gus on the beach that day, when he looked constipated and she looked happy. Neither one of those things was particularly true. She wanted Baxter to stay on the beach with them until sunset, but she made it hard for him that day too—all she did was pace the beach looking for people they knew or arranged their blanket and umbrella so they were picture-perfect, or demand that he return to the house with a different set of board shorts (she'd already taken some photos of him in the pair he had on yesterday). It was no wonder he didn't last until sunset.

Not that this excuses him. He went and fucked Cici Fitzgerald! Years ago, evidently, and then again now. She thinks of Lindy's strident plea on the stoop, and she nods in the dark. She won't excuse it. She won't manipulate herself into believing she's to blame. But she has plenty to blame herself for too. Like how she didn't stop taking those pills, couldn't stop taking those pills, even when Baxter was begging for a second kid. They started trying, but Annie's heart wasn't in it. It's not that she didn't love Gus—she loved him more than anything. But that first year was so wretched—the darkness, and the self-doubt, and Baxter wasn't around to help. No one was around to help. The idea of enduring that all over again after the baby came . . . well, she knew she should dump the pills down the toilet, but they felt like home to her then. She couldn't imagine living without them, how they armed her with more confidence, how they made her shinier, happier, made everything sparkle like an Instagram filter, really. She was taking too many, admittedly.

So it was her own fault when it happened, the miscarriage. They saw the heartbeat at six weeks, and she thought she could pull it off and be all things—the Annie she needed for herself, the dutiful, perfectly pulled-together wife for Baxter, and the mother that Gus and her new baby needed to thrive—and so she didn't dump those pills down the toilet. And then they didn't detect the heartbeat at ten weeks. And Annie had a D&C, and Baxter went back to work the next day, and then they halfheartedly tried for another nine months to get pregnant again, but nothing took. Still, she didn't quit. She knew it was her fault that the baby had died, slipped out of her in her doctor's office.

She didn't know if Baxter blamed her—they didn't discuss it, really—but she wouldn't hold it against him if he did.

So it's not like Baxter's the only one who's done something unforgivable. Maybe this is her penance. For not flushing the five-pill-a-day habit when she knew better. Maybe if she'd stopped *trying so damn hard*, she could have just enjoyed their life, enjoyed *her* life, and maybe it would have changed everything. Or maybe Baxter would have still e-mailed that penis picture; maybe it wouldn't have changed anything. But she'll never know now. She only knows she didn't quit until she realized she might lose him for good, and that was enough to startle her straight.

She deletes them one by one, all the old photos. Savoring them with a tightened chest, like her heart might actually stop, then unwinding with each click.

She thinks it will feel better than it does. It's supposed to be an exorcism, after all. Of the years she was someone else, of the memories that weren't really memories—they were what she projected them to be. That's not life, that's not memory. That's fiction.

What she remembers, honestly, of Baxter, is that once, way back when, he was a good man. Maybe not today. But it wasn't like this always. She was looking to be saved, after Texas and after Colin and Lindy and Bea, and after the day-to-day life she'd found to be so overwhelming. It wasn't actually overwhelming, though. It was just life. How did she never see that? Why did she never see that?

Everyone does that, she considers. Everyone should be forgiven for that, at least in their youth. At forty, it's probably time to start living with your eyes wide-open. At forty, it's time to stop being rescued.

After a while, her eyelids are heavy and tug her toward sleep. She's deleted nearly all the images by now.

She'll wake up tomorrow with the pictures of their old life gone. She can't go back to that. Baxter drove here tonight thinking he could finally be her white knight. How could either of them have known that she'd finally realize she no longer needed one?

A fresh start.

She'll rise tomorrow and meet him for breakfast and say, "I've erased everything. Maybe you too. Maybe not. I don't know."

She'll say to Lindy, "I've erased everything. So let's be OK now."

She'll say to Colin, "I've erased everything. It's OK to let it go."

She'll say to herself, "I've erased everything. But found a piece of myself while doing so."

࿏

She'd forgotten about her letter, that old letter to herself that Bea insisted on salvaging. The next-door neighbor is igniting late-night fireworks, and they shake her from her rocky sleep. She tiptoes through the living room, which still smells a little like Catherine's French toast. Owen's passed out on the living-room couch, so she's careful because she wants to do this alone.

The letter is still in the box, the last one left. The others were gutsier than she was, more willing, more ready to tackle their failed ambitions, the ways their dreams had diverted from reality. (Well, maybe all of Lindy's had come true.)

Annie removes the letter from the box gently, like delicate heirloom china.

Her hand flies to her throat, the gasp of air audible.

She's confused at first, turning the frame over, then over again.

She's certain she'd scratched everything out, that it had been an illegible, amorphous blob of blacked-out aspirations.

But then, gradually, she gets it.

Bea.

Annie runs her fingers over the glass, the heat of her body leaving streaks that are there for a moment, then disappear into nothing.

The letter is blank. The page is blank.

Bea knew from the start. Bea brought her back here because she always knew, always cared, always promised to watch over them.

Annie took a little longer to catch on.

There is only a vast white space onto which Annie can pen her future.

Annie smiles now.

She had to come all the way back here to figure out where she needed to go.

There'd been a time when she'd post those musings online—she had a bookmark on her computer that turned cute little quotes into gorgeous works of art. Annie liked to post them on Instagram. They made her feel wise, made her think others would find her wise too.

Now she keeps this for herself.

∽

Later, when she's ready, she rests the frame back in the box, back where that blank page belongs. It's only then that she notices the envelope flattened against the very bottom of the cardboard, nearly undetectable.

Her brow furrows as her fingers graze the bottom of the box, then the envelope, and then she lifts it.

The handwriting is Bea's.

The letter is Bea's.

Of course Bea wrote her own letter twenty years ago too.

What did Bea hope for in twenty years? Who would she be? What did she dream of?

Annie stills her shaking hands and then presses the envelope to her chest.

She won't open it yet, not here, by herself.

They'll do this together; they'll do this as one. They're a six-point star, after all. They're family.

41

BEA

Dear all of you:

This isn't the letter to my older self you thought it would be; it's my letter to you guys, the best parts of who I was back when I could still be it. Maybe it would be more poignant to have included that other letter too, but I'll be honest—I read it before I wrote this today, and I thought, Oh my God, what did I know back then? Sheesh, I was a little bit of a navel-gazing, self-important idiot!

So this is the letter to your older selves that I'm writing.

I hope you forgive me for not being brave enough to tell you the truth about me, about my illness. I couldn't face you all when it came down to it; despite all my bravado, my devil-may-care breeziness, I wasn't brave enough to say good-bye. It was easier not to, to slip quietly away, though I realize it might not have been easier for you. I hope you forgive me for that selfishness too.

I hope that you've forgiven each other for the indiscretions of our youth. I hope that you've forgiven yourselves for those indiscretions too. Look, and I feel like I can say this now without sounding like someone's mother, being family doesn't mean that you don't hurt each other. It means that you might nick each other from time to time, but you love one another anyway.

I hope you all still love one another anyway.

I wish I could be there to meet Catherine and Owen's children, to gather around your dinner table for the most mouthwatering meal I'll ever taste; I wish I could be there when Lindy, on- or off-stage, realizes that she has nothing to prove but what she proves to herself; I wish I could be there to witness Annie discover happiness she doesn't think she deserves; I wish I could be there for Colin when he forgives himself for coming when I called; when he finds peace. I can't be. I won't be; but not because it isn't my greatest wish.

You were the best part of who I was for twenty-seven years.

That's all I really want to say.

A five-point star is a symbol of strength.

I'll carry you with me always, farther than you'd ever imagine.

Your friend,

Bea

They've gathered on the roof after Annie wakes them, shakes Colin, then Catherine, then Owen, and finally Lindy, on the shoulders, and says, "Come on, come on, this is important." Now, they've fallen quiet, reverential, I suppose, though I wasn't asking for reverence.

"She would have been forty. Forty and one day now." Annie wipes her damp cheeks.

"Oh, Bea." Catherine's voice cracks too. "Happy birthday." In this moment, Owen looks at her like he used to. Catherine doesn't notice, but I do. Maybe one day soon, she'll notice too.

"I'm glad she made us come back." Lindy eases back on the chaise and stares up at the sky. She turns toward Annie, who meets her eyes, neither of them afraid, neither of them angry, old grudges fallen like drawbridges. Then, because she's Lindy, she adds, "I know, I know, who'd have imagined it? I'm admitting that I'm happy."

"Holy shit!" Colin says, his palms to his cheeks in mock astonishment.

"Fuck off, Colin."

Everyone laughs, their tentative mirth spilling out into the Philadelphia night.

Annie, still clutching my letter, beckons Lindy, then the rest of them, over to the roof ledge. From the perch, there's a sliver of a view of the lights on campus, through the street lamps and the oak tree branches and the haze of memories that color everything.

"She made us come back," Annie says after a while, "to remind us that remembering where you came from helps clear the path for where you actually need to go."

Colin grabs her hand, then reconsiders, partly because she doesn't need him to, partly because he doesn't need to either. Instead, he smiles at her widely, eyes bright, heart open, and she gamely does the same. They'll never be more than they are now, on this night, in this heartbeat of time, with the July heat fading and distant stars in hazy view, old gunpowder floating through the air. This night will be enough. This night will be the start of something new.

I was never meant to be here forever. None of us are. I told Colin all this when he came to see me in New York and stayed with me until I was gone. I told him that day, when my throat was sandpaper, and my muscles were anchors, and my skin was fire. Some of our stories are shorter than others. Some last a hundred years. It's not how long you live; it's how you do it while you're lucky enough to have the chance. Not to sound like a cheesy country song. Maybe Lindy will write about me one day, though.

I don't know. Maybe I would have done some of it differently. Not because I regret death, but I regret that my death didn't only change my trajectory, it changed theirs too. They cratered after that, detonating any last bonds that could have been salvaged after the wedding. But I couldn't have known that; I couldn't foresee everything. I only could ask David Monroe to ensure that they showed up here, present, accounted for, under one roof once again, to form a new star.

Tonight, on the Fourth of July, on the evening I would have turned forty—though that was never in my stars, written in my destiny—they stay there on the roof's ledge for a while, my old friends just staring at the lights of the campus. The neighbors grow bored with their backyard fireworks and retreat inside. The alley settles into quiet again. The night sky no longer bursts with light. The roof falls into total darkness, and then Annie leads them toward the trapdoor when they're ready, grasping one another, trusting the others to lead them home.

ACKNOWLEDGMENTS

I have long wanted to write a reunion book, and I am grateful to Danielle Marshall for seeing the glimmer of potential in my early drafts and recruiting me to the Lake Union family, where I have been nothing short of dazzled. I'm further grateful that she had the wisdom to pair me with Tiffany Yates Martin, editor extraordinaire, whose guidance and insights were joyfully collaborative, and who helped elevate the book from something I was pretty happy with to something that I'm truly proud of. The entire team at Lake Union, including Gabrielle Dumpit, Christy Caldwell, Dennelle Catlett, and Tyler Stoops: thank you for your advocacy and spirit.

My agent, Elisabeth Weed, has been my friend and ally for more than ten years now. I've thanked her profusely in each book, and many times in person, and via text and e-mail too. She remains, simply, the best. My publicist, Ann-Marie Nieves, is a true dynamo, and I'm always glad she's in my corner. Thanks also to Kathleen Zrelak for her enthusiasm, wisdom, and tenacity.

Others without whom I could not have written this book: Christine Pride, for her early excellent and insightful editorial guidance. Laura Dave, for many things. Catherine McKenzie, for her counsel.

As I approached the end of my initial draft of this story, I shattered my leg and was hospitalized. The book was placed on hold while I, along with my family, recuperated, recalibrated, and got our bearings. I owe an enormous debt of gratitude to the friends who got us through those months: Jen Lancaster, Katherine Eskovitz, Erin Mand, Jennifer Chiarelli, Erica Fisher, Shirley Lu, Melanie Ornes Boock, the women on the dinner rotation who kept us fed, my parents (my dad, who moved in to help!), my in-laws, and many more. It might seem odd to thank them for something so far removed from writing, but nothing is far removed from writing, especially not friends and family, all of whom buoyed my spirits, delivered meals, drove my kids to a million different practices and parties, and allowed me to return to the book sooner than I anticipated.

I'd be remiss not to thank all of my Penn friends who championed my recovery in time to get to my own twentieth reunion. I'd also be remiss not to add that absolutely nothing from this book (other than the initial teal-and-blue house, which served as my starting inspiration) has anything to do with or is based on any of the wonderful folks I know from my years spent in Philadelphia.

Last, my husband, Adam, and my children, Campbell and Amelia. This book is about creating family wherever you can, and not a day passes that I'm not aware that I'm the luckiest gal alive to call you my own.

ABOUT THE AUTHOR

Photo © 2015 Kat Tuochy Photography

Allison Winn Scotch is the *New York Times* bestselling author of six novels, including *Time of My Life* and *The Theory of Opposites*. She lives in Los Angeles with her family and their dogs.